t Y

ransform You!

Christina Bacilieri

THE LAST REFUGE

THE LAST REFUGE

CHRISTINA BACILIERI

Edited by Jennifer Rees and Tenyia Lee
Cover art and design by Kim Dingwall
Interior map art by Elizabeth Nazarova
Interior design by Kelly Carter

Library of Congress Cataloging-in-Publication Data
Names: Bacilieri, Christina, author.
Title: The last refuge / by Christina Bacilieri.
Description: First Edition.
LCCN 2023916928

ISBN 979-8-9886618-1-8 (hardcover)
ISBN 979-8-9886618-0-1 (paperback)
ISBN 979-8-9886618-2-5 (ebook)

First Edition: November 2023

CRESCENT INK
PUBLISHING

To my grandma Nancy, for reminding me
that the ones we love are always with us.

DREAMER

S leep is a time when our bodies quiet and our minds open, allowing the veil between the seen and unseen to thin. That's what Kiera's mother had once told her.

"Nothing good comes from dreaming," Kiera sighed into the darkness.

She threw back her bed covers, shaking away the visions burned into her memory. This dream had dogged her for weeks now. It was the same each time—water rippling over stone, the glint of iridescent scales, and a flash of golden eyes with flecks of amber around the pupils—always leaving a deep longing in its wake. The sweat sliding down her back made her skin prickle in the crisp morning air, but she welcomed the chill. It banished the ache in her chest.

The sun was hours from rising, which would provide her some cover on the street at least. Kiera peeled off her nightclothes and tugged on the dark pants and jacket she'd laid out the night before. If she was going to make it to the train station, she needed to leave soon. It wasn't too late to change her mind, she thought, as her hand brushed the backpack filled with an assortment of worn shirts and trousers. Her hesitation didn't last though; she couldn't pass up this opportunity. She hoisted the bag over her shoulder and crept out of her room into the still house. Nook was curled up in his bed. The tawny-furred hound cracked an eye open as she passed.

"Go back to sleep, buddy," Kiera said as she knelt down to stroke his head.

She'd found him behind a dumpster years ago on one of her lonely walks back from academy. The fact that a puppy had managed to elude the nightly drone sweeps was remarkable. She'd smuggled him home in her backpack, and her mother decided they could keep him, admitting the two of them were kindred spirits.

A hint of a smile tugged at Kiera's lips, but it faded as her eyes trailed to her mother's bedroom. The door was open, but Rose wasn't home. She was pulling a triple shift and had slept at the medical center. The steady flow of ill and emaciated patients had tapered off some in the last year, but the hospital was still understaffed, and she was the best nurse they had.

Kiera stood and ran her fingers over the doorframe where her mother had ticked off her height each year. Emotion tightened her throat as she thought of her mother gently cupping her cheek and making the mark over her head. It'd been the two of them against the world for as long as she could remember. The wood dug into her palm as she steadied herself against the doorway. Her father had left them before she was born, her mother telling her she believed he'd relocated to one of the southern continents. The only photo Kiera had of him was stuffed in a drawer in her room. She went numb every time she stared down at the handsome stranger whose light hazel eyes matched her own. When people asked, she simply told them her father was dead. She was more than happy to deny his existence if he was willing to abandon them to a life of poverty. Rose's sheer willpower had prevented that outcome.

Her mother had a gritty optimism that'd gotten them through it all. She'd made Kiera's childhood a bright patch in an otherwise dark world. Rose could make a game out of anything. She'd taught Kiera how to grow a windowsill garden and stitch up everything from cuts to clothes. Their belongings were secondhand, and they'd relied heavily on oatmeal for a couple of years, but Kiera went to bed every night knowing she was loved. That was something the kids who ended up in the Ruling Board's youth centers didn't have.

Kiera's stomach clenched at the thought of the Ruling Board, the world's governing body. The six merciless leaders, each from their respective continents, controlled Atterah with unflinching authority. The board hardly ever let single parents keep their children, insisting they couldn't provide a secure lifestyle for them. It was an easy excuse to take kids and indoctrinate them into the system. Everyone knew that children who grew up in youth centers ended up padding the board's lowest military ranks. Her mother had vowed that wouldn't happen to her. The government had conducted multiple in-home interviews, but she'd passed every inspection.

Kiera shoved down her unease and flicked her eyes around their tight space—it'd been her home for sixteen years. She knew every crack in the plaster, every run in the carpet. With luck, they'd be leaving it soon. If she could play her part today, she could buy them a fresh start. Her mother deserved that, even though it meant Kiera would be breaking their agreement. She swallowed the lump in her throat and scribbled a quick message about spending the day at the library and set it on the coffee table. Something would've gone terribly wrong if she wasn't back before her mother found that note, but it wouldn't be for her anyway. If things went sideways, that piece of paper would be evidence to the Ruling Board that her mother hadn't known about her plans.

When the front door clicked shut behind her, Kiera loosed a breath she hadn't realized she'd been holding. The weather was on her side; a light fog hung in the air. She pulled the hood of her jacket on, tightened her grip on her bag, and ducked into the lane beside their townhome. She kept to the alleyways; it would take longer to get to the station, but it was the most inconspicuous route. The majority of commuters wouldn't be up for another couple of hours, and academy was out for the spring equinox, so it was unlikely she'd encounter anyone.

Kiera kept low and close to the brick walls and peered up at the rooftops and darkened windows every so often. When the cracked asphalt paths gave way to cobblestone, she knew she'd made it to the business quarter. The train station was situated between the shops and the fine up-town homes. It'd always irritated her that the station wasn't closer to her side of town, especially when the uptown residents relied on it the least.

The sweepers had already made their rounds here, as the lane was dry and clear of litter. She'd timed her departure to avoid them. The cleaning equipment wasn't dangerous, it was the larger machines designated in purple that were the ones to watch out for. Their violet hue signified them as security drones outfitted with weapons. Still, Kiera didn't let her guard down around any of them. Every single one could transmit audio back to the government.

Blue light flared out of one of the stockrooms, drawing Kiera up short. She dropped to the ground and pressed her body against the brick. The light was coming from a window just over her head. It was at the rear of the shop and had been left open a crack, letting the voices within spill out onto the street.

"As long as you follow our orders, you'll be protected from the effects of magic," said a rumbling male voice.

Magic. The word sent a jolt through Kiera, and she had to press her hand to her mouth to quiet her breathing. It was illegal to utter it in public.

"Yes," came an icy reply, "we can ensure that it will remain safely contained within the borders. We stand before you as a united front, vowing that this endeavor will not jeopardize the peace and prosperity that Atterah has witnessed these last one hundred and fifty years. Mr. Hallowfeld's plan has been deemed a trustworthy solution."

The conversation was one she'd heard many times, and it hit her that it was coming from a television. Heat rushed to her cheeks. In her panic, she hadn't recognized the prerecorded voices. This was the same broadcast the board aired each time the gates of Etabon opened to the public. The previously uninhabited swathe of land was situated near the top of her own continent, Hytheis, and was the last refuge for magic, the only spot on the planet where it remained.

It'd been this way once a year for the last eight years. The first time she'd heard the broadcast, she'd been in the market with her mother. An ancient television had crackled to life and echoed throughout the store to deliver the shocking news that the board would be opening Etabon's borders for an annual festival.

The elderly woman beside them had whispered, "I never thought I'd live to see the day."

Her mother had snatched Kiera's hand, and they'd raced home. Along the way, they'd heard people murmuring that the announcement must've been a trick, but it wasn't. It was the board's desperate attempt to heal their withering planet. The broadcast had played on a loop for the remainder of the day, as it does every year now on the spring equinox.

Kiera tilted her ear closer to the window; she had to find out if there was someone inside. She couldn't risk anyone spotting her and reporting suspicious behavior to the authorities. The last thing she needed was a drone showing up to do a security check. All she could make out was Board Member Marcus's voice, the leader of Hytheis, rattling on about how the Founding Ruling Board had liberated their planet from an age of darkness. The board claimed magic corrupted people, turning them into monsters whose sole mission was to wage war. The story went that Atterah had been on the brink of destruction because magic thrived on chaos. One hundred and fifty years ago, the six members of the Founding Ruling Board rose up and contained magic within the borders of Etabon, establishing a civilized society outside of it.

Her jaw clenched tight at the comments. The only thing that could've made being trapped against the wall any worse was having to listen while the board spewed propaganda about an imaginary peace. They'd sat back and watched their people suffer for generations, disregarding the droughts, the shrinking forests, and the rising infertility rate among animals and humans alike. Those who spoke out about the worsening crisis disappeared. It wasn't until the waning crop yields recently began impacting their own tables that they'd stepped in. With the cost of food and medicine skyrocketing, they couldn't ignore the problem any longer. All the Founding Ruling Board had done was condemn them all to a slow death.

Kiera took in a measured breath to tamp down her frustration. She couldn't get wrapped up in her feelings about it. What mattered was securing a future for her and her mother, and right now, that future was waiting at the train station. At some point, there'd be a break in the speech. That would be her chance to catch signs of movement inside. As if on cue, Board Member Marcus paused for the oath of Atterah to play. As the technicians queued up the music, it gave Kiera ten seconds to determine if it was safe enough to take a look. Nothing within broke the silence, so she lifted up on her heels to peer into the window, and relief washed over her. The chair across from the television and the room beyond were empty. The shop owner must have forgotten to turn it off before leaving for the night.

A shudder ran through her as she pressed off the ground and back onto her feet, the monotonous pulse of the oath fading behind her. She jogged the rest of the way to make up for the delay. The light thump of her backpack against her shoulder blades and the soft scrape of her boots on the cobblestones were the only sounds as she flew through the remaining pathways. She had to make it down one more narrow corridor, and then she'd be able to cross over to the backstreet behind the station. Kiera's heart was pounding so loudly in her ears that she nearly missed it, but she caught the faint whirring of gears a second before she turned the corner. From her angle against the building, she spotted a distorted reflection in a group of waste bins.

A security drone floated forward, a glossy hovering ball of metal and lights, but she wasn't fooled by its polished appearance. The firepower within just one could decimate a city street. Its red light skimmed over the bins, hunting for stray humans and animals. If it discovered her, it'd be over. Its mechanical voice would demand to know the reason for her outing, and it was dangerous business to lie to a drone. Once it scanned her, it'd flag her heart rate as being elevated, and if it inquired about the contents of her pack, there'd be no guarantee that her answers would satisfy it. If the impromptu questioning didn't check out, she'd be escorted to town hall for a formal interrogation. The only option she had was to stand motionless on the other side of the wall and hope that the drone had already inspected the way she'd come. It drew back and slowly began to rotate, calculating its next target. Right before it swiveled to face her, it made a soft chirp and then zoomed off down the passage and disappeared onto the street.

Tears pricked at her eyes, but just for a moment—she'd come too far to stop now. Kiera rushed to the end of the corridor and glanced both ways before darting across to the station's backstreet. Midway down, a cluster of six figures were engaged in a furious whisper of conversation.

"Let's forget it. She's not coming, and there's no way we can go without knowing what to do."

"Calm down. I'm right here," Kiera said to the group.

They startled at her presence and turned to face her. The party was made up of her classmates from academy, three girls and three boys. They'd attended school together for years but weren't close. Uptown kids didn't typically mingle with people outside of their neighborhood. Even if they'd wanted to, most of the kids from her quarter left academy for trade work by the time they were thirteen. Kiera had asked to do the same to help with bills, but her mother had refused. Rose wanted her to get an education and wouldn't let her take on anything more than part-time weekends at the library. That's where Cassidy, the self-imposed leader of the bunch, had approached her with this absurd scheme.

"Nice of you to join us. We were starting to think you weren't going to show." Cassidy's face was set in a sneer. Kiera was starting to think that was its permanent state.

"I was held up a few streets over, and a security drone is prowling around. Are you sure that thing is working?" Kiera gestured to the silver disc in the girl's hand.

Cassidy's sharp umber eyes flashed to one of the boys. Her boyfriend, Ethan, gave her an encouraging nod. He was training to be an engineer and had been the one to repair the device. It was called a screen, and if it detected any type of monitoring equipment in the area, the light in its center would flip from green to red. The screen was an assurance that their conversation would remain private. Kiera had only seen one other device like it, so she'd been surprised when the girls had cornered her in the library's bathroom with it the other day. It reminded her that it didn't matter where you lived, everyone was afraid of the board's presence.

Kiera crouched down and began pulling the clothes out of her bag, tossing a set to each of them. The girls' outfits were easy—she'd packed some of her oldest things—but getting the boys had been more of a challenge. Some of the garments came from the library's lost and found, and others from its donation box. She'd promised herself that she would replace the donated items later. Kiera looked around at their shoes and couldn't help but wince. The fact that they looked brand new shouldn't have surprised her, though she'd told them to bring a used pair.

Gemma followed her gaze and bent down beside her. "I'm sorry, these were the oldest I could find," she said.

Out of all of them, Gemma was the friendliest. The two of them had been lab partners one semester at academy, and she'd been shy but kind.

"That's alright, Gemma. We can make it work." Kiera picked up a rock and marked up her glossy slippers, rubbing dirt into the grooves with her thumb. She lobbed the rock over to Cassidy and instructed the others to do the same.

When they'd finished getting ready, Kiera motioned for them to pay attention. "Keep your heads down, don't speak more than you absolutely have to, and be polite at the ticket counter." She directed that last comment at Cassidy. "When the clerk asks the nature of your visit to Tydden, we'll say we're going to the library to research our career paths"—Kiera waved to the boys—"and you three will say you're interviewing with future companies. Remember to buy the cheapest seats, that'll put us all in the last carriage. I'll go first so you can watch me."

That's why they needed her: None of her classmates had ridden the train before. They'd never needed to, as their families all had personal transport crafts. Monique handed her a couple of coins. Part of the deal was they had to pay for her ticket to Tydden, the capital of Hytheis and the closest city to Etabon.

"I'm glad you're coming with us," Monique said softly.

Kiera nodded and replied, "You're positive the ticket inspector won't check us for entry bands?"

Before Monique could get a word out, Cassidy spoke over her. "Tristan won't give us away. On the off chance that anyone notices we missed our stop, he'll say we got caught up talking, so we rode it to the end and back and didn't leave the train."

Kiera's eyes narrowed at Cassidy. "Why would he agree to this? He could lose a lot more than his job."

"For love, of course. Monique has always wanted to go, and he can get her there. You just have to make sure we blend in and set up in the right spot," Cassidy snapped back.

Kiera pressed her lips together to stop her next words. She'd never been in love, but if it made you do something this foolish, she wasn't interested. Cassidy stepped forward and thrust a delicate box into her hand. "You get the bracelet now and the title of purchase and a person-alized note from me once we're there."

The day they'd approached her in the bathroom, Kiera had initially told them no and to find someone else willing to chaperone them. Cassi-dy had blocked the door and pulled out a diamond bracelet. Something inside of Kiera had raged at the fact that it was another insignificant trinket to them, but it'd be life-changing for her, and Cassidy knew it. That bracelet could cover a house with a vegetable garden for Rose, plus Kiera's tuition for specialized education. Like the cost of groceries, rent had been climbing so fast they'd fallen behind. Owning a house outright would mean freedom.

Her chin lifted a fraction as she took it and placed it in her bag. Kiera had demanded the note and title; that way, Cassidy couldn't reconsider and claim she'd stolen it.

"If anyone is having second thoughts, this would be the time to go home," Kiera said.

Gemma, Monique, and Ethan shook their heads, but Darius and Grant were visibly trembling. Cassidy rolled her eyes at them.

"We're not going to get caught, and technically we're still considered minors. We've all taken the placement exam, but we don't have our professions yet. They wouldn't try us as adults."

So that's how she'd rationalized it, Kiera thought. She frowned. The board didn't discriminate when it came to sedition, and it wouldn't be the first time they'd executed a kid or the last. Cassidy's mother was a news anchor, and her father was a high-ranking government advisor. The rest had parents who worked in technology and banking. Kiera searched their faces. Maybe they hadn't been told the worst of it. Rose didn't hide the reality of the world from her.

"I wouldn't count on that…" Kiera began to say.

Cassidy raised her hand to stop her. "You can keep your opinions to yourself. We brought you along as a guide, not a consultant. So, are you going to do your job or what?"

Kiera arched her brows. The others exchanged a concerned look, but none of them protested.

"Alright, you all know the risks then."

Outwardly she was composed, but inwardly, her nerves were fraying. A secret part of her had always imagined going on this journey, but to admit that it was truly happening felt dangerous. If you wanted something too much, it could break you. There were consequences for being impulsive, but even that hadn't smothered her curiosity. Kiera told herself she was only doing this for the money, that nothing else had drawn her to this venture, but you can't lie to the truest parts of yourself. This dream had lived in her head for countless nights. Today she was setting it free.

A wild thrill ran down her spine.

"Let's go to Etabon," Kiera whispered into the shadows.

INTERLOPER

The landscape blurred by in a sea of colors as the train hurtled toward the festival. Kiera watched as dust particles danced in the watery sunlight filtering in through the windows. The rays obscured the arrival time scrolling across the digital ticker. When they passed through a thick forest, the cabin was thrown into shadow, revealing they were twenty minutes from their destination. The last carriage of the bullet train was musty and cramped, but Kiera's thoughts had drifted beyond the confines of the cabin.

She let her mind pick apart the circumstances that had brought her here. Etabon was a three-hour bullet train ride from her hometown of Mendinburrow, about ten minutes by way of a decent hovercraft, but her classmates had chosen this method of travel for a reason. Air travel meant flight plans and passenger lists had to be filed with the government, even if they were private crafts. If this excursion was to go undetected, they couldn't afford that kind of paper trail. Trains made multiple stops, it was easier to remain unnoticed amongst the numerous passengers, and there was the added excuse of missing your station.

Kiera used the reflection in the window to watch her classmates whispering in the seats behind her. None of them had applied for the board-certified bands required to enter the festival grounds. They didn't want it documented that they'd set foot at Etabon. If any of their parents found out, they'd be disinherited. The very thought of their children being sullied by magic was abhorrent to them. Over the years, it'd become common for the wealthiest and the poorest citizens to visit the site, but it was taking time for the practice to permeate the bottom half of the upper class and middle class. Even with the board granting amnesty to those who made the trip, in their social circles, it was still considered improper.

Her thoughts were interrupted by a burst of laughter over her shoulder. Kiera's hand traced over the window's cool glass. It always felt like she was standing on the outside looking in. Her attention settled back on herself, and she brushed her sable hair away from her face. The stress from earlier had left her warm olive skin looking washed out, but the real shock had been making it aboard without any trouble.

The train started to slow, and she could make out structures in the distance. Their plan was to get to the site, watch a few people cross over, and catch a ride back in the same passenger car within an hour. Her head buzzed at the idea of seeing Etabon up close. Try as she might, she'd never been able to shake her burning curiosity for magic. On nights when her dreams chased her from sleep, she'd climb out on the roof of their townhome and stare out at the stars that touched the horizon. She wasn't sure how, but she knew in her bones that she was gazing in the direction of Etabon.

A rustling caught Kiera's attention. Cassidy had moved up to sit in the seat across from her and was scanning her with distaste.

"I told you Tristan wouldn't let us down."

She jutted her chin toward the door of the passenger cart. The young man winked at them through the door's window but didn't enter to do final inspections, then turned around and walked away. He'd done the same at the train's previous stop in Tydden. Monique's excited giggles resounded through the cabin. As Kiera had anticipated, it was empty except for the seven of them.

"Checking for bands on the train is more of a formality, you don't really need them until you cross the gateway into the festival," Cassidy said as she flipped her auburn hair over her shoulder.

Kiera tilted her head to the side but didn't respond. She was pretty sure the Ruling Board wouldn't agree. To even acquire an entry band, you had to submit paperwork for admission to your local town hall. At best, their visit fell into a gray area. As long as they didn't enter the gates, they wouldn't technically be breaking any laws, but Kiera hadn't heard of anyone visiting the grounds to spectate. Then again, no one was permitted to discuss anything remotely related to magic in public, snuffing out most gossip on the topic.

As much as their government despised magic, it was the resource that sustained the world. When it passed through a living being, the interaction created energy. That energy was absorbed into the planet; it's what fueled the core. Whatever the truth about the dark ages, the board had convinced the public that the energy produced from the plant and animal life at Etabon would be enough to support the entire world. It turned out they were wrong. By cutting off its access to a sufficient energy source, they'd effectively been strangling the planet. The annual four-month-long festival at Etabon was their response, but over a century's worth of damage can't be fixed in less than a decade. There was a steep cost to disrupting the natural order of things.

Cassidy was rolling the screen back and forth in her palm, watching her. The light had remained a steady green the entire ride. Kiera had suspected they wouldn't waste surveillance equipment on the last cart. Being underestimated by those in power was an advantage she didn't take for granted.

"You could at least try and look grateful. It's not every day that you get to go to Etabon without it staining your record. But I guess it doesn't matter much for your long-term prospects, does it?"

It wasn't clear if Cassidy was referring to the fact that attending the festival would disqualify her from applying for government professions or socializing with certain families. Any person who hoped to garner a position in government couldn't attend the festival. It was an unspoken rule that the board didn't want its ranking officials tainted by Etabon's magic. Either way, it was a ridiculous comment but a clear picture of the other girl's desires.

Kiera pressed her knuckles to her mouth to hide her wry smile and said, "So, why is it that you all want to visit so badly?"

Cassidy's eyes smoldered beneath her lashes. "You're telling me you've never longed for something you can't have?" Her focus slid to Kiera's bag as if she could see through the material to the bracelet inside, and then back to her. It wasn't often that this girl was told no, and apparently, it didn't sit well with her. Cassidy was used to getting what she wanted, and visiting the festival was no exception.

Kiera held her stare. "Some of us don't have that much idle time on our hands."

"I suppose not," Cassidy replied as she casually looked down and picked at the shirt Kiera had lent her. She settled back into the chair and drummed her nails over the armrest. "I'm interested to see if there really is any lingering connection to this place. Some people say it lives in our genes, but I didn't get the dreams as a child."

The blunt remark threw Kiera off guard. There weren't any other topics more personal or taboo than this one. Most kids stopped having the dreams by five if they got them at all. In the eyes of their government, a child who dreamed of magic was the greatest shame a parent could bear. The dreams were considered remnants of old trauma from past generations, and parents were warned to swiftly rid their children of the feverish delusions. If a child was suspected of having them, they were ordered to be medicated.

Kiera's earliest memory was sitting at their kitchen table, coloring. Her tiny hand had drawn bright green hills full of people with wings and wolves that could walk upright. When she'd held the picture up for her mother to see, Rose had known what it meant. She'd just smiled, kissed the top of Kiera's head, and told her that it would be their secret. It was one they'd kept to this day. To her credit, Rose never gave her even one dose of the potent sleeping sedative that left kids quiet and glassy-eyed. Kiera hadn't outgrown the dreams, and a small piece of her heart was grateful for it. There was a strange truth to them that was absent from the waking world. On nights that she wandered through her dreamscape, she felt completely whole, but when dawn came, she was left fragmented again.

"I heard some kids are sent to the reeducation centers for having them. Even if they get classified as rehabilitated, it devastates their future job opportunities. It's probably for the best, we wouldn't want some kind of delirium to spread," Cassidy said haughtily.

Kiera's grip on her own armrest became painfully tight. A mix of fear and resentment swirled inside of her. She'd managed to avoid the centers, but that dread never really left her. If her "condition" was discovered at sixteen, she could only imagine what they'd do. Before she found her voice, a snippet of the oath of Atterah broke through the white noise coming from the front of the carriage.

The commotion distracted Cassidy, who scrunched her nose at the television mounted on the wall there. Its picture had wavered from fuzzy to entirely static throughout the ride. The jostling of the cart had cleared up the image revealing a clip of Eugene Hallowfeld shooting the camera a charming grin. There was a terrifying hunger in his eyes that gripped Kiera—it was like staring into a wildfire. It was rumored he'd be appointed as a seventh board member if his plan worked. For now, he'd settled for the warden of Etabon.

"My fellow citizens," Hallowfeld said in his silky tone, "we're going to revitalize our world through controlled chaos. As the board can confirm, I've made it perfectly safe within the borders of Etabon, and with my system in place, there will be no adverse effects from your time spent at the festival. Not only will our magnificent leaders pardon those who join me, but they offer their gratitude as your very presence will provide a vital service. As a reminder, the laws on this side of the border will remain unchanged. Discussion of magic or your visit to Etabon is strictly prohibited. Violators will face maximum penalties."

"I'll give that charlatan one thing, he knows how to draw in a crowd,"

Cassidy said.

"He panders to bored elitists while targeting vulnerable people. What a talent," Kiera muttered. The words left her mouth before she could stop them.

Cassidy's face lit up with wicked amusement. "I was surprised that you didn't drop out and apply for a work visa yourself, considering your situation. Why is that?" Kiera had her reasons for avoiding the festival. Ones she wouldn't be sharing with Cassidy, of all people.

Hallowfeld's honied words filled the silence between them instead, "I'll live at this paradise year-round, so I'll extend that honor to a select group of you. The rest will have the privilege of attending during the four-month-long festival window. The first way to enter is through a work visa. I'll need plenty of hands to set up and will provide room and board along with triple the wages on my side of the border. Impress me, and you could be chosen for my year-round staff. The second way to attend is a spectator's permit. For a small fee, you can experience a retreat in this breathtaking location. Your permit will automatically enter you into a lottery to win a perpetually stocked home in my exclusive community. The third and most admirable way is through the sponsor-competitor relationship. Sponsors will be given a commission and resources to prepare our fighters. Winners are guaranteed a lifetime of luxury, the finest homes in my community, and an annuity transferrable to their families. These brave competitors will battle in tournaments to satisfy magic's need for chaos. Their contribution will safeguard all those doing their part within the border and ensure that society prospers outside of it."

Cassidy scoffed, "You know that arrogant snob doesn't invite my family to any of his private galas. I think the board's gone soft where he's concerned. What's your opinion?"

Eugene Hallowfeld had been seventeen when he'd approached the board with the proposal to hold a festival at Etabon, barely older than Kiera was now. If any other citizen had suggested the idea, they would've been executed for treason, but not a Hallowfeld. The Hallowfeld family had holdings in all the major metal mines, and they were staunch loyalists. Their mines produced the materials needed to create technology, from monitoring equipment to security drones. It was no shock that the board had always been agreeable with them. When Eugene's father passed away, he took over the family inheritance. That's how he got an audience with the board. He used the opportunity to sell his idea to them, guaranteeing reinforced borders, records of all attendees, and a healthy percentage of the festival's proceeds.

Cassidy's bitterness hung in the air between them. Kiera drew in a long breath. She wasn't under any illusions that the other girl wanted her perspective, the question was just an outlet for her indignation. Apparently, fear wasn't the only reason the adults in Cassidy's social circle hadn't embraced Etabon's festivities; they'd been snubbed. Hallowfeld was known for his extravagant celebrations, and the festival was rumored to be his grandest event on a public scale. When the gates had opened, affluential citizens had flocked to the site for the promise of the ultimate diversion—the tournaments. They treated Etabon like their playground. It wasn't as if people in their positions entered the matches. Although Cassidy had spoken the words for selfish reasons, they were true; when it suited the board, they overlooked the actions of their favored citizens. Kiera wasn't foolish enough to admit that out loud. Questioning their integrity in any capacity was a high crime, and she wasn't about to insult them directly.

"He must be quite the diplomat," Kiera said flatly.

"That's a pretty unoriginal thought coming from someone who set the curve for the placement examination," Cassidy replied. Kiera shrugged a shoulder and gave her an unruffled smile. Cassidy pursed her lips and spat, "Did you know your scores knocked me out of the running for the government and media positions?"

Kiera refused to shrink back. "No, I wasn't aware."

A rush of understanding wrapped itself around her heart. Cassidy's choice had been taken from her. The placement exam was the cornerstone of their futures, one brutal written exam that decided their fate. Your score in the class ranking determined which professions you were allowed to pursue. It forced students to vie for a handful of openings in each. The board could create more but chose to pit them against one another instead.

Kiera couldn't afford the specialized education required for the roles her scores qualified her for. Her original plan had been to request to remain at academy to finish her basic education. If approved, she'd likely be eligible for a low to mid-income career, and the government would add a hefty education tax to her wages for the rest of her life. This venture had changed her fortune. The funds she'd get from pawning the bracelet would open an unexpected path for her. It would give her options she wouldn't have otherwise. Kiera felt herself softening toward Cassidy. She shifted her body away from the window to face the other girl.

"I wish they'd let us choose for ourselves what suits us best. You'd have made a good broadcaster," Kiera offered.

A dark grin played across Cassidy's face as she said, "Tell that to my parents. They expected a newscaster or a magistrate, now I'm just an embarrassment in their eyes. Anyway, I've decided to forgive you since you came with us." Kiera didn't get a chance to reply because the boys decided that was the perfect moment to crowd into the chairs around them.

Grant was wringing his hands and asked, "Do you think it's safe to be this close?"

Ethan shook his head. "Magic can't touch us on this side. Anyway, we all know people who've visited. They seem fine to me." He bent toward Grant. "I bet you'd turn into a goblin if you went through."

The boy emitted a gasp and shot a reflexive look at the screen. Cassidy snickered and reached over to interlace her fingers with Ethan's. She gestured for the others to lean in, and then she pulled a pamphlet from her bag with her free hand. The Ruling Board's emblem was stamped across it, but there was a phrase beneath the insignia that Kiera hadn't seen before. In bold print were the words: *Human above all else.* Cassidy unfolded the document, revealing that she'd obtained a cataloged leaflet about Etabon.

"I nicked this from my dad's desk the day I took the screen."

Cassidy's father had left the security door to their home office disengaged; that's how she'd pilfered the device from his collection of confiscated items.

"It's true, people change when they enter the gates." Cassidy tapped a graph at the bottom of the page. "There's an approximation here from the data they've collected. It says only eight percent of Atterah's population would remain human if they crossed the border."

"What does that mean?" Darius hissed.

"Pay attention, you twit. It means that something about the magic turns people into different creatures when they cross over," Cassidy said.

Kiera knew Cassidy wouldn't have risked sharing the information with them anywhere else. Her fingers skimmed a list of cataloged magical forms as she read out their descriptions. Kiera watched the other's eyes widen in amazement. She wondered if Cassidy fully grasped what would happen to her and her family if she were caught with that classified report. Kiera didn't admit it to the group, but she'd heard some of these descriptions before.

She furrowed her brow. It turns out the board couldn't seal every pair of lips. It was precisely how she'd picked up bits and pieces about Etabon over the years. From scraps of whispered conversation between the professors at academy and shopkeepers in the market. She'd even overheard a couple of tales about the scheming nature of the warden himself. Her mother had taught her the skill of appearing unassuming and distracted while carefully gathering details from passing exchanges. The board curated all written and broadcast news, making word of mouth the only way to obtain independent information. Her mother's most important lesson was never to get caught eavesdropping. Secrets are life and death, and people will choose to survive at any cost.

Rose valued the truth and was open to discussing details about the festival in private but had made Kiera promise not to attend. It wasn't the magic that worried her so much as the person who ran the site. The whole point of the occasion was to convert as much magic into energy as possible to nourish the core. Hallowfeld claimed the tournaments were entirely voluntary, but there was something sinister about his cloying grins and exuberant speeches. Every person in attendance was a conduit for the needed energy, but it was the tournaments that drew in those crowds and allegedly appeased the magic's wild nature. Who's to say he couldn't force workers into the matches if he wished? It was cruel, but all the board cared about were results, and the planet was showing incremental improvements.

So, Kiera and Rose had agreed it wasn't worth risking their lives for the earnings they could make at the festival. Kiera had never broken a promise to her mother. That was, until now. She hoped it would be worth it. Her stomach churned with guilt as the bell trilled through the cabin signaling their arrival.

A jarring hiss shook the train as it rumbled to a stop. Kiera remained in her seat as the rest of the group elbowed one another to be the first to exit. Instead of heading to the carriage's passenger door, they crowded around the back of the cart. There was the sound of a latch being lifted, and then the metal door slid open to reveal Tristan standing on the other side, grinning.

"Come along, you filthy stowaways," he chuckled.

The others hooted and cheered as he helped them out and over to the platform. He kissed Monique's cheek before turning back to assist Cassidy. She twisted in the aisle and waved the documents in her fist back at Kiera.

She purred, "You didn't come all this way to back out now, did you?"

Kiera stood stiffly and trailed her to the exit. She clutched the cool metal of the door for support until Tristan's calloused hand gently took hers and swung her onto the polished mahogany platform. When her feet hit the planks, the weight of her decision faded from her mind. Her hand lifted to shield her eyes from the blinding sun. Mountains rose up on either side of them, tucking the festival grounds into a sprawling valley ringed by an evergreen forest. Glittering streams tumbled down the mountain ridges cutting paths to the valley floor. The air was fresh and carried the sweet earthy scent of flowering vegetation. A flutter bloomed in the pit of Kiera's stomach. It was like Etabon's rolling foothills were sloping down to greet her, leaving a comforting warmth surging within her.

A feather-light pressure tickled Kiera's palm. Cassidy was pressing the note and title into her hand.

"Cheers, you earned it," Cassidy murmured.

A heaviness Kiera had been carrying for far too long fell away as she read the flowing script. Possibilities stretched out in front of her now. She folded the papers, tucked them into her pack, and flashed Cassidy a small smile.

The other girl curled her fingers, beckoning her over to the group. With the addition of Tristan, the eight of them clustered together and faced the platform's stairs. They joined the other guests heading to the entrance and were funneled off the platform into organized queues that snaked toward the gates. When the entry pillars came into view, Kiera was at a loss for words.

The moonstone columns loomed forty feet high, and both were topped with sculptures of serpents readied to strike. The massive wrought-iron gates between them were thrown wide open. Kiera covered her mouth as her eyes roved over the scene. A figure was stationed in the middle welcoming the droves of visitors and scanning their certification bands for admission. A jolt ran through the group when they realized the figure had delicately pointed ears and sapphire swirls adorning his long, graceful arms and legs. They were witnessing their first magical form. A faerie. The sign hanging above him read, *Warning: Bands Required Beyond This Point.* When the group made it closer to the front, they peeled off from the line and tucked themselves in a spot against the wall near one of the gate's smooth columns, where they could watch without being seen.

Kiera peered around the column as a woman who looked to be about her mother's age approached the boundary. When she passed through the gateway, great feathered wings emerged from her back. Her wings rose over her shoulders, silky gray feathers melding to ink black ones that cascaded down to her heels. She tilted her chin to the sky in rapture, fanning out her wings, the plumage becoming incandescent as it caught the sun's rays. Ethan's eyes glazed over as he prattled about the magnetism of the alary people, reciting the description from the pamphlet. Kiera gasped at the alary, recalling her first childhood drawing. It was her dreams incarnate—there had been truth to her wild imaginings. Elated tears pricked behind her eyes.

A second later, another visitor had their band certified and stepped past the pillars to make his change. On either side of his head, furry oval-shaped ears flared out, and ridged horns curled through his raven hair. Below his torso, he grew a short, upturned tail and glossy ebony fur that stopped at his cloven hooves. Kiera heard her companions confirm that he was a faun from his features that resembled a goat's. The next guest moved forward to fill his place. The woman grew a foot taller in front of their eyes, and her ears reshaped to end in fine points. A breeze sprang up from nowhere, dancing around her, leaving soft silvery swirls along the woman's arms and legs. She winked at the other faerie checking entry bands as she glided past into the festival.

Kiera hardly had time to catch her breath between each guest's transition. Cassidy leaned over to her and said, "If you move close enough, you can actually smell the magic when they change."

Kiera tipped forward and watched as an old man passed through the gates and turned into a dazzling fire sprite. The tiny sprite made a fiery arc in the sky and then zipped off into the crowd. There was a tang in the air and a smell of burnt branches. "That's amazing," Kiera marveled.

She peered back at Cassidy, catching her gaze in a moment that seemed to suspend them in time. The intensity of her stare prickled the hairs on the back of Kiera's neck. Suddenly Cassidy lunged forward, snatching away Kiera's bag and shoving her toward the gate opening. The crowd lurched. People yelled in protest. Kiera realized what was happening too late as she tumbled through the pillars, but not before she caught Cassidy by the wrist, dragging her down with her.

3

LYNX

P ebbles went skittering as they careened through the threshold. A metallic taste coated Kiera's tongue, and electricity crackled against her skin. A garbled cry for security rang out above her. Starbursts of color bloomed across her vision, and her head throbbed horrendously. An ache tore its way through her body, radiating out through her limbs. She and Cassidy rolled end over end before landing in a tangled heap.

Kiera squinted her eyes against the cornflower blue sky, forcing her vision to clear. Gem-toned banners flapped in the wind overhead. The gravel path beside them led to a sprawling mass of tents where a variety of creatures were milling about. Some had stopped to gawk at them. Her heart sank when she got her bearings. They had landed in the grass a couple of yards from the entrance. Kiera's bag lay in the dirt beside them. She looked over her shoulder and saw their classmates' stunned faces among the crowd on the other side of the gate. The faerie gatekeeper who blocked the exit stared at them open-mouthed.

A sound like a howling animal split the air. Kiera touched her chest and, to her disbelief, realized the noise had come from her. Her hand was covered in midnight fur, and long talons were poking through the ends of her fingers. She held it out in front of her, gaping, unsure of what she'd become. Her heartbeat juddered against her ribcage. Below her, Cassidy had transformed into a nixie, her auburn hair replaced with long viridescent strands resembling seaweed. Her webbed hands and feet slipped against Kiera, searching for purchase to throw her off. The mottled greenish-gray skin covering Cassidy's body left a residue on Kiera's satiny fur.

As the haze cleared away, reality set in. She shoved off Cassidy and stood, taking stock of herself. Power thrummed through her sleek feline frame. Kiera had grown a tail that slashed back and forth in the air behind her. Her mind raced to catch up to her temper until her brain latched onto a thought.

"You shoved me on purpose," Kiera choked out.

Cassidy wriggled to her feet and sputtered, "I need your scores invalidated. I deserve those positions. You don't understand, that kind of future would be wasted on you."

Kiera let out an incredulous laugh. "You did this for career options. Do you know what the board does to trespassers... to their families?"

Terror registered across Cassidy's face. It had been her intention to abandon Kiera and run, not cross over herself. Kiera's breath lodged in her throat as her own words sunk in. This selfish vulture had condemned them both. The board wouldn't believe a word Kiera said. They'd only see two undocumented traitors who'd crossed the border, and the punishment for treason was death. Cassidy let out a frightened scream as Kiera prowled toward her. At the very least, she could haul her over to the gatekeeper and make her explain the situation. There could be a slim chance he'd let them go if they convinced him that their intrusion was a mistake.

Before she could grab Cassidy, a glaring crimson light flared up in front of Kiera, thrusting her backward. She tried to shield her eyes but found she couldn't move her limbs. The tang of magic laced the air as it popped and sizzled around them. She and Cassidy both fell to the ground, their hands and feet bound by the crimson light. When Kiera tried to open her mouth, she found it was bound shut, too. Delicate leather slippers paced into her view, and the edge of a blood-red cloak snapped against Kiera's face.

Standing above her, staring daggers, was a woman with frost-blue eyes that emitted an uncanny glow. Her lips parted in surprise as she bent down to inspect Kiera, her strawberry blond hair falling over her shoulders. Instinctively, Kiera jerked away from the woman, whose palms were crackling with the same crimson light that'd shackled them. The blood in Kiera's veins ran cold—they'd been detained by a witch. A hulking figure, double the size of an ordinary human, stalked up beside the witch.

The being's mighty lupine body bristled with hostility. Like a moth to a flame, images from dreams past fluttered into Kiera's rattled mind as she tried to make sense of the being. Details wavered at the edges of her consciousness, and when he leered down at them, the description came back to her—he was a werewolf. Kiera craned her neck as far as her restraints would allow, studying the placement of his knees and how his clawed feet were elongated to support his frame.

A snarl peeled the wolf's lips back from his teeth as he said, "What are your orders?"

The witch's breathy voice was so hushed Kiera had to strain to hear her, "Bring them to the Ascendant One immediately. I'll handle the crowd."

He lifted her and Cassidy up and tossed each of them over a shoulder as if they were nothing more than sacks of flour. His clawed hand scooped up Kiera's bag, and he padded off in the opposite direction of the witch. Kiera watched the witch as she marched toward the gateway, her ruby cloak billowing out behind her. With each step the wolf took, Kiera's hope of escape slipped further away.

Thankfully they didn't travel far. The wolf's loping gait was making Kiera's stomach unsteady. She couldn't twist around to see where they were, but from the outline of the shadows cutting across the gravel path, she could make out that he'd brought them to the nearest cluster of tents. His gravelly voice sent a fresh wave of dread crawling up her spine as he requested permission to enter. There was a muffled reply, and the wolf pressed through the flaps of the ebony silk tent. The silver-furred wolf dumped them onto the floor and bowed his head. A plush handwoven rug broke the worst of their fall, but the impact still knocked the air from Kiera's lungs.

"These are the two that caused the disruption at the boundary," he growled.

Her eyes stung as she tried to breathe. It was made all the harder by the heady scent of sweet vanilla and leather that hung in the air. If she hadn't just come from outside, she could have believed it was the dead of night; somehow, the tent's material blocked out any trace of sunlight. Its interior was dimly lit, the only source of light coming from cut crystal lanterns that peppered the space, but she could make out a silhouette approaching from the back of the chamber. A devastatingly handsome man in a tailored pewter suit emerged from the darkness and walked between the two girls, glancing from one to the other as he adjusted one of his silver cuff links in the flickering candlelight.

He prodded at their wrists with the toe of his loafer and tsked.

"No entry bands on either of them," the werewolf reported without being prompted.

"Well, isn't this an interesting surprise? I can say with confidence I've never had an animal shifter trespass into Etabon," the man crooned.

Kiera stared up at him, not comprehending what he meant by animal shifter. Her head was still pounding from the magic she'd been hurled through, making her sluggish. There was something familiar about him. He looked to be in his mid-twenties with extraordinarily white teeth and neat hazelnut curls. A flick of his wrist released the hold over Kiera's mouth.

"What?" Kiera managed to rasp.

His smoky brown eyes, almost black, sparked. They radiated the same eerie glow as the witch's. "That entrance is spelled. Without a band, you both should have been thrown back at full force." He quirked a groomed eyebrow, "You not only managed to pass through unharmed but ready to fight as well."

Kiera blinked slowly as white-hot anger banished her fear. "I didn't trespass. I was pushed through by that rancid gray worm over there." Cassidy let out a stifled whimper of protest.

His sultry lips curved in amusement. "Be that as it may, I'm the warden of this magical oasis, and rules state that those who attempt to enter without a certification band, will be put at the mercy of the Ruling Board."

Her brief rush of courage ebbed away. If this man said he was the warden, then she'd come face to face with none other than Eugene Hallowfeld. She couldn't imagine what the board would do to her, much less to her mother, for her leaving the train without documentation and trespassing into Etabon. How could she explain that this was an accident when the evidence pointed to the contrary? Kiera had one desperate option left. She wasn't entirely sure it would work, as she'd learned about it through slivers of gossip. It may not even be true, but she had to try.

She cleared her throat. "Mr. Hallowfeld, I hear you're a man who likes to make bargains."

Rumor had it that bargains were the warden's preferred currency, particularly when they were advantageous for himself and a last resort for others. Even with this knowledge, Kiera had no choice but to ask his price.

Hallowfeld clapped his hands, and the bindings disappeared from Kiera's wrists and legs.

He offered her a hand up. "Let's do hear what you have to say, my feline friend."

Cassidy's face crumpled into a pleading expression, and Kiera's shoulders sagged in frustration. As much as she disliked her, she wouldn't leave her stranded here. Who knew what would happen if she left her out of the deal. Kiera wouldn't have that weighing on her conscience.

"What would it take for you to forgive us and spare the board the headache of dealing with our case?" Kiera asked.

Mirth stole across Hallowfeld's face at Kiera's careful choice of words. A pinprick of daylight pierced the gloom behind her as a water sprite flew into the tent. Its humanoid form was swathed in an undulating cerulean aura that kept it suspended in place. Hallowfeld waved the tiny man forward, and the water sprite mouthed something in Hallowfeld's ear before hastily dismissing himself.

Hallowfeld's attention fell back on Kiera. "You're including the treacherous gray worm, but what about the rest of your companions?"

So, he knew about the others. That must've been what the sprite had told him. Kiera swallowed hard; she was hoping they'd gotten back to the train unseen, but the witch or the gatekeeper must've noticed them. From the looks on their faces after Cassidy pushed her, Kiera had to believe that they'd been oblivious to Cassidy's true plans for their journey to Etabon. Even if they knew, if it meant the board wouldn't find out about their infraction, Kiera was happy to have them included. She nodded her head at him.

"I'm not sure it's worth my time to make an arrangement with you. How long will it be until your little gang is registered missing? Once that happens, the authorities will be contacted, and questions about your whereabouts will arise. Sounds like a nuisance to me. Better to hand you over now and be done with it," he chuckled.

"I won't be missed until tomorrow morning, but yes, it'll be reported if they're not back for dinner," Kiera said. It wouldn't do her any good to lie to him. If he held her classmates here and their parents contacted the authorities, their misconduct would be discovered. Either way, she'd lose her chance at protecting her mother's life.

Hallowfeld tapped his foot impatiently as he mulled his decision over. "Very well, you'll have to do," he sighed. "And what is it that they call you?"

"Kiera," is all she said back.

His eyes glinted when he responded, "A real pleasure to meet you. I'm Eugene Hallowfeld."

The werewolf addressed Hallowfeld, "What do we do with this one?"

He was pointing to Cassidy, who was flopping around like a dying fish at this point. Hallowfeld snapped his fingers, and her bonds disappeared.

"Remove her and the company she came with. Make it clear that if any one of them speaks so much as a word about what happened here today, they'll have the wrath of the Ruling Board to deal with. Let's hope their friend here manages to make good on our bargain so they get to keep their dismal lives," Hallowfeld replied.

The wolf grunted at Kiera, kicking her backpack with a clawed foot. "This yours?"

She nodded her head and bent forward to collect it. Kiera proceeded to pull out the extra pair of flowing khaki trousers and a loose cotton shirt she'd brought along for the boys. She fumbled with her claw to cut a hole in the trousers for her... tail. It was a perplexing thought to have a tail and claws. The concept made her pulse quicken. She gathered every ounce of strength within her to stay calm and pulled the garments on. They fit her new frame well. Her transformation and the ensuing scuffle had left her other clothes in tatters. It's not that the fur coat she donned didn't cover her whole body, but the clothes were comforting, a shred of normalcy she could cling to.

The wolf nodded to Hallowfeld and picked Cassidy up from the ground by her shoulders. Kiera's muscles tensed. She'd been the one to suggest the bargain, so she knew that meant Cassidy and the rest of the group were free to go while she was left to deal with the aftermath. Besides, she was the only one who could stay without drawing scrutiny. If she didn't deliver on whatever arrangement Hallowfeld settled on, they'd be facing the same fate as her anyway. Kiera banished the injustice of it from her mind. It wouldn't change the situation, and she'd need a clear head to keep her and her mother safe.

Hallowfeld made a parting gesture with his hands, and the tent flaps swept open for them. Fresh air wafted in, and relief washed over Kiera when she saw the sunlight. There'd been a moment there when she'd thought they wouldn't be seeing it again. Hallowfeld turned away, jerking his head for Kiera to follow. He glanced back at her as she watched the werewolf lead a trembling Cassidy back to the gates.

"We can't have them spilling their guts that someone was able to break my spell around the site now, can we?" he said.

Kiera was wondering herself how they'd managed that feat. The entrance checkpoint clearly wasn't for show; Hallowfeld took the verification of his guests seriously. He flicked his wrist toward the spot at the gate she and Cassidy had tumbled through. For an instant, the air glowed there, and it looked like tiny golden strings were knitting themselves back together, and then they vanished, leaving the entrance looking completely ordinary again.

The force of Hallowfeld's magic left Kiera's fur standing on end. She had no doubts now; he fit the description of a wizard exactly: unnerving glowing eyes that distinguished him from an ordinary human, and the ability to manipulate magic on a whim through gestures and spells. She was afraid to imagine what would have happened to them if that spell had worked properly. When the site had opened years ago, Hallowfeld became known for being a powerful wizard when at Etabon. At the time, she hadn't understood what that meant, but it was a prolific rumor. One that had gotten people killed for repeating it in the vicinity of monitoring equipment. He seemed like the type who'd spread it about himself.

She side-eyed him and asked, "What about the crowd of people that saw us fall through the gate?"

Hallowfeld snickered. "Clever girl. They'll assume you both had bands and were itching to fight each other before my tournament started. Since the nixie was the one who instigated the tussle, I let you remain while she's been banned for life. Well, that's the story my little birds will be telling anyway."

Hallowfeld strolled up to a booth and motioned to the five pixies inside. The tiny women and men flapped their translucent wings, sailing forward to speak with Hallowfeld. "Give me a minute to have a chat with my friends here," he said.

Kiera nodded, turning her attention to the crowds meandering up and down the gravel pathways around them. It was remarkable, all these different beings together when the whole world looked one way outside the borders of this place. To her surprise, several of the creatures were staring back.

Kiera drifted forward to a stall across the way, which was bursting with artwork. There was a werewolf inside with wheat-colored fur sketching an aerial view of the festival on a canvas. The piece was filled with hot air balloons suspended above Etabon's landscape; thousands of tents were scattered over the valley with a neighborhood of solid buildings and a manor house situated near its northeastern corner, streams curved through the terrain, and the deep emerald forest encircled the site. Kiera drew her eyes away and perused the stall. She was captivated by the mix of pieces hanging or leaning against any available space.

There were charcoal portraits of all manner of creatures and watercolor renderings of the mountains surrounding Etabon. Kiera picked up an illustration that caught her attention, a small canvas with a hand-drawn map of Atterah, the name of each continent written in elegant gold script above them: Fortayne to the North, Karveir and Andaine to the East, Erriem and Renival to the South, and their continent of Hytheis to the West. She let out a surprised noise as she noticed Etabon had been included among the city locations named, written at its rightful place near the uppermost part of Hytheis. On any other map, Etabon would have been left off, as the board refused to acknowledge it.

The werewolf turned her silver eyes to Kiera, nodding cheerfully. "It's beautiful to see the world as it truly is, no?"

Kiera smiled back at her, shaking her head in agreement. She wandered over to the next stall, its sign promising tea leaf and palm readings. A gauzy fabric was draped over its doorway, and floor-length antique mirrors leaned against either side of the entrance. As she passed, a flash of her reflection in one of the mirrors stopped her short, and a sharp intake of breath escaped her. This was not the face Kiera had seen staring back at her for the last sixteen years, but it felt remarkably familiar.

Her sable hair had vanished along with her upturned nose that matched her mother's. Beneath her clothes, shimmering black and gold fur covered her entire body. Kiera blinked her luminous amber eyes. They'd swallowed her light hazel color entirely. She ran a shaky hand over her mouth. Her full lips were now thin and accompanied on either side by long black whiskers, and her teeth were pointed and sharp to mirror her claws. She flexed her fingers and toes; even though she had pads on the underside of her hands and feet, some part of her was still human-like. She couldn't imagine not being able to pick anything up.

"Are you quite done admiring yourself?"

Kiera flinched as Hallowfeld stared over her shoulder, chuckling. He'd crept up behind her. His laugh sent icy tendrils lashing through her veins.

"Yes, well, I guess I would stare, too. You do realize how rare a solitary animal form is, don't you?"

Kiera ignored him and twitched her tufted pointed ears. She was positive Cassidy's pamphlet hadn't described her magical form and couldn't recall overhearing anything about animal shifters. It was fascinating how comfortable she felt, like her human body had been a dream, and she was waking up for the first time.

"So that's why you decided to hear me out," she replied coolly.

She realized her tail was swishing with impatience and stilled it. She'd have to learn to mask these new tells.

"Ah yes, about our bargain," he said.

4

BARGAIN

Hallowfeld led them into a cavernous ivory silk tent with the name Nautilus stitched across its flaps. It was a bar of some kind, with gilded chandeliers hanging from the ceiling and beautiful golden trinkets littering the room. A rectangular pearl counter ran the back length of the tent, and glass bottles of sparkling liquid lined the shelves behind it. Kiera nearly missed a step when she noticed the elegant beings inside. Mermaids and sirens were flitting around the room, bringing colorful drinks to the patrons.

"This is a private establishment for my esteemed guests, so we'll be able to speak freely here," Hallowfeld said.

He strode up to the bartender, who looked to be Kiera's age, and called out, "Attalin, mix us up your finest concoction."

Kiera wrinkled her heart-shaped nose, her whiskers tickling her face. As of this year, she was of age, but she rarely drank. Rose had let her try white wine, but her mother had warned her never to mix strangers and alcohol.

A pang of guilt fisted Kiera's heart. If Rose only knew where she was, she'd be devastated. Her mother had worked relentlessly to make a stable life for the two of them. She vowed she wouldn't ruin it due to a reckless mistake on her part.

Kiera lifted her eyes up to take in the mermaid behind the counter. She was incredible, her blonde hair streamed down to her waist, and glimmering orange and pink scales ran up and down her forearms and legs. She tucked a few loose strands of hair behind her ear, revealing her delicately stacked piercings. Her nails shimmered iridescent like the pearl bartop in front of her, but it was her eyes that stopped Kiera in her tracks. They shone like the last rays of sunset, golden with flecks of amber encircling her pupils. Night after night, Kiera had seen those very eyes cascade by in a breathtaking flash. Every nerve in her body settled in Attalin's presence; oddly enough, it felt like finding her way home after a lifetime spent desperately searching.

Attalin smiled warmly at her, breaking Kiera from her trance. She was cautious when meeting new people, but something about Attalin put her at ease. Questions unfurled like petals in her mind. How was it possible to know the eyes of someone you've never met? Was this tied to whatever pulled her to Etabon? Cassidy's words on the train about a lingering connection rang in her ears. Hallowfeld sat down at one of the pearl stools along the bar, throwing Kiera an impatient look. For now, her questions would have to wait. Kiera shifted uneasily onto the stool beside him; she was going to have to get used to this tail.

Attalin beamed at her again as she set their lavender drinks down in front of them. "This is your first transition, I take it."

"Is it that obvious?" Kiera replied.

Attalin's eyes flicked to the ceiling and back. "Well, I don't recall seeing a desert lynx at Etabon before. Singular animal form magic is rare, you know?" Actually, Kiera didn't, but she wasn't going to admit that in front of Hallowfeld.

"That's enough chatter, Attalin, you're monopolizing my new guest here. Go make yourself useful," Hallowfeld snapped.

Attalin shrugged a shoulder and moved off down the bar. Kiera's temper flared back to life. Her jaw clenched against the urge to tip Hallowfeld off his chair and onto the ground; she'd do anything to wipe that superior look off his face.

He smirked at Kiera. "So let's discuss the matter of you trespassing into Etabon."

She clutched her drink tighter. Kiera had managed to coax her claws back into her hands and feet earlier, but they were threatening to poke back out.

Hallowfeld went on, "When I was a boy, my father took it upon himself to try and rid the world of any remaining literature on magic. He'd store the seized manuscripts down in the cellar with the wine and turn them over to the Ruling Board in batches. The man lived for their approval. Between you and me, he was rather dull and didn't read a single book on the subject. An utter waste of knowledge if you ask me. I had no such qualms. That was until he caught me, of course." He let out a smug laugh, but if Kiera hadn't been watching him out of the corner of her eye, she would've missed how he subtly winced. He ran a hand absentmindedly through his tresses, revealing a silvered scar across his temple.

He lifted his glass to his lips and drew a mouthful before continuing. "It so happens that one of the oldest volumes briefly mentioned the potent magic of animal shifters. Your kind takes on a solitary animal form; you don't necessarily fit neatly into the defined categories of magical forms, you see. Where there's any number of, say, witches, werewolves, and fauns, the text stated that only one—at most, two—shifters are in existence at a given time. There was some drivel about balance, but what I gathered is every so often, your kind is born into the world with no rhyme or reason. The point is, I'm intrigued by your magic and would like to see what you can do. I can't say I believe the words of whatever raving lunatic wrote that journal centuries ago, but I care if there's a shred of truth about the energy you could generate. My business here is to restore our planet. I'll allow you the chance to make a useful contribution to that undertaking. This is the bargain: If you entertain my guests by fighting in the opening tournament today and win, I'll let you walk away with your freedom, and the Ruling Board won't learn about your violations."

Kiera considered him as he nonchalantly sipped from his drink, as if he hadn't just told her to gamble her life in the arena. Her hands trembled at the idea, knowing the odds were against her. She'd heard her professors whisper about people who trained year-round for Etabon's tournaments. Opening day was for the untried contestants to showcase their skills, but still, many were prepared fighters.

Her mother had taught her the fundamentals, like how to throw a punch and where to strike to target the sensitive parts of the body. She walked alone to and from academy and often spent evenings by herself when Rose had the night shift, so she couldn't be too careful. She was practiced at wielding and throwing a kitchen knife and knew how to disarm someone in case of a desperate situation, but Kiera knew next to nothing about her new body and magical abilities. Still, what other option did she have? From somewhere deep inside her, a small voice whispered that she could do this. At the very least, she had to try.

Kiera swirled her claw around in her drink. "And if I fail to win the tournament, what happens then?"

"Hmm, yes," Hallowfeld murmured, "then I'll have to turn you and your cohorts over to the Ruling Board. They'll likely incarcerate your family and collect whatever assets you have as reparations for the strain you put on my magic and the risk you posed to the safety and wellbeing of Etabon's guests."

Kiera flicked her tail and leveled her eyes at Hallowfeld. "That sounded rehearsed. You've said that before."

He leaned back, placing his hands on the bar. "That may be true, but never to an animal shifter, I assure you."

Kiera swallowed. She certainly didn't feel assured. She asked, "Fighters have sponsors, don't they? I don't even have a certification band, so who will I be fighting for?"

Hallowfeld snapped his fingers, and a gold and black certification fighting band appeared on the bar. The band had no symbol to signify whom she'd be fighting under.

"We'll have to keep it anonymous. It'll add to your mystery, and no one will have to claim the humiliation when you lose miserably," he said.

"So, winning would guarantee our safety and freedom. You won't report us to the board."

Hallowfeld wasn't a man who enjoyed repeating himself. "Yes, with our agreement, you and your classmates will have your freedom, and your indiscretions will remain undisclosed."

Before terror could paralyze her, Kiera reached out and shook his hand. "It's a deal."

Kiera snatched the band off the counter and shoved it onto her wrist. Magic hissed, locking their bargain into place.

He drained his drink and shoved off the counter. "Attalin will take you to the rings to prepare. Good luck, my feline friend. I look forward to the show."

Hallowfeld's cheerful farewell disturbed her. Kiera's nails were biting into the pearl countertop. Her tail thrashed wildly, and the air around her ears prickled with magic. She knew she needed to center herself and focus; she didn't have the luxury of giving herself over to despair. The fate of everything she held dear was on the line with this bargain.

"He's vile, isn't he?" Attalin huffed.

Kiera startled. Attalin had made her way back over on silent feet. She wanted to agree, but Attalin did work for Hallowfeld.

"I'll be honest," Attalin said, eyeing the exit he'd disappeared through, "I've never seen him so intense about a guest's magic before. You should be careful."

"It's a little late for that," Kiera muttered.

"Oh, I see," Attalin squinted as if she could see into Kiera's thoughts, "a bargain. I'm paying off my father's debts working at Etabon. It'll be ten more years before I win my own freedom back." Kiera's stomach knotted. She didn't want to pry, so she nodded back instead.

"We should get you to the rings then. I heard him say you'll be competing."

Kiera didn't know why, but she mumbled, "It's my first real fight, I'll probably lose."

Attalin leaned forward. "That's not true. I heard you tackled a nixie just for looking at you the wrong way." Kiera couldn't help the laugh that slipped out, and Attalin gave her a knowing wink.

"I'm Kiera Vandyer, by the way." She reached her hand across the bar, and Attalin grasped it, sending a pleasant buzz spiraling through her.

"Attalin Porter. Nice to meet you."

While Attalin got herself ready to leave, Kiera waited patiently on her stool at the other end of the bar. A few moments later, she stepped out from behind the counter and spoke quietly with a siren who was throwing furtive glances at Kiera. The siren, who appeared to be a couple of years older than them, was shaking her head, sending her powder blue hair quivering across her back. The light from the chandeliers glinted off her nose ring and the sapphire scales along her cheekbones. Her long almond-shaped nails were digging into her arms which were crossed over her chest.

Unsteady footsteps drew Kiera's attention away from the conversation. A man with bloodshot eyes staggered over to their side of the bar. This was the first being she'd seen here that looked to be an ordinary human, so Kiera was fascinated. His chest heaved as he gripped the counter for support and sweat curled the graying hairs at his temples. He was multiple seats down, but she could still smell the liquor wafting off him.

"Where's Hallowfeld?" he slurred at the two of them.

Attalin's eyebrows shot up as she said, "Wendel, you should go home and get some sleep." Her voice was soothing and had an edge of concern in it.

"Where?" he pressed irritably.

"I'm not sure; you just missed him," Attalin replied, her stare hovering between him and the siren.

There was a flash of emotion behind his swollen eyes. "Get me a drink." His words were so garbled they were nearly incoherent.

"No, Wendel. You've had enough for today. I'll make you some coffee, just give us a minute," said the siren firmly.

The man went rigid, and then he began muttering erratically. He curled in on himself and then quieted. After a strained moment, Attalin turned back to their conversation. Kiera's ears tipped forward, and the hairs on the back of her neck stood on end. Instinct had her leaping off her stool before the threat completely registered. The man had slid a knife from his pocket and swung it at Attalin. Kiera narrowly made it, her body slamming into his, thrusting him aside before he could make contact. Shouts of alarm erupted from behind her.

He crashed into a table and chairs but managed to remain upright. Spittle flew from his mouth, and he flipped around, enraged.

"Put it down," Kiera warned. Her claws had slid free, and she set herself in between him and the others. A pained cry escaped his lips, and he charged at her. She dove forward to meet him, catching his wrist and curling her talons around it. He yelped, and the knife fell from his grip, clattering to the floor. Kiera pressed him back and pinned him to the ground. He flailed against her hold, but his strength was no match for hers.

A werewolf with gold fur burst into the tent and stormed over to them, barking, "What's going on here?"

Kiera kept her voice steady as she said, "He tried to attack them."

The wolf's eyes settled on the knife. He picked it up and sniffed the blade, immediately jerking his head back. "This is poisoned. It could've killed someone in seconds."

Attalin stepped forward and addressed the werewolf. "Patrick, it's my fault. He got upset when I refused to serve him. He's not in his right mind. He needs help."

Kiera realized Attalin was protecting the man by telling a half-truth. He was already agitated when he couldn't find Hallowfeld, and it hadn't been Attalin that'd told him no.

The wolf bared his teeth at her. "It's not up to you to decide what he needs." He wrenched the man from Kiera's grasp and hauled him onto his feet, keeping his arms locked behind his back. The force wasn't necessary; all the fight had gone out of him. Silence filled the tent as the werewolf pushed the man through the exit.

"I take it back, I'm not worried," the siren said with a hand on her hip. Her eyes scanned Kiera and flicked to Attalin. "You'll be fine with this one."

Attalin stepped forward and set her hand on Kiera's shoulder. "That was brave. Thank you for stopping him. I owe you my life." Her eyes held Kiera's for a charged moment.

Kiera dipped her chin. "Happy to help." It was lucky her adrenaline had kicked in and that her body had reacted on impulse.

"We'd better get going. Jade, I'll see you later," Attalin said. The siren gave her an encouraging wave and then proceeded to right the scattered table and chairs. Kiera grabbed her backpack from where it'd fallen on the floorboards and hurried back over. Attalin pressed gently against her arm, directing her toward the tent flaps.

When they'd made it outside, Attalin put a hand to her abdomen and closed her eyes. Her chest rose as she inhaled a deep breath, letting the breeze tousle her hair.

"Are you ok? We can sit," Kiera said.

She'd understand if Attalin needed time to decompress. The encounter had been jarring, and Kiera's own palms were slick with cold sweat. The fur along her spine had settled, but the confrontation had left her jumpy.

Attalin chewed her lip. "I'm alright. It's the fact that I should've seen this coming. Wendel's been on edge for weeks. I've been visiting with him, but in the preparation for opening day, I missed how bad he'd gotten."

Kiera hadn't believed the hype around magic's chaos, but this had her questioning. "Was it magic that caused him to react that way?" she asked quietly.

A grimace contorted Attalin's face, and she reached up to clasp the gold chain around her neck. "Magic doesn't do that to people. What we witnessed in there was grief."

Confusion had Kiera opening her mouth only to shut it again. This was clearly upsetting Attalin and really none of her business.

She didn't want to put her through any more stress, so instead of inquiring further, she said, "Whatever he's going through, I'm sorry for the suffering it's caused him and you."

Attalin's eyes softened, emotion shifting in them like she'd made up her mind about something. She looked around and then linked her arm with Kiera's, drawing her into a walk.

She kept her voice low when she said, "I'm certain that blade wasn't really meant for me. Wendel is a good man who made terrible choices today. He and his wife came to Etabon after he received a grave diagnosis. They didn't have the funds to pay for a healer when they got here last year or the time to save up for one. Even if the witches want to heal someone for free, Hallowfeld sets the minimums, and he enforces them. Most wouldn't take that risk for a stranger. The one place where funds aren't exchanged for their services is for competitors in the arena. Wendel was too weak to compete; plus, humans aren't allowed to enter. His wife's magical form was an alary. She made a bargain with Hallowfeld. A healer would cure Wendel, and she'd compete in three one-on-one matches. He was cured, but she didn't make it out of the last match."

Kiera was gutted by Attalin's words and all they meant. A woman's life had been unnecessarily cut short because Hallowfeld truly preyed on people's misfortune to lure them into the arena. In his anguish, Wendel had wanted to go after Hallowfeld.

Her throat tightened with repressed tears. "Will he be ok?" Kiera asked.

"If anyone was paying close attention to what he said before he turned that knife on us, then no, he won't be." Attalin gritted her teeth. "It'd likely take more than a poisoned blade to stop that black heart from beating anyway."

Kiera understood she meant Hallowfeld. Bitterness coated her tongue, and uncontrollable shivers rocked her body.

"Hey," Attalin tightened her grip, leaning her shoulder against Kiera's, "we won't let anything happen to you. I've got your back." The steel in those gilded eyes of hers had hope rising in Kiera. She leaned into Attalin. She was still frightened, but at least she wasn't alone in this.

PRECIPICE

s Attalin and Kiera hiked toward the rings, she looked around and took in the site. The festival grounds stretched for miles. A mix of stalls and tents were scattered over the space, some near the streams and lush banks and others closer to the chaos of the fighting and entertaining arenas. The canvas and silk tents were filled with restaurants, sleeping quarters, and clubs, while the stalls boasted magical goods and services.

Kiera waved her hand in the direction of the arenas. "The rumors didn't do this place justice."

Attalin nodded. "I thought the same thing when I came here with my father; it can be overwhelming. He's a seer when in magical form and brought me along when I was thirteen to help out with his stall."

Kiera shifted her eyes to Attalin and said lightly, "Does he still tell fortunes? I could really use a premonition on how to win this tournament."

Attalin smiled, and then she bit her bottom lip. "He was banned from attending Etabon three years ago. Plus, it'd be an automatic disqualification. Hallowfeld prohibits fighters from using magical assistance beyond their own abilities in the tournament."

Kiera shook her head. "Have you been here without either of your parents since you were thirteen?"

"Yes, but my friend Jade, who's in a bargain of her own, and a handful of other great people, have looked after me. I'm permitted to leave once a year to visit my family." Attalin kept her chin up as she spoke as if she was straining against the heartache that threatened to drag her down.

The fear of being separated from her mother had hung over Kiera her whole life. It was cruel that Attalin was denied access to her family; she imagined it'd be like having a piece carved out of you.

"It's not right that he's keeping them from you. Once a year isn't enough. I'm sure that's hard on you. I wish there was something I could do."

Attalin slowed their pace and peered into Kiera's eyes. "Thank you. I miss them, but this is the only way I can keep them safe."

"I understand. I'm doing this to protect my mom, but it's my fault she's even in danger. I wanted to make our lives easier, and I ended up making things worse," Kiera replied. She explained the reason she'd come to the festival grounds in the first place and how she'd gotten caught up in the bargain.

"Your classmates are responsible for leaving the train, too. That's awful that they left you to handle this on your own. Cassidy sounds like a real piece of work." Attalin's face was flushed with outrage for Kiera.

She nudged Attalin's arm and said, "They didn't really get a choice in staying. Who needs them anyway. I've got you." Attalin's expression brightened at her words, the light in her eyes sent a rush of butterflies fluttering in Kiera's stomach. They approached a bridge that arched over a crystal-clear stream. Its eddying waters burbled along as if murmuring in a timeless voice that spoke to the deepest parts of her soul. As they crossed, Kiera bent over the iron railing to watch as their reflections rippled against each other in the swirling current.

"So," Kiera said, wanting to lighten the mood, "other than an affinity for catnip, do you know if there's anything special my form can do?"

Attalin cracked a grin. "For starters, I bet you could scare the wits out of every rat in Etabon. By the way, how will cleaning yourself work if water freaks you out now?"

Kiera pointed a claw at Attalin. "Ugh, I swear if you say anything about hairballs, I'm going to be sick all over you." They both pressed their hands over their mouths to stifle their shaky laughter. The tightness in her chest loosened—it was nice to release some of the tension from earlier.

"Seriously though," Attalin said, taking a breath, "I don't know very much about animal shifters. I don't think anyone does. I've only ever heard of one other solitary animal shifter, Nieyla; she's a badger form. I haven't met her myself, and no one's seen her at Etabon in years."

"What about the werewolves? Is their magic like mine?" Kiera replied.

Attalin tilted her head from side to side. "Not really, they're pretty common. I've seen entire families transform into werewolves when they enter the gates together. They do resemble animal shifters the most, but other than a nasty bite and amplified strength, their magic feels standard, although it is heightened during a full moon. It's not like yours—yours feels vast and almost slippery. I can't get a read on it. It may be how you swept through Hallowfeld's entry spell without a scratch on you."

"You can sense magic?" Kiera gaped.

Attalin rubbed the back of her neck, saying, "Yes, it's an uncommon skill, but some beings have the ability to sense magical energy. It's an impression I get. It's kind of like the tingling feeling that makes you look up to find that someone is staring at you from across the room." Kiera bobbed her head in understanding. She was familiar with that strange feeling, it happened to her at academy more times than she could count. People give off weird energy when they're trying to figure you out.

"Apparently, those with an intense attachment to Etabon tend to be inclined to the gift," Attalin said with a tinge of bitterness in her voice that caused a question to tumble out of Kiera's mouth.

"Does that mean you had dreams about magic as a kid?"

A blush crept across Attalin's cheeks, but she nodded yes. Kiera wanted to kick herself for being so blunt.

"You don't have to be embarrassed. I still get them," Kiera said, hoping to reassure her.

Attalin's eyes widened, and then her shoulders dropped in relief, "You might have the ability then too. If you do, you'll start to feel it after spending some time here. I'm not sure about how Nieyla's abilities manifested, but I heard a rumor that those with the gift could sense power coming off her in waves. It feels like that with you."

Kiera frowned. "I was hoping to know more about my magic to have a better chance in the rings."

"Don't doubt your form, Whiskers. It's good that your opponents don't know what abilities you have. They've trained longer, but they'll have no idea what to expect from you."

Kiera's lip twitched up. "Whiskers, huh?"

Attalin's eyes glinted with mischief. "They're the fiercest thing about you." She leaned forward and rumpled them.

Kiera snorted and batted her hand away. "Smartass. But you make a fair point—the others have more experience, but I'm an unknown, so I can use that in my approach to the fight."

"You still have a few hours before the matches begin. I'll share everything I know with you until then."

"Will Hallowfeld want you to go back to the bar?" Kiera asked.

Attalin wiggled her eyebrows. "He said to bring you to the rings, he didn't say when I had to return, and Jade agreed to cover my shift for me."

She came to a stop, and Kiera halted beside her. They'd arrived at the towering obsidian gates that held the fighting pits within, and Kiera couldn't help but feel she was standing on the precipice of her entire future.

The fighting rings were grander than Kiera had anticipated. They were made up of three monstrous pits dug deep into the ground. Each pit was surrounded on all sides by a cage of sheer russet metal that ran all the way up to form a dome at the top. They were crowned with what appeared to be measuring devices with numbers and a dial. The rings were situated in a way so that the massive U-shaped stands could have the best view from all angles.

"Do fights take place in all three rings at once?" Kiera asked, her eyes scanning the contestant area, taking in the beings already warming up among the tournament tents.

Attalin dipped her chin in confirmation. She moved to the outer edges beside one of the gray canvas tents.

Attalin kept her voice low as she said, "Try not to look too curious about the pits, it may tip some of the others off that you haven't trained in a ring before, and we want all the edge we can get." Kiera turned her focus to the other fighters. From what she could tell, there were all manner of beings competing—wizards, werewolves, faeries, and sirens, and that was only what she could see.

Attalin turned her back toward the others and leaned close to Kiera. "You see the metal surrounding each ring?"

"Yes," Kiera murmured back.

"That's not just to keep the crowd safe from the magic taking place inside the match but also to prevent any outside magic from assisting the opponents within." Kiera realized now that the strange thrumming she'd felt as she had walked toward the tents must be whatever magic was powering the domes.

"Those instruments on top of the pits measure the energy produced from the fight taking place within. Remember, once you accept a match, you're on your own and no one can help you. The only way out is to win, submit to your opponent, or die," Attalin whispered.

Kiera's body recoiled at the thought of death, but she gritted her teeth against it and chose to ask a question that'd bubbled up instead. "Do contestants tap out often?"

Attalin scowled. "Hallowfeld only allowed it to be an option because he says uncertainty adds to the chaos. This way, in every match, there's heightened anticipation and possibilities of who could live or die. A contestant can only surrender the match if there's a clear winner who can deliver a death blow. Most people don't give their competitors the chance to tap out—they go in for the kill."

Black dots pressed in at the edges of Kiera's vision, and her breath stuttered in her chest. Her grip on her composure was slipping fast.

"Easy there." Attalin put her hand on Kiera's arm, and a calm washed over her, reeling her back from spiraling into terror. "Let's start with your opponents' vulnerabilities. Magic is impressive, but if you pay close enough attention, you'll see there's a chink in everyone's magical armor."

Kiera shook the tension from her shoulders. "If that's true, then what's yours?"

Attalin hesitated but dropped her voice again. "My powers drain quickly if I'm not careful. I'm a mermaid but inherited a magic similar to the sirens. Where sirens can sing and mesmerize others, I touch the being I want my magic to influence, and it can impact their decision or reaction." Kiera didn't mean to, but she made what she could only imagine was a horrified face. Was everything she felt around Attalin this whole time a lie?

Attalin's eyes darkened. "I want to be honest with you—the only time I've used my magic on you was just now when you were about to pass out. Plus, my abilities only push a person toward the reaction I want. If they resist, it's difficult for me to change their course because it takes a lot of energy to use this part of my magic."

Kiera had that sensation from deep within again. Something in her bones was propelling her forward, telling her to trust herself and Attalin. If Attalin had wanted to keep this hidden from her, it would've been easy enough. Instead, she'd told her the truth, and after feeling the way her magic had altered her mood, somehow, she knew that she'd be able to sense her influence if she touched her with it again.

Kiera grasped Attalin's hand. "I believe you. You've been straight with me this far, and I'm sure it can't be easy to tell someone you could hijack their brain if you wanted to."

Attalin scrunched her nose. "Honestly, outside of my family, a couple of friends, and Hallowfeld, almost no one knows. I've lost a few good relationships that way. It's hard to open up to someone if they think you're making their decisions for them, but I'm not nearly that powerful anyway."

Kiera shrugged a shoulder. "Well, I think anyone would be lucky to have you in their life."

"That's really kind," Attalin said, giving her a soft smile.

Kiera was glad for the fur that hid the flush spreading over her face. Outside of her mother, she'd never been so candid with someone, especially not someone her age. Attalin made it easy for her to say what was on her mind.

Attalin rubbed her hands together. "Alright, we have a ton of magical knowledge to coach you on and not much time to do it." Over the next hours, they went through the tournament's roster. Whether it was dumb luck or a mistake on Hallowfeld's part, Kiera's name and form hadn't been added to it.

Attalin explained her opponents' magical defenses, like how the sirens put their adversaries in a trance. Kiera practiced pinning her ears and making growling noises in the back of her throat to drown out the hypnotic effects of their song. Attalin told her that the competitors who relied entirely on their magic would be easier to beat because their strength would drain faster. It was the ones who were not only skilled with magic but trained in combat that would be her greatest challenge.

Kiera cocked her head to the side. "So you're saying a trained faun would be harder to beat than a wizard?"

"What I'm saying," Attalin replied with a finger raised, "is there are limits to magical strength. We can only draw on what's available to us. Some say our ability to store magic has diminished since our ancestors' time."

Kiera wrinkled her brow. "Diminished? How?"

Attalin paused as they watched two alarys soar by overhead toward the warm-up ring. When they'd passed, she said, "If you trust in legends, centuries ago, beings could draw on their magic for days before depleting their cache and needing to recuperate. A wizard could cast spell after spell without getting exhausted. Now most of them only have enough for basic ones or a select few potent ones daily. Faeries with elemental magic used to be able to grow a thicket at the snap of a finger or call up a storm on command. Today, they can manipulate vines or scatterings of water."

"If that's true, what altered our capabilities so drastically?" Kiera asked.

"Speculation is that our capacity to store magic shrank over generations, and that it happened because we didn't have access to our magical forms until recently. Our ancestors evolved to accumulate and process magic constantly, but we've been separated from it for over a century, so it takes our bodies longer to complete the same tasks."

Kiera ran her tail between her hands. "I hadn't imagined our ability to hold magic as something that could diminish, but it makes sense that there'd be unintended consequences from severing our connection to our magical forms. So, we truly absorb magic in its raw form?"

Attalin nodded and said, "My father's a hovercraft engineer, so he explained it all to me this way: Magic is all around us here, and we're like rechargeable batteries that draw in and store that resource. Then we convert it into our own form of magical output to power our abilities. The higher the demands on that store, the quicker it'll drain. It takes time to fill back up and convert that energy again. The converted magical energy we release is what's absorbed by the planet."

"I wonder if our bodies could eventually revert back to their native states, like if we could expand our wells of magic over time," Kiera said.

Attalin leaned her head closer to Kiera's. "Funny that you say that because I've noticed a change. When I'm pushing my powers, I reach the end of my reserves about an hour later than I would during my first year here. I think living here has enlarged my cache. An hour doesn't sound like much, but in a tournament, it would make a difference."

The reverberation of the alarys' weapons clashing in the ring carried across the grounds to them. Kiera stilled, and a shiver went through her. "How long does it take to recuperate once you're drained?"

"If someone pushed themselves to the limit? Their bodies would need a sustained rest to replenish, like a night's sleep without accessing their magic."

Kiera's eyes trailed over to the grappling alarys, then to the individuals scattered around the contestant area. "Is there a way to measure exactly how much magical capacity someone has?"

Attalin shook her head. "No, someone like me can get a general sense of magical energy, but it's not exact." She followed Kiera's gaze. "I can say this for sure: You have more than anyone I've felt before."

Kiera crossed her arms over her chest. "I wonder what makes me different."

"Maybe your form naturally has a bigger store than the rest of us. Whatever the reason, some beings' magic won't last through the tournament, so that'll give you some advantage. The point I'm making is you'll need to use this," Attalin tapped Kiera's temple. "Be smart, draw your opponent in, and force them to deplete their powers, then strike when their guard is down."

Kiera dipped her chin in understanding. Attalin was right—if she had any chance of winning, it was going to take cunning. It'd be a dangerous mistake to fixate on her opponents' magical abilities and dismiss their other skills. A thought struck her: Attalin had said she contained more magical energy than anyone she'd felt before... Did that include Hallowfeld?

"Attalin, do you think Hallowfeld's capacity for magic is like mine?"

Attalin shuddered. "From what I can tell, he can hold a great deal but not to your level."

"Do you mean he's hard to read, too?"

The color had drained from Attalin's face. "His magic is disturbing. I try my best to block out sensing it when he's around, but yes, it's evasive."

Kiera's heart sank at the idea that she was anything like him. "So, we're the same in that way."

Attalin frowned. "I said your magic was slippery. It's elusive in a playful way, not deceitful. Comparing his magic to yours would be like comparing a deep grave to a boundless night sky. Your magic has a warmth and depth that his doesn't."

That reassured her. "I witnessed him use his powers when we were together. He seemed unstoppable."

"I've certainly never heard him complain about his spells draining him after casting, but you can't trust a single thing he says or does." Attalin shook her head. "He's devious. Don't let him distract you; what matters right now is you focusing on winning these matches."

She had a point, Kiera thought. "Alright, who's next on the list?"

With only thirty minutes remaining to the start of the tournament, Kiera had completed a crash course in magical history. She'd learned that werewolves have a lethal bite and that the faeries she was about to face could harness the elements: one was skilled in water, one in fire, one in wind, and the other in nature. She was hoping she wouldn't have to fight the fire elemental. If she was being honest, she'd had a fear of fire since she was a child.

Of all her opponents, the faeries seemed to be the ones with the least vulnerability to exploit. Attalin said their only real weakness was to amethyst. Kiera didn't know where she was going to find a rare amethyst stone before the tournament, so she'd have to rely on forcing her opponents to tap out. A trumpet sounded to call the contestants to prepare for the start of the matches.

Attalin took her by the shoulders. "We'll be moving over to the stage and stands—keep your chin up. You're brimming with magic, which makes you a real contender. You have claws and fangs now, so don't be afraid to use them. Tap into that primal instinct; there's wild magic running through those veins, so let it guide you. If a person believes you might truly kill them, they'll submit."

Kiera blinked at the blend of encouragement and brutality in Attalin's words. She swallowed. "Whichever way this goes today, I won't forget how you've helped me."

Attalin caught her by surprise and hugged her. "You've got this, Whiskers."

Kiera clutched her back, grateful she had Attalin to hold on to while this tempest raged inside her. Fear burned her throat, but coiled beneath that panic was an untamed power that'd been shaken from its slumber. Magic stirred in her bones, ready to be unleashed.

COMMENCEMENT

They wove back through the tents to the main pit area. They'd nearly made it to the stage when a nature sprite streaked up to them with a scroll in hand. Kiera stopped in her tracks and studied the petite being. Attalin had told her that although sprites were a similar size to pixies, sprites' powers manifested in the four elements like their larger faerie counterparts. The sprite landed and gave them a shy smile.

She was panting hard as she handed over the scroll. "A message from Hallowfeld," she said in a lilting tone. Kiera took the message, thanking her. She unrolled it and read,

Each contestant has their choice of one weapon to bring into battle with them, and I do not want to hear that you did not get a fair shot when you lose our bargain. Follow Imena to my personal weapons tent and choose wisely, my feline friend.

The nature sprite leaped into the air, her verdant aura suspending her in place. "If you'll follow me, please. We'll need to get you a weapon before the tournament begins, and we don't have much time left. Hallowfeld will crush me if you aren't back for opening ceremonies."

Attalin let out a whistle. "A pick from Hallowfeld's personal collection… What's he playing at?"

The nature sprite swayed in the air. "Sorry, Attalin, if it were up to me, you could come, but Hallowfeld's exact words were 'only the shifter is to enter.'"

Attalin exchanged a knowing look with the sprite. "It's ok, Imena, I understand."

She turned her eyes to Kiera. "You'd better hurry to make it back in time. I'll see you at the rings."

Kiera jogged along to keep up with Imena, her slight emerald form flashing ahead of her as she darted through the crowd. She was hoping Hallowfeld's weapons tent was within the tournament grounds, or else she was going to miss the start of the matches and would probably be disqualified. Was that his plan all along? Attalin had said Hallowfeld was conniving, and she may have walked right into one of his schemes. The crowd parted for them, some making startled noises and pointing as she went by. She watched Imena land in front of a gold silk tent, gesturing for her to hurry. Kiera skidded to a stop in front of the tent flaps.

"We have about fifteen minutes before the ceremony starts."

Kiera looked down at the trembling sprite. Could she have meant what she said before about Hallowfeld crushing her? That wizard is heartless, she thought. Kiera ducked into the tent and then froze as she took in what lay inside. The tent was stocked wall to wall with weapons of every make and material. It struck her at that moment she had no idea what to choose. There was an overwhelming number of options to pick from. She turned in circles, taking in the labeled tables.

There were bows of polished elm and oak, next to a table laden with crossbows and maces. She moved along, taking in a rack of sparkling gold and steel swords. Hanging from the adjacent wall were enormous staffs and axes. Kiera closed her eyes. Her skin was starting to tingle all over, and her fur was standing on end. This was the first time she had been alone since this insane nightmare started. It was as if the walls in the tent were closing in on her. What was she doing here? She was such a fool to have any hope of making it out alive, much less winning.

Tears welled behind her closed eyes, and she began taking in big gulps of air, trying to calm herself. She backed herself up against one of the tables and leaned against it, pressing the pads of her hands to her eyes. Her mother's voice drifted to her out of nowhere, a memory from her childhood rising up to the surface: *"My brave girl, you've never been one to back down from a challenge."* The memory made the side of her lip curve up.

She recalled that one of the boys a few grades above her had been bullying kids in her class, shoving them to the ground and stealing their toys. He was a government administrator's son, so the instructor had excused his behavior. When words hadn't worked with him, Kiera had taken it a step further. The boy had been massive, but she'd fought him viciously, the instructor having to pull them off each other. The headmaster had ordered her mother to inflict a harsh punishment, but that wasn't Rose's way. That evening as her mother cleaned the cuts and scrapes on Kiera's face, she'd said, *"Kiera, don't feel ashamed for standing up for others. We do our best to make peace, but some fights are worth having."*

Kiera's eyes flew open. Her mother's words from that day rang true. She may not have much, but she had grit. She wouldn't shy away from this fight. She'd battle for Rose and prove to Hallowfeld he couldn't use intimidation to force her to give up. Kiera knew his real reason for sending her to this weapons tent, and it wasn't charity. He'd wanted her to doubt herself, but that viper didn't realize the rage he'd lit inside of her instead.

Kiera pushed herself off the table and scanned the room, she felt something like a tug in her belly button area and followed it toward a table covered in throwing stars and daggers. She ran her hand along the blades until she touched a bandolier filled with glittering throwing knives with a vein of purple running down the length of the steel. It was like the blades had chosen her—she felt it in the pit of her stomach, these were her weapons. The answer had been in front of her this whole time. These certainly weren't kitchen knives, but they'd do just fine. She snatched the bandolier up and ran for the tent flaps, bursting out into the sunlight.

"Follow me!" Imena sang. "We don't have much time to make it back to the podium. I'll lead you there."

She let out an affirmative growl. Imena sprang into the air and made a beeline toward the pits. Kiera charged after her; she refused to miss the start of these matches.

Kiera couldn't believe how agile she'd become. She flew over the gravel paths at a blistering speed, dodging visitors with ease. Her eyes narrowed in on the podium outside the fighting pits, where all the contestants were standing on stage waiting for Hallowfeld's opening speech. A banner hung behind them displaying all their names and forms, and she could make out her own form at the bottom. Where her name should have been, it said Lynx. A surge of energy propelled her forward. As Hallowfeld held up his arms and opened his mouth to begin the ceremony, she crouched and leaped in a frantic attempt to make it on stage. To her surprise, she landed gracefully beside him. He stared at her with round eyes, a spark of anger glinting in them.

It was an accident, but she decided to go with it and let her fangs flash. "I couldn't help but make an entrance." Kiera waved to the crowd, her tail flicking. They roared and stamped their feet in excitement. Hallowfeld scanned her and the bandolier she had strapped around her.

"I don't tolerate tardiness; one moment later, and you wouldn't be participating in the events today."

"Yes, and whose fault would that've been?" Kiera hissed from low in her throat.

"Go take your place," Hallowfeld ground out. Kiera swept past the other contestants, most of them openly glaring at her as she marched to the end of the stage. She caught a glimpse of Attalin in the staff area, a hand over her mouth, and Kiera winked at her.

Kiera forced herself to keep her eyes forward toward the stands. She wanted to glance down the line at her opponents, but that would make her look nervous. She'd be standing in the ring with any one of them soon enough. Attalin had explained how the brackets worked in the competition. The event would start out with sixteen contestants facing off one-on-one. By the second round, eight would remain, and by the third round, there would only be four, and then the final match would take place. That meant that she'd have to successfully beat four opponents to win the competition.

Kiera turned her attention back to Hallowfeld, who was addressing the crowd using some spell to amplify his voice.

"My honored guests," he bellowed in his pretentious tone, "do I have an exciting tournament planned for you. Today, as always, to kick off Etabon's festivities, we'll see our first-time fighters battle to become the opening day champion, but I have a special treat in store." Kiera felt herself wince at his words.

"For the first time in Etabon's history, we have an animal shifter competing for the title," he paused for effect, "represented under an unmarked banner, no less."

The crowd buzzed with curiosity. Kiera wanted to shrink back from all the eyes on her, but she tilted her chin up to the crowd instead.

"The rules of combat remain the same. Contestants may bring one weapon of their choosing into battle and cannot have any outside assistance. The only way to leave the ring is by victory, submission, or death. Any deviation from these rules will result in immediate disqualification, and I'll personally deal with the transgression."

This sobered the crowd up a bit. Kiera could only imagine what this buzzard did to contestants who disobeyed him.

Hallowfeld lifted his hands up to the crowd. "May Etabon's magic flow freely through you all!" The crowd roared back as Hallowfeld turned to make his way off the stage, sneering at Kiera as he passed.

The contestants filed off after him, heading to small tents dotted around the ring's edges, marked with their banners. Attalin was standing next to her banner. It matched the armband Kiera was wearing, solid black with a gold strike running down it to mark that she was unsponsored. She ran her hand along it, admiring how the stitching caught the sunlight, shining like the gold in her fur.

Attalin bounced on the balls of her feet as she said, "I don't think I've ever seen Hallowfeld that ruffled before, people are going to be talking about you interrupting his opening for weeks." She gave Kiera a once-over, taking in the bandolier of throwing knives. "You look brilliant. The other contestants won't know what to make of you. Since these are a set like a bow and arrows, they'll count as one item. Way to find a gray area, Whiskers." Attalin looked back over at the podium. "You should have seen when everyone first went on stage and noticed that an animal shifter was added to the roster. It caused a panic."

Kiera kept her eyes trained on Attalin and clasped her palms together to keep them from quivering. Her nerves were live wires, every sense painfully amplified. The bandolier chafed against her fur, and her ears flicked at the hum of the crowd. The scent of their sweaty bodies packed too closely together causing her stomach to roll and saliva to flood her mouth. "Let's hope they keep believing that I'm the contender they're making me out to be."

Attalin blinked at her. "It's what *you* believe that matters. Remember what I said, trust your instincts, and let your magic lead you through these fights."

Kiera turned toward the tent. "So, who am I up against first?"

If she was wishing for an easy first match, she wouldn't be getting one. She was slated to go against Asha, a siren. Attalin had told her that Asha's sponsor, a wealthy weapons manufacturer, spared no expense in training his apprentices for the fights. He used the matches to charm potential clients. Kiera grimaced at the twisted ambition of it all, how the elite used their time at Etabon to advance their social status outside of it.

The board may despise the existence of magic, but apparently, this place had become significant to the prosperity of Atterah's so-called finest citizens. Kiera imagined the board members sitting around arguing about the merits of opening the site in the first place. She gritted her teeth—those greedy hypocrites. Kiera shook her head to clear it; she needed to concentrate. She watched as the other fifteen contestants made their way to the starting lines marked in front of their tents. Kiera understood now why there were three fighting rings. It would move the matches along quicker with three fights taking place at once, especially since there were eight to get through in the first bracket alone.

Kiera and Asha's names appeared in blood-red smoke in the air above the rightmost pit. Attalin had told her earlier that smoke displaying her name would be her cue to enter the ring, and once she passed through, it would lock the match into place until completion. Kiera threw her shoulders back and moved toward her side of the entrance. She wasn't strong in any form of faith, but for good measure, she sent a prayer up to any of the old gods who were listening and to the magic that had led her along this far. She'd asked Rose once about religion, curious about the true believers who still practiced in secret, risking the board's condemnation. Her mother had told her of a time before when many gods and faiths were accepted. Now people were only permitted to revere the board.

Kiera whispered under her breath, "Let your magic flow through me."

The thrill of magic buzzed around her, as if in response. She gazed across to the other side of the ring to see Asha taking her place, resplendent in a cobalt tunic. The sun played over her scales, a strip of navy and lilac running the length of her cheekbones. The same blend adorned her hands and feet. Asha's raven hair was braided into a tight crown atop her head, making her look every bit a warrior queen. She had some type of golden short sword strapped to the outside of her left forearm. Kiera would have to move quickly to make sure she didn't use that. Asha sent her a dazzling smile that she could only assume meant death, so in response, she flicked her tail in the air and let her claws slide free.

Their eyes were locked as they stood in tense anticipation, waiting for the trumpet to sound to start the match. The cheers from the crowd faded away—she wasn't sure if that was the effect of the metal cage around them or her adrenaline kicking in. The trumpet rang out, causing them both to flinch. Asha immediately began singing, testing Kiera's susceptibility to her magic. They circled each other, Kiera with her ears pinned, making snarling noises in the back of her throat to drown out Asha's voice. Her brain began to scramble for how to attack. In Attalin's lesson, she'd said the sirens' song was combated with specially designed tuning instruments to throw them off kilter with their shrill pitch.

It was Asha that made the first move when she freed her blade and lashed out in a fluid movement. Kiera reacted in the nick of time, sliding through the sand, the blade nearly missing her midsection. The siren's eyes flared with delight. Kiera hoped her speed would throw Asha off; it only seemed to spur her on even more. Asha lunged, again and again, her swift movements like a dance back and forth, faster and faster. Kiera was starting to falter, her throat getting dry, her concentration on her snarling flagging. There was no way she could keep this up. She was thankfully a fraction quicker than Asha by some form of her magic, but her training was clearly no comparison, and Kiera could sense she'd tire before Asha's singing would give out.

In her moment of distraction, the tip of Asha's sword found its mark, clipping Kiera's shoulder and sending a jet of blood spraying over the sand. Kiera's snarling rose an octave as pain lanced through her. The slice wasn't deep, but it incited Asha. She needed to get away to regroup.

As Asha raised her blade to land another strike, Kiera pushed her legs to the limit to leap out of the way. She ended up launching herself higher than she planned, colliding with the side of the dome. Her claws sunk into the metal and caught her before she plummeted back to the ground. Asha stared up at her with blood-chilling intensity. She stretched out her fingers and beckoned her.

Kiera read her lips as she sang, "Come here, you filthy mutt."

She forced herself to maintain her growling as her eyes darted around frantically, searching for options. An idea struck her, and she violently raked the claws of her left hand through the dome's metal, jerking it back and forth as she made the cut.

Sparks flew, and metal screeched between her fingers. She watched with relief as Asha fell to her knees, covering her ears in agony, and with that, Kiera released herself from the dome, falling to land on top of Asha. She pinned her to the ground, her claws firmly against her throat.

Kiera leaned down and whispered in her ear, "Submit or die."

Asha looked utterly shocked. Her blade had been knocked away and lay in the sand a few feet from them.

"Choose, or I'll rip out your vocal cords," Kiera said.

Blood pooled in the crevice of Asha's neck as Kiera's talons punctured her skin. She felt far away—was it really her saying these terrible things? Asha's eyes widened, and she thumped the ground tapping for submission. The dome's magic hissed to mark the completion of the match. Kiera pushed off Asha, staring down at her as she rose. "How does it feel to lose to a mutt? You can tell your friends the Lynx let you live." The stands exploded with applause as Kiera stalked out of the ring. As she exited, her eyes drifted to the instruments above the pits. While the other two dials leaned to the lower numbers in the left corners, hers stood straight up in the middle.

The fight was already replaying in her head. The squealing noise her claws had made against the metal had been sharp enough to save her. Kiera barely made it through the flaps of her small tent before she collapsed on the ground, vomiting up the contents of her stomach. She heard the tent's canvas rustle, but she didn't have the energy to pull herself up off the ground. Attalin crouched down beside her.

She tried to talk, but Attalin hushed her and said, "Drink this," pushing a container of water to her lips.

Kiera hadn't realized how thirsty she was until she started to drink. It was like she'd never drink enough again as she gulped down mouthfuls of it. Attalin rubbed circles on her back.

"You should slow down, or you'll be sick again."

Kiera nodded, struggling to get into a sitting position. She couldn't quite right her thoughts to get words out; there was so much she had to say, but her mind wouldn't stop buzzing.

Attalin said, "Deep breaths, your adrenaline is still in high gear from the fight."

Kiera breathed in and out, trying to focus only on that and taking small sips of water. When she felt steady enough, she rasped out, "How long?"

Attalin understood that she meant how long until her next match and replied, "You have time to get settled. The second part of round one will need to take place, and that should be twenty or thirty minutes—that's the benefit of being part of the first matches."

She looked over to the simple chair in the tent and turned back. "Are you ok to stand?"

"Yes," Kiera said.

Attalin helped her move over to the chair. Kiera swiped her hands over her face.

"It was pure luck that I won that match. I didn't even get a chance to use my weapons."

Attalin shook her head, handing her a damp towel for her face and shoulder. "Don't you realize you didn't need them?"

Kiera glared at her and then stared down at the ground. She wasn't angry with Attalin—she was upset for so many reasons. For how out of control she felt in the fight, for what she'd said to Asha, and the uncertainty of the rest of the tournament.

"I'm sorry, I know you're only trying to help."

"Kiera, listen to me," Attalin said in a tone that made her look up. "I haven't seen someone fight like you did today, especially not against someone trained like Asha. It's like you were anticipating her moves. I know you say what you did was luck, but I watched you, and if you saw what I did, you'd see things differently. I think your magic manifests in an innate ability to fight, which makes sense because your form is a predator animal. You wouldn't believe the amount of energy you put off; it's more than I've ever seen in one match."

Attalin went on, "It was clever to rip through that metal to stun Asha, but you're underestimating your physical abilities; they got you through the first half of that match. You beat a trained warrior, and you should have seen Hallowfeld's face when you did it. He looked even more stunned than Asha." Kiera snorted at that.

"Now that you've fought once, it'll get easier, and your next opponent isn't as agile or skilled as Asha. With the first three matches over, they've already moved you on and paired you up with your next opponent. You'll be facing Garrison. He's an orc, and all he has going for him is brute strength—I saw his last fight."

Kiera leaned forward in the chair. "Well, I need to focus in this next match. Panic nearly lost me the last one. Whatever magical instincts you're seeing probably won't last the whole tournament."

Attalin shrugged. "Fine, that's fair, but I have a feeling the next match will go smoother for you. I need to take a look at your wound."

"There are bandages in my pack," Kiera said.

Attalin got them from her bag, but when she bent over her to inspect the cut, she gasped. To their amazement, the slice across her shoulder had knitted itself back together—apparently another perk of her magical abilities.

Kiera took the next half hour to gather herself. It's not that she wasn't grateful that she'd managed to win the match, but she was fearful of the part of herself that'd enjoyed it. She would've liked to step out of the tent and watch the remaining first-round matches, but she still felt shaky. She couldn't have the other contestants spotting her and thinking she was vulnerable.

She tilted her head against the chair's coarse fabric, pressing her fur down against her face. Attalin poured water on the ground and threw a towel down over where she'd been sick. Kiera had forced down the bar of rolled oats Attalin had pushed at her, saying she needed to keep her energy up, and she couldn't do that on an empty stomach. Attalin had to be one of the kindest people she'd ever met; she reminded her of Rose.

"You don't need to do that."

Attalin waved her away. "I've seen far scarier messes at the bar—trust me, this is nothing."

The next words left Kiera's lips before she realized what she was saying, "Did you hear everything I said to Asha in the ring?"

Attalin paused and then said, "Yes, everyone did. The magic of the dome allows the audience to hear what's taking place within. It amplifies it and filters out the effects of persuasive magic, so we weren't caught up in Asha's song."

Kiera remained silent, partly because she felt too ashamed to keep speaking, and partly because she was stunned by the arena's powerful spellwork.

"Kiera." Attalin had moved over to crouch down in front of the chair. "I understand what it's like—I'm in a bargain with Hallowfeld too. When I look at you, I see myself a few years ago. I would give anything to go back and change what happened to me and my father. I can't do that, but I can make a difference in what happens to you today. You can win this bargain. Yes, what you said to Asha in the ring was brutal, but remember, you're fighting for your life. You're demonstrating to Hallowfeld and the other contestants that you're a force to be reckoned with. Don't let the mask you're wearing for these people make you doubt who you truly are inside."

Kiera spoke around the lump forming in her throat. "I didn't believe before today that I could say or do things like that to someone."

Attalin smiled sadly. "It's scary what we're capable of when we're forced to survive, but there's a difference between bluffing and making the real choice to end someone's life. My hope is you won't have to find out what that's like today."

Kiera pushed herself up from the chair. "Attalin, I don't mean to pry, but what happened between Hallowfeld and your father?"

A trumpet sounded three times to signify the completion of the first round. Attalin's head snapped to the tent flaps and then back to Kiera. "That's the signal that your next fight will start soon."

Kiera grabbed her bandolier of knives off the floor where she'd discarded them earlier and strapped them back on. She was headed toward the exit when Attalin took her hand, her hair rippling in golden waves around her as she said, "What happened… It's a long story, but I promise I'll tell you after the tournament."

Kiera didn't have the heart to say *if* she made it through the tournament, so she gave Attalin's hand a reassuring squeeze instead.

PREDATOR

Kiera walked back to the starting line in front of her tent and looked up, marking the sun making its lazy descent toward the western hills. That meant they had a couple more hours of daylight. Hallowfeld probably had some ridiculous spell that could light this place up like noontime if the matches bled into the night. She glanced over at his box to find he was staring right at her, a sour expression on his face. Kiera grinned, waving her tail in the air toward him; she could practically hear his disgusted snort from here.

Kiera cast her eyes around the arena. The eight remaining contestants had lined up at their tents. She wondered what their sponsors made of her. Some of them had to be furious with her last-minute entry after all the time and money they had poured into preparing their fighters. Maybe that's why Hallowfeld was agitated—some of his "esteemed guests" might not be thrilled with him due to the surprise contender.

Red smoke filled the air over the three rings forming into the names of the competing contestants. Her name appeared next to Garrison's above the rightmost pit. Perhaps this ring would bring her luck a second time. She noticed they'd already patched the spot in the metal she'd damaged earlier.

It felt silly, but as she strode toward the pit, she whispered under her breath again, "Let your magic flow through me." She willed Etabon's magic to guide her, and a flicker of warmth danced around her.

When Garrison came into view, her fur stood on end. He towered at least four feet over her, and she couldn't guess at what he weighed. His light gray skin had darker gray welts pocked all over it, and his wings, splayed out behind him, were tipped with jagged points. He was dragging a colossal axe through the sand. As he leveled his red gaze at her, Kiera realized it wasn't his form that unnerved her but the unhinged way he was glaring at her. She felt her stomach flip at the putrid stench that hit her when she passed through into the ring. Garrison's body was crusted with dried blood; his axe was splattered with it too. He'd even swiped some on either side of his face like some sadistic badge of honor.

Curse her new heightened sense of smell. She was narrowly holding herself back from retching in front of everyone. She couldn't help herself as she choked out, "You smell like hot garbage."

Garrison's voice boomed out, "Aw, is the poor kitty worried I'll get her pretty fur dirty? How about I make your pelt into a nice towel to clean myself off with after battles."

She spat on the ground, "Really, *kitty*? You're so unoriginal."

This time she didn't plan to be caught off guard. She readied herself for the starting trumpet. Moments later, it rang out across the arena. She dispatched a throwing knife from her bandolier, flinging it at Garrison's chest. To her surprise, it flew toward him with laser precision, but the point bounced harmlessly off him, falling to the sand. It didn't leave so much as a mark behind. Garrison guffawed, amused at her attempt to penetrate his incredibly thick skin. He advanced on her, emboldened. Attalin had warned her, while orcs were not nimble, their skin was like stone, making them difficult to take down.

Garrison swung his axe toward Kiera, but she spun out of his way, landing lightly on her feet. It was easier to manage her body after the first fight, but she needed to make her move soon. One hit from his axe, and she'd be finished. Garrison lumbered toward her; he was trying to pin her up against the ring's wall, so she baited him into moving forward. There was just enough room as he raised his axe for her to leap up and over him, somersaulting in the air to land on his back.

She'd learned from Attalin that orcs had one physical feature they were particularly partial to: their wings. If you knew where to look, they were also their greatest weakness. That's why they rarely ever turned their backs on their enemies. They had thinner skin there, and although it would still take a huge amount of force and scalpel-like cutting ability to get through, they could be damaged. With all her might, Kiera slammed her claws into the top of Garrison's right wing, the force making her bite her tongue. He instantly began bucking and shrieking in pain.

"That's enough!" she screamed. "You'll make me shred your entire wing off if you don't quit."

He slowed to a stop, black blood oozing from his wound in between her claws. "It's your choice. Submit, or you can let me tear through the artery here, and you'll bleed to death."

Garrison fell to his knees, bellowing in rage as he slammed one giant fist against the ground, tapping out of the match. She yanked her claws free and jumped to the ground as black blood showered the arena floor. Kiera shoved down her nausea at the gore. She turned toward the exit and realized she could hear the crowd chanting, "Lynx, Lynx, Lynx!" Hallowfeld was going to love that. Kiera studied the dial over the pit. It hovered near the middle again.

She sprinted back toward her tent. This time she wouldn't have long to recuperate before the next fight. Attalin was standing outside with a container of water and a towel in hand. Kiera nearly whimpered at the sight. She could smell that Attalin had doused the damp towel in lavender oil.

She tossed it to Kiera, holding her elbow over her nose. "You reek!"

Kiera gagged. "You're telling me."

She began rubbing Garrison's sweat and the mixture of dried and fresh blood off herself. It was going to take more than a damp towel to get rid of this odor, but at least it would be bearable for now.

Attalin passed her the water, beaming. "I told you that you'd beat him easy."

Kiera coughed around her water. "You call that easy?"

Attalin opened her mouth to reply, but the trumpet sounded three times to mark the end of the second round. Kiera let out an exasperated breath, her body was starting to wilt from the constant strain. Attalin looked up at the roster as the markers settled, and Kiera noticed the concerned expression ripple across her face before she could master it. She'd seen the names realign too. She would be going up against Xavier, the nature faerie. From the reverent way Attalin had spoken about them earlier, she thought the faeries would be her most formidable opponents.

If she let herself worry, she'd crumble, so she said dryly, "You think he knows to grow me irises? They're my favorite."

Attalin let out a strained laugh, and Kiera turned back toward the starting line. She lifted her eyes up to the sky to watch the red smoke coalesce into her name, hopefully, not for the last time. Kiera murmured, "Let your magic flow through me," and her skin prickled with the hum of magic.

She'd be in the leftmost pit this time, closest to Hallowfeld's box, but she refused to look over at him. He wouldn't get the chance to rattle her. Instead, she peered through the latticework of the dome as she rounded her side toward the entrance. Xavier was striding toward the entryway on the opposite end, and even from a distance, she could tell he had the grace of a dancer. His hair was the color of fresh clay with strips of hunter-green mixed in, and it curled around his finely pointed ears. Intricate swirls of jade marked his arms and legs.

They stepped into the ring at the same time, taking their positions. Xavier wiggled his nose, scenting the air. Kiera shrugged and gestured to herself, "I didn't have time to send it out for a wash, what can you do?"

Xavier raised his chin, flat-out refusing to answer. She arched an eyebrow and threw him an obscene gesture. He let his lips quirk up; he was striking, she had to give him that. The trumpet sounded, and Kiera immediately felt the ground beneath her quake. That's not a good sign, she thought.

Vines ripped their way up through the middle of the pit's floor, shooting into the air and arching to aim for her. Kiera sprang out of the way, rolling in the sand and up onto her feet, but the vines kept coming. She dodged left and right, lashing out with her claws to cut through them, but they continued snaking their way toward her, creating a barrier between her and Xavier.

She needed to get to him; if she could engage him face-to-face, it'd be harder for him to focus on using his magic. Kiera turned away and sprinted for the ring wall. She'd use the dome to her advantage again and climb up and over them. She squatted and jumped into the air only to feel a vine grasp her ankle and slam her back down to the ground. The breath whooshed out of her, and she gasped, trying to force air back into her lungs. The rest of the vines were on her now, slashing at her face and making cuts on her cheeks and upraised forearms. She rolled, but that tangled her legs further in the vines. The thorns shredded through her fur and skin.

Her breathing was coming in pants—*No, no, no,* her mind screamed. She was suddenly yanked off the ground, and the vines shot up, suspending her in the air, high above Xavier. The jerking movement embedded the thorns deeper into her flesh, dragging a cry out of her. He sneered up at Kiera. She was a fly caught in a spider's web, and he was slowly wrapping her legs and torso tightly. Her left arm was pinned to her leg. She let out a strained huff, recognizing she wouldn't be able to breathe soon. Tears pricked behind her eyes from pain and fear. She needed to think.

Xavier's gaze was bright with excitement. He must've known it would be seconds before she'd have to tap out or be fully encased in the vines and suffocate. Kiera still had her right arm free and was trying to slash her way loose, but it was no use with the other vines trying to tear at her face and eyes. With that, she remembered her blades; they were her only chance. She ripped one free of her bandolier as a vine tore a deep gash across her exposed neck and made a haphazard shot at Xavier.

He wasn't expecting it and didn't dodge in time, taking the blade squarely in his shoulder. The impact knocked him to the ground. The vines were instantly released. Kiera knew a fall from this height would kill her, that this was it, but she still turned over in the air, the ground coming up fast beneath her. She landed with a hard thud on her feet. It took her brain a moment to catch up. She wasn't currently a human, she was an animal shifter, and this body was infinitely more resilient. Kiera turned to find Xavier on the ground yelling in pain and clawing at the blade that was buried in his shoulder to the hilt. His screams were jarring, like that of a suffering animal. She reacted on instinct and ran to him and knelt down.

"Xavier?" He writhed away from her. She looked up and saw panicked faeries running back and forth near the ring entrance, but they wouldn't be able to get in until the match was complete. Whatever was happening to him couldn't be good if his sponsors were reacting like that. He was gaping at her like a fish, as if he couldn't speak.

"Tap out!" she yelled in his face. He didn't react. She couldn't watch him suffer any longer—it had to be the blade. It could cost her the match if he was acting, but she wouldn't watch him die. She grasped the hilt and wrenched it free. He collapsed in a heap, and there was a strange sheen to his skin.

"Xavier?" She crawled closer to him. "Are you ok?"

He didn't respond, and she couldn't tell if he was breathing. She choked out, "Please," and mopped the sweat from his forehead.

Her mind spun... Could she have killed him? He stirred lightly, and she watched as his pinky finger tapped the sand. The ring's magic crackled, ending the match. She let out a gasp of relief. The entrance exploded open, and faeries poured through, running toward Xavier with a stretcher, shouting about poisoning and amethyst. Kiera couldn't comprehend how that could have happened until she looked down at the blade in her hand, realizing now what the thin vein of purple was running through them.

She had been wearing the faerie's greatest weakness this entire time and hadn't even realized it. She stood on stiff legs as she watched them carry Xavier away. Kiera felt hollow, and the pain from her wounds pushed through her shock. She stared numbly up at the dome's measuring instrument, the dial leaning past the middle to the right. It took everything in her to walk out of that ring back toward her tent.

Attalin was waiting inside with wide eyes and open arms. Kiera collapsed into her embrace, sobbing. She had almost killed someone, and she wasn't entirely sure if he was going to make it. The other two fights felt like child's play compared to what had just happened. Her own cruel death threats from earlier replayed in her ears, feeling real now.

Outside of the tent, she heard Hallowfeld's voice boom over the stadium, not fully comprehending what he was saying.

"My dear guests, we'll be taking a thirty-minute intermission to let our contestants prepare for their final match. Best of luck to our last pair!"

Kiera couldn't get Xavier's limp form out of her mind. It was like her thoughts were trying to spool out of her head. She was trembling uncontrollably. Attalin began singing lightly, it was some type of sailor's lullaby. Her voice was soothing. Kiera felt like she really was on the waves hearing the ocean lapping up against a boat. She settled in Attalin's embrace, listening.

"You're a beautiful singer," she whispered.

Attalin gave her a kind smile. "I learned at the bar. You pick things like this up when you hang around a bunch of sirens and mermaids for too long. We get lots of requests for old-timey ballads and shanties. You'd think our patrons would realize most of us have never even been on a boat." Kiera smiled back at her. She hadn't asked about Attalin's aquatic abilities.

"Have you ever been to the ocean?"

Attalin nodded. "Yes, hundreds of times. It sounds silly, but I feel like a small part of magic must exist outside of this place because I swear it calls to me. Honestly, it's said mermaids can choose to access their tails in any body of water, but with Etabon's magic not extending beyond its borders, I don't know how true that is. I can confirm that in the streams and bathtubs here, I can call up my tail on command."

Kiera nodded. "I wondered how that worked. So, if I splash you with a cup of water, your tail won't pop out."

Attalin rolled her eyes. "No, the tail and gills are fully optional." She wiggled her fingers. "The scales not so much, but I like those."

Kiera inhaled a deep breath, moving to get up. Attalin helped her up from the ground where they'd ended up after she'd collapsed.

"I appreciate you taking my mind off what happened with Xavier—I was unraveling."

"I know, I could see it in your eyes. Kiera, you have to believe that was out of your control. How could you have known those blades had amethyst in them?"

Kiera paced back and forth in the small space. "It wouldn't have changed my decision to throw it either way. I have to win this bargain, consequences be damned."

Attalin stepped in front of her. "Stop beating yourself up. Xavier and the other contestants wouldn't have thought twice about killing you. What you did today could change things. When you chose to help Xavier, you broke the standard that Hallowfeld set for everyone. You showed mercy and still won the match."

Kiera looked into Attalin's eyes. "When I realized he was hurt that badly, I could've tried to tap out myself, but I didn't."

Attalin pursed her lips. "It wouldn't have worked. In his condition, he wasn't threatening your life in any way. We can debate all day about what you could've done, but the reality is you showed a kindness that others won't extend to you, and maybe it'll start a discussion about how contestants operate in the rings."

Kiera wanted to break something. "If the instrument above my match proves anything, it's that you don't have to slaughter anyone to produce energy. There's so much good here, I can feel it in the magic. I don't buy that garbage about it feeding off chaos; if anything, it responds to mercy. There has to be a way to heal the planet without people losing their lives. Magic has this awareness to it, it's intuitive.

This bloodbath fits the board's narrative, it makes this place out to be wicked, but that's nonsense."

Attalin bobbed her head. "Yes, and it's people like us who can continue to fight every day to make changes for the better." Attalin gripped her shoulders. "Listen, you need to understand your next opponent won't take mercy. You'll be facing Rowan. He's a wizard and is as wretched as Hallowfeld. He was trained personally by him and fights under his banner."

Kiera's jaw clenched. She wasn't sure she could force herself back into the ring. The last match had fractured something inside her. How could she justify saving herself at the expense of the other contestants? Didn't that make her a conspirator in this madness? Once she'd learned the rules, her plan had been to inflict the least amount of damage possible to make her opponent tap out, but she'd been naive to think she could control that. She opened her mouth to say this to Attalin, but her throat tightened with emotion.

Attalin touched her cheek. "Kiera, the world isn't black and white, there is no clear-cut good or evil. There's just us in the middle of all of this and the choices we have to make. Remember that when you're battling for your freedom in this next match." A rustling came from the tent flaps. Kiera turned in surprise.

"Pardon the intrusion," said a melodious voice on the other side.

Recognition flashed in Attalin's eyes. "It's Imena," she murmured.

Kiera gestured that it was ok for her to enter.

"You can come in," they said at the same time. The nature sprite hurried in and landed on the chair's arm.

"I have news about Xavier," she trilled.

Kiera compelled herself not to sway in place as Imena said, "The witches were able to reverse the effects of the amethyst poisoning. He'll make a full recovery."

Her body sagged with relief. "That's great news, Imena, thank you for delivering it. If I can ask, who sent you?"

Imena squared her shoulders and stood up to her full height. "You deserved to know, so I decided to send myself. I saw the way you reacted in the ring. You were kind to help him. A few moments longer and the amethyst would've shut down his organs. We should have more participants like you at Etabon."

Kiera blinked at her in astonishment. "I appreciate your kind words, Imena." The sprite beamed at her, then flitted over to plant a soft kiss on Kiera's cheek. Then she looped through the air and disappeared through the tent flaps.

Attalin stared after the nature sprite and then looked at Kiera with a smirk. "Sounds like you've started a mini-revolution, Whiskers."

She snorted. "I'll toast to that after this next match."

Attalin replied, "It's a deal then. Now, let's clean you up."

Her injuries were working to bind themselves back together, but Attalin had to bandage the gash on her neck and the worst tears on her arms and legs. It looked like it'd still be hours before they'd completely heal. Kiera was searching her forearms for the cuts the vines had inflicted, but only the deepest punctures remained.

She looked up at Attalin. "These powers are extraordinary, but I feel wrung out. How will I know for sure when I'm at the end of my magic?"

Attalin ran her hands through her hair, thinking. "I would describe it like finding a brick wall where there'd been a wide-open door before. For me, when I've burned through my magic, my mind goes quiet. I've spoken with others who feel it more gradually, like sand running through their hands. Everyone is different. With this being the first time you're using your magic, it's hard to say how far you can push yourself before you're depleted. You should be good for the next match, though. I can sense magic coursing through you. It isn't as intense as it was earlier, but there's a solid presence."

Kiera stood warily. "Rowan must be a powerful wizard to have made it to the final match. You said that witches and wizards have the physical strength of their human bodies, so his spells must be potent."

Attalin scowled. "Yes, don't underestimate him. He has a warped talent for spells that'll target your deepest vulnerabilities."

Kiera pinned her ears to her head. "He was mentored by a walking nightmare; I wouldn't expect anything less."

When they emerged from the tent, the sun was dipping down below the hills, making the red smoke stand out against the purpling sky. Kiera stared up at her name floating over the centermost pit next to Rowan's. It was strange how one day could feel like an eternity had passed. Whatever the outcome of this final match, Kiera's life had been altered—she couldn't unsee this version of herself.

She cleared her thoughts, focusing solely on the curious incantation that'd led her through the day. "Let your magic flow through me," she intoned, reaching out with her mind to Etabon's magic. It was like a cord was pulling her along, drawing her toward the middle pit. That familiar impression of warmth brushed her shoulders but was interrupted by an ominous shift in the air around her. A chill slithered up her spine. She looked across the ring and caught eyes with Rowan, his harrowing stare cutting to her core.

It occurred to Kiera that this was the reaction Attalin had described when she sensed Hallowfeld's magic. The awareness was overwhelming; it was horrible timing for this ability to surface. Rowan's eyes were piercing blue, he had a smattering of freckles across his cheeks, and soft auburn curls. It was unnerving that a stranger could look at her with such hate in his eyes. He inclined his head toward her, tilting the silver staff in his hand at her, too. The bottom of it was filed to a sharp point. That didn't feel like a sign of respect, more a gesture of farewell.

She took in the banner he wore across his chest, a serpent wound around a wooden staff. How fitting for Hallowfeld's coat of arms, Kiera thought. There would be no reacting to her opponent's taunts this time; she stayed supernaturally still. She locked her spine, barely breathing.

When the trumpet blared, she charged toward him, claws out, wanting to end this swiftly. He parried, using his staff to block her attack. He'd narrowly managed to deflect her. She readied to strike again, but he lifted the staff and slammed it down to the ground releasing a spell with a burst of light. Her vision went black, and she paused to figure out what manner of enchantment this was.

Kiera knew next to nothing about spellwork. Attalin had tried to equip her with the basics, but she hadn't had a fraction of the time needed to understand this type of magic. Attalin had explained spells were layered with complexity, they could be tangible, like calling an object into existence, or invisible to the eye and simply a feeling, like the magic that binds a bargain. Kiera wasn't sure if the entire ring was shrouded in darkness or if Rowan had taken her sight. Her ears twitched trying to hear where he was, and that's when the screaming started—she would know that voice anywhere.

Kiera whipped around frantically, searching the darkness. It was Rose crying out in pain, pleading for her.

"Mom, where are you?" she shouted.

Her brain was spinning—how could her mother be here? Had Hallowfeld located her and brought her to Etabon? She stumbled in the darkness, trying to determine where the cries were coming from. Rose's voice was breaking in anguish, and her sobs were becoming increasingly panicked.

"I'm here, I'll find you." Tears were streaming down Kiera's face now. Every whimper tore at her resolve until her grip on her conscience slipped away. "Rowan, I swear I'll end you," she yelled, but there was no response, only Rose's begging.

Kiera's heart was shattering. Something stirred beside her, but the turmoil had muddled her senses. She detected Rowan too late. He must've crept up to her while she was frantic. She lunged away but not fast enough as a searing pain cut across her thigh. Kiera gasped in agony and staggered back. Her hand flew to her leg. The wound was deep, blood gushing out around her fingers. She turned toward where Rowan's assault had come from, snarling with rage. Kiera steadied herself, trying to hear where he'd gone, but the screaming came again.

This time it was Attalin begging Hallowfeld to spare her family. She was imploring him to take her life and not theirs. Kiera slammed her hands against her ears, recognizing this wasn't reality. Rowan was using the spell to project her fears into the darkness. Covering her ears was a terrible mistake. She couldn't hear as he struck again, the sharp metal of his staff dragging across her back. Kiera roared as the slice made a burning path from her shoulder blades to her lower back.

The impulse to flee kicked in, and she lurched forward, trying to make her way to the ring's wall. She slammed into it, clinging to it to keep herself upright. The blazing rupture along her spine threatened to drag her into oblivion, but she refused to lose consciousness. Rowan's plan unfurled in her mind. He was distracting her and then inflicting as much damage as possible so she'd weaken and bleed out before her magic could heal her.

The screams began again, a blend of young and old voices. This time they were accompanied by Hallowfeld's crowing laugh as he ordered them into the fighting arena. She shook her head—she wouldn't give in to the illusion. Kiera forced her brain to focus, struggling against her magical cache. It was nearly depleted. She felt close to her breaking point. Intuition cautioned her that if she strained against her reserves any harder, she was going to burn out. Beyond that limit was an abyss, and if she tipped into it, she wasn't sure she'd be coming back.

Kiera spoke into her mind, *You're a predator, dammit, so act like one.* Her eyes searched through the darkness, her pupils dilating, and she caught a flicker of movement approaching on her right. She rallied her strength. She'd have to wait until the last possible moment to react. Kiera reached out with her senses, feeling for Rowan in the dark, beseeching Etabon's magic to keep her conscious for a few minutes longer. She let her body slacken against the wall. Rowan approached confidently, believing she was spent. He raised his staff above his head, and that's when she pounced.

Her body slammed against his rolling them to the ground and scattering sand in all directions. The impact shattered his spell. The world came hurtling back into focus. Kiera felt an excruciating ache in her shoulder, Rowan's staff was clean through it, protruding through her skin and fur. Her heartbeat was pounding in her ears as she let her jaws close around Rowan's throat, her canines ripping through his skin. Kiera tasted the copper tang of his blood on her tongue, mixing with hers. She felt herself slipping away, but she was taking him down with her. Rowan made a strangled noise. She was close to his jugular now, she felt his pulse thumping in time with hers, a millimeter away from ending him.

More blood spilled into her mouth. All she had to do was dig her fangs in a fraction more, and it'd be over, but she hesitated. The rage in his magic eddied feebly against her, but she couldn't bring herself to inflict any more pain. All she felt for him was deep sorrow. She wouldn't let her last act in this world be a cruel one. Kiera released her hold on him, and her world went black.

She felt herself floating away into darkness, being pulled to a quiet, solitary place. There was a nagging behind her though, like she'd left something she desperately needed. She struggled to turn around, but she was so tired. Kiera saw two strange figures, one of amber and one of ochre, calling to her, beckoning her back toward a dazzling light.

"They need you, Kiera. Your journey isn't over." She wanted to tell them that she didn't have the strength, but she couldn't find the words in this strange place.

"It's ok, child, we'll help you get back, you just have to let us in."

She wanted to cry out that she didn't know how, but her instincts took over, and she whispered into the void, "Let your magic flow through me."

8

FORGED

Kiera jolted awake. Her eyes flew open to take in a dim canvas ceiling.

"Oh, thank the old gods."

That was Attalin's voice. Kiera was so disoriented she flailed her arms, trying to get up.

"Steady now," came a comforting voice. She felt gentle hands pushing her to lie down on her back.

"Where am I?" Kiera sputtered.

"You're in a recovery tent. You need to calm yourself down, you had a rough go of it and my magic is still trying to do its work," said the same voice.

Attalin came to stand next to Kiera's head, looking disheveled. Her golden hair was matted with Kiera's blood, and her face was red and blotchy.

"Are you alright?" Kiera said, looking up at her.

Attalin let out a choked sound. "Am I alright? I should be asking you that." She reached out and took Kiera's hand. She looked a bit dazed as she said, "Your heart stopped."

The sweet older woman tending to Kiera gave Attalin a disapproving glance, clearly not thrilled she was sharing the news with her while she was in this condition. Healers wanted their patients relaxed, not agitated.

Kiera murmured, "I had the strangest dream. I was in this dark place, and there were these two shining figures."

The woman and Attalin shared a concerned look. Kiera decided not to go on before they thought she was hallucinating and gave her a sedative or something.

The other woman spoke again. "You've lost a great deal of blood. You'll need to stay here and rest for an hour or more before you can move. I'm afraid I've used all my magic to heal the worst of your injuries. I'll have to send for another witch to finish replenishing your blood and to get those wounds completely patched up."

Kiera's hand shot to her arm. The battle came crashing back to her. Her shoulder ached horrendously, but Rowan's staff wasn't sticking out of it anymore, so that was a good sign. Kiera looked at the woman, her eyes widening, comprehending how close she had been to dying.

"Thank you for saving my life," she said.

She gave Kiera a warm smile that lit up her sea green eyes and wiped the sweat from her brow, moving her short salt-and-pepper locks from her forehead. "It's my greatest joy to help others in need, plus any friend of Attalin's is a friend of mine."

Attalin gave the woman's shoulder a squeeze. "Gabby is the best witch in all of Etabon. You were in good hands."

Gabby patted Attalin's arm. "Maybe in my younger years. Your friend here is a fighter, that's the reason I was able to bring her back to us."

She began packing away tools and vials into a worn leather bag sitting next to Kiera on her cot.

"Someone will be here shortly to take my place." She pointed at Kiera and said, "I saw you fight in the rings, I know you're stubborn, so don't get the idea that you're invincible. You need to let my spells work. Your magic's drained, and your body needs to rest."

Kiera nodded as vigorously as she could manage. This woman could give even Rose's fussing a run for its money. Gabby picked up her bag and nodded to them both.

Kiera said quickly, "Is there any way I can repay you for your kindness?"

Gabby turned at the tent flaps, her bright eyes sparking. "Keep fighting for the right reasons, Kiera, that's all you need to do to repay me." With that, she was gone.

Kiera let her shoulders press into the pillow under her, and a twinge went through her injured side. Her whole body felt heavy. She turned her head toward Attalin, wanting to hear how the tournament went after she'd blacked out. She was dreading the outcome, but she needed to know.

"Attalin, what happened after I passed out?"

She bit her lip and moved closer to the bed, sitting down on the edge of it. That can't mean good news, Kiera thought.

Attalin pressed a hand to her cheek, worry clouding her eyes. "Kiera, I'm not sure Rowan is alive."

Kiera wasn't expecting her to lead with that. She hadn't imagined that Rowan wasn't alright. She'd assumed that he'd outlasted her and been healed after she'd fainted.

"I thought you said my heart stopped—wouldn't that technically make him the winner?"

Attalin flinched. "Your heart didn't stop until you were back here in the recovery tent when Gabby removed the staff from your shoulder—you started hemorrhaging."

Kiera stared at the tent flaps. Her mind had gone blank. Attalin shifted on the cot. "Rowan tapped out right before you collapsed. They ran in and pulled you two apart. The gash on his neck looked horrible. Your fangs must've ripped deep because he was drenched in blood. They rushed him to a recovery tent too, but I haven't heard if he made it. Normally Gabby would've tended to him, with him being Hallowfeld's apprentice, but she chose to work on you instead."

Kiera gazed at Attalin. "She did it because we're friends?"

Attalin smiled at her. "Yes, and Gabby has a soft heart for kind souls.

She watched your fights. Anyone with sense would have chosen to help you over Rowan."

That put a bad taste in Kiera's mouth. Even if Rowan was despicable, she couldn't come to terms with being chosen to live over him. It didn't feel right. Attalin fixed her with a look that said she wanted to say more about Rowan. It was bad form to speak ill of the dead, and since they didn't know what had happened to him, it seemed she wasn't going to go on about it. Kiera dug her claws into the cot's soft down, remembering the things she'd heard in the ring.

"I don't think I could've prepared for the spell he used on me."

Attalin's eyes were full of wrath and sorrow.

She replied, "When he cast the spell, the whole ring went dark, but then the dome's magic cut through the illusion to show the crowd what was happening. We couldn't hear what he was making you hear, but it was pretty clear when you called out for your mother what he was forcing you to endure."

Kiera felt a tear slip down her face.

Attalin leaned forward and brushed it away. "People train for years to combat illusion spells—you did the best you could."

Kiera suppressed a sob. "I was foolish, and my fear took over. I should've realized he couldn't have summoned my mother inside the border because magic can't travel beyond it. She's never applied for a band, so Hallowfeld couldn't have brought her here either. There was more; I heard Hallowfeld tormenting you and other innocent people. It felt so real it was excruciating."

Tears filled Attalin's eyes now. Kiera gingerly moved over on the cot, and Attalin laid down next to her. Both of them stared up at the ceiling. It felt safe to be near her, lying there, shoulder to shoulder. She could almost pretend they hadn't met under such terrible circumstances.

Attalin's voice quivered. "I'm sorry, Kiera, for all of it. I should've done a better job of warning you, especially about the burnout. I didn't anticipate you reaching the end of your magic; you had a decent amount when you went in. It's dangerous to try to access our powers when we're depleted. When we force ourselves past our breaking point, our bodies will faint to protect themselves. It's a way to stop the strain before we harm ourselves. Every second that you fought to stay conscious, you drove yourself closer to death, and it would've been my fault."

Kiera answered firmly, "No, I won't let you take responsibility for my actions. I understood exactly what I was doing when I pushed myself over the edge. It turns out I do have the ability to sense magic too, and it kicked in at the start of the match." Attalin inhaled sharply.

"Exactly," Kiera said. "I'm lucky it surfaced when it did because I relied on it to find Rowan, but with my body trying to repair itself at the same time, I used more magic than either of us could've predicted." Kiera leaned her head on Attalin's shoulder. "Don't question yourself for one second, you're the reason I made it through the tournament. Without your knowledge and support, it would've been impossible."

Attalin interlaced her hand with Kiera's. "Hallowfeld may be crafty, but you beat him. You took back your freedom even when he stacked the odds against you. You did something many of us have wished to do—you gave others hope."

Kiera blinked up at the ceiling. Today had been the worst day of her life, but she'd succeeded. She could feel it now. The magic from her bargain had dissipated—she wasn't bound to Hallowfeld. She'd won. It hit her that stumbling into Etabon had been a disaster and a miracle. She'd found her magic, met Attalin, and discovered that there was so much she didn't know about her world. It'd shown her that she really did have the power to change her fate, even in the smallest way. Before she could say this out loud, a faint voice called at the tent flaps. Attalin sighed, sitting up.

"That'll be the other witch Gabby sent for. I'll let her in, then I need to go clean myself up and get back to Nautilus for a bit with the matches letting out."

Kiera felt lost for words. There was so much she needed to tell Attalin. She wasn't ready to say goodbye after all they'd been through together.

Attalin's lip quirked up. "Don't worry, Whiskers, you're not getting rid of me that easy. Come to the bar after you've regained your strength. I'll get your post office information, and we can write each other. Didn't you know the best friendships were forged in blood?" Attalin tugged at her wrecked tresses.

Kiera snorted. "So dark for such a shiny mermaid." They laughed together as Attalin headed toward the exit.

Kiera was fascinated as she watched the other witch do her magic. Attalin had told her that witches and wizards could replenish blood and other elements of the physical body when healing another being, but they couldn't refill magical stores. No one could—the body had to handle that on its own. Light flared from her hands, stitching together her wounds that hadn't fully healed. She could feel her strength returning as the witch murmured incantations, her hand resting gently on Kiera's chest.

"Were you entirely drained from the tournament?" the witch asked.

"Yes, I believe so," Kiera said.

"I could swear I sense wisps of magic here." She lifted her hand from Kiera's torso, shaking her head. "I must be wrong. That'd be unheard of to regain power so quickly." The witch let out a bemused laugh. "I'm probably just getting tired myself."

She'd wished Kiera well and reiterated Gabby's instructions to rest, and in another half hour or so, if she could stand without feeling light-headed, then she could do as she pleased. Kiera was itching to leave the tent, but she was determined to listen to the witch's advice. She had no idea how the damage someone sustained at Etabon affected their body once outside of it. Kiera was sure it wouldn't be good if she had unhealed wounds before she left, and she'd need to get back home before Rose did.

Her mother was working a triple shift, so she wouldn't be home until morning herself, but Kiera would need to catch a bullet train back, and she had no idea what hour it was. She stood from the cot, slowly testing her arms and legs for soreness, but felt none. She ran her hand across her shoulder and down her back along her spine, searching for scars, but there wasn't any trace of the injuries she'd sustained earlier. If only the damage inflicted on her mind could heal as easily.

Kiera collected her bag from under the cot where Attalin had stowed it for her. She pushed through the tent flaps, and warm night air rushed to meet her, ruffling her fur. Kiera breathed in deeply, savoring the calm and quiet surrounding the recovery tents. She scanned the area; there was something she needed to do before she went to find Attalin. She scented the air, catching traces of blood in it... her blood. She followed it until she was standing outside of a black silk tent. A sinking in her stomach confirmed that Rowan would be inside.

She faltered, unsure if she should go in. Could she handle what she'd find? As she was reaching for the opening, a woman in a dark red cloak, carrying a leather bag like Gabby's, breezed out, giving her an irritated glance.

"Excuse me," Kiera said.

The witch's shoulders tensed, and she turned back toward her. Kiera's fur prickled. This woman's body language indicated she wanted nothing to do with her, but she'd come here for answers, and she wouldn't leave without them. When her frost-blue eyes landed on Kiera, she realized it was the witch from the gateway earlier. Her mouth went dry, remembering the way her magic had silenced her voice. She wasn't sure how to phrase the question.

"Is Rowan... recovering?"

The words felt strange on her lips. It was odd to ask if someone was still living, especially someone she'd harmed. The witch's eyes narrowed, but she replied. "He was barely hanging on to life. We had to put him in a spell-induced coma to heal, but his heart rate is stable. It's expected that he'll make it through."

The witch grasped her cloak, and Kiera caught sight of a tattoo on her wrist. It was of the moon nearly eclipsing the sun, feeble rays of light speared from the top of the crescent. The witch turned and stormed away. Kiera knew she should feel guilty, but she only felt empty.

No other sounds stirred around her, so she crept into the recovery tent. It was similar to hers, bare except for a simple cot, and it smelled of antiseptic. Rowan lay sleeping, bandages covering his throat. His breathing was ragged, and in this condition, he appeared far younger.

Kiera kept her voice low and smooth, "Rowan, I came to say I'm sorry my actions put you in here. I hope Etabon's magic heals you quickly." She reached out to brush his shoulder, and a stabbing pain rooted her in place. Blue light radiated between her palm and where she made contact with Rowan. After a moment that felt infinite, she jerked her hand back and watched as the blue light pulsed within him and then traveled up to his throat before fading away. His body relaxed, and his breathing leveled out. Kiera rubbed her hand and released a breath. For a beat, she'd been concerned that she'd hurt him, but he seemed okay, calmer even. Maybe the light had been some kind of defense mechanism. She decided not to push her luck and backed out of the tent.

She'd made it a couple of steps away before another witch passed her on the path and entered Rowan's tent. Good, she thought. Now that someone would be looking in on him, she was less concerned about how she'd left after their interaction. She let relief wash over her, thankful she hadn't taken any lives today.

9

GALA

Kiera wandered back toward the bar, trying her best to take the emptiest route, but when she did pass anyone, they recognized her from the arena. Instead of going through the bar's front, she headed around back to see if she could meet up with Attalin without braving the crowd within.

As Kiera rounded the corner, a phantom wind surged around her, and from out of nowhere, a charcoal box with a matching envelope floated into her arms, and then the wind dissipated. Intuition told her who it was from before she opened the letter. She tucked the box under her arm and flipped the envelope over to see a wax seal with Hallowfeld's coat of arms on it. Her claw shredded the seal, and she pulled the message out. The letter was written in glowing crimson script. It read,

My feline friend, we have a few loose ends to tie up before you can depart. I'll see you at my manor, dressed accordingly. Enjoy the gift.

A glowing cord of crimson light shot out from the letter and snaked away into the night. She wiggled the letter back in forth in her hand, and the crimson cord wiggled too. Was she supposed to follow it to his manor? She pulled the lid back on the box to reveal a gown of ivy-green silk. A groan escaped Kiera's lips, and her hackles rose. It'd been too easy to think she was done with him. There was no way the gatekeeper would let her out before she went to see him. Kiera decided she'd say goodbye to Attalin before going to Hallowfeld. It'd be best not to drag her into any more drama. When Kiera made it behind the tent, she found the siren who'd spoken with Attalin at the bar that morning sitting atop a whiskey barrel. She twirled a strand of powder blue hair around her nail and tilted her head to the side when she saw her.

"You must be predictable because she said you'd come back here looking for her instead of going in."

Her words were direct, but she'd said them with gentleness. Kiera's nerves were frayed, she needed to speak with Attalin, deal with Hallowfeld, and then head home as soon as possible. The siren was watching her tail swishing back and forth. Kiera stopped it. She realized her anxiety was coming off as rude.

"You're Attalin's friend who covered for her while she was at the tournament." Kiera took a breath and looked into her eyes. "Thank you for doing that. I couldn't have made it through the matches without her. I'm Kiera."

The siren dipped her chin. "I'm Jade," she said as she hopped off the barrel.

Kiera smiled at her. "Nice to meet you."

She made a move toward the bar when Jade stepped into her path. "Attalin's not in there. Hallowfeld sent her to his manor to bartend for his opening day gala."

Sweat broke out along her palms, and she glared down at the letter in her hand. That slippery snake. Jade pursed her lips, her eyes narrowing in recognition as she noticed the envelope.

"Hallowfeld's sulking, and it's pretty clear to me he knows you wouldn't consider leaving without speaking with her." She crossed her arms over her chest and watched Kiera carefully. "Attalin put her neck out for you earlier, and Hallowfeld's focus is on her now more than ever."

Kiera felt guilt in the pit of her stomach—she'd been thinking the same thing. It was clear that Jade was concerned for Attalin's safety and honest enough to speak freely to her about it. From what Attalin told her earlier, she knew they looked out for one another; they were like family. Kiera had gotten her freedom back today while Attalin was still under Hallowfeld's control, and likely to bear the brunt of his resentment. Her spine stiffened, and she turned to Jade with fire in her eyes.

"You're right. I'll have to give the prideful toad what he wants."

Jade straightened and raised her eyebrows, she looked at Kiera with approval. "Well then, what'd you have in mind?"

Kiera respected her courage, but if her plan backfired, Jade could get caught up in Hallowfeld's wrath too. "Are you sure you want to be involved?"

Jade grinned. "If it'll help Attalin, of course. Plus, you're growing on me. It's about time someone beat Hallowfeld at his own game."

Kiera let the weight of her remarks sink in, she felt Jade was giving her far more credit than she deserved. They shared a conspirator's smirk.

She waved the envelope at her. "Want to go to a party?"

Jade flicked her wrist toward a silver tent situated behind them. "Before we go anywhere, you need to clean that mess off you. We get ready in there sometimes before our shifts. There's hot water and towels."

Kiera frowned down at her matted fur and ruined clothes. "Right."

"I'll meet you back here in fifteen," Jade said over her shoulder.

She hustled into the tent. There was a counter with a large mirror and chairs at the front and then stalls at the back with showers. Kiera set the box on the counter and tossed her backpack on a chair. There were large glass jars with small, packaged soaps and combs next to the towels. She grabbed one of each before rushing to the nearest stall. She turned the dial up to nearly scalding and stepped under the stream, watching as red and black grime from the day slid off her.

When she was done, she dried herself off, and then she swiftly combed out her coat, leaving her fur glossy with a pleasant citrus smell. She grimaced at the charcoal box, but she didn't have any other options, so she pulled out the smooth, featherlight gown and slipped it on. It irritated her that it fit like a glove and even had an opening for her tail.

Jade was striding up in a glittering smoky blue dress as Kiera emerged from the tent.

"Perfect timing. I got us a ride." Jade gestured to some type of motorized bike with colossal wheels behind her.

Kiera walked over and ran her hand along the leather seat. "Is Hallowfeld's manor far?"

"Yes, it's on the other side of the grounds. Around here, most people walk, but we don't have time for that leisurely tourist stuff," Jade said, handing her a helmet and clipping one on herself.

"Thanks. Where'd you get this?" Kiera asked.

Jade hiked up her dress and climbed onto the bike. "From a friend. The tires are made for rough terrain, but he had them enchanted too, so we won't have trouble getting there."

"That was nice of him to let us borrow it," Kiera said as she got on behind her.

Jade pressed her chin to her shoulder, tilting back to wink at her. "He's the best kind of friend. Now, get that letter back out; we'll need it to get us through the residential barrier. Hang on tight."

Kiera wrapped her arms around Jade's waist, the letter firmly in her grasp. The crimson light speared out in front of them, a blazing summons cutting through the dark. The bike purred to life, and then they were rocketing along, chasing the red cord into the night. Balmy air whistled by them, shaking every cell in Kiera's body awake. They skirted the forest, branches whipping by them in a sage blur. Kiera could've sworn she'd seen flashes of eyes like a tapestry of floating lights in the gloom, but they sped by too fast to know for sure.

Jade eventually turned the bike onto the first paved road Kiera had seen at Etabon. She decreased their speed as they passed by a sign that read: *For residents or by invitation only.* An electric tingle zinged against Kiera's body as they passed it by.

"That was the warding spell. We're almost there—the manor is past the resident's neighborhood," Jade called to her.

Kiera's mouth dropped open as Jade steered them down the lane. The street started out with lovely stone cottages with manicured lawns, and as they drove farther in, the stories of the houses increased, and their yards expanded to include mature trees. Gold orbs bobbed alongside the street, each one igniting as they approached to light their way. The glow from the orbs and homes illuminated the area enough that Kiera caught glimpses in between the houses of the land that sprawled out behind them.

Kiera leaned closer to Jade's ear and asked, "Are those barns and crop fields back there?"

"Yes, there's even an orchard. Hallowfeld has it maintained by a fleet of water and nature faeries. People all over Atterah may be starving, but Hallowfeld and his lackeys have an abundance to pick from here. It's another reason sponsors and visitors are drawn to the festival."

Towering hedges loomed up ahead of them, and in between the greenery was a wrought iron gate similar to the one at the festival's entrance. Jasmine wound through it, making its sharply pointed spires less menacing. The crimson cord became taut and flared brighter as they approached, prompting the entryway to split open for them. The same electric prickle pressed against Kiera's body as Jade coasted the bike forward. If the neighborhood had been picturesque, this was breathtaking. A long drive lined with tall, bushy trees led up to a circle drive with a lighted fountain at its center. Lacquered oak doors were set into the four-story stone manor, its many balconies thrown open to let the breeze in. The tinkling of glasses and laughter wafted out and over to them.

Jade parked the bike in the shadow of one of the trees. Kiera murmured the plan to her, and she put her hand on her hip, giving Kiera a quizzical look.

"Are you ready for this?"

Kiera swallowed her uneasiness. "I have to be," she said firmly, not entirely sure if she was reassuring Jade or herself.

Jade clicked her tongue. "It's not that I don't have faith in you... it's just, I swear the type of guest that attends these things can smell fear, and their attention is going to be all over you."

Kiera tilted her head back, drawing her eyes up to the night for calm. The moon was bright and chasing the stars across the sky. It had to be close to midnight at this point.

She responded, "If they can smell fear, maybe I should've skipped the shower. It could've worked in our favor."

Jade laughed and put her hand on Kiera's back. "I see why Attalin likes you."

She turned her attention toward the doors and the golden-furred werewolf standing guard at the entrance.

"That's one of Hallowfeld's main guards, Patrick—he knows I work at Nautilus, so he should assume I'm covering the bar here tonight and let me enter."

"Just in case," Kiera said, handing her the envelope, while she kept the note.

"Smart move. Alright, here we go," Jade whispered.

Jade walked out of the shadows, throwing back her shoulders as she approached Patrick. She gave him a confident nod, brandishing the envelope, and he opened the door to let her pass. Kiera tilted her ears forward, straining to hear Jade, waiting for her cue. The party was roaring inside, and Kiera worried she might not hear her, but—attribute it to her siren abilities—her voice reverberated above the rest with ease.

"That lovely lynx is on her way and ready to celebrate! Where's the champagne at?"

She waited a few beats, wanting the party's full attention to be on the entrance, anticipating her. Kiera buried her discomfort and sauntered up to Patrick with the note in hand.

"Hallowfeld should be expecting me." The werewolf bobbed his head and swung the door wide for her. She stepped inside and paused. Two grand mahogany staircases cascaded down into a foyer with vaulted ceilings. A crystal chandelier suspended high above bathed the space in a warm glow. Off the foyer was a vast ballroom overflowing with guests, the polished marble floors reflecting off the glasses in their hands. Kiera scanned the crowd, searching for him. She found Hallowfeld leaning casually against the bar at the back of the ballroom, one hand on the velvet lapel of his tuxedo. Kiera spotted Attalin in a fitted, blood-red satin dress at the counter behind him. Jade wasn't kidding—the entire room turned their focus on her. Even the servers carrying trays of champagne and delicate desserts ceased their activity to look up.

She strode through the crowd and called to Hallowfeld, "You were absolutely right earlier. That tournament of yours was incredible, your contestants were trained by the finest sponsors."

Kiera stopped in front of Hallowfeld, his eyes calculating, and bowed her head. "It'd be an honor to fight under any of their banners, but especially yours. Maybe you'd do me the kindness of discussing it in the future."

Jade appeared next to her with two flutes of champagne. She handed one to her and the other to Hallowfeld. Kiera turned to the crowd lifting her glass in the air.

"To our illustrious host Eugene Hallowfeld. If not for his cunning and graciousness, we wouldn't get to enjoy all that Etabon has to offer."

Kiera downed half the glass in one drink to the cheers and applause of the crowd. Every word coming out of her mouth was like ash on her tongue, but she knew this was the only way to spare Hallowfeld the humiliation of losing, and it would ultimately help Attalin. She faced him, and he was leering at her. That drink might not have been the best idea—the look on his face was making the bubbling liquid in her stomach turn. She held her glass out to him. He waved his with a flourish and clinked it against hers.

"We're happy to have you, Lynx. Etabon welcomes you and hopes to enjoy your presence for years to come."

The crowd was beside themselves at this point, cheering and whistling. Hallowfeld gestured to the quartette in the corner, they picked up their instruments and began playing a bright melody.

"Dance with me?" he asked.

Kiera wanted to spit at his feet. Instead, she let him take her hand and lead her onto the floor. They began dancing along with a handful of other couples.

Hallowfeld lowered his voice. "That was clever."

Kiera gave him an innocent look. "I have no idea what you mean."

They moved around the ballroom. She cursed herself for drinking that champagne; her head was starting to feel fuzzy.

"It's exactly what I wanted to discuss with you, in fact."

Kiera blinked at him. "Me fighting for you? I think I've had enough of the arena for one lifetime."

He lifted his arm and spun her in a circle, catching her by the waist. She felt like she might very well be sick on his shiny leather shoes at any moment.

Hallowfeld's grip on her tightened. "Well, how about I convince you to reconsider? Your victory secured you a permanent home here."

The alcohol was burning its way back up her throat. Kiera drew a deep inhale through her nose to force the bile down. It was a miracle that her voice didn't waver when she said, "I won the bargain today. You told me I'd have my freedom, and you'd keep the violations from the board."

Hallowfeld raised his eyebrows. "Oh, you're free to go, my feline friend. I'll allow you to return to your hovel tonight. I'll need time to secure you a valid entry band, and until then, you can go about your life and keep up appearances. We don't need people asking questions. You'll return in two months' time. I have my quarterly meeting with the board in eight weeks, and your name will be on my list for expedited approval. If you were to go through the ordinary channels, you wouldn't get a certification band until next year. Lucky for you, I'll be your new sponsor. That's more than enough time to get your affairs in order. You'll have access to the funds I'll provide immediately. They'll be filed under an academic grant. I hear you're a gifted student, so it won't appear out of the ordinary. Do as you please. Within reason, of course. I'll be watching you from now on." He winked at her.

"You can keep your home and funds," Kiera replied. "I don't want any of it. I'm not interested in coming back here."

His hand clenched painfully over hers, and she had to restrain her claws from poking out. "Look at it this way, dear girl, all tournament winners are rewarded with these gifts—it's unheard of to refuse them. Don't you think it's selfish of you to keep your magic from the world? After witnessing your powers, it'd be negligent of me to allow you not to return. The energy you produce could heal our planet in years instead of decades. In your state earlier, you didn't see the final match recording. Your readings were inching toward the scale's maximum. You did in one match what takes others weeks to do."

"This is all a game to you, isn't it? I'm not giving up my free will to come back and hurt anyone else in your sadistic tournaments. I said no," Kiera hissed.

The glow of his coal-fire eyes amplified. "Before they departed this morning, your classmates were rather helpful in filling in some details about you. Terrible accidents can happen outside of Etabon every day, so I'll acquire your mother a band as well. She'll be safe here with you. We wouldn't want anything to happen to Rose, now, would we?"

He knew her mother's name. Kiera felt herself stumble, but Hallowfeld had anticipated it and held her close to keep her upright. His sickly sweet, vanilla scent made her eyes water.

"How dare you threaten my mother," Kiera snarled.

He chuckled in her ear. "Threaten? I did no such thing, but if you want me to be uncouth, I can do so. If you refuse to come back, I'll set that shack you live in on fire with her locked inside."

This conversation was far scarier than anything she'd faced in the arena today. She needed to use her head.

"What happens if the board finds out that I've been here before? Won't that cause issues for you?" Kiera said.

"Let me handle that. As far as anyone here is concerned, your name is Lynx. No one of importance knows your real identity, and the insignificant few that do will be keeping it to themselves. When you return, you'll continue to be known as Lynx, and Kiera could be any number of other creatures that exist here. We can't just have you disappearing from the outside world without a trace, though; we need to go through the proper channels to set you up as a permanent resident first."

Kiera's mind scraped and clawed for a way out, but he had her. So, she'd have to work with the only leverage she had. "I'll come back. I won't give you any trouble, but you have to agree to my terms."

Hallowfeld snickered at her as if she'd said the most hilarious joke.

"If I got caught discussing magic in public between now and then or the board was to find out I'm a violator, I'd be killed. I'm no use to you if I die out there, right?" Kiera asked sharply.

His lips thinned into a tight line. "I'm listening."

"Once you've secured my band, I'll come back willingly, but my mother's life is safe. I need you to guarantee she won't be harmed in any way. No tricks. The same goes for Attalin, her family, and her friend Jade. When I return, I want you to forgive Attalin and Jade's debts completely. You can't add any more time on them or force them into another bargain."

His mouth twisted into a sneer. "You're a shrewd thing, aren't you? Fine, as long as you come back and continue to fight in the arena, your mother's life is safe. No tricks. For the others, how about this: The first sunrise after your first fight back, they're free to go. Their safety and that of their families' are guaranteed, and their debts will be forgiven with no further extensions. And I won't impose any additional bargains on them."

Kiera bowed her head and squeezed Hallowfeld's hand. "Agreed then."

She felt the tickle of magic go up and down her arms and legs as their bargain settled into place. The song ended, and they stopped dancing, clapping for the band along with the other couples on the dance floor. Hallowfeld took Kiera's hand and kissed it—she compelled herself not to rip it away and smack him across the face. A helpless fury burned behind her eyes, but she refused to let him see her cry.

He led her off the dance floor, murmuring, "Now keep away from your old classmates. My word is my word, but if they get bold and go running their mouths, that wouldn't be good for you or sweet Rose."

Kiera kept her face neutral and dipped her chin in understanding.

"Take my personal hovercraft tonight. It'll get you to Mendinburrow in ten minutes versus waiting on a bullet train. You'll have more time with my guests and your friends. Attalin's shift is complete, so she can show you where the hangar is when you're ready. Your bank account information will be on board for your records," he said.

"Won't that require a passenger list?" Kiera asked.

Hallowfeld scoffed, "Rest assured, I'll have it managed."

It didn't sound like he'd have trouble manipulating the system. After today, she wouldn't put anything past him. She turned her head and spotted Attalin behind the counter watching them. Kiera nodded to Hallowfeld in acceptance. She'd need the lift to have time to talk with Attalin and get home before Rose did at six.

"Until next time, my feline friend. Remember, I'll be watching," Hallowfeld crooned.

Kiera glided toward the bar in a daze. She walked up next to Jade, who was standing at the counter across from Attalin, and said softly, "I owe you one."

Jade took a sip of her drink and nudged Kiera with her shoulder. "Let's call this one even. You did well."

Kiera gave her a halfhearted smile. "We made a pretty good team."

Jade bit her straw and smiled back in amusement. Attalin was giving them a stern look. She leaned forward over the bar. "That was a huge gamble you two took. What did you do, Whiskers?"

Jade glanced between them. "I'm going to head out—my good deeds are done for the day. I'll leave the bike for you two."

She gave them both a warm wave. Kiera watched her stride away. "She really cares for you. I imagine that's what it's like to have an older sister."

Attalin was still glowering at her. "Kiera, please don't tell me you made another agreement with him."

Kiera managed to keep the hitch out of her voice as she bent toward

Attalin and said, "I don't need to tell you that we have a ton of eyes on us right now. Hallowfeld said your shift is complete. Can we talk? I have to leave soon."

Attalin's lips thinned into a line, but she conceded. She lifted up a hinged section of the bar and stepped out toward Kiera. They pushed through the swarm of bodies and headed to the door. They walked in silence to the bike. Kiera lifted the seat up and hauled her backpack out of its compartment and over her shoulders.

Attalin studied her with concern now. "I know a quiet place we can go."

Kiera responded wearily and mounted the bike behind her. She tucked her arms around her and rested her cheek against Attalin's back, closing her eyes as she guided the bike away from the manor. Kiera couldn't stop the tears that leaked out and were whisked away on the wind.

Attalin drove them out to a grassy knoll close to one of the streams. It was peaceful out there, separated from the constant buzz at the heart of the festival grounds. Water gurgled over the rocks in the stream, and crickets chirped softly to one another. A deer paused its drinking at the water's edge, droplets sliding down its snout to its auburn coat, to watch them approach. It blinked its liquid gold eyes at them, turned slowly, and vanished into the tree line. Attalin dropped herself down and patted the ground next to her. Kiera sat, running her hands over the stalks of grass. It was strange she could sense the magic in the land; it felt alive and wild. Attalin's eyes flicked back toward the way they'd come.

"We're far enough away now that no one will overhear us, and I don't sense anyone's magic sniffing around." Attalin's hair fell to the side as she placed her hand on Kiera's cheek. "Kiera, what happened in there?"

The tears streamed down again as she told her everything that was said between her and Hallowfeld.

"I should've realized when he made those comments at the bar this morning about shifters' powers that he'd never let me go." Kiera's voice cracked.

Attalin scooted close and embraced her. "I'm so sorry I scolded you.

Of course he'd do something monstrous like this."

They were quiet for long minutes until Kiera could find her voice. She began ripping stalks of grass out by their roots and letting the wind carry them away.

Attalin watched her with tear-rimmed eyes. "What you offered to do for Jade and me... our families. There aren't words for that kindness."

Kiera slid her hand across the grass to rest on Attalin's. "If he thinks he's going to take my freedom and keep yours too, he's got another thing coming."

Attalin shook her head at her. "Forget about us. You and your mom can run, get out of Hytheis. You don't need to use his money to do it. What about the bracelet? You can pawn it and use the funds to go to one of the southern continents and hide out. I've heard whispers about people vanishing into the dunes of Renival or the jungles of Erriem."

"The board requires travel papers to relocate. That could take years, so we'd have to find a way to cross illegally. We can't risk it. He said he'd be watching us. My classmates told him about my mom, he knows my hometown and where I live. It sounds like he has someone following her already, and if we try anything and he catches us, he'll have her killed." Kiera closed her eyes and suppressed the urge to cry. She was done with tears for now. "Before I go, I just want to be here with you for a while."

The intensity drained out of Attalin, and a look of understanding passed over her face. They both laid back in the grass and stared up at the moon and millions of twinkling stars. Attalin turned her head toward her, and as she tucked her hair behind her ear, the moonlight glinted off her scales.

It felt like she'd lived this moment a hundred times. Kiera's hands became clammy. "Attalin, there's something I've been meaning to tell you. I've been trying to think of a way to say this that doesn't sound completely creepy, but there really isn't one, so here it goes. I've been dreaming about you, *erm* your eyes, I mean." Attalin propped herself up on her hand, listening intently.

Heat climbed up Kiera's neck, and it felt like her heart was lodged in her throat. "This is coming out all wrong. You know how I told you I dream of magic still? Well, the last couple of weeks, I've seen your eyes exactly. It's like we were supposed to meet."

Attalin's lips parted in astonishment, and Kiera wanted to go find a rock to hide under.

Before she could do just that, Attalin pressed her hand to Kiera's and murmured, "I think you're right." Kiera nearly passed out from relief.

Attalin's brow furrowed. "I'm like you, I had the dreams past five years old, up until I was thirteen. I haven't had them in years though. I thought it was because I lived here, but the last couple of weeks, it's been the same one every night." Attalin's skin visibly prickled as she looked around them. "It's more sounds than anything. I hear water burbling, crickets chirping, and a voice. Your voice. I thought I recognized it when you came into the bar, but when you shouted at Wendel to put the knife down, I was certain. There are people who believe magic is entirely benevolent. They say the dreams are Etabon's magic calling to us, trying to guide us." Attalin's eyes crinkled at the corners as a smile tugged at her lips. "I didn't know how to explain it either. I was worried I'd made it up somehow, but I think we're connected in some way."

Kiera returned her smile. Attalin's expression faltered as if she remembered something, and she gazed back up at the stars. "I think there are some things you need to know about me. I promised I'd tell you the story about how I ended up in this bargain, if you still want to hear it."

There was deep sorrow in Attalin's voice that sent an ache through Kiera. "If you're sure, then I'm here to listen, but this sounds deeply personal, so only if you truly want to."

She set her hand on Kiera's arm. "I want to."

The crickets quieted around them, as if they'd hushed to hear her story too.

10

SHATTERED

A ttalin sat up and pressed her hair back from her face as she said, "I remember the day my father came home to tell us the news that Etabon had been opened to the public. He and my mother talked for hours about the risk of coming here. She didn't trust Hallowfeld's motives, but he saw it as an opportunity. With my mother being a teacher and him a hovercraft engineer, they made a decent living, but he wanted more for us. He wanted to see how magic could benefit us, so he applied for a spectator's permit."

Her hand dipped into her pocket, and she clutched something in her fist. "You should know that seers are rare, nearly as much an anomaly as animal shifters. The kind with the amount of power and clarity my father possesses are one in billions. He told me once that visions don't always tell the whole story. He explained that they come in bursts, and while they're reliable, there are things even beyond the scope of what his magic can see. That's what got us into trouble with Hallowfeld in the first place—he never saw this coming."

Attalin opened her fist to reveal a miniature mirror hanging from a silver chain. The mirror looked shattered, but upon further inspection, each reflective shard of glass was a different color. It was a mosaic of burgundy, lapis, marigold, smoky black, and emerald.

Kiera watched the moonlight sparkle across its surface. "What is that?" she asked.

Attalin laid it in her palm. "This is a looking glass. Each shard is a fragment of memory." She took a steadying breath. "My father's memories, to be exact. He gave it to me the night he was banished, to explain the things he didn't have time to tell me. It was keyed to my mind so only I could view the memories. It's empty now—it was only good for one use. I keep it purely as a reminder. When I start to miss him, I'll pull it out and remember his choices are the reason I'm trapped here."

Kiera placed her hand on Attalin's. She intertwined her fingers with Kiera's and squeezed her hand. Attalin swallowed hard. "He let me see everything. When he came to Etabon, he had a vision the moment he stepped through the gates. It led him to his mentor's tent, the only other seer here, Sheena Francosie. She was a kindhearted older woman in her late eighties. Sheena told him she'd seen him coming too—it was like a bridge between them. She called it a psychic connection and said that Etabon's magic had drawn them together."

Kiera's tail flicked slightly, and Attalin tilted her head. "Sound familiar? Well, my father and Sheena grew close. He assisted her with her stall, and she coached him on how to use his abilities. Like all magic, her powers couldn't reach beyond the border. She could only see events within Etabon. She taught him that a seer must have a focus for their magic. It's not the case that they're all-knowing and able to anticipate every event in the time to come." Attalin's body tensed. "The truth about Sheena is she'd been to Etabon before it was legal to visit."

Kiera tightened her grip on Attalin. "How is that even possible?"

"Sheena was part of something she called the Alliance. A secret society that would risk journeying to Etabon. As a member of their network, she'd helped to orchestrate the crossings, and their mission was to reunite beings with their magic. They believed magic was not about power but about deep meaning and connection."

Kiera frowned. "I had no idea that a group like that ever existed."

A sigh escaped Attalin's lips. "Apparently they worked in the shadows for decades. When the network discovered Hallowfeld's plan to assume stewardship of Etabon and learned that the board had sanctioned the deal, they sent Sheena in as a spy to monitor Hallowfeld and his intentions for the site."

"Wasn't she afraid of being caught?" Kiera asked.

Attalin tossed her head. "She had the Alliance enact a memory-wiping spell on her. It was crafted to target certain memories. She couldn't recall the locations or members of the Alliance, so she couldn't compromise her people. She believed it was her duty to take on this final task for them. That way, she could relay intelligence back to her network, with no liability involved. They didn't have contact with her, she just had a designated drop point where she'd leave her encrypted reports. The Alliance was her family, and it was her last wish to protect what they stood for. I guess my father found the notion of all this romantic, and that's why he chose to conceal the truth from Hallowfeld the day he came to visit Sheena's stall."

Kiera's eyes widened. "So, that's how he crossed Hallowfeld."

Attalin gave her a sad smile. "Exactly. He came into Sheena's tent in search of something. He brought a pair of enchanted scales along to weigh her words and ensure she was telling the truth. Hallowfeld made her hold on to this tattered piece of black silk fabric with a faded moon and stars pattern on it to see if she could find an item associated with it. She couldn't locate anything, so he grabbed my father and made him try. He told Hallowfeld there was nothing at Etabon linked to it. It was the truth, but my father *had* seen something. An image of a sprawling city surrounded by dunes and the front of a bookstore."

Kiera gasped. "Dunes? He saw Renival, but that's beyond the borders."

Attalin bit her lip. "You're right. He did something unheard of that day—he saw outside of Etabon, and it shook him to his core. Hallowfeld told them they were both entirely useless but left without realizing my father's half-truth. The encounter with Hallowfeld had taken a toll on Sheena, too, so they left Etabon that night. He brought her back to live with us in Tydden. We only had a couple of weeks with her, but it didn't matter; she was easy to love. The world lost a magnificent soul the day she passed." She choked on the last word.

Kiera ran her thumb over Attalin's hand. "You don't have to keep going."

"No, I'm fine," she said, swiping a tear from her face. "My father waited until they'd left the festival grounds to tell Sheena about his vision. He confirmed he'd seen a bookstore in the capital city of Arrdor, in Renival. He recognized it because he'd traveled to the city once before. Sheena warned him that there was dark magic at play and that the vision should've been impossible. She made him promise not to tell anyone and to get the information to the Alliance. The only problem was she couldn't remember how to contact them. She was so ill at that point she couldn't even recall where she'd been leaving her reports. Sheena died without giving him any guidance on how to reach them."

Tension pulsed in Attalin's neck, and she huffed to Kiera, "He never managed to make contact with the Alliance, but he went back each year to search for them. The year I turned thirteen, he let me attend with him. I helped with his stall in the market."

"He brought you even though he knew it was dangerous?" Kiera asked.

"At that point, I think he'd given up hope of finding the Alliance and had turned his attention to making the business successful. What really made this place so treacherous was my particular set of abilities. He discovered what I could do a few weeks after we'd arrived. We were in the market one day, and I saw a fire faerie steal a charm from the witch's stall next to us. When the faerie wouldn't put it back, I grabbed his wrist and used my powers on him to make him return it. My father realized then what I was capable of. He panicked, and we closed the stall early. When we were outside, he took me to an alcove of trees away from the crowds. He told me he'd seen what'd happened with the faerie at the market, and he wasn't mad, but we had to keep my gifts concealed."

Kiera put a hand to her mouth; the only sound was the rippling of the stream beside them.

Attalin clenched her teeth. "I pushed him on it because I didn't understand why I needed to pretend to be someone I wasn't. I didn't want to lie. That's when he said there were people at Etabon who'd exploit me. He said the man who runs the festival would want more power for himself, that he'd twist my magic up for his own gain. He told me he'd withheld something that the man had wanted once, and that I could too."

A sinking feeling crept over Kiera. "Someone overheard you two?"

"Yes. There were pixies in the trees we'd been speaking under. They'd gone straight to Hallowfeld." Attalin laughed darkly. "When we arrived back at our tent, Hallowfeld and a werewolf guard were there to greet us. He seized my father by the throat and demanded the vision from him. Hallowfeld told him if he valued our lives, he'd give it to him. My father took that tattered silk fabric in his hands and told Hallowfeld the crimson book he was seeking was in the cellar of a shop named Sylvie Strauss's Books and Antiques in the city of Arrdor."

Attalin glared into the depths of the forest. "Even after he got that vision, Hallowfeld said he'd have to turn us over to the board. He said there were rules in place to keep Etabon's gates open. He'd have to document my father's scheme to conceal the scope of his magical abilities from him and, ultimately, the board. The fact that he saw something beyond the border was unprecedented. Hallowfeld claimed the board would rightfully assume he was plotting against the citizens of Atterah."

Kiera's jaw ticked when she said, "He said something along those lines when he threatened me this morning."

Attalin's hands curled into fists. "He knows how to manipulate people. All I could think of was the board going after my mother and my little brother because of my father's actions. I couldn't let that happen, so I did the only thing in my control. The werewolf and Hallowfeld were facing my father, so the wolf didn't expect it when I reached out and touched his arm. I told him to leave the tent, and he did."

"You revealed your powers to Hallowfeld," Kiera whispered.

"He was captivated by them. I told him that if he spared my family, he could have access to my magic. The rest is history; he asked me to wait outside while he made the bargain with my father. When he called me back in, he told me I'd be under his guardianship and work for him for thirteen years. He promised my physical safety and that I could see my family once a year. If I agreed, it'd guarantee he'd never tell the board about my father. So, for them, I did."

The pain in Kiera's chest for Attalin made her shudder. That Hallowfeld could torment a thirteen-year-old girl like that made her sick. She touched her hand to her cheek and found that it came away damp.

Attalin shoved the looking glass back into her pocket and grumbled, "My father didn't know when to quit. He was so fixated on honoring Sheena's memory and getting that information to the Alliance that he forgot to tell his own family what was going on, and it cost us everything. Hallowfeld allowed him half an hour to say goodbye to me. With the time he had left, he had a friend craft the mirror and deliver it to me so I could see the whole story. I suppose he thought he owed it to me. Not that it mattered much after the fact."

Tears rolled down her flushed cheeks, and Kiera wrapped her up in her arms. Attalin leaned her head on her shoulder and released a quiet sob. "The worst part is, the morning after my father gave Hallowfeld the vision of that book, I overheard some of the guards who went with him to collect it. They were bragging about finding the headquarters of some group in a bookshop that called themselves the Alliance. They said they burned it down and executed the group's leader. They killed everyone inside, took out the whole network. Sheena would've been devastated. My father ended up causing exactly what she'd been determined to prevent. All that possibility snuffed out in an instant. If he'd opened up to my mother or shared this with me before my first visit, we would've helped him to see that it was too dangerous for him to come back here. We would've worked it out together."

Attalin paused for a moment to take a deep breath. "The only break we had was that Hallowfeld assumed my father originally withheld the vision because he was afraid that he'd turn him over to the board. He never learned about the Alliance from my father or connected Sheena to them. If he had, I don't think we would've walked away that day."

"You were just a kid. It's wrong that you had to take all of that on by yourself. I'm so sorry those things happened to you," Kiera said gently.

Her lip trembled. "Kiera, I get that you sense the good in the magic here, but evil has dug its talons so deep into this place that there's no coming back from that. Hallowfeld is toxic, and anyone associated with him, willingly or not, is too. If you can, you and your mom should try to run. Trust me, I believed this place was a sanctuary, and then it swallowed me whole."

Attalin untangled herself and went over to the stream. She splashed cool water on her face. "If you knew what Hallowfeld's demanded of me in the past, you wouldn't want to release me from my bargain. I don't deserve to be free."

Kiera rose and glided over to her. Their reflections wavered side by side in the stream. "You can't mean that."

"I do. Whenever he wants someone to become a resident, sponsor, or competitor, and they're uncertain, he brings them to the bar. He signals me with a wink, and I have to use my powers to sway them. Hallowfeld can be charming, so all they need is a gentle nudge in his direction, but that's typically all it takes for someone to go against their intuition. When I heard your voice this morning, I did everything in my power to avoid making eye contact with him. I couldn't bring myself to use my powers on you, but you ended up in a bargain with him anyway. There've been times when my magic isn't strong enough to influence someone. If they don't agree to his terms willingly, that's when he turns to threats."

Kiera crossed her arms and stared into the current. "You've done what you've needed to survive. I'm not excusing any of it, but it's reality. Your hand was forced into that bargain for your family's sake. Whatever Hallowfeld's made you do, that's on him. Look, it sounds like even if he didn't have access to your powers, he'd get what he wanted one way or another, like he did with me. Your magic just makes things easier for him. When I come back, it means it'll be your last festival. Your sentence will be over, and you won't be under his control any longer. Hopefully, from then on, you'll have the chance to set things right."

Attalin's eyes drifted to the stars. "Hope is dangerous. It makes people do odd things. In the end, it's why I chose to speak to my father again. Don't get me wrong, it took years for me to master my fury, but I understand he was blinded by his hope for this place. He had this childish fantasy in his head about what it could be like if Hallowfeld didn't run it. It must be why he was so eager to find the Alliance. I've come to accept he was doing what he believed was best, but that doesn't change the fact that we're still paying for his ignorance, and now my own choices are hurting innocent people. It's a vicious cycle."

Kiera let those words settle over her before replying, "You told me earlier that there's no absolute good or evil, just the decisions we make. I stand by this one. I can't judge you for what you've done; I've hurt people too and made a mess of things today. When you leave here, try to make the world a better place with your freedom."

"Kiera, promise me something, if you do have to come back," Attalin said.

"What's that?" Kiera asked.

"The beings Hallowfeld tricks or forces into being permanent residents can become obsessed with him. I think it's a coping mechanism. Many go on to become his most loyal followers and end up pledging their lives to him. They make up nearly all the residents, and they all get this eclipse brand on their shoulders or wrists. It's like a cult. Some of us have managed to avoid it; he only seems to want people who are completely willing, but you'll have to be careful."

The tattoo Kiera had seen on the witch popped into her mind. "Does Rowan have one of those brands?" Attalin nodded her head yes.

Kiera frowned and told Attalin what the witch said before she left her own recovery tent about feeling wisps of magic and what happened when she visited Rowan and touched his shoulder earlier.

Attalin pursed her lips. "I've never heard of that happening. It sounds like you had a reaction to him rather than the other way around, though. I don't know what it means."

They both gazed at the churning water. Movement in Kiera's periphery snagged her attention. Attalin was swaying on her feet. Kiera turned and caught her under the arms.

"What's wrong?" Kiera asked.

Attalin touched her forehead and then pulled a gold chain from her dress. A honey-colored stone with strips of brown in it was suspended on the end of the chain. "It's this tiger's eye stone. There are many different types of stones and crystals—this one is particularly suited for protection. We've been speaking longer than I'd anticipated. Unlike my father, I take multiple precautions when it comes to discretion, and this has been shielding our conversation. Gabby imbued it with intricate blocking magic for me. Hallowfeld isn't aware I possess it. It sustains its potency by pulling directly from my energy—that way, the spell won't fade. Unfortunately, it's warped magic like his. Fighting fire with fire seems to be the only tactic that works against him."

Kiera wrinkled her nose at the stone. "If it's powered by dark magic, is that safe?"

Attalin lowered herself to the ground with Kiera's assistance. "It's like everything else here—it's a calculated risk. It pulls minuscule amounts of energy when it's not in use; even when I do invoke it, the strain is limited. Gabby was hesitant to give it to me because if I use it when my power is spent, it becomes dangerous. If it can't take from my magical stores, it'll pull from my life force."

Kiera startled at that. "You're purposefully diminishing your life?"

Attalin closed her eyes. "By minutes, hours, days maybe. I deemed it worth the exposure to have a few scraps of privacy for myself. It's the only way I can ensure I'm hidden from Hallowfeld. There are some moments that are certainly worth the sacrifice."

Her eyes fluttered open. The air was charged between them. It was as if she was going to say more, but her head tilted back. "I can sense a group headed in this direction, and I'm too tired to shield us any longer."

Attalin dragged herself from the ground, murmuring lightly to her necklace before slipping it back inside her dress. Kiera linked her arm with Attalin's, and they hiked back to the bike. Clouds had rolled in, blocking out the moon's rays. Kiera managed to drive the bike slowly over to the hangar, with Attalin holding on to her tightly, providing directions as they went. By the time they could see the building up ahead, a light rain had started falling.

"We'll have to park here. No one's permitted to approach the hangar without express permission from Hallowfeld. The area's patrolled by a goblin named Nash. Your transport would've been communicated to her already, but don't let your guard down. She's got a foul temper and is particularly ruthless when it comes to her job," Attalin said.

They got off the bike and faced each other.

"Will you be ok to get back by yourself?" Kiera asked.

"I'm fine now, don't worry about me."

Kiera looked at her thoughtfully and reached out to tuck a few damp strands of hair that were stuck to her cheek behind her ear. Her chest tightened at leaving her like this. "This isn't goodbye—it's I'll see you soon."

Attalin opened her arms, and they embraced. "Alright, I'll see you soon, Whiskers."

Rain pattered softly around them, and they stayed like that for a long moment. When Kiera stepped back, she wasn't sure if it was raindrops or tears on Attalin's lashes. Although Kiera would be back in a couple of months, it took everything in her to wave and turn toward the hangar. She trekked the rest of the way in wistful silence. The rain faded to mist as she followed the path up to the gargantuan structure.

The fur at the nape of Kiera's neck spiked. She sensed an area over her left shoulder grow warm and turned around just as a goblin slipped from thin air to fill the empty space. Kiera remained still as they studied each other. She was petite with moss-green skin and clawed hands. Kiera was still marveling at the goblin's ability to materialize out of thin air when her narrow lips pulled back in a sneer to expose needle-sharp teeth.

"So, you're the dirty mongrel I was instructed to permit into the building."

Kiera twitched her tail. Attalin was right, this goblin was dreadful.

"Hallowfeld must be short-staffed if he'd employ someone dim enough to confuse a feline for a canine."

"What'd you say to me, mutt?" Nash snarled.

"I'll say it slow for you. I'm a cat, not a dog."

The goblin's pointed ears twitched like she couldn't comprehend the fact that she'd been insulted.

Her ash-colored eyes narrowed. "You're lucky you didn't face a goblin in the matches today. Someone with the ability to fade would've easily slit your throat."

Kiera rolled her eyes. "I knew where you'd show up well enough. As riveting as this conversation is, I need to go. So, are you going to let me in?"

Nash pointed toward the building. "Your craft has advanced software, so it'll be an automated flight." Kiera's attention was so focused on the eclipse brand on the goblin's wrist that she almost missed that she'd said there wouldn't be a pilot.

She didn't get a chance to respond before Nash flashed her teeth at her and vanished on a chill wind. Before the tournament, Attalin had explained the goblin's ability to fade, which meant they could pass through space unencumbered. The only way to know where they'd appear is a minute shift in temperature. Their weakness was that fading took a great deal of energy, so most couldn't do it more than a handful of times.

Kiera's ears picked up locks turning, prompting her to jog midway down the building toward a copper door. She detected a thrumming similar to the fighting pits, but she noticed that its force was diminishing. Kiera realized it must be tied to this place's defenses. The door swung open, and she ducked into the building.

She couldn't help but gape at the behemoth chamber. The walls were lined with a multitude of hovercrafts of varying sizes, Kiera'd never seen anything like it. Her attention snapped to a whirring noise that echoed through the hangar. An enormous mechanical arm extended down from the back of the structure and roved over to the middle of the space. It plucked a hovercraft from the wall and placed the craft in the center of the room. Kiera watched the spectacle with wide eyes.

The metal roof of the hangar peeled apart and slid back on either side of the building to reveal the night sky. Kiera breathed in the damp evening air. A ramp slid down from the hovercraft, and Kiera took it as her cue to enter. The inside was luxurious. A solid glass wall divided four aviation chairs and the control panel from the passenger space. The linen seating area ran along the back curve of the craft and was scattered with cashmere pillows and throws. Kiera watched from one of the many windows as the craft ascended.

Once the hovercraft cleared the roof, she seated herself, tossing a cashmere pillow out of her way with a grimace. The craft levitated a moment as the building's panels closed up. Even from inside, she could feel the spell below lock back into place around the building. Now that she was alone, she let herself decompress. She melted back into the chair and closed her eyes with a huff. Her rest didn't last long; movement in the cabin made her eyes snap back open.

Kiera spotted a section of the wall retracting. A petite oak table rolled out and over to her. Stacked neatly on top was a simple cotton dress and flats next to a couple of documents. She groaned, realizing she'd be back over the border in a few seconds and the gown she was wearing was far too flashy for the walk home. She stood and yanked off the gown, pulling the flexible material of the cotton dress over herself just as the magic of the border prickled her senses.

Her skin tingled as her fur vanished, leaving her feeling cold and vulnerable. It wasn't only her physical body that felt stripped, but her spirit felt drained too. Her certification band slipped down her wrist into her hand; she balled it up before tossing it on the table. She resumed her seat and jammed her human feet into the leather flats, which she'd be burning the first chance she got.

Kiera was tired of wearing things Hallowfeld had put her in. She muttered, "I wish I could summon my own clothes instead of having to wear more of this stuff."

She almost fell out of her chair as a melodic voice responded, "Salutations. Only certain beings have the ability to disperse corporeal items and recall them later, and entirely within the borders, of course. My database does not have that ability listed for shifters. You are the only individual in the shifter category at this time. Chronicles remain limited, citing speed, agility, and increased healing abilities."

She glanced around the room for the source of the voice, realizing the world looked a little less sharp through her human eyes.

"Who's that?"

"I am Hova, your hovercraft operations virtual assistant. I come standard in all crafts of this caliber."

Kiera let out a breath of relief. Hova was like the artificial intelligence that ran the indoor markets or maintained most homes in her town. She forced down her irritation at the fact that her abilities had been documented in Hallowfeld's system, but she shouldn't have expected any less.

Hova continued, "We will be arriving at your destination in nine minutes and fifty-five seconds. Would you like a refreshment?"

Kiera waved her hand, unsure of where to gesture to. "I'm alright, thank you."

She could only imagine all the information stored in Hova's system but held herself back from asking questions, knowing all her inquiries would be relayed back to Hallowfeld. Kiera hadn't realized how jarring it would be to return to her human body. Her movements felt sluggish as she turned back to the table and picked up the papers. She ran her fingertips over the statements and spotted the number he'd deposited in her designated bank account. It twisted her stomach to see an amount that large. It was outlandish that people like her mother would work their whole lives and never see anything close to this, while Hallowfeld tossed this kind of money around like a party favor. She set the papers in her backpack, trying to ignore the nausea churning in her gut, and stared out the window instead. Expanses of land and city lights whipped by, dragging her thoughts away with them.

11

SURVIVORS

K iera startled at the mechanical arm that tapped her shoulder. Hova must have said her name a few times to alert her that they'd landed because when she looked out the window, they were docked in a hangar.

"Apologies for disturbing you, miss, but we've arrived. Are you well?"

"Yes, thank you, Hova. Just tired, is all." She stood and collected her bag. The craft's door slid open, and the ramp extended down to the floor.

"This private hangar is two blocks from your residence. Would you like me to call you a car?"

Kiera's hand tightened around the bag's strap. It was ridiculous that a question like that was normal to someone like Hallowfeld.

"I don't mind walking. I appreciate you getting me home," Kiera replied.

Hova waved politely and retracted her arm back into the wall. Kiera walked down the ramp and studied the hangar. The space was quiet, likely because it was still before daybreak. The clock across the way read five-thirty. This hangar wasn't nearly as massive as the one at Etabon, but for a private facility, it was still large and stocked with a handful of crafts. She assumed he must have something like this in most cities.

Kiera rolled her eyes and headed toward a twinkling exit sign above a flight of stairs that led down to the street below. She descended the steps two at a time and pressed through the outer door with her elbow. In the dim light of the solar lamps, it took her a moment to orient herself. Recognizing a street sign across from her, she turned in the direction of their townhouse, keeping her head down. She didn't want to linger too long and draw attention to herself.

In her head, she repeated the story she'd provide if she was stopped by a drone. She was a student returning from a meeting with her donor, and she had the grant documents for her specialized training in her backpack to prove it. With each footstep, she let herself become that girl, hunching her shoulders to appear small and defeated, the board's favorite posture. Kiera kept her pace steady—it was best to seem purposeful but not overly hurried. The townhomes on her street came into view, but she forced her shoulders not to sag with relief; she was close but not home yet.

The houses in her neighborhood were crammed side by side, their roofs pinched at the top as if they were trying to steal a breath from the sky. They shared a wall with a family of three on one side and an elderly couple on the other. The sidewalk was cracked, and the teal paint on the building's eaves was peeling.

Kiera trudged up the creaky steps, her exhaustion like a living thing inside her at this point. She'd been awake for a full day and had barely eaten. She scanned her hand on their door's entry pad to let herself in. Where most houses had voice recognition and artificial intelligence, theirs only had basic security features. Not that she minded—it made it easier to speak openly to her mother without unwittingly giving the board the ability to tap in and listen to their conversations.

Living in an older neighborhood, they were able to avoid common technology without raising suspicion. The board would cough up the funds to update the neighborhood at some point, but not anytime soon. Even handprint identification had bothered her mother. It was the same method they used to access and transfer funds from their bank account, so she dealt with it. Paper money was mostly used at places like Etabon, but her mother kept a small stack in the safe in her closet, claiming the board could freeze virtual accounts in an instant. To Kiera's knowledge, they'd never dipped into the cash. That'd taken careful planning on Rose's part, but with them missing rent, it'd become apparent they'd have to withdraw from it sooner rather than later. As Kiera turned the handle, she heard snuffling behind the door and couldn't help the smile that tickled her lips.

"Morning, Nook," she said to the little hound who was hopping from paw to paw inside.

He stood on his back legs, sticking his nose next to her ear, ruffling her hair with his snorts. She closed the door behind her.

"Yes, I'm sure I smell weird. Are you hungry?"

Kiera dashed into her room, stripping off the dress and shoes, opting for a loose olive-green sweater and pants. She wrapped the discarded items in aluminum foil and stuffed them into a plastic bag. Kiera opened her window and dropped the bag into the bush below it. Hallowfeld could've bugged the clothes with listening devices. The aluminum would interfere with the signal if the tiny devices were embedded in the fabric, but it was better that they remained outside until she could get rid of them properly. For good measure, she wrapped her documents in the aluminum and set them under her bed. She'd put it in their safe later.

She padded out of her room to find Nook patiently waiting in the kitchen. His collar was on, so that meant he'd been able to use his access door to go in and out while she was away. His entrance was situated near the bottom of the back door. It did a retina scan for entry identification, but he had to have his microchipped collar tag on for the door to unlock for him. The back yard was a minuscule patch of grass that the tenets shared. She poured him food and set it down next to his water bowl.

"Sorry we missed our walk yesterday. I promise we'll go later."

His clever eyes assessed her as if to say all was forgiven now that he had his breakfast. Kiera leaned against the counter, getting lost in the familiar tinkling of Nook's entry tag against his bowl as he crunched his kibble. She blinked tiredly at the wall, letting her eyes fall shut. It was strange to be in a place that'd always brought her comfort and yet feel so exposed. If she'd learned anything today, it was that safety was an illusion she'd created to help herself sleep at night. Even her dreamlike notion of Etabon had twisted into some sort of nightmare, but when she closed her eyes, the phantom presence of her magic still lingered. The memory of it soothed her.

Her body desperately needed sleep, but she knew the second she gave in, she'd have to relive the day's horrors. She'd try to keep them at bay for a little longer. Her eyelids peeled apart reluctantly. Nook was watching her, his head tilted to the side, his tail wagging hesitantly. Kiera scratched his ears and went to wait in the living room for her mother. It wasn't long before she heard the front door unbolting. Nook bounded off to greet her.

Rose came down the hallway speaking warmly to Nook. Her bronze hair was tied back over her shoulders, and her gray eyes lit up when she spotted her daughter.

"Good morning, love," she said.

Kiera smiled softly at her mother. Even in her scrubs, she was lovely. Rose set her bag down and then scanned Kiera, her expression shifting to worry as she noted the dark shadows under her eyes. After so many years of choosing their words carefully around others, they'd learned to convey their thoughts to one another through looks and gestures. Their unspoken language made it impossible to hide what she was feeling. The last twenty-four hours crashed over her like a wave, and her mother read each emotion that swept across her face.

Kiera looked down at the scrap of paper she'd left on the coffee table. It felt like a lifetime ago that she'd scribbled that note, and the shame of it curved her shoulders. If she'd turned down Cassidy's offer and just done what she'd written, they wouldn't be in this predicament. The limited choices she'd had in her future had been taken from her the moment she'd been thrust across the border, and she'd stolen away her mother's as well. The ripples from that one event would determine their course forward for the rest of their lives.

Rose strode across the room and wrapped her in an embrace. She didn't want to hide the truth from her mother. Kiera rested her cheek against her shoulder, breathing in her calming scent of sage and honey. Rose stroked her back until the tension in her chest dissipated, and she could breathe freely again.

Her mother had made a life for them all on her own—she'd had to. Kiera's grandparents on both sides had passed before she was born, her mother's parents caught up in a street raid, and her father's parents in a hovercraft incident. Living multigenerational families were a rarity with the constant culling of dissidents. A long life was a privilege typically reserved for the wealthy and those faithful to the board.

When they stepped back from each other, Kiera flicked her eyes toward her mother's closet. Rose nodded and headed in that direction. She turned and picked up her mother's cell phone and removed Nook's collar, walked over to the microwave oven, and set both items inside. She plucked their miniature television from the kitchen counter and put that within too. Every house was required by law to have a television to tune into the board's weekly announcements. She shut the door, careful not to hit any buttons to turn the oven on. The microwave would block signals to or from the devices, reducing the risk of the government listening in. They couldn't be too careful. It was better to be cautious than to end up in the back of an unmarked car.

She turned back toward Rose's bedroom and hesitated—her feet wouldn't budge. Kiera shuddered as she imagined how her mother would react when she shared what'd happened at Etabon. Kiera rubbed her eyes. The echo of Rose's screams resounding through the fighting pit came back to her, the terror she'd felt earlier sinking its claws in deep. Her mother's life was in real danger now. Sweat trickled down her back, and she had to lean against the kitchen wall to steady herself.

Kiera cursed under her breath. If she was being honest with herself, it was selfishness that'd compelled her to get on the train to Etabon. It wasn't just the bracelet. She'd wanted an extraordinary memory to look back on before facing the next chapter of her life. Her plan after the

117

trip would've been to get specialized education, secure a decent-paying job, and marry someone tolerable. That plan would've ensured that her mother could come live with her and finally rest.

Her actions had ruined that life for both of them. Kiera dug her nails into the wall behind her, hating herself for stalling. Her mother had raised her to be stronger than this. She wouldn't run from her failure. She owed Rose every shred of truth. It'd serve her right if her mother didn't want anything to do with her after this, she thought. Kiera squared her shoulders, retrieved the bracelet from her backpack and the papers from under her bed, and walked into the master bedroom.

She scanned the closet space, taking in the familiar layout. Her mother's clothes were hung neatly to block the hinged cutout in the wall where their metal safe hid. The ancient clock that sat on the top shelf faithfully ticked off the passing seconds. Her eyes tracked the hand as it made its way around the clockface. They kept these conversations under an hour as a precaution. Luckily neither of them was claustrophobic because the closet was barely large enough for them to stand in together.

Kiera could read the question in Rose's eyes. *Are you ready?* they asked. She closed the door behind her, and Rose flipped on the audio jammer that she kept hidden under one of the closet's floorboards. The audio interference the small machine emitted was much higher than their voices, making their conversation undecipherable to eavesdroppers. If any listening devices were tuning in, it would sound like their equipment was malfunctioning. Rose had brought it home when Kiera had started showing signs of the dreams.

Her mother had managed to procure it from a friend who worked in the tech design field. It'd been risky because if either of them had gotten caught, it would've been considered an infraction of the highest degree. Rose believed it was worth the risk. Kiera had been at an age where she was bringing home questions that were too dangerous to discuss, even in the privacy of their own home. Other than Cassidy's screen, it was the only device of its kind that Kiera had ever seen.

Rose wanted Kiera to have a safe place where she could use her voice, so once a month, they'd go into her closet, and Kiera could ask her anything. Rose didn't always have an answer, but it felt good for Kiera to talk things out. It wasn't until she'd gotten older that Kiera realized the lengths her mother must've gone to, to get the device.

The likelihood of the jammer being discovered by a physical home inspection was minimal. Neighborhood raids were less common these days. The board was keeping a lower profile since the festival's inception, relying more on technology to weed out renegades. People were still disappearing, but the abductions had become targeted. Instead of multiple families on a block vanishing, now only one household would go missing.

Kiera met her mother's gaze and forced herself to be efficient in her recounting of the events. By the time she was done, her voice was hoarse from speaking so breathlessly. During her report, the color had drained from Rose's cheeks, but her eyes had remained bright with concentration.

Her mother's hand had grasped the gold pendant around her neck, running it back and forth along its chain, as she did when she was deep in thought. Kiera was surprised the metal wasn't completely worn flat from how often her mother clutched it, but the engraving was still pristine. The edges gracefully ringed in etchings of water lilies, and in the center was the profile of a fox, its snout pointed skyward. It was a family heirloom, the last piece Rose had left of her own mother. The story goes it was part of a pair, exchanged to celebrate a deep bond of love ages ago. Kiera wasn't sure if it was true or just a sweet tale that her mother had spun, but it was poetic to imagine that the necklace had a twin out there. At the moment, her mother was probably thinking there'd be no one to hand hers down to. Especially since she'd told her that she had to go back to Etabon to fight in the arena. Rose peeled back the foil on the documents and skimmed the pages.

Kiera pressed her sweaty palms to her pants. "I'm so sorry, Mom. I was out of my mind to think getting on that train could help us. I know I've put you in a terrible position. You don't deserve this."

Rose took Kiera's face gently in her hands, resolve gathering in her storm-colored eyes.

"There's nothing more important to me in this life than you. Do you hear me? We're survivors, and we'll get through this as we always have, together."

Kiera shook her head, the tears she'd been holding back falling onto her cheeks. Rose wiped them away with her thumbs.

"We had the element of surprise with the jammer. He wouldn't have expected us to have it, but he'll be watching our every move now. Attalin said we should pawn the bracelet and use the money to run, but if he finds out we're trying to escape, he said he'd have you killed…" Kiera's voice broke.

Rose pressed her lips together, her eyes crinkling at the corners in concentration. Her mother stared down at the bracelet and said, "They've reinforced the borders everywhere since the festival opened. There isn't time for travel documents, and even if there was, I'm sure he's paid off people on the inside. That way's out of the question, we wouldn't make it to a port or a hangar without him getting wind. For now, we'll plan like we're going back."

"I'll do whatever you need me to do," Kiera said.

"You've received your scores back from academy. We'll go down to town hall today to apply for your specialized education. We'll pick a career that requires heavy combat training, like a tech security guard. I have a friend who can get us connected with a decent mentor. There's plenty of money in that account, so we'll use added funds to secure expedited approval to get that mentor immediately."

Kiera's eyes flashed, understanding her mother's train of thought. "If I have to go back into the rings, at least I'll be fully prepared this time."

Her mother's voice wobbled subtly. She'd hidden her fear well, but Kiera could see in the way she was holding her body that she was distressed. "Yes, as a last resort, we need to make sure you can protect yourself. In the meantime, we'll move out of the city. You said Hallowfeld," Rose spat his name like it was poison, "wanted you away from your classmates, so we'll take him up on that. Fewer people and less technology will make it harder for him to spy on us. I don't doubt that he'll be keeping close tabs on us, but we won't make it easy for him."

Her mother leaned over and opened the safe. She placed the bracelet and paperwork inside. "We have two months to figure this out. Until then, we don't draw attention from him or the board. If there's another way out, I promise I'll find it."

"Mom, I ruined everything. Everything you've worked for," Kiera whispered.

Rose faced her and brushed Kiera's hair back. "You're alive and healthy. *That* is everything to me. Yes, your actions complicated matters for us, it was a big mistake, but I understand why you went. You wanted to change our fates, and you wanted to witness the thing that's been calling to your spirit your entire life. At your age, I was constantly searching for a spark to fill the dark hole this world can leave in our hearts. I'd all but given up wishing, but a few years later, you were born, and I found that light in you. What's done is done, love, now we move forward."

Kiera exhaled a tight breath. More tears threatened to spill over as she murmured, "I ended up seeing another side of myself at Etabon. The things I'm capable of are terrifying."

Pain flickered across Rose's face. "Kiera, in this life, we'll be faced with impossible decisions. There are times, no matter the choice we make, we'll either be disappointing ourselves or the ones we love. We do our best with the options we're given. Trust me when I tell you I've made plenty of mistakes." Her mother's attention skimmed to the clock above them—they were nearly at an hour. "I'll share them with you one day, but right now, we need to finalize the details of our next moves." Kiera squeezed her mother's hands.

They agreed they'd both rest for a few hours and then go into town to deposit Kiera's application and funds at town hall. They emerged from the closet with a solid plan.

Rose kissed Kiera on the forehead and said, "Get some rest. We'll head to town in a few hours."

When Kiera's head hit her pillow, she was so drained that she didn't dream. What felt like moments later, Rose came to wake her with a cup of black tea. She groaned and rolled out of bed, letting the steam from the tea wash over her face. Her mother was already dressed and had her education documents in hand.

"I made some calls, and that tech security mentor is accepting new apprentices. You'll need to sign the bottom."

Kiera picked up a pen, and her chest twinged. They'd discussed her career plans a thousand times. She'd considered becoming a librarian or a nurse, but she'd never imagined her choice would be made like this. Not that it really mattered either way, as the apprenticeship would be short-lived. Kiera lifted her eyes to catch her mother's. Rose's face was somber, mirroring her thoughts. Once she'd finished with the documents, she washed her face, her mother pinned her hair up for her, and she threw on slacks and a button-down. Kiera placed Nook's collar back on, and they left him staring after them as they slipped out the front door.

INTERROGATION

It was twelve blocks to the nearest public transport train. They made their way there in silence. The streets were nearly empty, but that was normal for midmorning; kids were still out for the equinox break, so they'd be sleeping in, and adults were at their jobs. A couple of drones whizzed by on their way to the station, but their brown and green colors marked them as grocery and retail carriers for wealthier citizens.

Kiera watched the bullet train slide into the station, its doors opened wide for passengers to board. Rose brushed her shoulder against Kiera's in reassurance as they stepped onto the train bound for the city center. They typically avoided this part of town as security was amplified around municipal buildings, but this type of legal procedure had to be conducted in person. Kiera snatched the ring above her head, holding on tight as the doors snicked closed. A soft ding resonated through the cabin to alert commuters that the train was about to burst into motion. A breath later, they were rocketing over the tracks and would be to their destination within minutes.

Kiera discreetly took in the passengers around them. Each had on the same mauve judicial robes that marked them as low-ranking government administrators. These were the individuals who processed education, lodging, and domestic documentation before it was passed on for final approval and certification. It was unnerving that they all had the same bleak stares on their faces. Although she wasn't surprised—they were the people who decided which families deserved adequate housing and which single parents could keep their children from being hauled off to youth centers.

Every time Kiera saw these robes, she was reminded of the years of anguish her mother had been put through, hoping they'd find her suitable enough to raise her own daughter. Her mother's cool fingertips grazed subtly across her arm, bringing her back to the present. Kiera's knuckles around the ring above her had gone white, and her fingernails were digging red crescents into her palm. She lifted her chin slightly to indicate to her mother that she would pull it together. She needed to get a grip. This wasn't the place to let her bitterness spill over. A display at the front of their compartment flashed, indicating that they were pulling into the city center station. Kiera forced calming breaths in and out of her nose to slow her racing heart.

The occupants of their cart filed out onto the platform. The station was directly across the street from the squat ivory town hall building. The place was nothing less than a fortress, with armed guards stationed next to each of the building's pillars. Kiera watched as security drones descended like grotesque pigeons from their perches at the top of the structure to scan the robed individuals before they entered the building's revolving doors. Rose followed her down the stairs and across the walkway toward the monstrosity.

The security in Mendinburrow was nothing compared to the measures that were taken in the capital city of Tydden. Rose had traveled there for work on occasion and mentioned getting around the city was a nightmare. They'd had a lesson on capital defenses once at academy; the instructor had blathered on about each board member residing in their continent's capital city and how no expense was spared to ensure the safety of their brave leaders.

Kiera's gaze caught on the emblem of Atterah, the massive banner thrashing in the breeze. The purple flag was emblazoned with a set of gold scales, three daggers balanced on each side. The symbol was supposed to represent their six righteous leaders distributing justice for all and doling out vengeance to traitors who try to tip the scales in their favor. Kiera wanted to scoff at how out of touch they were. She thought it would be more fitting if those daggers were tipped in red—at the very least they could be honest about how much they enjoyed making their people bleed.

Kiera stopped short as a drone hovered in front of them. She hadn't even noticed it float down from the rafters. It barked that a scan was required for each of them and to state the purpose of their visit. Rose stepped forward first, resting her hand on the machine's screen face so it could take her handprint.

"We're here to provide my daughter's documentation for further education."

The drone's screen blinked green, then pivoted toward Kiera. She echoed her mother's actions and placed her hand on the screen. The light blinked green for her, but the drone announced that Kiera's heart rate was significantly elevated.

Rose smiled demurely into the camera. "Yes, she's been excited to start her specialized education. With her transcript, she could end up working in the tech department at this very building one day."

The drone lingered a beat longer and then chirped and moved aside, satisfied with her answers. It drifted off to harass someone else. Kiera cursed internally. She could chalk her agitation up to a lack of sleep and nerves, or she could acknowledge that Etabon had awoken emotions buried deep inside of her. She swallowed her resentment and painted on a sweet smile as she followed Rose through the revolving doors.

While Rose politely conversed with a man at the front desk, Kiera skimmed the area under her lashes. The snowy marble floor was a stark contrast to the black glass cubicles that were distributed equidistance around the room. This initial space must be one chamber among dozens in this building. There was a catwalk overhead that ran around the top perimeter of the space, peppered with menacing sentries. Besides her mother's soft conversation, the only other sound was their boots clinking against the metal.

The receptionist picked up his phone and then pointed to a cubicle halfway across the room. Rose thanked him, and Kiera trailed her to the spot. Up close, there didn't seem to be an entrance, but just before Kiera looked back over her shoulder to the receptionist, the onyx wall slid open for them. They stepped in, and she instantly wanted to recoil, but the wall closed behind them.

The woman inside had the complexion of a shucked oyster. Kiera wondered if she ever saw the sunlight. Her watery blue eyes tracked Kiera's movements like a predator.

"Hello, dears. I'm Mrs. Hasselti. I'll be processing your requests. Please take a seat."

The administrator's office was sparse, containing a wing-backed chair set behind a desk with a lone computer atop it. The room's only other furnishings were two chrome visitors' chairs. They both offered subdued hellos. Kiera took her seat, briefly glancing above her. It made sense why the room beyond was so hushed—these were insulated prisms topped with clear glass allowing the guards above to peer through.

"Don't worry, dear, they're there for our protection," Mrs. Hasselti said.

Kiera compelled herself to channel Rose's charm and gave her a dazzling smile, gesturing above her. "This building is so orderly. It must be a joy to work among the city's finest."

Mrs. Hasselti's crimson red lips pulled back into an eerily cheerful grin. "The real joy is to see our youth upholding such model behavior. From your records here, I see you show real promise."

Kiera commanded her eyes not to trail to the bulging vein at the administrator's temple, which matched the pale purple of her robes. She bowed her head, looking to the floor instead.

"Thank you."

Mrs. Hasselti turned to her screen, her scarlet-coated nails tapping rapidly across her keyboard.

"They already processed in your vocational documents at the front. The instructor you've selected seems to fit your profile very well."

She knew this interview wasn't just so this woman could praise her moral fiber, she was pressure testing them. They were tight-lipped about this process at academy, but she'd heard a few professors whisper to each other about the havoc these interviewers could wreak on students' prospects. One wrong response or reaction could result in the complete denial of a pupil's request or worse.

"Your placement exam scores are terrific. With just your mother caring for you, that's a true accomplishment. What a gem you are to have developed as you did," Mrs. Hasselti trilled.

Her eyes flashed to Rose with thinly veiled contempt. Kiera felt the world sliding sideways. Did this woman just insult her mother?

She made herself swallow the cutting response she wanted to utter and replied, "I hope to lead a life that'll make the board proud."

Mrs. Hasselti's eyes traveled to her screen; she appeared slightly dubious. Could she detect the deceit in her words? Kiera would have to be more deliberate in her responses.

"I see neither of you has applied for a certification band to attend Etabon. Can you tell me why that is?"

Hallowfeld was true to his word; they weren't aware she'd been there. Kiera made a show of looking repulsed. "That place encourages deplorable behavior."

Mrs. Hasselti sat up straighter, thrilled by her response. "Well, I couldn't have put it better myself."

Kiera hadn't lied. Etabon's current warden did reward cold-blooded behavior. Mrs. Hasselti banged away merrily on her console, her eyes roving over the data in front of her.

"How are you planning to pay for your schooling?" The administrator flicked her cool gaze back to Rose with a challenge.

Kiera folded her hands under her legs—best to keep them pinned down, so they didn't end up smacking Mrs. Hasselti. "That'll be in my account," Kiera said.

She spouted off the checking number from Hallowfeld's documents; it was burned into her memory. Mrs. Hasselti prompted her to lean forward and place her palm on the computer screen she'd turned toward her for personal verification. When she beheld the amount in Kiera's account, she licked her lips.

"Could you please add whatever funds are required for expedited approval along with the tuition?" Kiera asked.

Mrs. Hasselti blinked at her before collecting herself. "Yes, of course." She jammed some keys in. "This grant is robust. It appears you had a generous benefactor."

Kiera knew she was fishing, but she wasn't going to offer up Hallowfeld's name. She didn't want to consider the line of questioning that'd bring on.

"I'm beyond fortunate that our government allows its prosperous citizens to take an interest in abilities like mine. It's a real privilege for desperate situations like ours," Kiera replied through a gritted smile.

Mrs. Hasselti bobbed her head in approval, giving Rose another nasty look. "You poor dear."

Her renewed disdain for Rose outweighed her curiosity to probe further. Mrs. Hasselti beamed at Kiera. "Well, that's all squared away then. With what's compiled here, I should have your approval by the end of the day. Your current academy will be notified, and your mentor will be sent your paperwork."

Kiera simpered, "That's a relief."

The self-righteous expression on the administrator's face almost had Kiera squirming in her seat. "I see there's a form here for housing as well."

Kiera nodded. "I believe there will be fewer distractions living outside of the city, and that lake house appears to be vacant."

Mrs. Hasselti scanned her screen. "Yes, I can procure this for you if you wish, dear, but the internal equipment is quite outdated. It doesn't have any automation."

That was exactly why she and Rose had found the location perfect—no recent technological updates. "It should be no trouble to get it retrofitted. I'll have that work commissioned for," Kiera said.

Just don't ask me when, she thought. Mrs. Hasselti pouted her lips sympathetically as if she couldn't imagine living without these comforts for any amount of time. It was pathetic that what distressed her was the idea of living in a home that couldn't scramble her eggs for her while there were citizens out there who could barely afford to feed themselves.

"What a dreadful place." She wrinkled her nose as she viewed their current townhome. "I'll process this at once to get you away from the riffraff in your current location."

Kiera thought of her kind neighbors and the fact that this was yet another insult flung at her mother. This woman was the person that designated citizens to live in these locations, and she had the nerve to demean them for it. A roaring had begun in her ears; she might lose it. Kiera was considering hurling Mrs. Hasselti's computer against the floor, but she caught eyes with her mother in the reflection of the dark glass behind her. Rose had maintained her serene demeanor the entire interview, and now gave Kiera a knowing smile. If they walked out of here without reacting, they'd be beating this spiteful toad at her own game.

"Would you like the yearly zoning fee to come from your same checking account?" Mrs. Hasselti asked.

Kiera dipped her chin in confirmation.

"Wonderful, I'll have you all moved in within two days. Will that be all?"

Kiera bowed her head. "Yes, thank you, Mrs. Hasselti."

The administrator stood and sidled around her desk. It seemed she might even try to reach out to hug her. Kiera stood and clasped her hands behind her back, she'd gag if this woman touched her.

"My thoughts will be with you, dear. I hope the arrangements we've made today have brought you closer to the future you deserve."

Kiera bared a toothy grin. "Here's to hoping you get the one you deserve as well."

Mrs. Hasselti's eyes softened, and she let out a patronizing sigh. She placed her hand on the wall, and the inky glass parted to release them.

"Good day," she snarled at Rose. To her dismay, Rose chirped a sweet goodbye and glided out the door. Kiera stole out behind her.

It took all her composure not to go sprinting out of the building, but they managed to stroll past the guards, down the steps, and back across the street at a leisurely pace. Once they made it onto the train, she reached out and wrapped her hand around her mother's, and Rose pressed her hand warmly. She knew what she'd say about this interaction because, unfortunately, this wasn't the first time someone had treated them this way. Rose had encouraged her to play into people's assumptions. If they believed you fit into their mold, they wouldn't look too closely.

Kiera knew Rose had sympathy for people like Mrs. Hasselti because, for them, it was blasphemy to think individual thoughts. They had been taught to see the world one way and to never deviate. What was acceptable to them was a quiet household with two compliant parents. The more money the household made, the more agreeable in the eyes of the board. Although Kiera understood that this narrowmindedness was a result of the board's influence, it didn't make it any less painful to pander to these people. Even though it felt like losing every time they bent to their judgments, what mattered were days like today when they bested the system.

13

SAGE

Kiera trailed her pen along the binding of her notebook. She was staring idly out the study window. There was a soft rapping on her oak desk.

"And she's back," her mentor said, his knuckles resting on the spot he'd knocked on in front of her.

Kiera gave him an apologetic smile. "It won't happen again, Mr. Tenserra."

Wrenley Tenserra was a compelling instructor, but even his charisma couldn't hold her attention today. A dynamic man in his early thirties, Wrenley had fierce brown eyes and dark hair cropped short to make sparring easier. Describing him as athletic didn't even begin to cover it—he was head-to-toe muscle.

This was the third time he'd caught her brooding, and it was testing his patience. There was very little opportunity to daydream when the course is exclusively for you. Kiera spent the majority of her week training with him. It'd been a big change for her at first, taking her private lessons in their home; but after nearly two months, she'd adjusted. There were days that she still missed their old townhouse where she'd spent her whole childhood. Leaving had felt like a betrayal, but they didn't have a choice. They'd moved to the lake house outside of the city, and her mother commuted in for work.

Wrenley studied her with perceptive eyes. "How about we cut the strategy lesson short and run through our drills."

This was the reason she admired him—he treated her as a person and not just another lecture to get through. He worked at Amplitude, the most successful technology company in Hytheis. He'd started out writing and designing defensive artificial intelligence code and had been elevated to a security manager for the firm. She was lucky to have him as a mentor.

His lessons ranged from strategic thinking to hand-to-hand combat. From their first day, he'd been candid with her about the fact that he trained his apprentices in the same techniques he taught his own staff. Wrenley expected his pupils to have minds as agile as their physical skills. His theory was to sharpen a person's mental fortitude, so they were better prepared to defend against any form of attack. He'd beaten Kiera at multiple games of chess to prove his point. Kiera appreciated that he included conflict resolution in his lessons; he stressed that physical force should be used as a last resort. She wished their leaders would adopt his philosophy.

Kiera sprang from her chair and followed him down the stairs. She tracked his steps through the back door and out toward the yard. A smile bloomed over Kiera's face when she saw Jax practicing his drills out on the dock. Jaxon Sage was Wrenley's apprentice. He was Kiera's age and had been under Wrenley's mentorship since he was thirteen. When his parents died, Wrenley had taken him under his wing. Jax had been her sparring partner from day one, and his kind advice and sharp humor had won her over within the week.

Kiera picked up her bamboo staff from where it leaned against the patio wall. It was a glorious day; the property was dappled in sunlight flickering through the trees that dotted the grounds. The breeze off the lake was already trying to tug strands of hair from her braid. Wrenley crossed his arms and took up a spot on shore to observe from.

"Remember to protect your left side. Don't hold back, kiddo," Wrenley said with an encouraging nod.

Kiera grinned. "Do I ever?"

Wrenley chuckled and motioned her toward Jax. Kiera kicked off her shoes, enjoying the feel of the grass between her toes before walking midway across the weatherworn wooden planks of the dock.

Jax's raven curls fell over his forehead, and his autumn eyes danced with laughter. They were a startling shade of green that melded into umber and gold. His bronzed arms flexed as he tucked his bamboo staff behind his head, resting it over his shoulders.

He kept his voice low. "You're early. Was he boring today, or did you just miss me?"

Kiera rolled her eyes. "He's never boring, and the only thing I missed was that look you get on your face when I best you."

Jax threw her a lighthearted smile. "Ready to drink some lake water, Kie?"

"Not a chance," she shot back with a grin.

During their initial sessions here, before her feet had calloused, she'd pulled out a decent amount of splinters. Wrenley had declared it was good practice for a distraction she could face during a real conflict. An enemy wouldn't patiently wait for her to remove splinters; they'd use any vulnerability to their advantage. When she pointed out that the odds of her having an actual altercation on an old wooden dock without shoes on were slim, he'd smirked at her and made her do fifty push-ups. Her skill had come a long way since then, and the exercises were an outlet for her anxiety, more so than she'd like to admit. On the days she had her sessions, she was too exhausted to have nightmares.

The two apprentices faced each other in their fighting positions and nodded. Kiera tried to center herself, forcing her mind to be present even though her thoughts desperately wanted to be elsewhere. She wasn't certain what answers the end of this day would bring. Wrenley called for them to begin. Jax darted toward her, and she raised her staff horizontally between her fists in time to block his blow from above. The loud crack of the staffs colliding shook her senses awake. Jax shifted his staff down and aimed for her lower body, but she'd anticipated that and obstructed his second attempt.

She clenched her teeth in concentration and rocked back on her heels, and then thrust forward with a burst of power as their staffs engaged in the middle between them. Her blood raced in her veins, sending adrenaline coursing through her, but she forced her breathing to remain steady. Their eyes locked, calculating each other's next move. She saw the glint in Jax's eye just before he slid his staff away and thrust forward, aiming for her midsection. She blocked it but lost a step backward. He immediately aimed for her head. She ducked but saw that he was coming back around to take out her legs. Kiera jumped, narrowly avoiding his hit. She landed close to the edge of the planks and righted herself before falling into the lake.

She was well aware, after weeks of training, that he'd knock her into the water without hesitation, either by a blow or backing her off the end of the dock. She didn't give Jax time to collect himself after his last advance and lashed out. He moved back, but she'd clipped his shoulder, sending a thrill through her. He retreated further, and she pursued him, all her fear and rage for what the next day would bring poured into her movements. She made to land what looked like an easy strike to his chest, but in her frenzy, she'd stopped paying attention to his tells. He knocked her assault away and burst toward her. She realized her mistake too late. He'd been drawing her in, and she'd left her lower body wide open. Jax caught her on the calf, and when she flinched forward from the pain, he snapped her across the back, sending her tumbling forward. She'd finally beaten him last week, but that wouldn't be the outcome today, she thought, as she plunged face-first into the lake.

Kiera sank deep beneath the lake's surface. Before swimming back up, she lingered, taking in the world around her. It was peaceful under the cool water watching the grasses sway and the fish darting through them. It made her think about the mermaids and nixies from centuries ago; they must've enjoyed the quiet below the surface. Her line of thinking made her thoughts skip to one mermaid in particular. Attalin's worried expression from their last conversation pushed its way into her vision. Could it only have been seven days since Attalin had been here? Kiera thought.

Her lungs began to protest for air, so she kicked her way back up, watching the sun's rays filtering down from above, the light shifting as she drew closer to the surface. When she broke out of the water, Wrenley was already leaning forward to offer her a hand up. Wrenley or Jax always helped her out after pushing her in. She'd only pulled Wrenley down into the lake once, and that had resulted in an extended sprinting session for her and Jax, but it had been worth the laughs. As he helped her up, Kiera took in a deep breath of air.

Wrenley chuckled. "You were down there a long time. I was wondering if I needed to send Jax in after you."

"That's what you get for making me learn to hold my breath for so long." Kiera plopped down at the end of the dock next to Jax.

Wrenley snorted. "That'll teach me."

He sat down on her other side and handed her a canteen of water.

"I think she was trying to avoid the embarrassment of losing to me for a little bit longer," Jax quipped.

Kiera nudged him with her shoulder. "Don't forget who beat you twice last week."

Wrenley leaned back, taking in the sky. "Your form was great until you let your emotions get the best of you."

Kiera wrung the water from her hair and sighed. "Pesky things."

Wrenley studied her but must've been able to read that she didn't want him to pry. "We have time. Do you two want to take a crack at the course before we stretch?"

Wrenley stood, offering her a hand up. She smiled and accepted it. It was exhausting trying to determine if someone was a decent person. Kiera had to be much more careful in her interactions now—she had no idea who Hallowfeld could've gotten to. Wrenley seemed like the type of man she hoped her father could've been, but did she really know him or Jax? She'd likely never know where their true loyalties lay.

"How could I say no?" she called to his back, as he stepped onto the lawn.

Wrenley glanced over his shoulder. "You can, but that means longer meditation."

Kiera didn't mind stretching, but meditation was difficult for her. Her brain never wanted to be still for longer than five seconds. She'd become more disciplined at it, but it was clear the effort would be pointless today.

Jax's body brushed past hers, and it sent a rush of warmth from her stomach to her toes. He turned around, walking backward over the dock to look at her. "Come on, Kie, it'll be fun." Jax winked. "Didn't you want to see that look on my face? That is, if you can beat me at something today."

She narrowed her eyes at Jax and shouted to Wrenley, "The course it is!"

Kiera could feel the heat radiating off of Jax's body as they crouched side by side at the start of Wrenley's gauntlet. It included climbing multiple rope obstacles, balancing across round stones, and crawling below vines with sharp thorns. Wrenley let out a whistle, and the two of them burst toward the course. Out of her peripherals, Kiera could see that they were evenly matched through each phase. It was down to the mad dash across the stretch of ground between the last obstacle and the finish line. A burst of energy pushed Kiera ahead of Jax. He caught the back of her shirt, but her hand grasped the finish line flag. Their momentum tipped them forward, and they collided, rolling through the leaves. Jax was sprawled over her, panting in the grass. Kiera's body was wracked with laughter as she thrust the flag into the air triumphantly.

He lifted up on his elbows over her, hooting, and pulled a leaf from her hair. "Fine, I'll admit it, you won that one fair and square."

Kiera realized how close his lips were, his torso pressed to hers, and her cheeks flushed.

Wrenley had his eyebrows raised. "That was your best time yet."

Jax rolled off her, and Kiera let out a breathy laugh, wiping sweat from her face, "I still can't believe you talked my mom into setting this up back here."

Wrenley's mouth twitched. "If you can imagine, it was way easier getting her to agree to it than it was getting you to use it the first time."

Kiera covered her face, hiding a fresh wave of embarrassment at the memory of her first flailing attempts on the course. She took the hand Jax extended to her and got to her feet. She could only imagine her mother's expectations for Wrenley when it came to her safety, but she seemed far more at ease around him than she'd anticipated. His mentorship came recommended by a friend, but they were still careful around them.

"We'll cut out meditation today since that was your best run."

Kiera and Jax whooped as Wrenley tossed them their stretching mats. They lined up next to each other and moved through their routine.

"Your mother let us know you two are going to take a short holiday, so just give me a call when you're back, and we can pick up our lessons after your break," Wrenley said.

"Are you going to miss your favorite student?" Kiera answered.

"Hey now," Jax said, putting his hand to his chest in mock outrage.

Wrenley sighed and shook his head at them.

Kiera smirked, but the idea of never seeing them again made her heart heavy. It bothered her that she was going to miss them so deeply— it felt like a vulnerability. Wrenley checked his watch and stood, rolling his mat up.

"It's time for us to head out," he said.

She pressed herself up off the ground and stepped forward. He gave her a gentle embrace and said, "Have a good break, kiddo. We'll see you after."

"Thank you," Kiera said as she looked up at him.

Jax tucked his mat under his arm and walked up to her, reaching over to pull another leaf from her hair. He twirled it between his thumb and forefinger. "Something to remember you by until next time," he beamed.

Kiera shoved his arm playfully. "What are you going to do without me?"

"I'll survive. Wrenley's given me some time off too. I may rest or do some traveling, who knows?"

Kiera gave him a crooked grin. "Sounds refreshing."

Jax's face became earnest. "Really though, I'll miss you, Kie. Have a good holiday."

Kiera's throat tightened. "I'll miss you too." He bent to hug her, and all she could think about was that his shirt smelled like cloves and pine. His cheek grazed hers as they pulled away from each other, sending sparks over the places where his skin touched hers.

She watched as he jogged to catch up with Wrenley, who was already halfway across the yard. Wrenley smiled at something Jax said, and they waved back at her before disappearing around the side of the house.

VISITOR

K iera rested her chin on her shoulder and stared out toward the lake. At last, she was left alone with her thoughts. After weeks of instruction from Wrenley and Jax, she realized how unprepared she'd been at Etabon last time. Although training in her human body had allowed her to appreciate just how agile her magical form had been, powerful magic had gotten her through those fights, or more likely, it had something to do with what she'd seen when she was dying. A shiver went down her spine at the memory of the ethereal voices calling to her after her final match.

There were still nights that those figures came to her in her dreams, whispering something she couldn't quite make out. She'd wake up with her skin pebbled in a cold sweat and would lie awake for hours. Her logical side tried to rationalize them as hallucinations she'd had from the shock and blood loss that day. The silhouettes could've just been Attalin and Gabby as she drifted back into consciousness, but deep down, she'd sensed the supernatural in that encounter. Had she unwittingly let something in that had the ability to plague her beyond Etabon's borders? Kiera wondered.

She jumped up from the ground, shaking off her uneasiness, and walked back to the lake's edge. Kiera picked up a smooth rock and threw it across the water, watching it skip, sending out ripples in all directions. She bent down and collected another, turning it over and over in her hand, reflecting on Attalin's impromptu visit at the beginning of the week.

It'd been in the early hours of the morning when the first rays were setting the lake's surface alight. Kiera had been sipping tea at the kitchen table when Nook barked at the front door. It sent alarm bells off in her head because their nearest neighbor was a mile away. They'd noticed the occasional drone flying over, but Hallowfeld hadn't been bold enough to physically send anyone, at least not that they'd seen. There was an abundance of greenery to hide in around the area, so they hadn't ruled it out. Rose was standing at the top of the stairs, her hair tousled and a hand in her robe. It was her day off from work, so she'd been sleeping in.

"Do you see anyone?" she asked.

When Kiera realized who was walking up the gravel drive, she did a double take, gasping, "Attalin?"

Her mother's expression was puzzled, but the tension left her shoulders. Kiera threw the door open and shouted hello.

Attalin's head snapped up, and she smiled, saying, "I'd know that voice anywhere."

Kiera cleared the front steps in a leap, and when the girls' eyes met, she saw Attalin mouth, "Hey, Whiskers."

They crashed into each other and embraced. It was exhilarating seeing her in her human form outside of Etabon. After a moment, Kiera leaned back, holding her by the shoulders. "What are you doing here? Are you ok?"

The light in Attalin's eyes winked out, and she pulled a charcoal box from the bag over her shoulder. "I'm here to deliver these."

Kiera's mouth went dry. There was a note attached to the box, and she recognized the handwriting on it. The looping script read:

See you in a few days, dear girl.

Inside, settled atop the red velvet lining, were two permanent resident certification bands.

"He had his meeting yesterday. Your permits will be approved by the end of the week. He has a hovercraft set up to take you back then," Attalin rasped out.

Rose came out and offered Attalin a friendly welcome, then ushered them both into the house. Once they were inside, her eyes settled on the box with knowing.

"I'm sorry," Attalin murmured.

"Hey now," Rose said, taking her hand, "this isn't your fault."

The day Kiera had returned from Etabon, she'd told her mother everything about how Attalin had coached her through the matches and what Hallowfeld had put her and her family through. The way her mother looked at Attalin now told Kiera she understood just how vital she'd been in helping her get back home in one piece.

"Why don't you stay for breakfast?" Rose asked gently.

Attalin lifted her head in surprise. "I have to board a flight back in a couple of hours, but I have time. That sounds great, thank you."

Rose set out fruit and oat muffins. They talked, not about anything crucial in case there were listening ears, but Kiera could tell by the way her mother leaned into their conversation that she liked Attalin instantly. If it hadn't been for the ominous box sitting on the counter, it would've been a perfect morning.

When they'd finished eating, her mother disappeared into the study to give them some space. Kiera took the box outside and set it by a cluster of trees. She'd rather not have it in the house if she could avoid it. They went out to the dock and let their feet dangle over the water. Attalin's eyes darted around nervously, and after a few minutes, her fidgeting was so pronounced that Kiera knew she was trying to tell her something. She stood and offered Attalin her hand. "I could use another cup of tea, want one?"

Attalin's eyes assessed her and flared in understanding. "I'd love one."

Rose had managed to smuggle the audio jammer along when they'd moved. They hadn't used it because they didn't want Hallowfeld to catch on that they had it, but this situation called for an exception. The two of them piled into Rose's closet. Kiera wrenched up the floorboard to flip the jammer on.

Attalin sagged against the wall. "It's a good thing you have this. I needed to warn you but didn't know how with this place under surveillance. You can't come back to Etabon. Hallowfeld is more erratic than ever."

Kiera couldn't mask the fear that passed across her face. "What do you mean?"

Attalin tucked her arms over her chest. "Since you left, he's been crueler than ever. He's traveled out of Etabon a lot. I think he's planning something big. He's recruited new sponsors, and he's grown his following—more residents have taken on the eclipse brand. He had Wendel beaten within an inch of his life right in front of me, as an example of what happens to people who don't fall in line. It's not safe for you or your mom."

Devastation wrapped around Kiera's ribcage, and it became difficult to breathe. She braced herself against her terror and reached out for Attalin, gathering her in her arms. "That's horrible. I'm so sorry." Attalin shuddered against her and then drew back.

"Hallowfeld sent me here as some kind of twisted reminder to you, but you can't let guilt bring you back. Do you have something to write with?" Kiera reached past her and grabbed the pen off her mother's calendar. Attalin's hands trembled as she took it and wrote down a name and address on Kiera's palm. It was an address for a bakery a town over next to the name Emeric.

Attalin's cheeks flushed, the intensity in her eyes turning their golden shade to molten honey. "Gabby managed to get this for me. She never had the chance to use it for herself. I need you to memorize that and wipe it off when we step out of here. She said the owners of this shop used to smuggle people out of Hytheis to the dunes in Renival. Ask for nine lemon and lavender cookies in a box. When they ask what color ribbon for the box, say orange. It's code that you want to be taken to Renival. It's been years since Gabby's left Etabon herself, so she doesn't know if they're still there, but it's worth trying. I know running is a gamble, but I'm afraid you won't make it out of the arena this time."

Kiera rocked back on her heels. "Attalin, if Hallowfeld finds out you tried to help us escape, he'll kill you."

She straightened with resolve. "We have a bargain. He can't harm me for nearly a decade."

"What about your family?" Kiera asked.

"If he can't have you, he wouldn't risk losing me, too. Hallowfeld covets my magic. If they're dead, it means I can't see them once a year, and that voids our bargain."

Attalin stepped forward, taking her by the elbows. She locked her eyes on Kiera's. "If you can use this to get out, then you go, and you don't look back. Do you understand me?"

Kiera whispered, "Ok, I promise."

They held each other for a while, Attalin's head resting on her shoulder, Kiera stroking her hair. Kiera gave her a final squeeze before stepping back. She flipped the jammer off and stomped the floorboard back down. That goodbye had been harder than their last one, both of them sick with worry for the other. When Attalin walked down the driveway, Kiera had forced her eyes to remain dry, but inside, she was fragmenting. Attalin was taking a piece of her heart back with her.

Kiera had waited a full day before signaling to Rose that they needed to use the jammer. Interference with technology did happen, but she didn't want it to be obvious enough to tip anyone off. She'd kept their conversation short, telling Rose about Attalin's warning and writing the name and address on her mother's hand. When Kiera asked if she'd discovered anywhere safe they could go, her mother had wavered in her response, staring down at her hand, emotions swimming behind her gray eyes. Kiera had always been in tune with her mother's train of thought, like they were of one mind, but lately, she had these fleeting moments where she slipped into someplace Kiera couldn't follow. Rose placed her hand on Kiera's cheek and told her everything she'd looked into had come up as dead ends, but that she'd keep searching for a way out. Rose had noticed someone tailing her to and from work. If she could shake them and get away, she'd look into the bakery.

A soft swishing of wings released Kiera from her reverie, drawing her back to the present. She'd spent a lot of time in her head these last few days. Kiera watched as a flock of geese landed gracefully on the lake. They dipped their heads under the surface to wash their feathers. Sometimes she wished she could fly—maybe her problems would feel smaller if she could look at them from above. The rock slipped from her grip, tumbling out of her hand. It plunged straight down into the water, startling the birds back into the air.

Each day this week, Rose had come home clearly unable to elude her tracker. Today would be her mother's last chance to visit the bakery. The hovercraft was set up to take them back the next morning. They'd maintained their normal routine. Rose went to work, and Kiera attended her sessions. They didn't want anything to appear out of the ordinary. When they'd spoken in her closet the other day, Rose said she'd call Kiera if she could get to the bakery, and if it checked out, she'd invite her into town for dinner. Over the phone, they would agree to meet at a café, but really, they'd rendezvous at a location near their old townhome. Both of them knew the alleyways there, so it'd be their best chance to throw off any pursuers and get back to the bakery.

Kiera was just turning back to the house when she heard her phone's blaring tone. She jogged into the living room and caught it on the last ring. The screen flashed Rose's name. This was it. The call was coming from her mother's cell phone and not a phone booth, so it was likely just to tell her the bakery was a bust. They'd be out of options and would have to stick to the last resort, the one Kiera had been training for, and go back to Etabon together.

"Hi, are you on your way back?" Kiera asked.

"No love, I need you to listen." Her tone made the hair on the back of Kiera's neck stand on end. "The board is allowing us to have this call on a secure line, so I need to be quick."

Kiera felt like the floor had dropped out from under her. Did they have Rose imprisoned somewhere? Had she gone to the address and gotten caught by the authorities, or had Hallowfeld gone back on his word and framed her for something? This wasn't right—he'd agreed her mother would be safe.

"I'm going to be out of contact for over six weeks. An incident happened with Board Member Marcus's father, and he requires urgent surgery. The government's assembling a team of the best doctors and nurses in Hytheis to care for him. I was chosen to be on that team. It's a great honor." Kiera forced down the sourness in her throat. An honor that no one could refuse without facing the penalty of death, which would occur anyway if they failed to heal him. "I'm only allowed to tell you this as I'm your sole caregiver, and you'll be on your own until I return. Our government was convinced this information could be shared with you. They agreed you're an upstanding citizen, and I assured them you'll use the utmost discretion with this knowledge."

Kiera forced her voice not to quiver, "Of course, I understand." No doubt one of the officials listening in told her mother to convey that message, and it implied she was not to run her mouth about the man's condition or there would be consequences.

Rose continued, "Good. I don't want you to worry about me, I'll be safe in a secure location. For me, this situation takes precedence over our travels, but you can still get out of the house and go on our trip."

It dawned on her that her mother was telling her she had to go to Etabon.

"Are you sure?"

"Yes, I'm positive. The borders into Hytheis have been shut down, but you're traveling privately within the continent, so you won't have any problem. Don't change your plans on my account. I'll come to you after Board Member Marcus's father is better." Rose paused. "Now do as I ask and take care of yourself. I'll be to you as soon as I can. I love you, Kiera."

She stared at the phone. "I will. I love you too." Then the line went silent.

Kiera sank into a sitting position. Her mother's words bounced around frantically in her head. There'd been intention in her remarks. She'd meant for her to listen to their actual meaning. To anyone eavesdropping, it would've sounded like a mother reassuring her daughter about the situation and urging her to maintain their travel plans, but to her, it was a directive. The phrases "get out of the house," "don't change your plans, and "do as I ask" burned at the forefront of her mind.

Kiera stood on trembling legs and began pacing. The way her mother had said those words practically shouted at her to go back to Etabon. She'd made the timeframe of her absence clear. She wouldn't be returning to the festival with her tomorrow. Her mother would try to get to her… if they healed Board Member Marcus's father. Kiera shook her head. She refused to think like that—not *if* but *when* they healed him. Rose had alerted Kiera straight off to watch her responses. They were always careful on the phone, but this conversation had been on a whole different level.

She couldn't fathom the courage it'd taken just to convince them to approve that call. Her mother must've known she would've gone searching for her when she didn't come home. Kiera would've been frantic and assumed it was Hallowfeld who'd taken her. She'd addressed that too—there would be no attempt at finding her. It sounded like the government would have her sequestered in some undisclosed military compound. It must've been why Rose referenced it. Kiera's hand went to her mouth when she realized she was trapped. Even if the bakery had been a viable option, the borders were shut down.

She rubbed her temples. Leave it to her brilliant mother to pack all of that into a sixty-second conversation. Another reason she'd alluded to getting out of the house; if they felt she would cause any issues, they could start digging into her background or do a "precautionary" raid on the house.

Kiera's training pushed through her flurry of thoughts. She took deep breaths, in through her nose and out through her mouth, forcing herself to settle. A concept from one of Wrenley's lectures surfaced in her mind: During a crisis, first steps were to prioritize resources and potential threats. She considered her prospective hazard level. She was one teenage girl with a nearly perfect track record who lived far outside the city. If she didn't give them a reason to, it'd be unlikely that they'd even devote one essential drone to monitor her.

The government's primary focus would be getting the medical unit and the board member's father to a secure location. After that, they'd allocate available resources to whatever threats they'd established. Her goal was to avoid becoming one of those targets. That gave her less than twenty-four hours of privacy before they made their decision about her. So, from what she gathered, she was supposed to leave in order to signal that she was just a harmless girl, who was more interested in her trip than interfering in the board's matters.

She chewed this theory over, looking up at the ceiling as if the sheetrock held answers. There still had to be more at play here. It felt weightier than just the board's perception of her for her mother to be sending her back to Etabon on her own, knowing full well what she'd be facing there. Whatever was going on, they'd shut down the borders for it. It occurred to her that when other board members' relatives had gotten sick before, it'd been a public affair. Their conditions were displayed on the news. It was like the board used their hardships as a way to humanize themselves.

Board Member Dalia, the board member of Fortayne, had a sister who'd had a stroke. A team had spent weeks trying to rehabilitate her. The broadcasts were incessant about her condition and called for nightly moments of reflection. When it was reported that she'd passed away peacefully in her sleep, there was a full week of mourning. Her medical unit hadn't been so lucky; there were whispers that Dalia had the entire team and their families executed for their failure.

Kiera shuddered at the recollection. Now, her mother was in the same position. She padded to the kitchen and flicked on their television. She watched for ten minutes, and there was no mention of Board Member Marcus's father. His condition would be major news, especially here in Hytheis. Her mother had used the word "incident" when describing the situation to her. She'd never heard of news of this nature being kept quiet, but there had to be a reason they didn't want it publicized. Could there have been an attack on a board member? Kiera wondered. It seemed inconceivable, but whatever was going on, her mother believed she'd be safer inside the borders of Etabon than trying to flee Hytheis on her own.

The end of their conversation pricked at her heart. If anyone could survive this, it was her mother. She allowed herself a few tears before drying her eyes on her shirt sleeve. As she stood there, the realization hit her that in a few hours, she'd be on a hovercraft bound for the festival, and she'd be going back alone.

15

SECRETS

Kiera closed her eyes and leaned her cheek against the cool glass of the hovercraft's window. It felt soothing against her swollen face—the lack of sleep was catching up with her. Memories from last night blurred together in a flurry of motion. She'd scoured the house for anything that could be considered unlawful and disposed of it. There hadn't been much on her initial list, the main item being the audio jammer. With all the memories tied to it, destroying it had been hard for her. Kiera had broken it down piece by piece in the closet.

When she'd pulled up the floorboard for the jammer, she also removed the paper money. There was too much to look inconspicuous, so she packed most of it to take with her. Traveling with it to Etabon would be easier to explain than a pile of it stashed under the floor. Nothing could be left to indicate that they distrusted the board. She'd put an acceptable amount in her mother's travel purse along with her certification band and left it on her nightstand. When she'd dug to the back of the space to make sure she hadn't missed any money, her knuckles had brushed against cold metal. Something had compelled her to withdraw her hand instead of seizing the item. She'd retrieved a flashlight and peered in to see what it was. It'd sent a jolt through her when she'd made out what was lying at the back of the compartment—thankfully she hadn't just gripped it.

Her mother had stowed a gun in their house. It was high treason just to have it, a guaranteed death penalty. She couldn't imagine how difficult it'd been to attain it. Only sentries with the highest security clearance were permitted to have weapons. It was possible she'd gotten it from the same friend who'd smuggled her the jammer, but that would have been reckless. For a few seconds, Kiera just stared at it, unsure of what to do. Then she reached in and carefully collected it by the handle. In her lessons with Wrenley, they'd gone over the basic features of a gun and in what cases they were employed instead of a security drone, but those were all diagrams in a textbook. She'd never held one in her hands.

Kiera marveled at it. This one seemed advanced, with a multitude of buttons. It took her a beat to find the safety and check that it was switched on. It'd be a disaster if she accidentally fired it. Kiera left it and the pieces of the jammer in the closet and stalked to the garage, where she found the fast-drying concrete. Her mother had bought it to set fence posts around the garden. Kiera mixed some up in a small duffle bag and brought it back to the closet, where she submerged the gun and jammer parts in it. She waited until dusk and carried the bag out under a cluster of towels. Her plan was to discard the bag of concrete in the lake under the guise of an evening swim. When she pulled the towels toward herself on the dock, she slipped the bag down into the water and let it sink to the bottom.

It was lucky that her mother had the opportunity to tip her off. If the board decided it was worth raiding their house, they'd come up clean now. When she'd finished, she'd only slept a few fitful hours, her dreams swarming with unanswered questions for her mother. The morning had rolled in on a cool mist. She'd looked through the blinds, leery of what could be concealed amongst the shifting vapors. Kiera had gotten up, dressed quickly, and collected her bag. She'd clipped on Nook's leash, and they disappeared out the front door, becoming another cluster of shadows in the haze. Thankfully their trek to the private hovercraft port they'd departed from had been uneventful.

Kiera was alerted to their arrival by the whir of hangar doors drawing apart below, prompting her to open her eyes and look out the window. The ride had been swift and quiet, as the craft Hallowfeld had commissioned was compact and autonomous, and she and Nook had been its only passengers. It landed in a relatively large structure located behind the bullet train tracks. She rubbed her face, trying to clear the unease that clung to her. She needed to place what happened behind her for now and focus on what was ahead.

Kiera tossed her bag over her shoulder, wrapped Nook's leash around her wrist, and descended the ramp with her chin held high. Similar to the last time she'd arrived at the festival, she was funneled into an organized queue along with other patrons that'd come by air. The difference was that this progression bypassed the larger line from the trains, feeding in near the front.

Memories from months ago gripped Kiera's chest. It wasn't long before the entry pillars came into view. Her feet were heavy as she studied them, shuffling forward. Kiera took off her shoes and placed them in her bag in anticipation of the change. She made it to the front of the line and watched as a couple turned their wrists over to be scanned. The familiar tang of magic filled the air, and a crackling and shimmering hissed around them. The man grew taller while long sinewy wings sprouted from his back, gray skin ran the length of his body, and his eyes turned a deep red. The woman radiated light, her auburn hair growing and tumbling down her back to her waist, and light blue and green scales formed, running up and down her forearms and legs. It was remarkable, smelling their magic—crisp ocean and smoldering pine—all in the same breath.

The water faerie manning the gate exhaled. "Welcome to Etabon, my lovely friends." She motioned them forward. The mermaid and orc thanked her as they passed.

Kiera moved to the entrance reluctantly. Once she stepped across that threshold, Hallowfeld would have her ensnared.

A wide smile split the faerie's mouth, causing her freckles to crinkle over her nose. "Another permanent resident. We're so very happy to have you!" She wiggled her fingers at Nook, and Kiera noticed the eclipse mark on her wrist and balked.

The water faerie waved her in, and she took a wobbly step forward, but then Kiera felt the pull of the magic as soon as she moved closer. She offered up her wrist for her band to be inspected and certified. The water faerie nodded, and Kiera sighed as she stepped over the border into the open arms of Etabon's magic. There was no other feeling like this. Kiera's fur sprouted along her back, golden black, and soft, rolling up her torso and down her spine. Her tail curled and sprang free, wrapping around her leg. Her claws pushed through her hands and feet, and her teeth elongated into points. Kiera licked her fangs and twitched her pointed ears. A warm comfort settled in her veins as her magic greeted her.

Kiera thought her transition would spook Nook, but he just sniffed at her, looked up, and wagged his tail happily. There was a new sharpness to his clever eyes.

The crowd behind her murmured, "The Lynx." She took a deep breath. *No,* she thought, *I'm Kiera Vandyer, and I refuse to be afraid.*

Kiera had intentionally worn baggy clothes for her body to grow into, loose-fitting pants with a spot stitched in for her tail and a long flowing shirt. After orienting herself, she headed toward the bars and restaurants, knowing exactly where they'd be going first.

Nautilus looked just as it had a couple of months ago, with Patrick, the stern, gold-furred werewolf, stationed out front. He gave her a terse nod of recognition and moved the flap aside for her to enter. Hallowfeld likely knew the second she'd stepped foot across the border, but she didn't see him inside. No doubt he was waiting to make an ostentatious entrance. She headed to the counter. Only a few individuals were milling about within. It was early morning, so most patrons were just waking up.

Kiera saw a flash of golden hair as Attalin came from the back carrying a crate of glasses. Seeing her dulled the sharp edges of emotion threatening to splinter inside of her. Attalin caught sight of her over the bar. Disbelief played across her face, but when she noted the devastated look in Kiera's eyes, her shock evaporated. Attalin glanced behind her, making the connection immediately. She peered back at Kiera with a questioning look. Kiera shook her head slightly, confirming she and Nook were here alone. Her concern for her mother threatened to bubble up to the surface. She knew she couldn't break down in here. It hadn't even been twenty-four hours since Rose had been seized by the board, and it was already getting to her.

Attalin was in tune with Kiera's feelings and hurried to grab a mug and a pot of coffee. She poured her a cup and handed it over.

"Morning, Whiskers, looks like you could use one of these."

Kiera forced a smile and took a gulp. The coffee was bitter and scalding hot, but sipping it banished the tears behind her eyes. Attalin wiped her hands on a towel and tossed it into a barrel behind her.

"I took the night shift to prepare the bar for today—I just finished up my hours. I had a feeling you might be here and wanted to be free." Attalin's tone betrayed the true meaning behind her words; she'd been hoping for Kiera's sake that she wouldn't be seeing her here.

In a look, Kiera tried to convey how desperately she'd wanted to act on Attalin's warning to stay away. It'd been daring for her to bring them that bakery address; she only wished they could've used it.

Attalin gave her a reassuring smile and said, "Why don't I grab us some food, and we can catch up."

Kiera stared down at the steam rising from her mug. "I'm not sure there's much to catch you up on."

Attalin leaned her elbows on the bar and considered her. Kiera wasn't sure it was safe to share even the simplest detail with her. If the board found out she'd leaked classified information, it could gravely impact her mother. In one of their lessons, Wrenley had said that agents rarely entered Etabon. The board didn't want their top talent exposed to magic, but there were always informers present, people who were more than happy to turn in their fellow citizens for money. In her case, Hallowfeld wouldn't want to part with her, so they'd probably work something out with him, but they could punish her by executing Rose.

Attalin dipped her chin. "Well, I'll tell you what I've been up to then, and you can eat at least. I'm going to go visit Gabby real quick. Why don't I take Nook and your bag and drop him off there."

Kiera rested her hand on top of his head. "Gabby will be ok with him being in the tent?"

"Absolutely, it's the best place for him, I promise. Meet me by the stream. I'll be there in five minutes." Kiera didn't have to say out loud that she was afraid to leave Nook alone, but she trusted Attalin's word. If she said he'd be protected in Gabby's tent, then he would be. She drank another mouthful of coffee and stood.

"Sure then, thank you," she said, giving Attalin an appreciative nod as she handed over her bag and Nook's leash. He trotted off to the back of the bar without a moment's hesitation, completely trusting Attalin too.

Kiera began walking to the front, but before she got outside, a charcoal letter breezed through the tent and pressed into her hand. She barely managed to restrain the growl in her throat.

Welcome back, my feline friend. Meet me at the arena in an hour. We have much to discuss.

Kiera crumbled it up and tossed it into a waste bin, then shoved through the exit. She wandered out to the spot by the stream where she and Attalin had talked at last time. During the day, the view was equally breathtaking. The sun streamed down through the trees, and clusters of wildflowers swayed in the wind, honeybees bouncing from blossom to blossom. A hummingbird buzzed by her ear, and she could've sworn it tittered with laughter when she jumped aside. Kiera studied the dumbfounding way the tiny bird could fly backward to watch her. The creatures here seemed joyful. She wondered if it had anything to do with the concentration of magic in the land. Etabon had a way of allowing you to appreciate its beauty even during the worst of times.

Kiera dropped down and laid back in the grass, letting the sun warm her, slowly dissipating the tension in her muscles. Her ears picked up Attalin's approaching presence at the same time her magic felt her coming. Kiera turned her head and watched as she drew closer. Attalin sank down next to her in the grass and handed her a foil package from her bag.

"I see you're enjoying sunning yourself. I could swear you were purring."

The joke was halfhearted, though Attalin could clearly sense there was something very wrong. Kiera sat up and ripped back the foil to find a fried ham and egg sandwich.

"Thanks," she said before biting into her breakfast with satisfaction. Around a mouthful, she remarked, "I got a letter to be at the arena in an hour."

Attalin wrinkled her nose. "He's such a pretentious weasel."

Kiera's eyes glinted. "That's an insult to weasels everywhere."

"We'll have you back in time." Attalin put her hand to her mouth, chuckling.

"I was just realizing that the animals here look like they can sense magic too. Nook's eyes looked a little different when we crossed over," Kiera said, waving her arm around them.

Attalin glanced around the clearing and then replied, "Gabby told me once that even animals feel a deep connection to magic. She explained it like an ember that burns inside all of us, and every being accesses it in different ways. I try not to think about all the creatures that are severed from that connection outside of Etabon. Once I was aware of it though, I did notice a glint in the eyes of the animals here that I don't see beyond the border."

An idea occurred to her. "If magic manifests differently for beings in their magical forms, I wonder how it affects those who don't have one? The people who remain human, I mean." She knew that asking a question like this, even within the borders, was treading into illicit territory. Attalin had told her that there'd been debate among those who were physically changed by the magic. They referred to their magical forms as their true forms, instead of their human forms outside of Etabon. Kiera glanced back toward the way they'd come.

The tents were off in the distance, but she didn't want to be careless. Attalin patted a spot on her dress where her tiger's eye hung beneath, indicating she'd activated it.

"I was curious about that too, and asked Gabby about it a few years back. Being a healer, she's a wealth of knowledge when it comes to the body's connection to our magic. She explained that those who maintain human bodies within Etabon have a magical connection that allows them to tap deep into their creative abilities. So, they may not be able to harness the elements or craft spells, but their connection allows them to delve into the deepest corners of their mind and produce innovative ideas."

Kiera flicked her tail. It made sense. In her tech lessons, Wrenley had detailed the history of technological advancements, and she'd noticed that the truly groundbreaking developments had stalled over the last century. There were still inventions and modifications to already existing designs, but she wondered how much more true innovation there could be if humans had access to their magical impulses. An even darker thought was that their government detested magic so much that their world was missing out on technology that could help people. Kiera wondered what it'd be like if magic and tech combined, how many lives could be impacted for the better. She recalled a conversation she'd had with her mother once after she'd had a hard day at work. It'd been on the same night as one of their monthly talks. A child her mother had been caring for had succumbed to an infection, and Rose had taken it hard. It'd been during the months that Etabon was closed to the public, so the child's parents couldn't take her to the site to seek help from the witches.

Her mother had explained, the idea that individuals would choose to heal themselves through magical means was blasphemy to the board. They wouldn't even use it to save their own families, believing that magic taints the mind. She'd found that funny coming from people who didn't appear to have consciences. Kiera felt her mood shift as her thoughts turned to her mother. Attalin was watching her. She crumbled up the foil from her own sandwich and threw it into her bag, then tilted the sack so Kiera could toss hers in too. Kiera turned and stared vacantly at the water rushing by.

Attalin dusted breadcrumbs from her fingers and walked over to the stream. She bent down, speaking over her shoulder, "I want to show you something."

Kiera's head jerked up. The distraction prevented her from falling headlong into despair. Attalin had waded into the deepest part of the stream, her sunflower-yellow dress drenched, water creeping up its edges. She closed her eyes, and a soft glow emanated from her, the air around her wavering for a moment. Kiera was on her feet and at the water's edge before she realized what had happened. Attalin's legs had been replaced by an elegant tail. Her tail fin was a semitransparent golden color that tapered up into the orange and pink scales that normally donned her calves. Attalin's dress billowed out as she circled around in the stream, revealing that her scales ended in a V on either side of her belly button. Behind her jawline, faint pearlescent gills flared subtly, and the scales that normally ran the length of her forearms now climbed all the way up to her shoulders.

Kiera was gaping at her when Attalin lifted her tail and sent a wave of water spraying all over her. This woke her from her daze, and she spewed out the water that'd splashed into her mouth. An uninhibited reflex had her shaking off her fur, which left it standing on end. She gave Attalin an incredulous look that had her doubled over with laughter. Kiera peered down at her reflection and burst into laughter too.

Once they'd both gathered themselves, Kiera found a rock to sit on the bank's edge, and Attalin propelled herself back to the shallows to join her. The air wavered as her legs reappeared, and she rose out of the stream, droplets running off her hair and residual scales. She rummaged around in her bag, pulling out a canteen and a small, bundled item. She murmured to the bundle before dropping it back into the bag and then plopped down beside Kiera with the canteen in hand.

A realization struck her: Attalin had revealed her tail to cheer her up. Kiera got the impression that, like her persuasive abilities, this was another part of herself she didn't often show to others. It must've taken a great deal of bravery to open up about such a personal aspect of her magic. They sat with their feet in the water for a few thoughtful moments before Kiera spoke.

"Thank you for sharing part of your form with me."

Attalin gave her a warm smile. "I feel like I can completely be myself with you."

She took a sip from the canteen and handed it over to her. Kiera took a swig and realized it was fresh apple cider.

"I know exactly what you mean," Kiera replied. Attalin trailed her fingers through the reeds in front of them.

"I don't make the change often. It's a piece of my magic I typically reserve for myself." She nudged Kiera with her shoulder. "And a few special people, of course." Kiera grinned and passed back the canteen.

Attalin took a sip before saying, "Sometimes I'm afraid I won't want to turn back. It's difficult to tear myself away from that side of my magic, it's so wild. It's essential to who I am, but I rarely get the time to enjoy that side of myself."

Kiera nodded. "I wish you had more opportunities. You deserve to let go and embrace who you are. Your tail is breathtaking, by the way, it's like a sunset." Kiera wasn't sure why, but she felt nervous to have admitted that last part.

Attalin's eyes glistened with unshed tears. "That's so kind. I used to feel shy about it." Kiera flicked her eyes back up from where they'd settled on the ground, relieved she'd been honest. Mischief glinted in Attalin's eyes. "Plus, you can admit it, it's a bit cooler than your tail."

Kiera snorted, grabbed the canteen, and took a sip. She shook the jug at Attalin. "Is this what you went to Gabby's for? It's delicious."

Attalin's face became serious. "She did make it homemade, but that's not all I picked up when I went by." She stood and motioned for Kiera to join her.

They followed the stream farther away from the crowds. After a few minutes, Attalin darted ahead of her and ducked into a grove of weeping willows. Kiera looked between the fluttering leaves but didn't see her within. She parted the curtain of branches, which softly grazed her whiskers as she entered. Kiera looked around the small clearing, but Attalin seemed to have vanished.

"Down here."

Kiera jumped. She peered around one of the trees and looked down. Attalin had climbed down into a rocky hole.

"I'm sorry, I didn't mean to startle you. I just wanted to check and make sure no one was in here. It's clear, I don't sense anyone's magic." Kiera shook her head and climbed down after her. She squinted her eyes. Her vision allowed her to see that there was a tunnel that led further back and then slanted down.

"You're good with tight spaces, right?" Attalin asked her.

"I got over claustrophobia a long time ago. You know how many conversations I've had crammed in a tiny closet." They exchanged a sad smile, both thinking of Rose.

"Follow me," Attalin said.

16

ABLAZE

They journeyed deeper underground. The tunnel, barely wide enough to squeeze their shoulders through at first, opened into a cavern with a crystal-clear pool at its center. The air was damp and cool, and Kiera must've turned in circles three times to take in all the stalagmites and stalactites. She was examining a massive stalactite, staring up at it muttering, "A buildup of redeposited minerals…" when Attalin came to stand next to her, looking up too.

"That's fascinating. How'd you know that?"

Kiera tilted her head thoughtfully. "From a book. When I was a kid, I was terrified of making friends. I was convinced that they'd sense I was different, like they could somehow see the dreams marked all over me like tattoos. Maybe some did get that impression, but it didn't help that my own fear pushed others away. I ended up at the library more often than not. At the time, books tended to be better company than other people my age."

Attalin blinked up at the formation. Her lips quirked up. "I'm glad you made an exception then."

Kiera flicked her tail. "Only for shiny mermaids."

Attalin winked at her, and then they turned their attention toward the pool. The water was so still, even as far down as they were, it felt unnerving.

Attalin cleared her throat. "Most people don't know about this place. Gabby told me witches have been coming here to practice spells for generations, or that's what the speculation is anyway." Attalin pointed to markings on the far wall. "That's supposed to be a language from a millennium ago. Gabby still comes down here sometimes, as do a handful of the other witches." Kiera nodded, still not entirely sure why she'd brought them here.

Attalin crouched down, retrieving the small bundled item from her bag.

She unwrapped it from its casing and spoke in a hushed tone. "There are things we need to tell each other, and this is the only way we can do that."

Kiera sensed a shift in the energy around her, she felt pulled toward the pulsing force of the object Attalin was holding. It was rough with jagged edges and was the color of the darkest night.

"What is that?" Kiera asked.

Attalin dipped her head toward it. "The stone is black tourmaline, but the spell inside of it is a cloaking magic, unlike anything I've experienced before."

Kiera hovered her hand toward it and felt a calming sense of security. She furrowed her brow at the rock and stepped back, uncertain if she should trust her feelings.

She looked back to Attalin. "This must've cost a fortune."

Attalin shook her head, her hair falling back over her shoulders. "No, this is what I went to Gabby for. She's like a second mother to me. She was the witch who came to retrieve me the night my father was banished, and she's looked out for me ever since. I'm not sure that I would have gotten through my time here without her."

Kiera's heart swelled for the kind witch that'd saved her life. Attalin held the stone between her fingers. "When I went to her, I told her you'd come back, but she could see it written all over my face that something was wrong. I didn't have to say anything—she knew your mother was supposed to accompany you here since I'd told her so weeks ago. She activated the spell to explain to me what it does, and then she put it in my bag. Not only will other beings be unable to hear us, like the protection my tiger's eye stone offers, but it'll shield us from eyes and malignant magic too. Whatever we discuss here will be safeguarded. This stone has over tenfold the amount of power my tiger's eye does. Gabby told me it took a coven, a group of thirteen powerful witches, to create it. Unlike my stone, though, it doesn't pull from a life force, so once the energy of the spell is expended, this will turn back into a normal black tourmaline stone."

Kiera felt reassured and stepped closer, letting her fingertips brush the tourmaline. A sense of protection washed over her again. Her eyes widened in amazement. Attalin whispered, "I feel it too. Gabby explained this spell is potent because it's filled with the love the coven had for one another. They were like family to each other, and that kind of bond can create very pure magic." Kiera trembled. Even if she was encased in a powerful cloaking spell far beneath the ground, she was still terrified about what the board could do to Rose if they caught her spilling their secrets.

"I know you're afraid, and I'm sure for good reason, but I trust this spell will keep us safe. Gabby said this stone was crafted centuries ago when covens could meet without restrictions. Hallowfeld only permits a few witches of his choosing to do magic in groups now, and only for his benefit. That's why I brought us down here; besides it being secluded, I thought if we were surrounded in a place covens used to practice, it could possibly give the spell a boost of energy."

Kiera found her voice. "Gabby let us have this? It sounds like an irreplaceable relic."

Attalin reached out and took her hand. "She wouldn't have given this to me if she didn't think what I need to share with you and what you need to tell me was worth the sacrifice. Gabby doesn't believe in coincidences. She thinks you're special; she told me so after you left."

Kiera blinked in surprise. Attalin tucked the stone into their clasped hands, saying, "Gabby sees what I see, someone with a great deal of power who wants to use it beyond themselves, and that was more than enough reason for her to share this gift with us." Kiera swallowed down her apprehension. She recognized the familiar feeling pressing against her bones, insisting that this was the right path. Kiera nodded for Attalin to proceed.

In her other hand, Attalin had the casing the stone had been wrapped in; there were words scrawled on it. "Gabby activated the stone back at the tent. I checked it by the stream earlier. It's been concealing us, but I think we should recite the spell down here to reinforce its energy."

Attalin reached out, the stone still clasped between them in one set of hands, and the casing now in the other with the words face up for them to read. Kiera scanned the words and realized she was familiar with them. The fur on the back of her neck spiked. She'd spoken a variation of them each time she'd entered the rings.

"I've experienced a chant like this before," she said to Attalin, whose face darkened.

"You've probably heard Hallowfeld spew something that sounds like this. The teachings in these words are ancient, from a period that Gabby calls the time before. The idea behind them is to treat magic as its own entity, working in harmony with you, and letting it guide you. Hallowfeld doesn't actually respect that philosophy. He believes he's the supreme ruler of his success; he'd never give credit to anyone or anything but himself for his abilities. He thinks it makes him a better showman to say things like this."

Kiera replied, "Yes, I heard what he said before the tournament last time, but I experienced these words in another way. I said a phrase similar to these before each fight, and it was like the magic heard me." Kiera paused a moment, letting the memories from her prior visit rise up, the echo of one completely coming back to her. Kiera's pupils flared. "When my heart stopped, I saw two figures, and they said I was still needed, that my journey wasn't over. I spoke the words 'Let your magic flow through me' to them. I think that's how I gained the strength to come back, with their help."

Attalin let out a gasp of astonishment. "I hadn't realized you were using invocations. I remember you said you'd seen those figures, but I thought you were in shock."

Kiera took in a deep breath, shaking her head no. "I think the magic is trying to guide us in some way, like it did the last time." The stone between their palms warmed a fraction. They both stared down at it and then back at each other. Attalin blinked slowly as if she suddenly grasped something.

"This is what makes you different, Kiera. No one taught you to have trust in magic—you knew what to do from the beginning. My guess is it trusts you back. That's probably why it manifested in forms you could, comprehend, or it somehow allowed you to commune with past spirits that day. Either way, it's remarkable." Attalin's gaze traveled back to the casing. "Are you ready?"

Kiera believed she was meant to have this revelation with Attalin; remembering set so many things right in her head. The disorienting nightmares over the last two months seemed to have been her brain trying to piece this memory back together. The voices didn't feel ominous now that she recalled they'd saved her, but she was still wary about the fact that she possibly could've been communing with the dead or magic in a visible form. At any rate, Attalin's statement rang true—it felt as though a gentle presence had been guiding her through her trials at Etabon. This presence had been watching out for her, and she sensed it wouldn't fail them now. Kiera's eyes settled on the words again. She let Etabon's magic embrace her and fill her with courage. "Yes, I'm ready," Kiera replied steadily.

In tandem, Attalin and Kiera spoke the words, "We call upon your combined gifts, seeking your protection. We lay our fate at your feet and ask your magic to flow to us, around us, and through us."

After a charged moment of silence, a phantom breeze began to swirl around them, and then the breeze broke out into an indigo blaze, encasing them in an orb of dancing flame. The idea of being trapped among flames was something out of Kiera's nightmares, but it seemed even that debilitating fear couldn't reach her in here. She tilted her head back and stared up at the shifting inferno, marveling at the idea that this spell was meant to burn their secrets away. At this distance, the heat should have been unbearable, but this wasn't an ordinary fire, so all they felt was a soothing warmth and sense of tranquility. Kiera's ears twitched as she tried to make out the choir of muffled voices surrounding her. It sounded like thirteen women lightly singing in harmony.

She felt Attalin squeeze her hands. "We don't have a second to waste."

Kiera knew she was right. She launched into a recounting of her phone call with her mother and everything she'd surmised afterward from her words. She told Attalin about the gun she'd found while clearing out the house. When Kiera had finished, the threat to her mother's life hung in the air between them.

Attalin looked solemn. "I'm here with you. You're not alone in this."

She worried at her lip. Kiera could see guilt gnawing at her. "When you came into the bar earlier, I could see your relief when you saw me. When you were reluctant to talk, I assumed you'd wanted to share what was going on, but that you needed privacy. It took a lot of courage to trust me with this, and I'm sorry I added to your worry by asking you to share it."

Kiera felt a rush of gratitude for her. "No, I'm glad I told you, I wanted to. It would've eaten me up inside to pretend I didn't have this massive secret weighing on me. That's what the board does, what they've always done successfully. They make us feel isolated, so we can't seek help from one another. It's been the key to their control, using fear to make us abandon each other. Etabon's magic is powerful—I know it'll shield me. This," Kiera looked to the flames, "is beyond the board's understanding."

Attalin replied, "There's no tracker or listening device from the outside strong enough to penetrate this spell, that's for sure. You're right, the board underestimates magical abilities, but that benefits us because they can't anticipate what they don't understand." Attalin squinted thoughtfully. "That could be one of the reasons your mom wanted you on this side of the border. The board's determined to remain as withdrawn from magic as possible. Even if the medical team fails and they want to retaliate against their families, I don't think they'd waste resources or personnel to hunt you down here. Their relationship with Hallowfeld is close. I'm sure they'd let you live if they knew he was interested in your abilities, especially if he told them you're going into the arena anyway."

Kiera glowered. "It's dark, but it would make sense. With my training and magic, my mother would've known I'd stand a chance in the rings at least. Out there, if the board wanted me dead, all it'd take is one security drone, and I wouldn't see it coming."

"It must've been an impossible decision for her, but if they shut down the borders, there was no place for you to escape to. Still, there are huge risks in here too. For whatever reason, your mom was spooked enough to get a gun so maybe she felt the threat was greater out there. If there really was an attempt to harm a board member, then I'm sure the danger is far beyond what we realize. We've seen how they react when they're challenged. I can only imagine what they're capable of when they're threatened."

"At first, I thought Hallowfeld took her or somehow had her selected for that team," Kiera ground out.

"It wouldn't make sense. He'd want her close by to keep you compliant. The board must've selected her on her own merit, and if they wanted her, their rank far outweighs Hallowfeld's," Attalin said.

Kiera grimaced in agreement, "What did you need to tell me?"

Attalin studied their interlocked hands before saying, "Hallowfeld's been coming and going from the site more frequently, which on its own is peculiar, but a couple of nights ago, I overheard a group of his followers. I'd had this dream that I was swimming at the stream we spoke at. It woke me up in the middle of the night, and the feeling to get to water was so intense that I ended up going out there. On my way back, I kept to the outskirts of the site to avoid running into anyone, but I had to move in as I got closer to my tent. I stumbled across four of Hallowfeld's inner circle standing outside of one of the bar tents, and they were all clearly intoxicated. They were so out if it they didn't notice me in the shadows, so I kept to the trees and was turning around to take another route back when I caught a snippet of what they were discussing."

Kiera could feel the pulse in Attalin's wrists pick up as she said, "The pack included Yasmeen, a powerful witch who worships Hallowfeld, and Illias, a faun who manufactures most of Hallowfeld's weapons, along with two werewolves, Patrick, who you've met, and his deranged cousin, Devland. Yasmeen was frantically telling the others that the Ascendant One was expecting it by the start of the festival, and they needed to find it on their next excursion or he'd end them. They were referring to Hallowfeld—that's what his followers call him. Patrick told Yasmeen and Illias that they'd better find it soon because the one-on-one match with the shifter was on the next full moon. They were bragging about the upcoming match, saying Devland would likely finish the Lynx off before Hallowfeld could see if she was useful. I tried to make out more, but after that, they'd gone stumbling back into the tent, slurring and howling. I haven't seen Yasmeen or Illias around since then. I'm not sure if that means they're still off looking for whatever Hallowfeld requested, or something worse."

"What do you think Hallowfeld's after?" Kiera asked.

Attalin's jaw ticked. "I'm not sure, but it sounds like he's been searching desperately for it. What concerns me is Devland. On a normal day, someone like him is dangerous, much less during a full moon. Three years ago, he was the winner of the opening day tournament, but his final opponent didn't make it. The siren had tried to tap out, but Devland kept mauling him; when the siren finally had a chance to yield, the healers didn't make it to him in time."

Kiera shuddered. She recalled Attalin's instruction from last time to avoid werewolves' fangs. A werewolf's bite is serious, and left untreated, the infection from the wound is deadly. Once the venom enters the bloodstream, it rapidly causes the victim's blood to clot and induces hallucination and organ failure. The damage from one bite seems more than enough to incapacitate an opponent. The fact that Devland was willing to inflict multiple bites on a wounded competitor told Kiera enough about him.

Attalin looked equally distressed as she said, "The next full moon is in two days, so we know when the match is set to take place. That's also when his power will be at its peak."

Kiera considered this. "At least I'm trained this go around. I'll also have the advantage of knowing exactly who I'll be going up against."

Attalin tilted her head side to side. "Devland is the worst of Hallowfeld's followers. He clearly has motives for pitting you against him. If those two are correct and Hallowfeld's using this as some sort of way to measure your usefulness to him, then we could be playing into his hands." Attalin's words echoed Kiera's own thoughts.

Kiera stared into the flames for a moment. "When we go to the arena, I'll bring up the matches. We'll see if he's willing to let me select my own opponent. If he conceals who I'll be facing, then we can assume the element of surprise is part of this test, which could benefit us. In the meantime, we can do our best to uncover what he's expecting to get from this match."

Attalin took in a breath, blinking slowly. "Etabon's magic brought me out to the stream. It led me to this knowledge for a reason, but I'm terrified to find out what that reason is."

Kiera gave Attalin a look she hoped was reassuring. "We can't let fear paralyze us. We have to act on what the magic's shown you. There's still time to figure it out before the match. Our next move is to find that buzzard and see what he has to say."

Attalin scowled. "Don't worry, if he's at the rings, I know exactly where he'll be."

17

HOLLOW

A ttalin was pleasantly surprised that their conversation had hardly used up any of the energy within the tourmaline. When they were ready to leave the cave, she whispered to the stone to remain active. The flames vanished, but its thrumming presence remained. She pocketed the stone, and they intended to drop it off with Gabby before heading to the rings.

They trekked back out of the cavern and emerged to the willows swaying in the breeze. Kiera couldn't help but want to remain nestled among the trees a bit longer. She touched the trunk of one, soaking in the stillness of the place as she moved to exit the clearing. Attalin fell into step with her and used her arm to move the branches aside for them.

"When you see these parts of Etabon, it's easy to imagine what it'd be like here if Hallowfeld didn't control it," Attalin said.

Kiera peered back. "It's comforting to know that peace can find a way even with him around."

Attalin led Kiera back toward the throngs of patrons. With the flurry of activity, as people moved about looking for their accommodations or shops, Kiera could almost blend into the crowd. They broke off from the main pathway and turned down a gravel lane with canvas lodging tents on either side.

Attalin motioned all around her. "This quarter is mainly where the temporary staff members stay. Spectators and nonpermanent sponsors reside in their own private tents, and permanent residents have their own houses in Hallowfeld's neighborhood, of course."

Kiera furrowed her brow. "Aren't you a permanent resident?"

"Yes, but those of us who haven't taken the eclipse mark are sent to stay in these tents during the festival. When it's over, we share small cottages in the neighborhood."

Kiera wrinkled her nose at that, and Attalin chuckled. "It's supposed to be a punishment to entice us to get the brand, but we love being together. It would take a lot more than good company in a small living space to turn me into a follower."

She stopped at the last tent on the row and ducked her head inside. "Looks like we missed Gabby. She must've left for the matches. We'd better get a move on ourselves to get you there before Hallowfeld's deadline. There will be plenty of time before the matches start. We wouldn't want to miss the riveting conversation that takes place before the fighting," Attalin said, rolling her eyes.

She'd mentioned Hallowfeld was sure to be in his suite at the arena, socializing with the worst sort of patrons as he always did before the matches. Attalin said the verbal sparring that took place before the fights was nearly as terrible as the event itself. It was mostly affluent guests jockeying for Hallowfeld's attention.

"Can't wait." Kiera's tail flicked with sarcasm.

"Give me a second to put my bag up," Attalin said.

Kiera waited, knowing Attalin had stepped inside to deposit the tourmaline back into its hiding spot. She hurried back through the flaps whispering to what looked like a glassy white crystal, then tossed it back into the tent behind her.

"Nook is napping on my bunk. No one else is in either. I share this tent with Gabby, Jade, and Viviana. You've met Gabby and Jade but haven't met Viv yet. She's the most incredible musician and an orc when in magical form. We'll need to go watch one of her shows. After the tournament, you can come in for dinner and meet her if you'd like."

Kiera shook her head. "I'm glad Nook's settled, and yes, I'd love that."

Attalin smirked. "It'll be spotless in there when we get back, I just set off the cleaning spell in that selenite crystal. I pulled the curtains around my bed though, so it shouldn't bother Nook."

Kiera winced. "You didn't have to use up that spell—no judgment here."

Attalin turned her head and raised her eyebrows. "You didn't see Jade's side of the tent. Amazing cook but self-admittedly the messiest person on the continent. That spell is her personal favorite of Gabby's."

Kiera's lips twitched up. It felt good to have a normal conversation with Attalin after their heavy discussion earlier. Most people wouldn't consider spells and crystals normal, but that was beside the point. It felt right to Kiera. They wove their way through the mass of creatures converging on the fighting arena.

After clearing the obsidian gates, they turned toward the stands. Kiera stared out over the rings. She could make out the contestant tents and warm-up area on the far side. It was odd seeing the arena from this angle. Attalin paused and then headed down the steps toward the lowest level near their side's pit opening.

Her face broke into a grin once they made it to the bottom, pointing for Kiera to look past her. Gabby waved to them from the healer's station situated in the middle of the lower level for the easiest access to each ring's entrance. Attalin went to her, and she gave her a hug. Something about it made Kiera's heart twinge for her mother. Gabby's bright green eyes landed on her, and she could see the compassion in them.

Gabby kept her voice low. "Hello, Kiera." She came forward and gave her a gentle embrace too.

When they stepped away from each other, she held Gabby's stare. Kiera wished she could thank her for trying to help them escape Hytheis with the bakery address and for giving her the opportunity to open up to Attalin with the tourmaline. But something about her kind smile told her the older woman already knew. Gabby's face shifted into a formal expression as she politely nodded at someone behind Kiera. The icy tingling at the base of her neck told her who it was before she looked. She turned around to see the leering grin that haunted her nightmares.

Hallowfeld was bedecked in a fawn-colored suit with solid gold buttons. He placed a proprietary hand on her shoulder, and she had to force herself not to show her fangs.

"Right on schedule. Welcome back, my feline friend."

Kiera nodded back smoothly.

Hallowfeld removed his hand to reach into his vest and pull out a gleaming pocket watch. He surveyed the time and then fixed his eyes on Gabby. "Is everything in order for the matches?"

She gestured to the healing station, unruffled. "I have all the tonics and salves prepared. My team is well rested in case anyone requires treatment."

Hallowfeld lifted his chin and hummed. "Very well then." It was a polite dismissal, but Gabby didn't shrink away.

She merely pivoted to Attalin and Kiera, saying, "I'll see you both after, for dinner."

Then she calmly strode back to her post. This wasn't the usual reaction Hallowfeld prompted, but it appeared that Gabby had enough skill to warrant being treated with a degree of respect versus the outright contempt he reserved for most people.

Hallowfeld tucked his watch back into his vest and addressed Kiera. "How about you and Attalin take in the show from my personal box?"

It would be the perfect opportunity to bring up her impending match, and from his tone, it was plainly a command, not a request. Kiera inclined her head. "Lead the way," she answered. He whirled around and escorted them past rows of gawking spectators.

A faerie with a shock of white-gold hair and pyrite-colored swirls running the length of his muscled arms stood guard at the entrance to the private level they'd come to. He bowed his head to Hallowfeld and moved the curtain aside for them to enter. Passing by him felt like skirting an open flame. She knew without having to ask that he was a fire faerie.

She flashed her eyes back at Attalin, who gave her a look of encouragement and rolled her shoulders back. They didn't need to speak for Kiera to know what that meant—keep your chin up and be confident. Kiera held her head high. No being in here had the ability to belittle her unless she gave that power over to them. Her magic stirred inside of her in agreement. She'd faced these kinds of people on the other side of the border thousands of times, but she wouldn't cower here. A predator's smile bloomed across her face. Let them see all of her.

Hallowfeld's box was expansive, sprawling over half of the level it was on. Guests seated next to his suite were notable but not desirable enough to make it in. Gauzy curtains hung on every side, the ones facing the rings were swept back and tied in place with silk cords. Plush couches and leather armchairs peppered the space. There was a long bar at the back holding prefilled champagne flutes. The lilac-winged alary standing behind it was fashioning mixed drinks for the guests inside. Next to the bar was a great table stacked with a multitude of tiered serving platters filled with sizzling meats, lush fruits, stewed vegetables, confections, and pastries. The tinkling of glasses and laughter quieted when they entered.

Kiera cast her eyes around at the creatures within. She couldn't help the roiling in her stomach. It wasn't just the overabundance that shocked her, it was the intense looks of envy and longing she was getting. Hallowfeld snaked his way to the bar and gave the alary a withering glare. The alary's smile faltered for a beat as he rapidly made a drink of muddled herbs and clear liquor and handed it over. He released a breath when Hallowfeld sipped it, nodded, and turned away. A chestnut-furred werewolf draped over a chaise nearest them had paused midbite. Kiera realized the whole room seemed to be holding its breath.

"Cheers!" Hallowfeld thundered, and the room burst back to life, cheering with him. It took a great deal of self-control not to audibly snort. *Was this man's ego so fragile that he needed an entire room to hang on his every move?* Kiera wondered. She forced herself to take calm breaths, shoving down the desire to turn and run from the suite. They'd come here for answers, and she'd be damned if they left without getting the information they needed. Hallowfeld made a beeline for a settee near the center edge of the balcony, open to the pits. Kiera kept her spine straight and prowled after him.

She could feel the focus of the room on them but ignored the attention and let it fade into the background. Everything truly fell away when she took in the view. It wasn't just the entire arena below that captivated her but Etabon's wild mountains around them. The world looked wide open from here, like anything was possible.

She was abruptly brought back to the current circumstances when Hallowfeld patted the spot next to him for her to sit. She coolly turned toward him and lowered herself onto the settee. She left enough room so they weren't touching, but his vanilla and leather scent still found its way into her nostrils. Attalin settled next to her. Her shoulder skimmed Kiera's arm, drawing her attention back to center.

She kept her eyes forward on the scene below, watching as a wind sprite fluttered back and forth, its silvery aura rippling as it filled in the tournament board with the contestants' names and forms. There was less than half an hour before Hallowfeld would make his opening remarks. She needed to have this conversation before he got distracted or any of the other beings here grew brave enough to approach them.

"What do you think?" he crooned.

"It's all certainly impressive." She kept her voice quiet and did her best to leave the contempt out of it.

His eyes rested on her with amusement. "Remarkable what a few months can change. Aren't you fortunate to be seated amongst such powerful company? I'm sure you couldn't have fathomed seeing it all from here before today."

She thought of the beings in this room and how miserable they looked underneath their artificial smiles. If having influence meant living a petrified half-life, even in magical form, she wasn't interested. Kiera felt the force of her magic flowing inside of her; none of these beings had given her that. It came from somewhere else entirely, but that logic seemed wasted on Hallowfeld. So instead, she shrugged a shoulder and gave him a cryptic smile.

Hallowfeld said, "Speaking of company." He pulled out a gilded key with a house tag dangling from it and dropped it in her hand. "You'll be amongst the finest in my neighborhood. This is your assigned home. It's a real shame your mother couldn't be here to accept it with you. A little bird on the outside told me she's an overachiever like her daughter. It appears she's been held up working on a private assignment for the board."

Kiera feigned bewilderment. She made a show of recovering. "It sounds like you're better informed than I am. All I know is that she couldn't come home or board the flight with me today. I thought you'd orchestrated that."

Hallowfeld emitted a grating laugh. "How comical. No, dear girl, it seems my comrades were in need of her skills, but when she resurfaces, I'll be sure to scoop her up and get you two reunited as soon as possible."

Kiera rubbed the back of her neck. She wasn't certain if Hallowfeld was pretending not to know about their board member's father, but either way, she wasn't going to reveal anything that could put her mother in danger. She needed to be convincing. "Our agreement was she'd be safe."

"And so, she shall be. Now, tell me, how was your trip to Mendinburrow? Did those funds treat you well?" he asked. Kiera picked at her claws to appear indifferent while her magic strained in her gut. She knew he was baiting her.

Her voice was soft but full of fire. "Considering you made sure it was the only option available to me, yes, I used those funds to move from the only home I've ever known and trained to live out my life as a competitor."

Hallowfeld's eyes sparked with cunning. "Dear girl, I did you a *favor*." The way he drew out the word favor chafed her. "Someone with your talents shouldn't have remained wasted among the rabble. Now you can pursue an existence that suits you. You'll be able to take your rightful place in society, and with my guidance, you can live up to your true potential."

Her attention snagged on the words "my guidance." He was insane if he thought her rightful place was anywhere near him. Did he somehow think she was obligated to him for using that bank account? Kiera thought. It was as if he assumed by taking those funds, she was aligning with his belief system. The weight of her decision bore down on her, the intense pressure squeezing the air from her lungs like a vice. A wave of nausea rolled into her as another dark thought surfaced in her mind. In the end, it *had* been her choice to accept his gift—had it really mattered that there hadn't been alternatives? There it was, the thought that'd silently haunted her dreams for weeks, the fear that she'd traded away a piece of her soul.

Hallowfeld had the choice to let her walk away with the rest of her classmates that day, but he hadn't. She'd had the choice not to use the money in that account, but she had. It was all a web of tangled up decisions, and she was caught in it. Her shame started to crest, threatening to drag her down beneath his gaze. Then she felt the warmth of Attalin beside her. Sometime during this exchange, their hands had found each other's and interlocked—and it hit her. These events had led her to connections with her abilities, with Attalin and the beings who came to Etabon searching for the magic inside of themselves.

She looked down at their joined hands. These decisions were threads in a tapestry, not a web. They wove together to form a complex and ever-changing story. Her life wouldn't be defined by one desperate mistake but by a collection of all her experiences. She'd do her best to learn from this one. Kiera lifted her chin. She owed this man nothing and wanted no part of the future he offered. If it came down to it, she'd choose death over becoming a follower.

"That's very kind of you, but I can manage on my own. I'm enjoying the combat training though, and I'd like to select my match date and opponent so I can test my skills."

Hallowfeld's posture sharpened, and his expression soured at the rejection of his offer. It was subtle, but she felt his magic writhing, desperate to lash out at her. That brush of unnatural iciness took her breath away. His essence felt hollow. If that's what dwelled inside of him, it was no wonder he was so rotten. Her own magic rose up to steady her, filling her veins with warmth. Hallowfeld adjusted a cuff link as he regained his composure. His eyes narrowed. Apparently, he hadn't wanted the conversation to turn in this direction.

"Well, aren't we rather sure of ourselves," he said as he pulled his pocket watch out of his vest and made a show of checking it. "I don't have time to discuss these arrangements in detail." His eyebrows lifted and teeth clenched in a mocking grin. "If you truly cared, you would've gotten here early. Instead, you spent an hour lazing about next to a stream." Kiera remained still, listening. "I'm a very busy man, and let's be clear: You work for me. So, you'll accept the match timeslot I have available, which is at sunset two days from now, and be content with whomever I can scrounge up for you." He sneered at Attalin. "It's not as if anything of great substance depends on the match."

Kiera clung to Attalin's hand for the willpower to remain calm. It was a surprise to her own ears when she spoke, and her voice didn't quiver with rage but sounded composed. "I hadn't realized you were keeping such close tabs on me."

Hallowfeld held up a polished golden orb on a chain that could easily fit in the palm of her hand. "I had a tracking spell placed on precious Attalin here this morning."

The orb filled with a swirling image of Attalin, with Kiera seated beside her. The image looked to be delayed by a minute—she leaned in and watched their conversation from seconds before playing out, ending with Attalin's shocked expression at Hallowfeld's last words. He snapped his fingers, and the orb fractured and turned to dust, its particles and the spell drifting away in the wind.

"From the moment you arrived at Nautilus this morning, I had the great misfortune of watching every move you two made, or should I say lack thereof." Hallowfeld gestured dramatically, "Blathering pleasantries at the bar, Attalin dashing away to drop off your mutt and fetch you breakfast, and more chattering with Gabby about how to make cider. Besides the bit about her wallowing around in the stream, it was quite dreary. What a waste of such an intricate spell. Some of my best witches are drained."

There was a buzzing in Kiera's head. She knew she should be happy about the fact that their cloaking spell had duped his tracking spell, because they certainly hadn't been at the stream for an hour, but all she could do was feel Attalin's humiliation. Out of the corner of her eye, she watched as a deep blush spread across her face.

Kiera replied with a laugh, "For someone who says their time is so valuable, you have an odd way of spending it. Then again, I might watch others who have a deep connection to their magic too, if I was longing for one." Her words were rash, but she couldn't help herself.

Hallowfeld's eyes had turned into depthless pits. "You're hilarious. All jesting aside, it's my responsibility to know everything that goes on inside of these borders to remain within the board's regulations, and I take that job very seriously."

Kiera let her head dip a bit and gaze lower to the ground. She was walking a fine line between sounding self-assured and provoking Hallowfeld. She needed to do her best not to cross it, if she hadn't already.

"Of course, and where would we all be if you hadn't convinced the board to open Etabon? I'm sure I'm not the only being who's grateful for that feat." Hallowfeld studied her and then folded his hands in his lap, placated for now. Still, there was emotion simmering behind his eyes that promised he wouldn't easily forget the blow to his pride.

Hallowfeld sighed. "My feline friend, you're equal parts cheeky and gracious. You're a paradox, and that's what I adore about you. Take some time to have a think on my mentorship; the offer still stands. I hope you'll reconsider."

Kiera pushed down the acid in her throat and crinkled her nose, pulling back her lips in what she hoped looked like a smile rather than a scowl, and nodded to him.

Hallowfeld stood. "I'm glad we had this chat, as my calendar will be full for the next few days. I look forward to your upcoming match. As always, I'll be watching."

MERCY

Hallowfeld snapped his fingers, prompting a piece of the stage to float up from the arena floor and hang in the air in front of him. He turned and stepped off the edge of the balcony onto it, giving them a wink before descending to the ground. The crowd around them broke out into cheers. Kiera was at a loss—an arena full of beings were applauding a man who'd just admitted that he believed some people were worth more than others. He'd literally invented a four-month-long holiday around violence. She looked around the packed stadium. To Hallowfeld, these beings were resources he could harvest, consume, and discard on a whim. She thought of the witches he'd used to create his tracking spell. They'd be left without access to their magic all because he'd demanded it.

She turned to Attalin, who was staring rigidly at the spot Hallowfeld had vacated. She wanted to talk to her about how the tourmaline had interfered with his tracking spell, but it'd have to wait. Kiera took stock of the room. This was their opportunity to find more comfortable seats in case Hallowfeld returned. They couldn't leave the box before the matches were over without offending him, but they didn't have to be seated next to him. There were display screens on the sides and back of the suite so that guests who got up to get food and drinks could still watch the tournament. No matter which way she turned, Kiera would be forced to take in the event. There was a cluster of empty armchairs farther to their right, with very few people around them. Kiera brushed her thumb across Attalin's hand, dragging her attention from the balcony. She nodded to the chairs, and Attalin gave her a reluctant smile.

They strode across the room and settled themselves into place. The view from this angle allowed her to see a bit more of the contestant tents behind the rings. Kiera's heart rate picked up as she watched the sixteen contestants make their way from the warmup area and file onto the stage. She couldn't help but wish each of them protection during their matches, from each other but also from themselves. The rings could change something inside of you if you weren't careful. Kiera was on the edge of her chair now, straining to make out each participant's form. Sweat collected on her hands at the idea that any one of them could be dead soon.

Hallowfeld had taken the podium and was giving his opening speech, but Kiera didn't hear a single word he said. Her eyes roved over the lineup, noting a young faun in the middle of the group and a tiny bobbing figure closest to the stands. There were contestants that looked eager, like the broad-shouldered fire faerie nearest to the podium. But even from this distance, she could tell some of those beings didn't want to be on that stage.

It tore at Kiera's heart to know there were those among the field each year faced with the impossible decision of fighting for the people they loved, whether they were lured into the pits by the sponsor money that would sustain their families or a desperate bargain. The crest of Atterah popped into her mind. A distorted image of the scales dipping back and forth with the daggers tipped either in the blood of an individual or their loved ones. Sponsoring fighters was a ruthless business. Kiera looked around the room at the creatures who enticed others into the ring for their enjoyment. It was a mistake, because she made eye contact with a wind faerie. The faerie grinned and sauntered up to their chairs.

Kiera was pretty sure she'd used her magic to waft over a frost-scented breeze that ruffled her fur and Attalin's hair. The hoary swirls along her arms matched her long silver hair that was bound back by a leather tie. Kiera noticed the eclipse brand on her shoulder, peeking out from behind the sleeve of her pastel blue dress.

"Good afternoon, you two. Attalin, are you going to introduce me to your friend here?"

Attalin side-eyed the faerie and said, "This is one of Hallowfeld's closest friends, Huxley Olinder."

Huxley gave Kiera a bow. "It's a pleasure to finally meet you, Lynx, especially after how thoroughly you beat my contender the last time you fought."

Kiera gave her a terse nod. She despised that people called her Lynx rather than by her real name, but she'd be irritated with whatever came out of this woman's mouth, considering the company she kept. Huxley's cold cyan eyes scanned her.

Attalin said softly to Kiera, "She sponsored Xavier."

Kiera's eyes flashed back to her as Huxley replied, "Yes, what a disappointment he turned out to be. He lost me a great deal in wagers. I was certain he'd be the one to finally win me the opening day competition, but Hallowfeld's apprentice fared as poorly, so it washes out in the end."

Kiera frowned. "So, you stopped sponsoring Xavier even though he nearly lost his life competing for you?"

Huxley sniffed her nose in distaste. "Actually, he's the one who chose not to renew his contract with me. He's opened up a floral art and sculpture shop in the market. A waste of talent if you ask me." She took their aggravated silence as a cue to explain. "He should be using his skills in the most lucrative way, not arranging flowers for the masses. I have colleagues that believe the festival is reprehensible—you know, magic and all—but there's money to be made here if you know how to bet on the right fighter." She wiggled her eyebrows. "To do that, though, I'll need a competitor more accomplished than Xavier."

Kiera leaned forward in her chair and gave her a pointed look. "It sounds like Xavier decided to use his talents to create something. Maybe he was sick of his magic being exploited."

Huxley crossed her arms and cocked her head to the side. "I don't agree. I think he just lost his nerve. It seems you managed to take that drive out of Rowan too." Huxley tipped her head in the direction she'd come from. "He doesn't want to participate in the matches anymore either. If I were them, I wouldn't squander my powers."

Kiera eyed the seating area over Huxley's shoulder and saw Rowan situated amongst the guests. Her jaw clenched when she saw the smirk Huxley was giving her.

"Have you fought in the tournaments?" Kiera asked.

Huxley looked affronted. "Absolutely not."

Kiera narrowed her eyes. "Then how could you claim to know what'd you do?"

Before she could reply, Attalin leaned forward and said, "You'd better get back to your spot, the tournament is about to begin."

Huxley sighed. "Quite right, I wouldn't want to miss the start of the show. Lynx, if you're not already spoken for and are interested in a sponsor, don't be shy." Huxley's greedy eyes raked over her, and a light wind skimmed her whiskers before she left.

Kiera was bristling with outrage. Attalin leaned close to her. "Like I said, the absolute worst."

Kiera turned stiffly. "You weren't joking," she said as she flicked her tail in the direction Huxley was drifting off to. "Did you?" She hadn't seen her touch Huxley but was wondering if Attalin had used her abilities on her. Attalin laughed and leaned into her chair's arm, resting her lips on the back of her knuckles. She stared defiantly at Huxley's back, then dipped her chin down to whisper to her tiger's eye. Kiera knew that Attalin would understand what she'd been getting at.

Attalin kept her lips covered as she murmured, "No, I didn't need to. She was trying to make a good impression on you and didn't want to cause a scene. Hallowfeld may not have told her yet that you're considered one of his competitors; he enjoys toying with people, even his 'friends.' If he hasn't already claimed you as a competitor, she wants a shot. Plus, if you were to become one of Hallowfeld's apprentices, you'd be in a powerful position, and she'd want your favor."

Kiera frowned and tucked herself down in her chair. "That's twisted on so many levels. He treats his own supporters that way?"

"The only person that matters to Hallowfeld is himself. If something pleases him, then he does it. Whether his followers would admit that he'd cause them suffering, even destroy them to get what he wants, is another matter." She watched as Attalin faintly breathed a word to deactivate her stone again.

Kiera tried to imagine what it'd be like to devote your life to someone only to find out your existence meant nothing to them, and the cruelty of it took her breath away. She couldn't stop herself from glancing over at Rowan and found he was peering back at her too. To her astonishment, his eyes were amiable, and he gave her a discreet nod. As they focused on each other, she could sense his magic. It was subtle, but she could feel a spark of warmth in him that wasn't there before, and she hoped her nearly imperceptible wave was enough to convey her desire for peace.

Kiera winced when the trumpet sounded three times to signal that the tournament was set to begin. Attalin reached over and took her hand. Her eyes were bright with emotion. A resounding cheer from the beings around them drew their attention to the arena below.

The smoke had filled the air above each pit, and the fighters headed for their marks. Hallowfeld had reappeared in the suite and was perched on his settee. Huxley and a couple other guests had joined him. There was a wavering semi-transparent curtain surrounding them. Kiera assumed it was a magical shield of some kind to give them privacy while still allowing the room to gawk at them. The small group spoke animatedly to each other, but you couldn't hear their voices, and the undulating shield made it impossible to read their lips.

The creatures around them looked put out by the divider, but Kiera felt some of the tension inside of her loosen with the separation. She took a breath as she watched the initial sets of competitors pass into the metal domes. The displays in the suite flickered to life, showing live close-ups of

the contestants. The young faun was going against the swaggering fire faerie, there were two werewolves facing off, and to Kiera's surprise, the tiny
bobbing figure from before, a nature sprite, was going to battle a siren.

Attalin and Kiera exchanged a stunned look as Attalin said, "This
is the first time I've seen a sprite in a tournament. Pixies and sprites will
usually only do one-on-one matches together."

Kiera marveled at the sprite. She scanned the contestant board, and
her heart sank when she read the name inked there.

"We know her. That's Imena," Kiera breathed.

Attalin closed her eyes, and Kiera could hear her whispering words
of strength and protection.

Kiera watched Imena's virescent aura ripple, keeping her suspended
in the air. She was clutching a slender weapon in her hand that Kiera
couldn't place. When the trumpet sounded to start the matches, it felt
like time slowed down. She kept her eyes on Imena and the siren in the
center pit. Imena's aura appeared to harden rapidly around her as the siren began singing. From the stands, the siren's song was garbled through
the dome's metal, removing its hypnotic influence so the spectators remained unaffected.

"Smart move," Attalin breathed, "she's reinforced the power around
herself, so noise won't pass through, but that could drain her powers
quickly if she keeps it up for too long."

The siren's pitch increased in frustration, and she pulled a bow and
arrow from her back. As the siren strung her bow, Kiera watched as a
plant sprouted from the ground and grew up to meet Imena. Her hand
reached out through her opaque sphere, plucked the fuzzy white flower
atop the plant, and disappeared back inside. Just as the siren released her
arrow, Imena's energy became transparent again. She dodged the arrow
with ease, and Kiera could make out her ears were stuffed with the fluffy
material from the flower. She couldn't help but smile at Imena's clever-
ness. She could fight back now that her ears were insulated.

The siren sent another arrow spearing for her. She darted out of the
way, but this time as she twisted back around to face the siren, she raised

her weapon to her mouth and sent a miniature projectile of her own back at her opponent. The siren's hand slapped against her neck where the needle-like arrow struck her. She wrenched the barb out and began to knock back another arrow, but then her weapon fell helplessly from her hands, and she cast forward into the sand.

"They're poison darts. She must've gotten the toxin for her arrows from part of the flower," Attalin murmured as the siren's body trembled in the sand.

Imena zipped back over to the plant and snatched a leaf off it, hovering close to the siren. The siren barely managed to tap the sand in between convulsions. The dome's measuring instrument registered the fight's energy on the lower left side of the scale. The magic released, and the gates flew open to let the healers rush in. Kiera noticed Imena had chewed some of the leaf and spread it on the siren's neck. By the time the healers made it over to her, the convulsions had stopped, and her color was returning.

Attalin raised her eyebrows. "The leaves must hold the antitoxins for whatever was in the flower. That was kind of her. Most competitors wouldn't have bothered; they'd have left it to the witches."

Kiera startled and touched Attalin's shoulder. "Look at the dial—it jumped up near the middle. Using her magic to heal the siren more than doubled the reading."

Attalin gripped her chair and stared. They watched the witches lead the siren off to their station. From their interaction on her last visit, Kiera got the feeling that Imena would've treated the siren even if she hadn't been able to concede. She remembered Imena mentioning that Etabon should have more participants that showed kindness.

Imena tucked the rest of the leaves into her belt, then faced the stands. She swept through the air, her green light leaving a trail behind her. She made a shape in the sky of a square with a line down the middle of it and then floated eye-level with Kiera and waved in her direction. Kiera let out a gasp of surprise and waved back. She recognized the symbol as the same that she'd worn on her own wristband. She didn't even have to look over at the contestant board to understand Imena's message. She was unsponsored and competing her own way. A portion of the stands erupted in cheers as she hurtled back to her contestant tent. Those who'd watched Imena's match gestured to her dial. The remainder of the audience was still wrapped up in the ongoing matches.

Attalin spoke under her breath. "She's got a point to prove. Seems like you left an impression on more than just your opponents."

Kiera smiled weakly. She was moved by Imena's bravery, but she'd just put a target on herself. Through the waterfall-like force field, Kiera could feel Hallowfeld's gaze on her. Instead of giving him the satisfaction of her attention, she focused on the match in the leftmost pit where the two werewolves were grappling in the sand. Their strength was evenly matched, and they were trading shredding blows with claws and teeth. The venom from their bites didn't affect their own kind, so the match would be decided by whomever could overpower the other. The fight ended abruptly when one of the wolves managed to get their jaws around the other's throat, prompting the ensnared wolf to yield.

Kiera's stomach felt queasy, and a low ringing filled her ears as she remembered how her own fangs had felt around Rowan's throat. She forced a deep breath in through her nose to remain calm. Her eyes panned over to the last remaining match. She'd been dreading this one. The faun's strength was flagging. He was wielding a sword. She remembered Attalin's previous explanation about fauns being master artisans. Often, they'd use their own weapons in matches because they were imbued with the magic that was channeled into their creations when they fashioned them. It was clear by the sword's ability to block the fire faerie's terrifying whips of flame that the sword was enchanted with the faun's magic, but his arm was trembling from the exertion. It took everything in her not to flinch at each of the fire faerie's onslaughts.

Kiera could imagine the unbearable heat of the flames, and her throat became dry. She watched the faun stumble forward after the faerie had rained down a brutal strike from above. The misstep cost him. The fire faerie gave a triumphant snarl as his flame coiled around the faun's arm. Kiera felt frozen with terror as the faun shrieked in pain, dropping the sword. The faerie sent another spiral of flame winding around the faun's other arm. The faerie's eyes locked on the faun's throat next, but he managed to use his hoof to tap the ground in submission. The fire faerie looked disappointed that he hadn't had the opportunity to inflict his death blow. His flames vanished, and the faun fell to the ground in a shuddering heap.

As the witches plunged through the gates to aid the writhing faun, the faerie turned to the stands to salute Hallowfeld. The snake and wooden staff banner was stamped across the fire faerie's vest. Kiera caught Attalin's eye, trying to convey that she was unraveling. Attalin discreetly slid her hand over and clasped Kiera's in hers. A wave of soothing magic flooded through her, and Kiera let it in eagerly. She released a huff of relief and squeezed Attalin's hand in appreciation.

In place of the panic Attalin's magic had washed away, she felt numb. The rest of the tournament went by in a blur. Kiera hadn't realized the matches would affect her this intensely. From a hazy perspective, she registered Imena's success in her next two matches and her dedication to healing each of her opponents, prompting the dome's dial to jump from the lower left corner up near the middle each time. Spectators were noticing her accomplishment with murmurs of wonder and bewilderment. The fire faerie was victorious in his matches as well, ruthlessly burning each of his targets more severely than the last. It was a testament to the contestants' foresight to tap out in time and the witches' healing abilities that he hadn't killed anyone yet. Kiera was no seer, but she felt like she'd known who'd make it to the final match from the beginning.

The shock from earlier ebbed away as she watched the last two participants, Imena and the fire faerie, take their marks in the arena. Both contenders looked worn out but determined. Kiera's pulse raced as she watched a sadistic smile spread over the fire faerie's lips.

He whispered across the sand, "Do you know what fire does to fresh kindling?"

Imena lifted her chin but didn't so much as blink at his words. Pride swelled in Kiera's chest for her. The trumpet sounded through a stadium, silent with bated breath. The faerie sent a stream of flame spearing for her, which she skirted by plunging low. Imena launched a dart straight at the faerie's face. He ducked, diving into the sand, and hurled a net of fire toward the sprite. She dodged it by rocketing into the sky as fast as she could carry herself and then flipped downward, sending another projectile at him. The faerie threw up a small blazing shield just in time to destroy the dart before it hit his jaw.

His flames were dwindling, revealing that his powers would burn out soon. He was desperate and hurled flaming orbs at her, each ball smaller and dimmer than the last. Imena was panting as she avoided each, biding her time until his magic was exhausted. The faerie swayed on his feet as he created his tiniest sphere yet, which took up only a quarter of his palm. He faked a throw in her direction, and she flitted downwards. The movement was enough to throw off her focus and give him a better chance to aim. The faerie released his sphere at her. Imena realized his tactic a moment too late. She moved so the orb didn't hit her full-on, but it made contact with her and licked up her left side from her ankle to her cheek. The force threw her to the far side of the ring, and she hit the ground with a soft thud. A collective gasp erupted around the stands.

Kiera wasn't sure when, but she'd stalked over to the edge of the balcony in front of their chairs, and her fists were clenched at her sides. Imena's aura flickered around her, reflexively hardening to shield her. The searing pain from the burns must've paralyzed her. She was hanging on to consciousness by a thread. The faerie had sweat dripping from his face as he conjured the last of his fire to create a slender flame. The fire dropped from his hand and then uncoiled to glide across the sand toward her.

Kiera understood with a jolt that he'd made a miniature blazing snake. It arched up and struck Imena's energy, trying to get to her. When it couldn't penetrate her force field, it began bearing down on her shield. Kiera realized if she fainted from her burns, the shield would drop, and she'd be incinerated. Her soft whimpers of pain were being amplified throughout the arena, along with the faerie's sickening laughter as he watched. Kiera felt as though she could see through Imena's eyes, as if she were the one watching through tears and a weakening aura as the faerie's magic battered her last defense. Kiera assumed that if she tried to use any energy to tap out, her protection might fail, or maybe she was suffering too much to even move.

The fire faerie was spent, though. His snake disintegrated into embers that floated off into the air. He let out a shout of frustration and stormed toward the other end of the ring. The green force field around Imena had vanished. Thoughts were eddying out of Kiera's head, and it felt like electricity was building in her chest with each step the faerie took. Attalin was beside Kiera at the edge of the balcony holding her hand. She knew they couldn't help Imena with the dome's magic in place, but she silently begged Etabon's magic to give her the strength to concede.

The faerie was inches from her limp form. He raised his leg. His magic hadn't been able to crush her, but without protection, his foot would. By some miracle, Imena lifted her head, staring up into the stadium, and then let her blistered cheek fall against the sand. The dome's magic hissed in completion of the match.

The faerie looked around in aggravation and brought his foot down toward her. Before he reached her, though, the arena's magic blasted him backward, laying him flat out in the sand. The rules of the arena were absolute: Once a participant yielded, the match was over. The faerie sat up, gasping for air as the witches entered the dome, rushing past him. Gabby was the first to go by to reach Imena. She cursed at him as she passed. The spectators seemed to be in agreement, because they withheld their applause at his victory. Instead, the entire arena began chanting Imena's name. The fire faerie's face turned a deep shade of red. He stood on trembling legs, saluted Hallowfeld, and stalked out of the pit. Kiera gaped down at the rings. Throughout her matches, Imena had, in fact, proved something. Showing mercy had generated more than double the amount of energetic output that violence had, and people were catching on.

Kiera felt Attalin tug on her hand. "We need to go before there's trouble."

She blinked at her sluggishly. The scene had unfolded so quickly that her mind was still trying to process it.

Attalin's voice became urgent, "Kiera, it's over—come on. Imena will be in good hands with Gabby. I've never seen her so agitated. It's probably because no one's been horrible enough to try to harm a fellow contestant after they've managed to surrender before."

Kiera moved to follow Attalin but couldn't help herself. She glanced at Hallowfeld's rippling curtain, and as she did, it dropped. He was looking right at her with a straight face. It hit her that during the intermission, before the final match, he'd vanished. He'd likely paid a visit to his contestant. It would explain why the faerie was so bent on destroying Imena even after the contest was over. His orders had been to kill her during the match, but he'd failed.

Kiera refused to take her eyes off him as they walked to the exit. She wouldn't let him see her rattled, but she did feel responsible for what'd been done to Imena. The exchange she'd had earlier with Hallowfeld had provoked him to flex his authority. He'd found the perfect opportunity when Imena had connected with her. The fact that she'd proudly displayed an unsponsored status and her acts of kindness in the arena had insulted him. Her death had been intended to punish them both and illustrate that defiance was met with consequences.

Kiera felt queasy. Hallowfeld's prim demeanor wasn't just a clever persona to impress his guests, but a mask for the evil lurking within him. Kiera clenched her jaw tightly. As she exited the suite, she could feel Hallowfeld's stare searing into her back. He'd delivered a message of his own. If she was foolish enough to resist him, anyone associated with her could be his next target.

BREADCRUMBS

Kiera clutched Attalin's arm as they followed the flow of spectators away from the fighting arena. The tone in the air was somber with a roiling undercurrent of indignation. She was lost in
thought and hadn't noticed that they'd turned off away from the crowd.
They were strolling down one of the gravel paths among the food stalls
and tents. Kiera stared up and down the row at the magical storefronts.

Attalin spoke gently, "I thought we could use something to calm
us down."

Kiera cleared her throat. "How is it that these shops look more permanent than some of the others?"

Attalin's eyes softened at Kiera's curiosity. "They've used magic on
their tents to make them function like fixed buildings. When the festival
comes to an end, it'll take the owners longer to strip down the spells layered on them, but they think it's worth it for the ambiance. I agree with
them, this is one of my favorite shops in Etabon."

They'd stopped in front of a red bricked sweet shop the size of a
midsized tent.

Attalin beamed. "It doesn't hurt that many of the occupants in this
section are witches and wizards. There's no added expense when you can

use your own magic to enchant your business."

The name on the door read Luna's Bakery. At first glance, Kiera thought the symbol on the door was a waning moon, but upon further inspection, it was really a crescent roll with stars around it, which made her chuckle. Attalin pushed through the door, prompting the little bell above it to tinkle. A plump witch with cheerful amber eyes greeted them. Attalin struck up a conversation with her and followed her over to the row of glass cases filled with an assortment of desserts and pastries.

Kiera ran her hand over the bricks on the far wall, enthralled by the store's spellwork. She'd wandered over to the display window and was watching a dozen tartlets bob about in the air when Attalin walked up beside her and handed her a hot, sweet-smelling drink.

"I got us some frothed caramels and a box of chocolate tarts to go with whatever Gabby's making for dinner."

Kiera had almost forgotten about dinner. She took a sip of the frothed caramel and let out a contented sigh. "I think this is the most delicious drink I've ever had."

The witch beamed at Kiera's compliment and waved as they headed out the door. Attalin hooked her arm in Kiera's. "We'd better head back to the tent." Kiera leaned into Attalin's shoulder. She was right; this had lifted her mood.

They arrived back at the tent after a few minutes' walk, and this time Attalin motioned her inside. Kiera was astonished at how much room there was within. The tent was lit by what appeared to be an inverted tree growing out of the middle of the ceiling. Its twisting branches curled across the canopy, and dozens of twinkling lights hung down from it. Bookcases lined the walls with heaps of stones, crystals, and books filling the shelves. The bookcases were broken up by a set of grand bunk beds on either side of the tent, and there was a kitchen area along the back wall with a miniature refrigerator, sink, cooktop, and oven. A door beside the kitchen led to a small, enchanted washroom. Under the tree chandelier was a table with candles and crystals decorating its surface.

Nook bounded off one of the lower bunk beds and cheerfully

launched himself at Kiera. She bent down to cuddle him, and he nuzzled into her neck. Attalin set the tarts down on the table and then selected a crystal from one of the shelves.

Kiera stood and breathed, "This place is unreal." She was staring at one of the bookcases taking in the labeled crystals and stones.

Attalin nodded. "I won't ever take Gabby's abilities for granted. We're lucky to live with such a powerful witch." She spoke to the crystal in her hand: "Uncover." The crystal glimmered a pale green that radiated throughout the tent. Attalin let out a relieved breath. "I activated the revealing spell in this labradorite. If there was magic on either of us that didn't belong, the color of the stone would've turned brown. Gabby has layered protection spells on the tent, but after hearing Hallowfeld placed a tracking charm on me today, we can't be too cautious." Attalin drew an enchanted box from the shelf and offered it to Kiera so she could keep Hallowfeld's gilded key in it. She dropped it in immediately, glad to be rid of it.

Attalin set the labradorite down, paced to the other side of the room, and pulled the tourmaline out of a hidden compartment in one of the bookcases. She took a seat at the table and gestured for Kiera to sit down too. "I don't doubt Gabby's spells or the labradorite, but I think our conversation could do with an added layer of protection." Kiera made a grim face of agreement. They invoked the stone, and its soothing force and indigo flames blanketed the tent.

Attalin shook her head. "Gabby must've known he was having me watched. When she put the tourmaline in my bag earlier, she warned me not to discuss anything important without it cloaking us. The good news is that he wasn't aware of my real interaction with her when I collected the tourmaline. He mentioned me getting breakfast, but I didn't discuss making cider with her when I was here. The spell must have backfilled our conversation with that information just like it backfilled the image of us near the stream when we were really in the cave."

Kiera nodded. "It sounds like the spells on this place and the tourmaline served their purpose."

Attalin looked miserable. "I still can't stand that we came that close to being caught, and it would've been my fault. If Hallowfeld discovered Gabby was concealing a powerful relic from him, he'd lose his mind." Attalin rubbed the back of her neck. "Not to mention what he would've done with the other information."

Kiera's heart fluttered at the thought of her mother. She shook her head. "He likely knew you'd be exhausted from your shift last night and probably had one of the beings wandering around the bar this morning put the spell on you when you were distracted. What matters is that the enchantment worked, and he's unaware of what we know."

Attalin rested her hand on her cheek. She looked discouraged. "Something has him off-kilter, and it's making him impulsive."

"I couldn't tell if he knew what'd happened to Board Member Marcus's father or if he was fishing for more information. Underneath his commentary, I felt like there was really aggravation about the board taking my mom."

"I'm sure he doesn't like being reminded he's not the most powerful being on the planet. He answers to them. It's sick, but in his mind, they're holding on to his leverage," Attalin replied.

Kiera's hands balled into fists as she let out a strained exhale. "Now we know for sure he's hiding my match-up to Devland. He acted like he didn't have a competitor chosen yet, and he definitely didn't want to discuss it."

Attalin pressed her lips together. "Yes, but I'm worried about the bad blood we created today. Hallowfeld doesn't handle rejection well." Attalin paused and pinched the bridge of her nose. "You should've let his comments about me go."

Kiera furrowed her brow and leaned back. "I'm sorry, I know you can speak for yourself."

Attalin put her hand on Kiera's. "I'm not upset that you defended me, I was terrified about how Hallowfeld was going to react to it. No one talks to him like that." What Attalin said was true. Kiera had felt his magic writhing angrily. Until today, she hadn't realized the depth of Hallowfeld's powers. That bitter cold brush of his magic was just scraping the surface; she'd sensed an abyss of darkness in him.

Kiera murmured, "You're right. I underestimated his magic and his ego. I knew he was trying to get under my skin—I shouldn't have reacted." Kiera held back tears. "He was trying to have Imena killed as a threat to me. What she was doing in the arena was ingenious; it was proof that although using magic at all produces energy, using it with goodwill produces twofold the amount compared to using it for violence alone. It substantiates that magic responds to compassion over aggression."

"It was remarkable." Attalin squeezed her hand. "Imena has an incredible spirit. Don't worry, Gabby will heal her."

Kiera felt the pressure in her chest building again. Attalin put her hand on Kiera's shoulder. "Are you alright?" she asked.

Kiera reached out and fidgeted with one of the crystals on the table. "If you hadn't used your powers on me, I'm not sure I would've made it through earlier. Watching the tournament was worse than I imagined it'd be." Kiera placed her hand on her chest. "After the calming effects of your magic passed, I had this feeling like my power was going to burst out of me."

Attalin bit her lip. "I felt that when I was holding your hand on the balcony."

Kiera searched Attalin's eyes for fear.

"Whiskers, your magic is unique, but it's not something I'm afraid of."

Kiera snorted. "Mind reader."

Attalin raised her eyebrows. "No, I can just tell you're worried about my judgments, but you don't need to be."

Kiera flicked her tail in frustration. "I just don't fully understand my magic yet, but it's nothing like what's living inside of Hallowfeld." A shiver went up Kiera's spine. Fear sparked in Attalin's eyes at the mention of Hallowfeld's magic.

Kiera wrapped her arms around herself. "It sounds like he wants me to be one of his apprentices. It's insane the way people blindly follow him." Kiera shook her head and tightened her grasp on her arms. "Attalin, I refuse to become one of those followers."

She blinked at Kiera thoughtfully. "We'll do everything in our power to stop that from happening." Attalin tugged the tart box over to her. "As a matter of fact, it was one of his sycophants who actually gave me an idea to try and uncover what he's up to." Kiera's ears perked up as Attalin continued, "When Huxley spoke about the market earlier, it occurred to me it'd be the perfect place to hunt for answers." She pulled a piece of paper from the tart box and laid it flat on the table. It was a glossy floor plan with names above squares and a legend that correlated the names with times and service descriptions.

"Luna's shop is absolutely one of my favorites, but I had another reason for visiting her. She's part of the group that coordinates the weekly market days. She registers which shop owners and vendors will be in attendance and their locations in the tent as a guidebook for guests to use to find what they're looking for. She's a close friend of Gabby's, so I trust her. I was curious if any of Hallowfeld's inner circle had inquired about the register. It turns out that Yasmeen paid Luna a visit today to collect the guidebook for tomorrow. She didn't ask about anyone specific; she just wanted the list."

Kiera sat forward and examined the service descriptions. "Yasmeen is the witch you overheard telling the other followers she needed to locate what Hallowfeld wanted from outside the border, and now she's back," Kiera said. She flicked her eyes up to Attalin, who dipped her chin.

"Exactly, and the fact that she was sent to get this roster tells me Hallowfeld is still searching for something. Yasmeen is a formidable witch. She doesn't usually get ordered to do footwork, so this is significant. If I were Hallowfeld and I wanted someone to get me answers that they couldn't find on the other side of the border, this is where I'd send them. The market is where a multitude of beings converge to share magical services and knowledge. It's a convenient place to go if you're seeking information. Plus, it doesn't take much effort to track someone down if you know their exact location and what time they'll be there. I'm sure that's why Yasmeen got the list."

Kiera leaned back. "Attalin, you're brilliant. Not only do we know that Yasmeen is back, but now we know where she'll be tomorrow. We'll just have to track her down and see what booths she visits."

Attalin twisted her hair into a knot on top of her head and rolled back the sleeves of her dress. She dragged an ancient looking book sitting on the table over to her. "I'll dig around for some spells. Maybe Gabby can create one that can help us eavesdrop from a distance. We can have her take a look at the list, too, when she gets in and see if there are any beings who stand out to her. If we can narrow down who Yasmeen will be paying a visit to, that'll make it easier for us to stay out of her way at the market. It'd be best if we watch from a distance. We don't want her spotting us and running back to tell Hallowfeld."

Kiera twitched her ears. "An animal shifter form doesn't exactly lend itself to anonymity."

She patted the book. "I think Gabby can help with that too." Before Kiera could ask how, a rustling under one of the bunk beds caught her attention. Nook's ears perked up, and his tail wagged playfully.

Attalin grinned. "I can't believe I forgot to introduce you to Jasper." At the mention of his name, a black cat poked his head out from under one of the beds. He was sizing Kiera up.

Attalin muffled a laugh. "I think this is why Gabby's so fond of you. The two of you look a lot alike."

Kiera stuck her tongue out at Attalin and called to Jasper to come over. He approached cautiously, rubbing against Nook on his way past and flicking him in the face with his tail. Nook didn't seem bothered by it. Jasper's watchful eyes noted Kiera's own tail twitching. They became fast friends once she started scratching him behind the ears though. He jumped up on one of the chairs to join them.

"Alright," Attalin said, "now let's see about these spells."

She was just focusing her attention on the book's pages when a crystal bracelet on the table flashed a soft white light. Attalin turned toward the tent flaps. "When that garnet bracelet flashes white, it means a friend is here. If it ever flashes red, that means trouble."

A few seconds later, Gabby pushed through the tent flaps leading with her bag. There were dark circles under her eyes, but she gave them both a warm smile.

"It's nice to come home to those bright faces. Give me a moment to put my things away."

Gabby headed to one of the bookcases, placing her bag on it to unload its contents. She glanced over her shoulder, noting the tourmaline and the labradorite.

"Everything alright, Atti?" Attalin looked over at the labradorite. Its color had remained pale green when Gabby entered. She and Kiera exchanged a grateful look.

"We're good, thanks to you," Attalin replied.

She finished unpacking and faced them. "I see. Let me get dinner going, and then we can talk about that."

Gabby pulled a deep blue stone from one of the shelves and rubbed it across her forehead. A dull light flowed from the stone into her temples. She sighed and set the stone on the table. "That's better. It'd be bad form to fall asleep in the pasta."

A smile tickled Kiera's lips. She leaned forward and picked up the stone. Addressing Gabby, she asked, "Which one is this?"

Gabby pointed at it. "It's chrysocolla, and it had a re-energizing spell within it. My powers are drained, and my physical body is exhausted. If I hadn't used it, I'd need to go to bed immediately. As you know, it won't replenish my magic, but it'll give my body a boost."

Kiera rolled it in her hands. "You have a stunning collection. Are all the spells in the stones and crystals yours?"

Gabby radiated joy. "Some are gifts from other witches, some I bought at the market, but the majority I've imbued myself. I typically create these in the month leading up to the festival when I'm not casting as heavily on a daily basis."

Attalin grinned, waving the selenite crystal at her. "Those of us who can't cast appreciate it."

Gabby chuckled and nodded. "Yes, the stones come in handy for those who can't create spells, but these days, I'm relying on them more than I'd like to as well."

Kiera twitched her whiskers. "With your power, I'm surprised to hear that."

Gabby sighed. "I'm afraid my body gets tired faster than it used to. That's when I lean on my premade spells." She smirked. "I may have to admit my age is starting to have an impact." She plucked another crystal from the shelve. "This carnelian is imbued with a preparation spell." Gabby whispered to the crystal and tossed it at the kitchen area.

The stone burst into millions of tiny red sparks that dissolved into the fridge, a pot, pans, and an assortment of kitchen utensils. All the items that the sparks infused sprang into motion. It was like an invisible person was preparing their meal. Kiera's mouth hung open. Gabby gave her a wink. "Normally, I'd do dinner by hand, but I'm beat, and it sounds like we have a lot to discuss."

Attalin and Kiera exchanged a serious look, and both nodded. Gabby bobbed her head and sat down heavily in one of the chairs.

She frowned. "What's happened?"

RIPPLES

A ttalin quickly filled Gabby in on what had taken place in Hallowfeld's suite and everything they'd been discussing before she'd arrived. Gabby had saved Kiera's life and had attempted to aid with the bakery address, and now the stone. Kiera trusted her, and that familiar pressure of magic settled in her body in consensus. She didn't hold back and spoke up to add in details about her mother and her strange interactions with Rowan from the current and prior visit.

Gabby eyed the indigo flames. "It makes sense now why you two have the tourmaline activated. Kiera, I'm sorry about your mother being taken."

She stared down at the table, hoping to suppress the tears that burned behind her eyes. "Thank you."

Attalin pulled her legs up in her chair and wrapped her arms around them, and said, "I imagine the tourmaline will continue to be useful with Hallowfeld in his current state. How did you realize he had that spell placed on me?"

Gabby picked up the garnet bracelet. "I wasn't sure of the exact tracking spell, but before you entered the tent this morning, the bracelet flashed white but was tinged with black. It was a warning that a friend was entering but afflicted with deceitful magic." Gabby set the bracelet back down gingerly. "I had my suspicions he was up to something when a handful of witches didn't turn up for tournament preparation. Knowing he needed multiple witches to create a spell and with Kiera being back, I guessed it was a surveillance charm. We know he can't use harmful magic on you due to your bargain with him, so it made sense that it was an intrusive spell and not a destructive one."

Gabby gestured to the tourmaline. "This relic has been in my family for generations, lying dormant until we called on its power today. It was the only enchantment I could think of that would be powerful enough to protect you both from any spell of that scale. When you came to drop Nook off, I didn't know how long we'd have since you and Kiera had separated. Removing the spell would've taken time we didn't have, and that would've alerted Hallowfeld to the fact that we discovered it, so counteracting it was the best course. I was already worried he'd send one of his guards to the tent to see what you were up to, or I would've taken more time to explain."

Kiera considered the tourmaline and then Gabby. It must've taken deep faith for the members of her family to risk hiding it without knowing if it'd ever be used. The board has wiped out entire families for keeping memorabilia like that.

Kiera said, "It couldn't have been easy to activate an heirloom that your family has kept safe for so long. I appreciate that you entrusted it to us, but what made you sure this was the right time to use it?"

Gabby stared up at the flickering chandelier for a moment before responding. Her eyes looked a bit misty as she said, "My mother told me I'd know when to draw on it. She said sharing our gifts is our choice and a privilege." She placed a hand on her heart and then looked back at Kiera. "It's difficult to explain, but it was a knowing. I felt it in my body this was the right moment."

Kiera and Attalin exchanged a curious look. That sounded similar to their dreams and the feelings Kiera had been getting.

"So, your magic guides you too?" Kiera asked.

Gabby reached out and touched her cheek warmly. "It guides us all—we just have to know how to listen."

"So, the figures I saw and the steady presence I've been feeling really are my capacity to commune with magic?"

"I would say so. It took me years to look inward and make sense of the fact those deep feelings of knowing were spurred by my magic. There were times I ignored my intuition, not realizing it was a force greater than myself trying to guide me. I've spent hours of deep meditation to cultivate the relationship I have with my abilities. The fact that discernment came to you on the first day you transitioned is extraordinary," Gabby said.

Kiera smiled at her and asked Attalin, "What are the odds your magic called you to the stream and Gabby's encouraged her to lend us the stone within the same week?"

Attalin paused thoughtfully. "It doesn't seem like a coincidence to me."

Gabby's eyes gleamed. "You know I don't believe in happenstance. Something has the magic stirring in us. It's a sign that change is on the horizon."

Attalin chewed her lip. "Whatever it is, Hallowfeld's got his dirty hands all over it. I meant to tell you sooner about overhearing that group, but you left the tent early the other day to prepare things before the next tournament, and then I had to work last night."

Gabby held up her hand. "Of course, I understand, and Hallowfeld's been on edge. It worked out that we ended up discussing this under the protection of the tourmaline. That was a good idea bringing it to the cavern, Atti." Gabby's forehead creased as she explained to Kiera, "Sacred ground can give a boost to the power in a spell. The cave is such a place. It's what witches would describe as a vortex or a place where magic swirls in heightened amounts. The magic there is pure."

"You said the stone could be boosted from the energy at the vortex. What about Attalin's tiger's eye stone? Is it like the tourmaline?" Kiera asked.

Gabby closed her eyes and took a deep breath. "No, it's not. That stone defies the balance of nature. The way it manipulates energy exists outside the natural order. I'm sorry, Kiera, but I won't discuss how it was created."

Kiera flicked her eyes to Attalin, whose hand was hovering protectively above the spot on her chest where the necklace hung. "All you need to know is there's no other stone like it, and mark my words, I don't intend for another one of its kind to be made. It was an experiment of mine when I was trying to grow my understanding of magic. I wanted to test if I could force a spell never to fade. I wish I knew then what I know now: there's a price when we abuse our magic. All things have their time, and by ripping magic out of its natural cycle, I warped it into something awful. That stone must feed from a host to maintain its permanence. I regret making such parasitic magic."

Gabby's shoulders curved inward. "The energy that makes up our magic is benevolent. Our bond with it is sacred. The creation of the spell in that tiger's eye confirms that it's our choice to distort magic with our animus."

"So, it's true? Magic doesn't feed on bloodshed and chaos?" Kiera asked.

"That's utter nonsense the board spread about magic. It's an outright lie they used to sow fear and maintain supreme power outside the borders. Magic doesn't create chaos—our actions do." Gabby studied Attalin with worry. "Nothing good can come from something that siphons life from another, but I made a promise to Atti that she could use it until I determine how to safely destroy it. I wear it for the short periods when she leaves Etabon to maintain it, so it doesn't fall into the wrong hands."

Kiera hesitated before speaking again. "Can't you simply stop wearing it and let the energy run out?"

Gabby shook her head. "I'm not certain what would happen if we tried. The magic that powers it is unpredictable, another burden of meddling in the dark unknown. I have no idea if the magic within got desperate enough, if it would try to somehow acquire another host."

Kiera's pulse quickened. "I see."

Gabby gave her a sad smile. "My magic is rarely depleted during the off months, so when Atti needs a break from it, the stone is manageable."

Kiera wondered what leverage Hallowfeld had in order to keep Gabby here permanently. She stopped herself before she could ask though, because she caught the subtle shake of Attalin's head. Whatever it was must be dreadful.

Attalin said quietly, "I know there are times it takes from my life force, but it's also given me moments to cling to, which I wouldn't have experienced without it. I believe it's provided me as much life as it's taken away."

Kiera put her hand on Attalin's knee. It was painful to hear that she had to go to such lengths to feel secure. Attalin interlaced her fingers with hers and said, "Even so, when you've worked out how to unmake it, I'll gladly help you."

Gabby's eyes softened, and she inclined her head, saying, "For the sake of understanding magic, let's leave the tiger's eye out of our discussion. It's an exception to natural phenomena."

She stood and pulled a small worn book from the same compartment the tourmaline had been in and brought it back to the table. Gabby patted the tome. "This book is like the tourmaline, a remnant from the time before. It may shed some light on your abilities. You said the night you had the interaction with Rowan, there was a blue light radiating between him and your palm." Kiera nodded her head and blinked inquisitively. Gabby flipped through the pages and ran her finger down a section near the back of the book. Kiera stared down at the text Gabby was skimming through. It looked like the markings on the cave wall.

"What's peculiar is what I found when I went to look in on Rowan that night. I brought over some stones I thought would speed up his healing process, but when I got there, he was awake. I witnessed him sitting up, using a spell to illuminate the tent, and he was looking at the spot on his shoulder where his eclipse mark used to be."

Kiera turned her palms up and looked between Attalin and Gabby, baffled. "From everything you've explained, there doesn't sound like a logical explanation for that. He was injured, and his powers were drained. How could he have been using a spell without recuperating? And how did he manage to break his pledge to Hallowfeld?" Kiera said.

Gabby hesitated, her eyes flitting down to the pages and back up. "I believe *you* are the reason for his speedy recovery and the brand vanishing." Kiera was stunned. She could hear her heartbeat in her ears.

"Rowan was grateful he'd been released from the blood oath of the eclipse brand. We didn't know how he'd managed to escape it, but I promised him I wouldn't tell Hallowfeld. He's been hiding the fact that he no longer has it and is trying to figure out how to flee," Gabby said.

Attalin cocked her head to the side. "If he escaped the brand, that means he felt there was something to escape from. Apparently, once they get those marks, their allegiance to Hallowfeld isn't exactly optional. It sounds like a curse."

"How could I have released him from that curse and renewed his magical stores?" Kiera croaked.

Gabby pointed to the book. "Early text indicates shifters as a sign of balance from the universe. I'm unclear on its exact meaning, but there's reference to them being the primordial convergence of harmonious energy. Similar language is used to describe the vortex." Gabby squinted. "There's more indicating shifters are unsolidified vessels. My interpretation is that it means shifters are a source of raw power. Like the vortex in the cave, it appears energy is drawn to you, but it seems you have the ability to channel that raw energy through you."

Attalin pressed her forearms on the table. "After the tournament last time, your magic was already replenishing. This explains why your stores refill so extraordinarily fast."

Kiera wanted to jump up and pace around the room. "Why am I the only being like this?"

Gabby shook her head. "It's a gift, Kiera. This is conjecture, but if I'm understanding the use of the word 'primordial' here correctly, shifters could've been the first magical beings to manifest on our planet, making your essence closely related to the source energy. It would explain why your bond is unencumbered. Where the rest of us muddle our magic with the constant inner struggle for control, your form allows you a peaceful partnership. Power passes through you effortlessly."

Kiera leaned forward and stared down at the floor, trying to catch her breath. A meditation Wrenley taught her came to mind. She imagined herself sinking down into still water unaffected by what was happening on the surface above. Her breath leveled out and coherent thoughts began to form.

Truthfully, this conversation was illuminating. She was familiar with the inner turmoil Gabby described; the difference was that's how she felt outside of Etabon, and not when she was in her magical form. She'd never felt more at home in her own skin than when she was connected with her magic. On the other side of the border, her greatest fear had been being a misfit. When she'd arrived here, she'd realized it was the greatest gift she'd ever received. Although this information overwhelmed her, learning about it revealed another layer to who she truly was. Kiera sat back in her chair and scanned Attalin's face.

Attalin said gently, "Are you ok, Whiskers?"

Kiera emitted a shaky laugh. "I just found out I'm an oath-breaking primordial vase—never better."

Gabby and Attalin smiled at her, both settling back into their chairs. Attalin gestured to her. "She said vessel, actually."

Kiera smirked at her, and then her expression darkened as an idea surfaced in her mind. "His followers indicated that Hallowfeld is trying to see if I'm useful. Do you think he has some idea about how my abilities work?"

Gabby rubbed her temples, saying, "We should assume he knows enough to be dangerous. He's a fierce collector of any remaining historical artifacts he can get his hands on. His justification being that he's seizing and managing them for the board. He could've acquired an ancient relic of his own, and he has some bright minds at his disposal. Whatever he's pieced together, he likely wants to investigate if your connection to your power has deepened since your last visit. The initial transition can be jarring. Our bodies take to it much easier each subsequent time, allowing for our powers to stabilize the longer we spend here."

"That could explain why I'm feeling my magic more intensely this time. I've had more time to settle into my body, but my powers feel like they want to burst free," Kiera said.

Attalin frowned. "Hallowfeld's probably counting on the fact that you haven't fully developed an understanding of your gifts yet."

"He'd be correct in that assumption," Kiera muttered.

"We can start working through that together," Gabby replied soothingly. "Attalin said you felt your power manifesting at the tournament earlier?"

Kiera touched the spot on her chest. "Yes, I felt it gathering here."

Gabby nodded. "Would you be willing to try practicing with it?"

"I can try, but I'm not sure what I did that night in Rowan's tent," Kiera replied.

Gabby faced her so they were knee to knee. "That's alright. Don't worry about what you did then. Just focus on that tightness in your chest and imagine yourself gently releasing that pent-up energy into my hands. You don't have to push."

Kiera swallowed. She couldn't imagine if something went wrong. "What if I hurt you?"

Gabby shook her head. "I trust your magic."

Kiera considered Gabby's words. "If you're sure."

Gabby reached over and placed her hands in Kiera's. Kiera closed her eyes and did as Gabby instructed. She could almost imagine her powers leaping with excitement at the opportunity to be released, which brought a smile to her face. A few seconds later, Attalin's sharp intake of breath pulled Kiera's attention back to the present. Her eyes were wide with wonder and Gabby was beaming. Kiera watched as rays of cobalt light radiated from her palms and vanished into Gabby's. They all stared as the glow waned.

Attalin put her hands over her mouth. "That was stunning, Whiskers."

Gabby bobbed her head. "Are you tired?"

Kiera gestured to her chest. "Not at all, I feel alive." Her eyes scanned Gabby. "What about you?"

Gabby blinked slowly. "Wonderful, but let's see what I can do."

She surveyed the room and then opened her palm and flicked her wrist. A book floated off one of the shelves and over to her.

Gabby marveled at the book in her hand and peered up at Kiera. "I feel like I've rested for six hours. That's how long it takes me to personally recuperate my magical stores. You have a very special gift. Witches can heal the body, but you're the only being that can renew a magical cache. The pure magic in you must've burned through Rowan's curse—that's how you set him free."

Kiera touched her chest. "I could feel the energy rushing through me, but not exactly from me. It was more like sharing an abundance rather than taking from my personal strength."

Gabby nodded. "You're a natural channel. You're drawing from the environment, not your life force."

Kiera asked, "I'd be able to tell the difference?"

Attalin cringed. "Trust me, you'd know. It feels like something's trying to dig out a piece of your soul."

Kiera crinkled her nose. She wanted to snatch the tiger's eye necklace off Attalin and stomp on it, but there was no telling what destroying it would release into the world.

Gabby rubbed her forehead. "If Hallowfeld gained access to your abilities, he'd be unstoppable. He'd see you as an untapped generator. I'm concerned he does, in fact, have a notion about your capabilities, and he's trying to draw them out."

Kiera and Attalin said at the same time, "How?"

Gabby opened the book she'd summoned and flipped through it. She set it in front of them. The pages had an illustration of a werewolf, a description of their abilities, and the antidote for their venom. "With the match. It makes sense now why he'd want you to face a werewolf. Their bite can lower inhibitions, induce hallucinations, and cause their victim to lose control. Kiera, you said it felt like your magic wanted to burst out of you earlier. Hallowfeld could be expecting you to unleash some kind of power surge. With the protection of the dome, it'd be the safest place for him to test that theory."

Kiera's mouth went dry. It would also explain why Hallowfeld had himself wrapped in a forcefield earlier. She locked eyes with Attalin, recalling her moment of delirium on the balcony. "If that's true, I could've hurt you today?"

Attalin put both of her hands on the table. "No, you wouldn't have. You're stronger than you think. I don't know what Hallowfeld's expecting out of you, but all I felt on that balcony was courage." Tears were threating to well behind Kiera's eyes.

Gabby said softly, "Every one of us struggles when our powers build up. We get restless when we don't exercise our magic; you just have a great deal more flowing into you than the rest of us. Plus, we have no way of knowing if a surge of your power would be destructive." She tilted her head down. "Do you feel that way now?"

Kiera shook her head no. "That's good," Gabby said. "Now we know how to help you burn some of it off and relax. Hallowfeld won't know that you've found an outlet for your energy."

Kiera stared into space for a second. "If he even suspected some kind of outburst from me, how could he risk an arena full of people?"

Attalin's face distorted in loathing. "He'd capitalize on it. He'll be in no real danger with his magic and the powerful beings in his suite to shield him. It'd more than likely be part of his plan, to push you to your breaking point and see what you're capable of." Kiera's claws slid free in anger.

Gabby looked between them. "It aligns with his typical pattern. He was hoping to draw you to his side with bribery. When that doesn't work, he uses fear. His last resort will be brute force."

Kiera rubbed her face. "That's why he went after Imena. He was using the tournament as a warning."

Gabby's eyes filled with grief. "You're right. Hallowfeld is the law here. He kills as readily as the board does. Where Etabon is concerned, consider him a seventh board member, but he's far worse. He is umbra, the darkest part of a shadow. I don't believe that creature has anything left of his soul. He wanted to send a message with Imena that insubordination won't be tolerated. Hallowfeld ordered me to make sure she succumbed to her injuries."

Kiera made a strangled noise, and Attalin paled. It was like someone had sucked all the air out of the room. Kiera stood, knocking her chair over. It was her fault that an innocent being died today. That message had been for her, and Imena had been the unlucky victim Hallowfeld had delivered it through.

Gabby stood and steadied Kiera under her elbow. "I didn't let Imena die." Kiera stared at her in confusion. "I'll explain." She gestured back to the table, and Kiera righted her chair and sat back down. "I convinced him that with the severity of her burns there was no way to save her even if I tried. He underestimated my abilities and her will to live. She'll be scarred from her neck down the rest of her life and will likely deal with a degree of pain from the skin grafting I had to do, but she'll make it. I've concealed her with a trusted friend to finish healing. She's a small being, so we won't have trouble keeping her hidden until we figure out our next steps."

There was terror in Attalin's eyes. "Gabby, if he finds out…"

She gave Attalin a firm look. "He won't. I was careful. I even spread ashes in the stream to look like a burial rite." Gabby turned back to Kiera and said, "Hallowfeld is accountable for his choices. You're doing him a favor if you let his wickedness eat you up inside."

Kiera felt emotion climbing in her throat. "It's more than that. Imena acknowledged me at the tournament, I think because she was inspired by my participation last time. I feel responsible for her competing."

Gabby replied, "Your actions gave Imena the courage to stand up for what she felt was right. She wanted others to know that you don't have to be the cruelest being to make an impact—strength comes in all forms."

Kiera cradled her arms. "It was never my intention to encourage anyone here to put themselves in danger."

Gabby nodded. "The danger isn't new, Kiera, but the courage to face it is. You set something in motion that's bigger than yourself. It's not just Imena; others are starting to see that Hallowfeld's way is not the only way. The idea that magic thrives on compassion, not chaos, is spreading. I know it's daunting, but our actions create ripples. Those ripples will inevitably fan out and touch the lives of others. I spoke with Imena when I healed her. She wasn't under any illusions about what entering the matches could mean for her life."

Gabby reached out and touched her arm. Kiera could feel her hand trembling. "Do you think I wasn't afraid today when I helped Imena? People like Hallowfeld make it easy for us to convince ourselves that inaction is the only way to survive, but choosing to watch others suffer is still a choice we make and one that we have to live with." Kiera put her hand over Gabby's as Gabby said, "We can choose every day to hold space for kindness. I can tell you from experience it's not the easiest path, but I have no doubt it's the most rewarding."

Kiera blinked back tears and said, "I'm thankful for your courage to save her."

Gabby smiled and looked from Attalin to Kiera. "She wanted me to tell you both, thank you for going to the balcony. Seeing you there reminded her she wasn't alone. It gave her the willpower to push through the pain and tap out."

Attalin's eyes were bright. "She's a survivor like us."

Kiera leaned over and hugged Attalin.

"The fighting pit has containment properties. Hopefully, that'll provide spectators with protection on the off chance my power really can be explosive. I don't want to hurt anyone, so I'd rather Hallowfeld try to draw my energy out there than anywhere else in Etabon," Kiera said.

Attalin was worrying her lower lip. "We know his plan involves werewolf venom. If we can find out what Yasmeen is searching for at the market tomorrow, maybe that'll reveal more about what he knows and his overall plan."

Kiera flicked her tail. "Who knows, there could be a way to convince him I don't have whatever power he's expecting."

Attalin picked up the guidebook and Gabby eyed the tart box. "That was clever going to Luna's, Atti."

Attalin flashed a grin. "I learned from the best." She handed the chart to Gabby. "Is there anyone in particular on there that stands out to you as someone Yasmeen would want to meet with?"

Gabby's eyes roved over the list. "If she's personally going, it'll have to be someone of significance." She lingered on one name. "Here, Larkin will be there. He's a photographer, but that's his cover. I met him a couple of years ago. He came to Hallowfeld's manor under the guise of taking his portrait. His real business is selling antiquities to a few of the elite. The photography allows him to travel to each continent without drawing attention." She glanced up. "I'm surprised he's back. There was speculation when he didn't attend the festival last year that the board incarcerated him. Out of everyone on the roster, he'd be the most likely to have something Hallowfeld desires, but you two need to be careful where he's concerned. His nickname is the Jackal for a reason. He's opportunistic and will advance himself by any means necessary."

Attalin gestured to the spell books on the table. "Do you have anything that could amplify his conversation with Yasmeen? If we have to interact with Larkin, we will, but we're hoping to avoid it."

Gabby rested her chin on her hand and squinted at the book. "I believe there's an enchantment in there that'll do."

Kiera leaned in. "That's great, but what about the fact that I'll draw attention to us? And I'm sure a number of beings can recognize Attalin."

Gabby rose and strode over to a bookcase on the far wall. She picked up two small necklaces with stones that sparkled with an array of colors. "I imbued a couple of opals with disguising charms a while back. We can activate them in the morning. Jade and Viv will be leaving early tomorrow for their shifts. The market won't open until mid-morning, so I'll get you two situated before I head over to the arena for the day."

Gabby peeked at her watch. "It's getting late—the others should be here any minute. Kiera, you're more than welcome to stay with us after dinner."

Kiera put her hand to her head. She'd completely forgotten about where she'd be sleeping with everything that'd happened today. "If it's not too much trouble. I don't want to stay in Hallowfeld's assigned house."

Gabby snapped her fingers, and a cot appeared out of thin air next to the nearest bunkbeds.

"It's no trouble at all, especially with my magic replenished," she said, winking at Kiera. "Now, let's see how this meal turned out." On her way to the kitchen, Gabby plucked the tourmaline off the table and deactivated it. She closed it back in its compartment and then collected two serving bowls off the counter.

Attalin set the table while Gabby placed the food in the middle. One bowl was filled with chicken pasta and the other had a heap of mixed vegetables. Kiera's stomach growled at the smell.

"This still looks hot." She'd noticed the commotion in the kitchen had stopped before their conversation had ended.

Gabby smiled. "The perks of a magically made recipe. It maintains the perfect temperature."

Attalin nodded, "They're great for days like today when we all get home at different times." The bracelet on the counter began flashing white light. Her eyes flicked to it. "Speaking of." Jade and Viviana came through the tent flaps at the same time, heatedly discussing who was more high maintenance, alarys or sirens.

Jade put her hand on her hip. "Alarys for sure, what's with all the preening." Viviana let out a breathy giggle and flared her semi-transparent wings.

"These do take a lot of upkeep. I can't imagine how much more time it takes to care for all those feathers."

Jade rolled her eyes. "He was twenty minutes late last time."

Viviana's rose gold eyes danced with laughter. "Weren't you an hour late to the first date?"

Jade pointed at her scales. "They don't polish themselves."

Viviana held her hands up in mock surrender. "You're the one who agreed to another date with him."

They'd been so caught up in their conversation, they hadn't noticed the other three watching them with amusement. Attalin's eyebrows were raised, and she was resting her chin on her knuckles. "My vote's for sirens."

They both looked to the center of the room as Jade said, "Of course you would." Her face split into a grin when she saw Kiera. "I wondered when I'd be seeing you back." She walked over and gave her a strong embrace. "Attalin told me about your agreement with Hallowfeld. That took guts. My bargain would've lasted another seventeen years. Thank you for caring."

Kiera hugged her tightly. "I'd do it again every time."

Viviana came over bashfully. "I didn't realize we had a guest." She held out her hand. "I'm Viviana. You can call me Viv."

Kiera took her hand. "I'm Kiera. It's great to meet you. Attalin was telling me you're an amazing musician."

Viv's wings lifted with excitement. "It's my passion. I can play a few different instruments."

Attalin pointed across the room. "She's being modest. Gabby had to enchant that trunk over there so she could store all the instruments she plays."

Gabby smiled and motioned to the table. "Let's eat."

Kiera had noticed Attalin had left the labradorite activated. It'd sustained its pale green glow when Jade and Viv had entered, which comforted her. Everyone settled in their seats. The next hour was filled with delicious food and vibrant conversation. Before bed, Viv even played them a heartrending melody on her violin. When Kiera laid her head down on her pillow, she felt optimism rising in her chest. Nook was curled up by her feet, his warmth soothing her. Today had been full of uncertainty, and she knew tomorrow would be more of the same, but tonight had been uplifting. She missed Rose, but she knew her mother would be glad that she was among friends that made her feel safe and welcome.

Kiera watched as the twinkling lights on the chandelier winked out one by one as if it could tell the room's occupants were winding down for the night. Attalin was on the bottom bunk across from her cot, peering over.

She tipped her chin up at the chandelier. "It's spelled to taper off as we fall asleep." Kiera motioned to the others. Attalin snuggled down into her quilt. "They have the curtains drawn around their bunks. Gabby spelled them so they cancel noise, so we're not disturbing them."

Kiera marveled at the hangings around each individual bed. "Magic is so beautiful," she said.

She turned over to face Attalin. Her eyes adjusted to the growing dimness. Night vision will never get old, she thought.

Attalin murmured, "I'm glad you stayed. You know I would've given you my bed and slept on the floor in a heartbeat."

Kiera smiled into the dark. "I know, and I wouldn't have let you."

Attalin laughed quietly. "Who's more stubborn, shifters or mermaids?"

Kiera chuckled. "Mermaids—definitely mermaids."

Attalin said sleepily, "Night, Whiskers."

Kiera whispered back, "Good night, Atti."

Attalin had this way about her. She could make the world feel lighter even when everything around them was so heavy. As she drifted off, she couldn't help thinking it was because the grooves of their souls fit together seamlessly.

REFLECTIONS

The next morning, Kiera woke to the smell of scrambled eggs and tea. It took her a moment to orient herself to her surroundings, but when she saw a kettle pouring itself over a mug, she remembered exactly where she was. She looked over to the table and saw Gabby reading from one of the spell books. Attalin was carrying her breakfast over from the kitchen. She had a bowl of eggs in one hand, half a piece of toast in her mouth, and she waved at Kiera with the fork in her other hand. Kiera rubbed the sleep out of her eyes, groaned, and rolled out of bed. The mug she'd seen filling with tea floated over to her.

Kiera glanced over at Gabby. "Thank you, but you'd better be careful, you won't be able to get rid of me."

The corners of Gabby's lips curved up. "You can stay as long as you'd like. Jade and Viv feel the same way." She pointed to a piece of paper next to her. Kiera had been so tired she hadn't heard them leave this morning, but they left a note saying they hoped she was staying again.

Kiera walked over next to Attalin and nudged her with her hip. "What about you?"

Attalin swallowed a bite of eggs and grinned. "You forget, Whiskers, I'm the original member of the shifter fan club."

Gabby smiled into her cup and said to Kiera, "Why don't you grab some food, and then I'll walk you two through this." She motioned to the spell book.

After they ate a quick breakfast, Gabby laid out the necklaces, a fiery orange stone, and a page she'd marked in the spell book. She'd pulled the tourmaline from its compartment and enacted it. She set it next to the other items and then picked up the orange stone.

"This is topaz—it has an invisibility enchantment in it. Before you two leave the tent, hold hands, and say 'obscure' to activate it. I would bet anything that Hallowfeld is having the tent watched, so this will allow you a few minutes of cover to leave, but don't push it. The spell will deplete fast, so give yourselves five minutes coming and going, ten minutes total. Don't forget to disengage it—that way, you can use it to get back into the tent unseen."

Gabby put it in a leather satchel and handed it to Attalin. She reached for the necklaces next and placed them around their necks. "The opals will last about two hours. Kiera, remember not to use your powers in public. We can't chance anyone seeing you. When those opals feel like they're dwindling, you need to get out of the market and find someplace safe less than five minutes away from here so you can enact the topaz." They both nodded at her.

She turned a mirror toward them. "Let me show you how they work. When you're ready, all you need to do is grasp them and say 'mask.' The enchantment will modify your physical features and imitate a form similar to yours. You can give it a try." They both held their necklaces and whispered, "Mask." Attalin's hair darkened to auburn, and her eyes turned to a deep brown. Her scales all shifted to a wine color and cropped up along her cheekbones.

Kiera blinked at her. "You look exactly like a siren." Attalin was speechless and took the mirror and turned it toward her. Kiera took a step back from the blue-eyed werewolf in the reflection. She looked down at herself and realized her fur had turned entirely pitch black, and her streamlined frame had transformed into the stocky build of a werewolf.

Gabby nodded. "They work perfectly. Remember, you only have that form's appearance, not their abilities. Now say 'unmask' so you can reserve the stone's power."

They did, and just as suddenly, they transformed back into themselves. Attalin touched her face. "That's wild."

Gabby cupped her hand and waved it over a cookbook. It changed to look like the ancient volume that she kept in the compartment with the tourmaline. She put it in Attalin's satchel.

"This is just in case you have to deal with Larkin. We can't risk him getting his hands on the actual book or a relic like the tourmaline, but this replica will get his attention." Kiera nodded. She didn't want to consider the fallout if someone like Larkin ever got his hands on the real items. Attalin reached out and picked up the guidebook to put it in her satchel, too. She studied it for a moment before setting it inside.

"Larkin has his stall open for two hours this morning and then a long break with another two hours open at the end of the day. Are we choosing correctly, going when the market opens?" Attalin asked.

Gabby sighed. "It's a gamble, but let's hope Yasmeen wants whatever it is badly enough to have an early visit with him. Whether you two get any information or not, you need to leave before these spells run out, so keep that in mind; it's not worth the consequences of being caught." Gabby had her bag close by and zipped it shut. "The market will open soon. Let me put this spell on you two before we head out." She dabbed tea tree oil on their ears and then cupped her hands and whispered the spell from the open book into them.

"When you two are situated, focus on the conversation you want to amplify and say 'intercept' to tap into the spell."

Attalin adjusted the satchel on her shoulder. "What's the timeframe for this spell?"

"For the sake of keeping all things equal, assume it and the enchantment on the cookbook will last two hours. They could remain longer, but there's no point staying at the market without the protection of the opal."

Kiera reached out and touched Gabby's hand. "You still have a full day of work ahead of you, and you've dipped into your magic. Can I restore it to full capacity?"

Gabby glanced apprehensively at the tent flaps. "I should have enough for the day. I don't want you two to miss the start of the market."

Kiera smiled. "I'll be quick." She brought her hand to Gabby's shoulder and slowly let that warm sensation flow through her to her fingertips. Since Gabby had only used a couple of spells, it just took a second to replenish her magic. "As good as new." Kiera grinned.

Gabby kissed her on the cheek and did the same to Attalin. "You two take care of each other. I wish I could come with you, but I'll just make it on time for my shift at the arena as it is. Not showing up for it would attract Hallowfeld's suspicions where you're concerned."

Attalin picked up Gabby's bag and handed it to her. "Don't worry about us—we have plenty of charms to keep us safe."

Gabby nodded. "I'll open the tent flap wide so you two can duck past me."

Attalin snatched the tourmaline up, murmuring to it as she deposited it back in its compartment. Then they followed Gabby over to the exit, joined hands, and whispered to the topaz as she reached for the canvas. The stone emitted a bronze light that spread and settled over them. Gabby swung her bag wide as she stepped out into the morning sunlight. Kiera and Attalin squeezed together and brushed by her as she said over her shoulder into the tent, "Bye, girls." Then she turned and walked away without looking back.

Attalin led Kiera in the opposite direction. They dodged and weaved around unsuspecting guests headed toward the market. At one point, they had to jump off the gravel path to avoid bumping into a group of rowdy alarys. Kiera stepped into a puddle. When she looked down, there was empty space where their reflections should've been. She was still gaping down at it when Attalin tugged her back onto the path.

Kiera counted off seconds in her head. After traveling for four minutes, Attalin steered them into a narrow alleyway behind some restaurant tents. They dropped behind a stack of rubbish crates. Attalin mouthed to her, "Ready?" Kiera clutched her necklace in her other hand and bobbed her tail in confirmation. They activated their opals before disabling the topaz and stowing it in the satchel. Then crept back out from behind the crates and slipped among the crowd as the crimson siren and dusky werewolf.

They didn't have too much farther to walk before they arrived at the marketplace. A line had already formed outside of the towering tent in anticipation of the opening. Kiera leaned back, staring up to take it all in. The beams holding it up must be colossal, she thought. She wouldn't be surprised if they had to be reinforced by magic of some kind. Attalin was surveying the line and muttered that she didn't see Yasmeen in the crowd.

A gong sounded, and a ruddy-faced wizard waved his hands in a parting gesture at the tent. Its flaps yawned open, and great braided cords tied back the folds so guests could enter. A thrill ran through Kiera as she glimpsed what was inside.

Attalin linked arms with her. "Keep close, it's easy to get separated in here."

The market was a flurry of motion. Guests jostled one another eagerly, and shopkeepers yelled out services from their kiosks. The tang of magic and burnt sugar hung in the air. Kiera was grateful that Attalin was guiding her along because it allowed her the chance to glance about.

They passed a stall where a wizard had his hands on either side of his human assistant's head. He called out, "Come travel the world without ever leaving the market!" He was displaying a spell that transported the mind into landscapes from each continent. A projection of what his assistant was seeing behind his closed eyes floated in the air above them. Kiera stared over her shoulder as the scenes flicked by of the assistant hiking the tundra in Fortayne, roaming through the mountains in Karveir, and staring out over the sand dunes in Renival.

The shop beside that boasted a witch's freshly made remedies, the terracotta jars of tonics and salves stacked neatly in rows for patrons to peruse. A soft glow radiated a few stalls down where a fire faerie was crafting handblown glass figurines. Chattering above Kiera's head drew her focus away from his flames. A mix of sprites and pixies soared by and landed at a tiny clothing shop situated on top of the fire faerie's stall. Kiera looked around and realized there was an entire miniature market taking place above them.

She felt Attalin slow beside her, and they came to a stop. There was a bottleneck ahead as guests filed into a space to their left in front of the stage and display ring area. Attalin let out a resigned sigh. Kiera spied the canvas wall not too far from them and nudged Attalin's shoulder.

"Couldn't we just slice our way out and then back in to get around?"

Attalin smirked and shook her head, "The tent's material was spelled a few years ago. Too many guests had the same idea and were making their own entrances and exits."

Kiera frowned. "It seems dangerous that there's only one way in and out of this place."

Attalin nodded. "You're not the only one who feels that way. Gabby was the one who convinced Hallowfeld to station medics and responders along the walls in case of emergencies. Now there are at least five water faeries on duty in case of a fire, and of course, Hallowfeld gets to take credit for being concerned about guests' welfare."

Attalin pulled out the map to study how much farther they had to Larkin's stall. Kiera took the opportunity to examine the booth beside her. The banner guaranteed a trained companion like no other. She was astonished to find an assortment of animals lounging inside the stall, and some were even settled on the counter together. A hedgehog was dozing next to an owl, both completely at ease. There wasn't a single cage in sight. It made sense why the animals were so docile—the shopkeeper was an elderly nature faerie. He had a ferret perched on his shoulder and was enthusiastically chatting to a customer about elks.

Kiera admired nature faeries' deep connection to the natural world. Their ability to commune with plants and animals fascinated her. Motion at the customer's hip caught Kiera's attention. Two large cream-colored ears had poked out of his satchel, and bright brown eyes looked up at her. Kiera recognized the creature as a fennec fox, known for dwelling in the deserts of Renival. It scampered out of its bag and came to rest at Kiera's feet. She crouched down and gingerly reached out to pet its small head. To her surprise, it made a sort of purring noise at her touch.

The young man turned around and said, "Thimble?"

His voice was familiar, and Kiera had to stop herself from gasping. There were forest green swirls along his bronzed arms, his ears were finely pointed, and he'd grown taller, but it was undeniably him. Jax's autumn eyes were unmistakable, like leaves turning in early fall. They matched his nature faerie form beautifully. He looked between the tiny fox and Kiera and smiled. "She doesn't usually take to strangers so quickly."

Kiera stared up at him, her pulse hammering in her ears. After an awkward moment of stunned silence, she did her best to mask her voice as she said, "Well, I'm honored."

A subtle evergreen sheen played over Jax's raven curls as he tilted his head to the side, studying her with curiosity. "Have we…" he began.

Before he could finish his sentence, Attalin, who was standing on her tiptoes beside her, said, "Good, the line is starting to move."

Kiera patted the tiny fox. "It was nice meeting you, Thimble. Good-bye, then," she said, nodding politely to Jax. Her magic was doing electrified somersaults in her stomach as she peeled her eyes away from him.

She linked arms with Attalin again as the crowd pressed forward. Instead of following the line into the theater area, they passed it and headed to the open food court ringed with concession stalls.

When they were far enough away, Kiera whispered to Attalin, "You know my mentor. I just saw his apprentice back there. He'd said he was traveling for his break, but I had no idea he'd visit Etabon. What are the odds?"

Attalin's eyebrows shot up. "That's curious—small world." Her voice raised with alarm, "Did he recognize you?"

Kiera shook her head. "Not a chance—I lowered my voice. We're friends, but there are a million reasons he can't know it's me."

Ones she didn't have to say out loud. They were currently undercover, and even if they weren't, it was dangerous to be associated with her. Plus, she still wasn't entirely sure she could trust Jax. Although, the hum of her magic said otherwise. The tension left Attalin's body at Kiera's words.

Attalin's attention was drawn to the stalls across from them. "Look, that's the booth."

Kiera would think about Jax later. They didn't have time for distractions, they needed to focus on the reasons they'd come to the market and get out.

Larkin's booth was diagonal from the food court, so they hastily purchased some frothed caramels and snagged a table at the edge. From this angle, it would appear that they were trying to get a view of the stage and ring, but really their position allowed them to look right into Larkin's booth. The flaps were tied back to reveal no one was currently in.

Kiera sipped from her cup. "Is it a bad sign that it's vacant?"

Attalin grumbled, "It's early. Most vendors that set appointments don't take their first one until fifteen minutes after the market starts. That way, customers have enough time to make it through the surge after the opening gong. I doubt we've missed them."

Attalin's tight grip on her mug was a telltale sign of her concern, though. She caught Kiera staring at her hands and smirked. It was hard to hide the truth when you noticed each other's quirks. Kiera tilted her head wistfully. She hadn't thought she'd enjoy herself so much since they were there under such serious circumstances, but being with Attalin had that effect on her.

"Do you come here often?" Kiera asked.

Attalin took a break from scanning the crowd to look at her. "No, I haven't been here in ages. I've avoided it because it reminds me of my father." Her eyes traveled over Kiera's shoulder to the stage. She practically glowed as she watched the troupe of nixies dance across the platform. "I forgot how wonderful the buzz of the market was, though."

Kiera beamed. "It suits you."

Attalin held her mug up to Kiera's. "You, too."

They clinked glasses. Attalin was still on alert, but their conversation was more relaxed after that. While she kept a lookout, they discussed the stalls they'd passed on the way in and which ones that'd been the most eye-catching. Kiera leaned back in her seat to watch the water faerie in the display ring. She'd been manipulating vapor into different shapes and then had formed a glistening liquid sword which she tossed into the air. The sword turned to ice, and the faerie dove forward and caught it just before it hit the ground. Kiera burst into applause along with the rest of the theatre crowd. Out of the corner of her eye, she saw Attalin's smile fade as she straightened in her chair. Kiera's breath caught in her throat. She must've spotted Yasmeen.

They both drew their cups up to hide their lips.

Attalin whispered, "She's here. The one in the red cloak."

To Kiera's disbelief, she recognized the witch standing in front of Larkin's stall from last time. She'd cast the spell that'd trapped her at the gate, and she'd had a brief interaction with her outside of Rowan's recovery tent. She had a swollen lip, a black eye, and her cloak was tattered at the edges now, but that was her. The eclipse brand, hardly visible beneath the sleeve of her cloak, confirmed it.

Attalin inclined her head, and they activated the amplifying spell. A goblin had scuttled up to Yasmeen. Attalin flashed her eyes at Kiera, and she tipped her chin down slightly to imply she'd caught who it was: Nash, the goblin that guarded Hallowfeld's hangar. Kiera forced herself not to jump when she heard the witch's breathy voice in her ear. It sounded as if she was sitting right beside her as she greeted the goblin.

"Any news, Nash?"

Nash leaned against the booth panting. "The update is they're still in their tent. Gabby went to the arena to prepare for the day's events." Kiera and Attalin exchanged a look. So, their ploy was working.

Yasmeen clenched her fists. "This assignment is beneath me. I can't believe I've been sent to meet this bloody vulture. Speaking of, where is Larkin?"

Nash crossed her arms. "He was riffling through some storage crates that were just delivered. He should be here momentarily." Yasmeen grimaced as she shifted her weight to her right leg.

Nash raked her eyes over her associate. "Why haven't you healed your injuries?"

Yasmeen lifted her chin. "I'm forbidden to until I've redeemed myself." She brought her hand to her busted lip and murmured, "I should be grateful that there's still breath in my lungs, which is more than I can say for Illias. It's our own doing. We failed to retrieve the object sooner. The Ascendant One won't be merciful with me a second time."

Kiera winced. She didn't know what was worse, that Yasmeen glazed over Illias's murder, or the title she bestowed on the killer himself.

Nash bared her pointy teeth in a grin. "I told you the Ascendant One has always favored you over Illias, or he wouldn't have given you another chance. What's so special about this artifact anyway?"

Yasmeen stared over her head at an alary that was headed toward them. "It'll ensure Devland's success tomorrow even if the oaf can't do the only thing werewolves are good for."

The alary strutted up to them, flexing his bone white wings, each feather tipped with gold.

"Larkin." Yasmeen's nose wrinkled when she acknowledged the alary.

"Apologies for the delay, but I've only recently acquired the piece." He had a film box and some canvas portraits tucked under his arm.

Yasmeen stared at him with distaste. "That was cutting it awfully close."

He sidestepped her and entered the stall. "I think the words you're searching for are, 'Thank you, Larkin, I'm eternally in your debt.'" He scanned Yasmeen with an amused look. "Then again, getting to see you in this state is thanks enough." She stalked in after him.

Nash said to her back, "I'll meet you here when you've finished." Yasmeen waved her hands, and the stall flaps dropped shut. They strained to catch more of the conversation, but the exchange had gone silent.

Attalin cursed. "We're being blocked. We should still be able to hear them. The tent must be enchanted with a shielding spell. I should've anticipated that."

Kiera put her elbows on the table and leaned forward. "It sounded like Yasmeen is getting what she came for. Even if we're missing her conversation with Larkin, we'll still have a chance to find out more." Kiera's eyes flicked to Nash who was perusing the nearby stalls. "She and Yasmeen seem close, so I bet she'll fill her in on what they discussed. We can trail them out of the market to wherever they're going and listen in."

Attalin nodded. "It's a plan." After a few tense minutes, Yasmeen threw back the curtains and emerged from the booth, hissing about Larkin's greediness. She had a slender bundle cradled in one arm. Kiera and Attalin readied themselves to go. They'd have to move quickly not to lose them in the crowd. Nash hurried over to Yasmeen's side while Larkin gave them a sly grin.

"It was nice doing business with you. Send him my regards." Larkin chuckled.

Yasmeen snatched Nash's hand, and they vanished. There was a beat of stunned silence between the girls, and then it was Kiera's turn to curse.

Attalin shook her head. "She's faded them straight out of the market and likely right to him. Apparently, Hallowfeld doesn't want to leave anything to chance."

Kiera calmly set her mug down. "We only have one option left." She stood and pushed her chair in. "Ready to meet the Jackal?"

Attalin rose beside her. "Born ready."

22

WINGS

The two of them linked arms and dashed over to the booths across the way. They couldn't risk Larkin leaving his tent again. Attalin took the lead as they strolled into the stall. The counter was set in the middle of the room, and the space was decorated with photos of varying sizes. One in particular captured Kiera's attention. It was taken off the west coast of Hytheis—she'd recognize the jagged cliffs and turquoise sea anywhere. She had to admit, Larkin was awfully talented for this being a pseudo profession.

He was turned around, hanging up a portrait on the back wall, and looked over his shoulder when they entered. What struck Kiera was his eyes that mirrored his wings—they were glowing white and ringed with gold. They seemed to blaze brighter as he took them in.

"Neither of you look like a human. I don't believe you're my next appointment."

Attalin let out an airy laugh. "No, but we've heard you were the one to see about one-of-a-kind pieces. I'm Nat, and this is my associate, Stella."

He straightened the portrait on the wall and faced them. "I'm Larkin, but it seems you knew that already."

He glided over to the counter, which held a picture of one of Andaine's colorful spice markets. Kiera realized it'd been among the photographs he'd carried in minutes before. The dismantled pieces of its frame littered the counter. The bottom section was hollowed out and the exact length of the bundled item that Yasmeen had been clutching. Now she knew how Larkin smuggled his objects in. Kiera felt him studying her and looked up.

"What do you think?" he asked.

Kiera kept her voice low and calmly held his gaze. "It's lovely, but not precisely what we're looking for."

He picked up the photo. "My last client wanted it reframed in something more ornate."

Larkin turned his attention back to Attalin and gestured to the room. "Who told you about my work?"

She gave him a coy smile. "A mutual acquaintance."

He chuckled at her. "Alright, you've piqued my interest." He reviewed a timetable sheet behind the desk. "My appointment will be here shortly, but I'll have a quarter-hour at the end of the day. Come back then."

Kiera stepped closer to block Attalin from anyone passing by as she drew the tome from her satchel. She held it up so Larkin could get a good look at it. "I think you've misunderstood me. Our acquaintance mentioned you're the best at your craft, but you're not the only one in the market that can assist us. We were hoping to conduct our business promptly."

Larkin's eyes narrowed on the book. "As a matter of fact, I believe I can spare a couple of minutes."

Attalin gathered the book close to her chest. "Excellent."

Larkin nodded to Kiera. "Can you close those curtains behind you for privacy?"

She did as he requested and enclosed them in the stall. When she joined them at the counter again, he snapped his fingers, and a candle on the edge of the desk ignited to produce a green flame. It cast an eerie glow over the room.

Attalin's eyebrows lifted. "You're resourceful. I've never seen a quelling candle in person. Is it true that it stops all sound from traveling beyond its glow?"

Larkin smirked. "Indeed. I came across it a few years ago at a dig site in Karveir—perks of the trade. We can't have anyone absconding with our secrets, can we?" Kiera and Attalin exchanged a knowing look.

Larkin leaned on the counter. "How did you come to possess your artifact?"

Kiera bared her teeth in a devious grin. "The previous owner didn't have use for it any longer."

Larkin snickered. "I see, so it was inherited in a way. That's how I come by many of my items as well."

Attalin set the book on the counter but kept her hand resting on it. "We're well aware of its worth as an ancient remnant, if that's what you're asking."

Larkin's eyes smoldered. "Well then, if you know its true value, what's your asking price?"

Attalin pushed the book closer to Larkin. "We don't want money, just information."

His face darkened. "Your acquaintance should've told you I'm a purveyor of relics, not gossip. I don't trade information—that's the fastest way to retire in my line of work."

Attalin drummed her fingers over the book. "Then I don't believe we can arrive at a deal."

He frowned and rustled his wings. "Very well. I'll make an exception. On whom can I provide you information?"

Kiera crossed her arms. "Your last client."

Larkin stared at the book with longing. His hand hovered above it as he debated. "As enticing as your offer is, I must decline. Even an item as historic as this isn't worth the possible fallout. We're done here."

Before he could pull away, Attalin's hand shot out to grasp his. "You'll tell us what Yasmeen was here to collect."

Larkin went stiff, and his eyes clouded. "It was an object to aid her ally in a match tomorrow." Larkin's teeth were gritted, and each of his words were clipped.

"Go on," Attalin prompted. Larkin's entire body began to tremble, and the murkiness in his eyes swirled. Kiera watched Attalin with concern. Larkin is under her influence; should he be this aware or combative? Kiera thought.

She must've sensed Kiera's unease because she rasped, "I've got it under control." Attalin planted her feet and pressed down. "Speak, Larkin." The two were locked in an intense stare.

Larkin gasped, "The remnant has only been used once, in a blood sacrifice." His wings had begun to slowly arch up on either side of her. Each feathers golden tip sharpened into a spiked point, but Attalin refused to concede.

"Stop stalling," she snarled. The glow in Larkin's eyes appeared to be piercing through the haze of her magic. At this point, Kiera didn't think Attalin would be able to escape his wingspan if he managed to break her sway. Her jaw tightened and without another thought she stepped forward and placed her hand on Attalin's shoulder. A soft blue light radiated out of her fingertips. Attalin gasped as Kiera began to channel energy to her.

"Do what you need to," Kiera whispered in her ear.

Attalin lifted her head. "Calm down and tell me."

Larkin's eyes became wholly glazed again, and his wings drooped to his sides. "Yasmeen came to collect a dagger crafted by a faun a century and a half ago. The faun created the dagger to draw a being's magic out of them all at once. Legend has it that its purpose was to spill power to fuel a curse."

Attalin bobbed her head. "Did she explain how it's intended to be used during the match?"

"I mentioned one cut would wipe out their opponent's magical reserves, so she was practically guaranteeing her ally's success. Yasmeen said, 'This will secure more than a trifling match victory.' She called the dagger an insurance policy if the shifter can't be bitten. The venom would give them enough of a reaction to test if she is ready for the next great reckoning. The dagger is only to be used as a last resort."

Attalin opened her mouth to ask more but was cut off by a voice calling on the other side of the flaps. "Hello? Is anyone in?"

Kiera squeezed Attalin's shoulder. "Time to go," she murmured.

Attalin tightened her grip on Larkin. "You'll forget this interaction ever happened. All you'll remember was someone came to the tent asking if you had appointment times available. You never turned around from hanging your photo when you told them you were booked for the day. They left without another word. Now close your eyes and count to twenty before coming back to awareness."

Larkin's head bobbed sluggishly in confirmation. Kiera let go and blew out the candle. Attalin stuffed the book in her bag, and the girls hurried out of the stall. Attalin deliberately bumped into the human man on the other side of the flaps.

When she reached out to steady him, she leaned in and murmured into his ear, "You'll apologize to Larkin for being late for your appointment, and you didn't see anyone coming out of this stall." The man's eyes fogged and then cleared, as he slipped into the booth.

Kiera felt weary. It'd taken all her concentration to stay connected to Attalin. A great deal of energy had been flowing through her for Attalin to keep Larkin contained. Attalin rubbed her temples and muttered, "I should be completely depleted but only feel half drained."

Kiera gave her a tired smile. She was glad enough energy had remained within her so she wouldn't be without her magic. She looked to the place where Attalin's tiger's eye hung beneath her shirt. Maybe it was in Kiera's head, but she'd imagined the presence inside it writhing away from her when she'd been channeling to Attalin.

Attalin grasped the opal necklace. "We still have enough time not to rush, but let's get out of here."

Kiera was about to agree when she felt a tugging feeling in the pit of her stomach. "We can't leave just yet." Attalin's eyebrows shot up, but she didn't protest as Kiera followed the feeling. It led them farther into the market to a weapons display tent.

A stocky faun was polishing an axe behind the counter. Kiera scanned the space and was drawn to a small blade labeled *butterfly dagger*. The faun wiped his brow and came around the counter to her.

"Fancy that one? I made it yesterday," he said, grinning. "I swear the template came to me in my sleep, just brilliant, it is."

He took it down from the shelf and unlatched the back of the knife to show her that a small vial was hidden between the metal handles. He pointed to the blade. "It's a syringe dagger. See how the needle runs down the middle of the blade? You can see the tip at the end here, and the plunger is a part of the hilt. You can fill this vile with any brew of your choosing, and your opponent wouldn't know what hit them."

Kiera felt a stirring inside of her, and a plan started to formulate in her head. She reached into the small pouch on her wrist and dug out some of the money she'd brought with her. She handed it over to the faun. "I've never seen such a clever design. I'd be honored to take it."

His face flushed with pride, and he insisted on getting her a sheath. Kiera ran her thumb over the blue butterfly that was carved into the dagger. When the metal was unlatched, a wing sat on each side of the hilt.

She whispered down to the blade, "It's like you were made for me." It warmed a fraction in her hand. After what they'd just heard from Larkin, she was certain there was something greater at play here—she could feel it.

Attalin moved to stand beside her. "Was this a knowing?"

Kiera tilted her head. "Yes, we'll talk about it when we get back."

The faun trotted back over and shook Kiera's hand. "When you didn't haggle on the price, I could tell it made an impression on you."

Kiera smiled at him. "For something this special, I wouldn't dare."

Attalin was clutching her opal as they said goodbye to the faun. She squinted to her left and right. "Let's head this way—it's the shortest way back to the front, and we need to leave right now. We don't have very long."

Kiera grasped Attalin's hand, and they plunged into the crowd.

They made it back to the stage area without trouble but then came to a dead stop as visitors spilled into the walkways. Attalin stretched to stare over the heads of the beings in front of them. She began bouncing on the balls of her feet.

"Bad timing, the stage performances just let out for an intermission."

Kiera swallowed and wrapped her hand around her necklace. Instinct told her that they had about twenty minutes before the spell would dissipate. They'd pushed it too close. If she turned back into a shifter in the middle of the crowd, it would cause a scene that would get back to Hallowfeld.

Kiera looked around desperately and murmured under her breath, "I'm not sure if you can hear me, but we could use some help." Nothing happened, and another precious minute ticked by. Shop owners on either side of them were using the gridlock to their advantage, showcasing their goods to the captive audience.

Attalin's attention had been drawn to a witch right next to them with a counter full of imbued stones. She called out, "Get a glimpse of these celebration stones. A spell from my collection is guaranteed to put any gathering over the top!"

The witch proceeded to show an interested orc a small-scale version of what one of her stones could do. She'd produced a miniature firework show behind her counter. It gave Kiera an idea. A solution could be within one of these booths. She turned in a circle and stared back the way they'd come. There had to be a stall somewhere with magic that could get them out of here unnoticed. If goblins could fade out of the market, maybe there would be one willing to take them. At the very least, there must be an enchantment that offered something similar.

Kiera felt a tugging in her veins to head farther back into the market, and she knew she was right. Attalin was facing the witch's table when Kiera turned back and caught her hand. "We have to go back this way."

Attalin's eyes widened. "Are you sure?"

Kiera put her hand on her chest. "We'll never make it if we go toward the front."

Attalin chewed her lip and stared at the mass of unmoving bodies ahead of them. "Alright."

The two pushed their way backward. The crowd thinned as they moved farther away from the stage. They raced down the line of stalls on their left until Kiera felt the pull grow. She stopped short in front of a large cubicle. "Here," she said breathlessly.

They peered in. It looked to be a gallery. There were patrons admiring a statue of an alary in the center of the room. Its golden wings were flared wide, its arms raised in a V above its head. Kiera and Attalin stepped inside. She hastily scanned the room hoping to see a goblin among the customers but was disappointed. None of the patrons evoked the stirring pull that'd brought them here. Kiera had the sinking feeling that she'd misinterpreted the message from her magic. Had she made the knowing up out of desperation?

She pivoted to Attalin to share her concern, but the framed piece behind her stopped Kiera short. It was a depiction of Etabon's mountains and rolling hills, but it looked so alive. She took a step closer and all at once she understood the artwork around them was made out of foliage. It made sense now why the wings of the alary statue looked so silky and delicate. They were golden leaves, and these framed hills were made out of real moss. She knew whose gallery this was.

She scoured the room again, and this time she saw him. Xavier was stepping out from behind a curtain made up of thousands of multicolored leaves that partitioned off the back of the cubicle. His eyes met Kiera's, and he gave her a friendly smile. The pull of her magic fluttered in her stomach, and he crossed the room to her.

He cocked his head to the side and emitted a surprised laugh, saying, "Hello there. This is going to sound bizarre coming from a stranger, but I saw you in a dream last night."

Kiera grinned. "Honestly, that's not the wildest thing I've heard today. I think I'm here to ask for your help."

Xavier's eyebrows lifted, but he didn't seem opposed. He pointed to the curtain. "Let's talk in the back."

They trailed him to it, and he held it open for them to enter. Kiera's shoulder brushed his on her way past, and he gave a subtle jolt. There was a small worktable with neat copies of sales slips and sketchbooks behind the partition. It looked to be where he created his drafts and finalized his transactions with his customers. Xavier plucked a small figurine off a narrow standing shelf and handed it to Kiera. The figurine was a combination of black and gold petals and was a perfect rendering of her shifter form.

He blinked shyly at her. "This is for you."

Kiera locked eyes with him. He put his hand to his shoulder. "I recognize your magic—I felt it just now. It has a distinct effervescent quality."

Attalin straightened, and Kiera could see in her eyes that she was considering using her powers on him. "I won't tell another soul about this. You're safe with me," he breathed.

Kiera's magic buzzed in her veins, and she smiled at him. "I believe you." Attalin's posture relaxed, and Kiera whispered, "Xavier, we don't have long—we have to leave immediately. Is there a way you can help us?"

His eyes lit up, and he nodded. Xavier crouched down and put his hand to the packed dirt floor. The surface trembled as he called to his powers. A moment later, a tunnel appeared in the ground. "The fabric is impenetrable, but no one said anything about not going under it. I use this passage sometimes when the market's overcrowded, but I've never shared it with anyone else. It'll let you out in the back of one of the storage tents behind the market."

Attalin still looked skeptical but said, "Thanks. I'll go first."

Kiera turned to Xavier and embraced him. "I won't forget your kindness."

To her astonishment, he squeezed her back, saying, "And I haven't forgotten yours. You saved my life in more ways than one that day. I was considering becoming one of Hallowfeld's followers. My life flashed before my eyes, and when you pulled that blade out, I decided on a different direction. Thank you for helping me change my path."

Kiera stepped back and lowered herself into the tunnel. "The one you chose for yourself is beautiful."

He chuckled and said, "I'm glad we found each other. By the way, you smell much better than the last time we met." Kiera and Xavier's laughs echoed through the tunnel as she hurried away. The passageway was wide enough that once she was within it, she could stand upright and sprint to the end. When she reached the far side, she looked up and saw Attalin squinting into the opening. She reached down to grab her hand. When Kiera had climbed out and stepped aside, Xavier's magic closed up the tunnel.

They moved toward the storage tent's exit, snaking their way through stacked chairs and tables. Attalin was clasping her necklace, shaking her head. Her face drained of color. "We're going to have to make a run for it. Gabby said to enact the topaz five minutes out from our tent, but we'll have to do it sooner. These opals won't make it to the five-minute mark."

Kiera whispered, "Get us as close as you can. I have an idea on how to handle it from there."

Attalin kept her grip on her opal to keep track of the waning spell. She intertwined her other hand with Kiera's, and they stole out of the tent. It took Attalin less than a second to orient herself, and then they began racing back toward the lodging quarter. Kiera matched Attalin, step for step, as they thundered over the gravel path whipping around other guests.

Attalin's breath rasped out of her, "It's fading. Up there." She pointed at a grouping of dressing tents off to their right.

Attalin heaved them into the narrow space behind the tents. It was stacked high with pallets of boxed clothing, and they dove behind one of the flats. Attalin snatched the topaz from the satchel, saying, "From here, I'd say it'd take seven minutes to get back."

Kiera noticed sweat had curled the hairs around Attalin's temples, and they were starting to lighten to her natural color. They enacted the stone, and the bronze hue took hold.

Kiera said, "Alright, jump on," crouching down so Attalin could get on to her back.

She let out an incredulous laugh but didn't waste time climbing on.

Kiera hiked Attalin's knees up on either side of her and stood easily. By the time they squeezed back out from behind the tents, they were back to their true forms. Kiera had been holding back before so Attalin could keep pace with her, but now she let all her power surge through her legs. The wind whistled in their ears as she hurtled toward the tent. She kept time in her head, counting off the seconds. Attalin had flattened herself on Kiera's back, her mouth close to her ear to quietly whisper directions and encouragement.

Kiera's heart leapt when the tents came into view. They were going to make it. She pushed herself even harder, picking up speed. Her sharp eyes spotted Nash a few paces ahead in between two tents keeping watch on theirs. She must have resumed her post after transporting Yasmeen to Hallowfeld. Kiera couldn't slow for risk of reappearing any moment now, but that meant they'd blow through the tent flaps.

She hissed, "Nash is going to see the tent flaps burst open."

Attalin shifted around on her back. "No, she won't. It's going to get loud, but don't stop running."

Attalin muttered a word that sounded like "ignite," and then Kiera heard a thundering crack split the air ten feet behind them. When they passed by Nash, her mouth was hanging open, and she was facing away from them toward the booming sound. Kiera lunged through the tent flaps. As their bodies hit the ground, the invisibility spell dispersed. The impact knocked the air out of Kiera. Attalin crawled over to the bookcase that held the tourmaline and pulled it out with trembling hands.

She activated it, and Kiera choked out, "What was that out there?"

Attalin sat with her back against the bookcase. "A fireworks display. I bought one of those celebration stones off that witch in the market. I nearly set it off then and there to scatter the crowd, so we could get out."

Kiera rolled over onto her back and stared up at the tree chandelier. The room was tilting a bit. "That would have been mayhem. I'm glad you saved it. It was much better as a diversion here."

Attalin wiped sweat from her forehead. "I had a feeling it would come in handy. You're not the only one who can tune in to your knowings."

UNLEARNING

Kiera startled awake. Her dreams had been frenzied. A fox had been leading her down a winding path, its thorny underbrush catching at them like fangs. They'd made it through unscathed and had come to a pulsating ruby, but when she'd reached down to collect the stone, it'd scalded her hand. She'd turned to the fox in confusion, and its eyes held an aching pain that took Kiera's breath away. Without words, Kiera understood what the fox was asking her to do. She'd taken a rock in her blistered hand and brought it down, shattering the ruby. The burst of light it'd released had flung her into consciousness.

Kiera blinked up at the canvas ceiling and flexed her hand to settle herself. She vaguely remembered dragging herself to the cot and agreeing with Attalin that they needed a rest. It felt like she'd slept longer than an hour. The clock on top of one of the bookcases confirmed her nap had bled into the late afternoon. Attalin was at the table, studying an open book. Kiera wondered when she'd gotten up. Her eyes connected with Kiera's, sensing her stare.

"Feeling better?" Attalin asked.

Kiera stood and stretched her arms up. "The room isn't spinning anymore."

She joined Attalin and scanned the stacks of books layering the table. The tourmaline sat atop a pile closest to them.

"You've been busy."

Attalin smirked and whispered to the stone before saying, "I've been up for an hour or so. I have a shift at the bar tonight and wanted to see if I could find anything more on Larkin's dagger before heading out."

Kiera tensed. "Did you?"

She closed the book in front of her. "No, I can't find any mention of it in the books that I can read. Some of Gabby's collection is in an old language I can't decipher, but she should be back soon."

Attalin was toying with the frayed edge of the book's cover. "I'm not sure what came over me at the market earlier. I was so sure I could get the information out of Larkin without trouble. He'd nearly burned through my sway when you stepped in." Attalin locked eyes with her. "I'm sorry I forced you to use your powers in public."

Kiera nudged her knee with hers. "With that quelling candle and your skills, it's like it never happened. I'm pretty sure you could've convinced Larkin he was a pigeon if you'd really wanted to."

A small smile graced Attalin's lips, but she still looked wilted. "What if his memories somehow come back when he's on the other side of the border? When someone's memory is altered, the effects don't normally wear off, but what if they did?"

Kiera knew this was likely where her thoughts were drifting. "I doubt he'll be leaving Etabon anytime soon. Plus, we were in different forms. The only way he could trace our abilities back to us is if he managed to track down and ask the select few people who know about them." Kiera's tail flicked for emphasis. "By doing that, he'd risk exposing his fault in spilling Hallowfeld's secrets. He's the Jackal, remember? I can imagine the only thing more valuable to him than his reputation is his life."

Attalin let out a tight breath. "True, admitting his part in it would destroy his client base, not to mention what Hallowfeld would do. So, you think it was the right move?"

Kiera reached into Attalin's satchel next to her as she said, "We're a team. I trust your judgment." She pulled out Xavier's figurine and the butterfly dagger and set them on the table. "I have a feeling everything happened exactly as it was supposed to today."

Attalin carefully picked up the sculpture and admired it. "He did an excellent job. He even has your one white whisker on this side."

Kiera brushed the whiskers on the left side of her face. There *was* a white one among them. It was funny the little details that Attalin noticed about her. "He may have a photographic memory or... maybe he dreamed about me. Did you hear him say he'd dreamed about seeing the werewolf form from the masking spell? We didn't even know before this morning what I'd look like."

"Yes, I heard that. Dreams really are a powerful gateway." Attalin's words stirred something inside of Kiera about her own dream. She launched into retelling it. When she finished, she noticed Attalin's eyes had settled on the butterfly dagger.

"Did it seem like a message about tomorrow?" Attalin asked.

Kiera studied her hand. There was no pain, but it tingled with the memory of the blisters. "It gave me the impression that I need to get rid of Larkin's dagger. If it can discharge anyone's magical reserves in one cut, it can't be meant for good. Do you think it's possible to destroy it?"

Attalin pressed her lips together. "Larkin mentioned a faun created it. I'd imagine it would be like any other faun-crafted weapon. If you alter them from their original form, they lose their magic."

"So, if I manage to break it, it'll become useless?"

Attalin's eyebrow twitched. "Yes, but I hate that you even have to go near it. If what he said about a blood sacrifice and curse are true, it's far beyond anything we've dealt with. There's little known about warping magic for those kinds of purposes. It sounds like there's some dark and twisted energy powering it."

Kiera's ears flattened against her head. She considered mentioning Attalin's tiger's eye but instead said, "I don't like the sound of 'the next great reckoning.'"

Attalin rubbed her eyes. "I wish we hadn't been interrupted. I wanted to ask Larkin what that meant. I can't find reference to it in any of these books either."

The words had filled Kiera with indescribable dread. "Whatever it is, Hallowfeld and his followers are clearly after my powers to make it a reality. So, I won't produce the reaction they want tomorrow. That should interfere with their plans and buy us more time to get to the bottom of this."

Attalin leaned toward her. "You'll have to destroy the dagger without being cut."

Kiera said, "Larkin told us that Devland will use it as a final option. My plan is to steal it away from him before he decides he needs it. He'll be so focused on infecting me with his venom at the start, that he won't anticipate it."

"Right, but once you take out the dagger, his only option will be to poison you. If your plan is to avoid revealing your powers, you'll need to beat him before he can infect you."

Kiera shook her head. "I need Hallowfeld to witness that the venom doesn't affect me."

Attalin's face flushed. "Devland's no genius, but he's not a first-time fighter either. You won't be able to trick him into thinking he's bitten you."

Kiera's tail flicked. "What if it's not a trick?"

Attalin narrowed her eyes. "Wait, you mean let him bite you? How do you plan on stopping the side effects?"

Kiera lifted the butterfly dagger, balancing it in her palm. "With this."

She opened up the dagger and pointed to the vial. "I can use it to inoculate myself against the venom right when the match begins."

Attalin took the knife, her eyes widening with understanding. "You'll carry the antidote into the ring with you."

Kiera nodded. "Exactly. Devland can land a bite, and I'll wait just long enough to show I have no magical reaction, and then I'll beat him. We'll be able to destroy the dagger and manipulate Hallowfeld into thinking I don't have the power he's looking for."

Attalin stared at her. "This is an insane plan."

"Do you have a better idea? If I don't do it this way, what's stopping Hallowfeld from dragging me into the ring in the middle of the night and doing it anyway? Right now, he believes he has the element of surprise. We won't get another chance like this."

Attalin's voice wavered. "This could go very wrong. What if Devland resorts to the dagger earlier than you expect, or your knife malfunctions and you can't inoculate yourself?"

Kiera cocked her head to the side. "I've trained for months to anticipate situations like that. I can handle myself."

Attalin crossed her arms over her chest. "I trust in your abilities, Whiskers, but Devland is coldblooded."

Kiera paused. "Do you think I can beat him?"

Attalin dipped her chin. "It'll be challenging, but yes."

"That's what matters. What I know in my bones is that I have to do this. My magic hasn't led me wrong yet."

Attalin's fingers brushed the knife. "I hope you're right. The antidote will have to brew overnight. Gabby has everything here for it, but we'll have to ask her if she can even assist you in making it. This is a bit of a gray area. The butterfly dagger is your weapon, so what's inside of it will be as well, but the tournament rules state you can't have outside assistance in the matches. Which means you may have to make the antivenom yourself."

Kiera glanced around the room at the books and jars of dried plants interspersed among the crystals on the shelves. She hadn't thought of that. At that moment, the garnet bracelet on the table started flashing white.

Attalin looked relieved. "Perfect timing, that should be Gabby."

No one entered the tent though. Instead, a high-pitched voice called hello from the other side.

Attalin and Kiera exchanged a puzzled look. Kiera snatched up the tourmaline and whispered to it, while Attalin went to the entrance and peeled back the canvas. A pixie waved at her. His translucent wings beat against the air as he hovered in place.

"Hello, Aspen," Attalin said.

"Hi there. Gabby asked if I could stop by and let you know that Hallowfeld has her and some of the other witches working late tonight. They're preparing for tomorrow's matches, so they'll be expected to bunk at the arena. She said she'd see you there tomorrow evening."

Attalin's hand tightened on the canvas in her grasp, but her voice was calm when she replied, "Thank you for delivering the message, Aspen." He gave her a friendly nod and then fluttered away.

Attalin let the flaps fall shut and cursed. Kiera muttered to the stone and set it back on the table.

"This isn't the first time he's had Gabby work into the night before, but this feels intentional. He's trying to isolate you, so you'll be less prepared for the match."

Kiera realized that without the antidote, her plan would miss its mark. She'd still be destroying the dagger, accomplishing one of her goals, but that meant Hallowfeld would come after her sooner rather than later. The point was to fail his test and buy them time while he regrouped.

Attalin glared at the clock. "I need to head to my shift soon."

Kiera gestured to the bookcases. "I'm going to try and make the antidote. If Gabby were here and told us to err on the side of caution with the match rules, I'd have to do it anyway."

Attalin bit her lip. "It wouldn't hurt to try. If it doesn't turn out, you could fill the vial with a less complicated brew and use that on Devland instead."

Kiera nodded. "I'll search for a sedative mixture if I can't make the antidote."

Attalin snorted, "For him, I was thinking more along the lines of poison. Do you have experience in making tinctures?"

Kiera rubbed the back of her neck. "Actually, I do. We usually didn't have the money for store-bought medication. So, my mom and I would make tonics and salves from our windowsill garden."

Kiera averted her eyes to the books covering the table. She pictured her mother's elegantly penned recipes, her handwriting just as meticulous as the instructions themselves.

"She has an absurd attention to detail. I received high marks at academy because she passed some of that on to me."

Attalin grinned. "We'll have to see if you can teach me. I'm the worst at following instructions—I tend to improvise. I've made more than one batch of salty cookies."

Kiera's lips twitched up, but her smile faded as she watched Attalin stand and gather her things to go.

"I hate that I can't come with you."

Attalin reached over and smoothed the fur on Kiera's shoulder. "You've got the harder task. I just have to babysit a bunch of liquored-up snobs. Plus, Gabby gave me this before you got up this morning."

Attalin plucked a bracelet off the nearest bookcase. It was deep blue with veins of gold running through it. She pushed it onto her upper arm and pulled her sleeve down over it.

"It's lapis lazuli imbued with a ricochet charm. If someone at the bar tries to use magic on me, it'll rebound the energy back onto the caster."

Some of the tightness in Kiera's chest lightened at that. She stood and gave Attalin a hug.

She squeezed her back tightly and said, "We'll figure this out, Whiskers. I'll be back in the morning. We can finalize the plan then."

Attalin grabbed her satchel and strode to the flaps.

"Good luck," Kiera said.

Attalin gazed over her shoulder and winked, "Back at you."

Kiera caught a glimpse of the purpling sky as Attalin left. She turned back to the table. Since she was alone, she picked up the tourmaline and stowed it in its compartment, then rifled through the bookcases until she found the volume she was looking for. It was the book Gabby summoned yesterday to explain the werewolf's venom. Kiera ran her finger down the page that listed the ingredients for the antidote. She recognized a few, like turmeric, coneflower root, and grapeseed oil, but the other six herbs were unfamiliar to her. She gathered them from the shelves and collected a scale, pestle and mortar, and pot from the kitchen.

Kiera's movements were fluid as she settled into the familiar rhythm of preparing the plants. She ground up the putty vine leaves and false daisy and dropped them one after the other into the pot with the powdered king of bitters and velvet bean she'd measured out. Each of the nine components had to be added in order. She held the dropper over the pot, keeping her hand steady as she released the beads of physic nut oil. The final element was butterfly pea flower. Once it was combined, the whole mixture needed to be soaked in grain alcohol. As she poured in the liquid, the flowers swirled to the top, dyeing the solution a bright shade of cobalt. Something about the whirling petals caused a distant memory to surface in Kiera's mind.

She was maybe five years old, sitting on the counter in their tiny kitchen, trembling. Rose was steeping violet tea. The delicate flowers tinted the water a light blue. Kiera had a nightmare that she'd lost her mother and couldn't find her no matter how hard she'd searched.

Rose had held her while she sipped the tea and whispered, "Don't be afraid. No matter what, I'll always be with you—in here," touching the space above Kiera's heart. "Just like my mother is with me." Rose had patted the same spot on her chest. "It's easier to face hard things when we remember we're not alone." The tea, coupled with her mother's caresses, had lulled her back to sleep that night.

Kiera drew in a ragged breath and took a step back before the tears rolling down her cheeks could fall and ruin the concoction. The recollection had torn open a cavity inside her chest, letting all the ease she'd felt seep out. A great deal had changed since that night. She'd been sure that she could prevent that loss by censoring the abnormal parts of herself. Her plan had been to stuff her desires deep down—then she and Rose could survive in peace. She'd thought if she could only curate an ordinary existence, they'd be safe from the board. That diamond bracelet had been their ticket to a predictable life.

When she'd stumbled into Etabon, she'd brought about her greatest fear, but she'd also found Attalin. Kiera realized that she'd been sleepwalking through life—her bond with Attalin had awoken something in her. It'd forced her to let someone else in, and now she couldn't stop collecting people she cared about. Kiera's body was wracked with an intense sob. The pain was so sharp all she wanted to do was close her eyes to it again. The more people you love, the more pieces your heart can shatter into when they're taken from you.

When it was just her and Rose, she'd gotten comfortable with the idea that they'd go unnoticed by the board. Even with their careful planning, her mother had fallen into their hands. In the end, it didn't matter what your status was or how obedient you seemed to them, it was all an illusion. If you had something they wanted, they could come to collect at any time. No words were truer when it came to someone like Hallowfeld. By some twisted turn of fate, he was infinitely more evil than the board. Kiera sensed he would devour every ounce of happiness she'd found in this life.

She slumped into the chair nearest her, fearful of why this memory had come up. She stared into the liquid, trying to collect herself. She would know if something happened to her mother. Major news like the passing of a board member's relative would reach her even here. A part of her believed she'd sense that devastation if it came to pass.

This felt different. So, what was gnawing at her? Maybe it was the absolute recognition that while the Ruling Board was in control, the people she loved would never be safe, and Hallowfeld was a horrific extension of the board. Rose was at their mercy, and if she freed Attalin from Hallowfeld, in reality, all of them would live as prisoners either inside or outside of Etabon. Kiera rubbed her face, then let her hands drop to study her reflection.

Tears were tracked through her fur, but she still looked fierce. Her body appeared to be stronger than she felt inside. Kiera watched herself in the serum. Hadn't she been brave today? She'd trusted her instincts, and they'd succeeded. Her wild, orb-like eyes peered back at her. Her mother had known that she'd manage here without her somehow. Kiera brought her hand up to rest above her heart and stilled, breathing in the woodsy smell of the brew. She let her eyes fall shut. A thought occurred to her, and she let out a noise somewhere between a sob and a laugh.

She realized now what her mother had been trying to explain all those years ago. The ones we love are always with us. Kiera's grandmother was gone, but she lived on in the wisdom she'd passed on to Rose. It was the same knowledge that Rose had lovingly poured into Kiera. No one could take that from her. Her mother didn't have to be here beside her to know what she'd say.

"My love, look inside. You're stronger than you know. I'm not lost, and neither are you. This is all leading to the same destination." Her mother had faith in her; she'd believed Kiera could meet what was coming with courage. Hadn't she raised her to do so? Kiera had grown up with one foot in two different worlds. The meek and the renegade. It was time to make the choice between who she was and who she'd been pretending to be. That was it then—she had to let part of her past fall away. The decision was hers. Her mother had known all along that she wouldn't be alone here. She was never meant to face this life on her own. Love. That's what would make her strong.

Kiera opened her eyes, thinking of Attalin and all the other incredible beings who'd guided her on this journey. She'd need those bonds to face whatever was next, and she'd be ready. The hair on the back of her neck bristled—she was done living a fragmented life. Done believing that playing by the rules of those in power could serve anyone other than them. There was no amount of shrinking or conforming that could protect her loved ones. Kiera was done hiding who she was to fit into a system that wouldn't accept her. To reach lasting safety, they'd have to find a new path.

Her thoughts turned to Imena and her act of defiance. She'd connected an entire stadium, and something about that had shaken Hallowfeld to his core. She'd proven to Kiera that one being could make a difference, even if it was just for a fleeting moment. Kiera felt her magic eddying in her veins. She knew in every fiber of her being that change was coming for Etabon. Kiera wiped away what remained of her tears and placed the lid on the pot. She carried it over to the kitchen counter and pushed it back against the wall. For now, she'd have to wait for the elements to settle, but tomorrow was a new day.

FRACTURED

Kiera crept around the tent on silent feet. Nook and Jasper were curled up together at the end of her cot, watching her. The other girls had left for the day, but Attalin's curtain was still drawn shut. With the enchanted shade in place, she wouldn't disturb her, but it was hard to break old habits. Late last night, Jade and Viv had come home looking as bone tired as Kiera felt. Jade had assured her that it'd been an ordinary night at the bar. Hallowfeld hadn't been by and Attalin had been fine when she'd left. After that, Kiera had fallen into a deep, dreamless sleep. She'd only woken once close to dawn to watch Attalin slip into the tent. She'd stopped by one of the bookcases to deposit her bracelet and consult the labradorite. When she'd noticed Kiera's eyes were open, she'd shaken her head and ruffled the fur on her cheek.

She smiled at the thought. Kiera made a pot of tea and hauled a microscope over from one of the shelves. As she sipped from her mug, she read the directions on how to verify if the antidote worked. It was straightforward enough.

She took a dropper full of the solution to test on some werewolf venom that Gabby kept in an amber vial. Kiera peered through the microscope at the clear bead of venom on the slide. She inhaled as she released the blue drop of serum over it. If it worked, the mixture would turn purple. If not, then it'd become a curdled black mass. Her heartbeat drummed in her ears as she watched the two drops mingle. Her next moves hinged on this dot. When the liquids merged into a bright shade of violet, she leaped up and did a silent victory dance.

"That must be good news," came an excited voice from the other end of the room.

Kiera spun around. "You're up!"

Attalin gave her a sleepy smirk. Her hair was tousled, and she was watching Kiera through a gap in the curtain. She shoved them open.

"You were so focused it was hard to tell if you were even breathing. I didn't want to throw you off."

Kiera grabbed the tourmaline, her mug of tea, and another cup for Attalin. She carried it to her, and Attalin scooted over so they could sit side by side on the bed propped up on her pillows.

"It works," Kiera said.

Attalin leaned into Kiera's shoulder and replied, "Your mom is going to be proud."

Kiera let herself relax against her warmth. She liked how Attalin had talked about her mother like she genuinely believed they'd be back together soon. Attalin was rolling the stone in her hand.

Kiera gestured to it. "We've used that a lot."

Attalin set it down next to them. "It still has plenty of energy in it. Speaking of energy, I hope I didn't keep you up when I came in this morning. You'll need all your strength today. Even without the venom's effects, taking a bite from a werewolf will be tough."

Kiera tilted her head back on the pillow. She thought of her drills with Wrenley. They'd had sessions on some frigid mornings, before dawn, where she'd been thrown into the lake, and then he'd pushed her to train through the burning numbness. On one occasion, she'd fallen from the course, and he'd had to pop her shoulder back into place. He'd taught her how to focus through pain, mastering it into a dull throbbing. Still, this would be the real test of his coaching. Kiera interlaced her hand with Attalin's.

"A part of this match will be mental. That's where I have Devland beat. He's fighting for Hallowfeld's cause, but I'm fighting for something bigger," Kiera said.

Attalin studied her with bright eyes. "If Devland knew better, he wouldn't show up today." She let out a breathy laugh and laid her head on Attalin's shoulder.

"Really, Kiera, I can sense it—you're stronger than before."

Kiera smiled softly. "Who knows what'll happen if I beat another one of Hallowfeld's followers? We could start a full-blown movement this time around."

Kiera spent the rest of the day preparing. Attalin had confirmed that Hallowfeld hadn't shown up at the bar last night. Although, she'd overheard a patron gossiping that he was skipping his typical socializing to host an exclusive gathering at his manor. If that were true, Kiera had to imagine it was no ordinary get-together. She guessed that he'd make a move right after the outcome of the match. If he'd rallied his followers last night, it reinforced that hunch.

She stretched out her tense muscles and even meditated to center herself. She needed to be sharp for the match. Attalin had explained that in order to avoid suspicion, she'd need to end the fight within fifteen minutes of being bitten. Once infected, most beings started showing signs of pain immediately; hallucinations followed that, and by a quarter hour, the venom would dispatch its victim.

Kiera ran through the fight in her head and practiced with the butterfly dagger. It was unlikely she'd fight with it, but she needed to manage holding it at a natural angle so she could discreetly inoculate herself. Before she knew it, the clock on the bookcase trilled that it was time for them to head to the arena. She dipped the dagger's edge into the serum and filled it with the dose needed for her size, nearly the entire vial. She and Attalin stood in front of the tent flaps, her hand on the canvas.

"Ready?" she asked.

Kiera rolled her shoulders back and nodded.

When they stepped out, the sun was low in the sky, casting their shadows across the grass like toppled ink. They made the trek to the arena in silence. When the obsidian gates came into view, Kiera could feel her magic rumbling awake in her chest. Her match was the last slated for the day, so the stadium was teeming with guests. A stillness fell over the warmup area as they crossed to her assigned spot.

Kiera halted when she came to the starting line outside of her contestant tent. Enchanted drums had been set up in front of the stage. Their beat thundered through the stadium, sending reverberations through the pads of Kiera's feet up through her spine. She gazed up into the crowd and saw Hallowfeld standing behind a podium situated on his balcony. His maroon suit looked like a bloodstain against the white marble terrace. Hallowfeld's head was angled toward them, but he made no move to leave his perch. He was keeping his distance today. Attalin touched Kiera's shoulder, and she turned to her.

"Kiera, I need to tell you something." Attalin swallowed. "Before we met, I think I'd been secretly wishing for you. I felt so guilty about that the first time you were here. It's like I'd summoned you here with those dreams, but if I'm being honest, I'm thankful for the stars that aligned so we could find each other. I didn't want to admit this before, but for the first time in a long time, I'm hopeful for what's next." Attalin embraced her. A swell of emotions burst through Kiera, and she clutched her back tightly.

"You've got this, Whiskers," Attalin said into the fur on her neck.

Before she could find her voice, a cheer echoed through the stands. She looked over her shoulder to see the red smoke rolling across the sky above the middle ring, beginning to spell out her name. Kiera stepped back and tucked a few loose strands of hair behind Attalin's ear. She straightened her spine and walked toward the pit. The sun had dipped below Etabon's western hills. Golden orbs began flickering to life to light the arena, floating within the pit and throughout the stands.

Hallowfeld's voice boomed across the arena, "Settle, settle, friends. The time has arrived for today's promised finale. It's the match we've all been waiting for. My lone Lynx will be facing… Huxley Olinder's mighty wolf!" Huxley stood beside him at the podium, waving to the stands.

Devland erupted from his contestant tent, a mass of silver fur. Hallowfeld had concealed him until the last moment. Kiera flashed her fangs. He'd been the wolf that'd delivered her to Hallowfeld's tent when she'd fallen through the gates.

"I believe this will be a show we'll never forget."

The stadium trembled with applause.

"Good luck, competitors. Here's to hoping Etabon's magic shines on you with mercy." Hallowfeld's irreverent words weren't lost on Kiera.

She looked toward the rising moon and breathed, "Let your magic flow through me."

Like electricity, she felt the ripple of magic surge around her, prickling her fur. Kiera unleashed her claws and let them kiss the dome's metal as she stalked toward her entrance. Sparks flew into the air, and the roar of the crowd crescendoed through the stadium. Attalin had jogged over to join Gabby at the witches' station. When Kiera's foot brushed the pit's sand, she felt a tickle confirming her bargain with Hallowfeld. Gabby was holding Attalin under the arm, and she had her hand pressed against her chest. So, she'd felt it too. At sunrise, she'd be free.

As the cage closed behind Kiera, she focused her attention on the threshold across the way. Devland passed through, bristling with violence. He was double her size, and his orange eyes glowed with an eerie light that mirrored the moon's. The dome sealed closed after him, and the sounds of the crowd fell away. When he came to his mark, he let out a chilling howl. Kiera flattened her ears and gave him a cool look.

That's when she noticed the dark sheath wrapped around his waist, the top of the dagger peeking out. She kept her hand wrapped around the pommel of her own blade. Unlike Devland, she'd carried her weapon in uncovered. She took her mark, angling the tip of the blade toward herself. The metal pressed against her outer thigh. Devland rotated his shoulders and pulled his lips back in a silent snarl. She kept her breaths slow to steady her heartbeat.

When the trumpet sounded, she slowly pushed the palm of her hand down into the plunger. There was a prick of pain and then she felt the serum coursing into her muscle. She and Devland watched each other for who would make the first move. She flicked her tail back and forth restlessly to keep his attention trained there. His patience snapped, and he charged toward her. Kiera needed to finish administering the dose, so she held her ground. A second before he closed the distance between them, her hand went flat against the hilt, and she spun out of his way. His jaws snapped around the space where her head had been. She crouched in the sand and smiled at him. His eyes narrowed.

He came at her slowly this time, pacing left and right as he wove back toward her, trying to herd her against the ring's wall. A twitch of his ears gave him away before he lurched at her again. This time she dove low to avoid him, but the impact knocked her knife out of her hand. It flew through the air and stuck in the sand, hilt up, a couple of feet from them. Devland laughed darkly at her, but it'd freed up Kiera's hands, so she let her claws slide free.

They circled each other warily. Then Devland brought his foot forward to kick sand at her. She blocked most of it, but some grit still found its way into her eyes. She knew what would follow. He tore toward her, but instead of falling back, she crouched and dove forward. Devland wasn't anticipating it, and his torso slammed into her shoulder. She leaned into his momentum, her legs straining as she rolled him over her back to crash on the ground.

Before he could regain his footing, Kiera turned and raked her claws across his face, narrowly missing his eye. He let out a yelp of pain, throwing up his arms to cover his face. She took the opportunity to reach for the dagger. The moment she touched it, though, a searing pain shot up her arm. She hissed and yanked her hand away instinctively, and that's when she saw it. At the top of the dagger, embedded into its hilt, was a blood red ruby.

Devland was on his feet now and his eyes widened as he realized she'd tried to steal his weapon. He let out a rumbling growl and wrenched the dagger from its sheath. He leveled the blade at her. She had to switch to the offensive before he could begin slashing toward her. She darted forward, jamming her elbow into his throat, using all her force to knock him over.

They careened into the ring's wall and slid down it together. This time she was ready for the pain when she grabbed for the blade. She caught Devland's hand in both of hers and smashed the back of the dagger against the wall with all her might. Kiera cried out as a tearing pain radiated through her shoulder. A sound like shattering glass split the air, and blinding light speared from the splintering ruby in the dagger's hilt. A breath later it exploded, blasting them away from each other. A ringing filled Kiera's ears, and the world went white.

RECKONING

Kiera tried to move her body, but it was paralyzed as if the magic that'd been released from the dagger had ensnared her. A scene flashed across Kiera's vision. With a horrifying start, she realized she wasn't seeing anything within the arena. She'd entered into some kind of dark memory state. There was a table with a crimson spell book opened to a page wet with scarlet ink that read *The Great Correction*. Kiera saw a young witch with auburn hair and coal-fire eyes imbuing a ruby as a faun hammered the ruby into the hilt of a dagger. With a sinking realization, Kiera understood it was the weapon she'd just encountered. The scene dissolved and flashed to another.

A mix of creatures had their hands placed on the dagger and they were chanting, "Human above all else."

Beside them was the young woman who'd imbued the ruby. She was clutching the crimson book and stared at something on the ground in front of her.

A man who appeared to be human took the dagger and held it to the throat of a different woman with smoldering amber eyes that marked her as a witch. Kiera recognized the witch's eyes and felt sick. She'd seen them in her dream—only then, they'd peered out at her through the face of a fox. The witch's hands were bound behind her back, and she was kneeling in the grass. The sleeve of her celestial print dress had been torn, and the matching black silk moon-and-star patterned scarf tying back her blonde hair was dirty and tattered as if she'd been caught in a struggle.

"You're a coward," the amber-eyed witch said.

Another wave of understanding crashed into Kiera. This was the voice that'd called her back from the darkness after her fight with Rowan.

The man spoke, "You have my word, Bren. No harm will come to them if you transform and yield willingly."

A voice cried out in the background, "Mother, no!"

The woman named Bren clenched her jaw and lifted her chin. Her eyes fell on the other witch with the book. "Odette Mona, why would you betray your people like this?"

The witch stepped forward and linked hands with the man. "It's Odette Hallowfeld now—we were married last week," he said.

Tears filled Bren's eyes. "Do you know what the consequences will be if you cleave magic from our world? Magical energy feeds the core of our planet—Atterah will crumble."

The man's eyes flashed with amusement. "Still superior, even now. You see this?" He drew the dagger away so Bren could get a look at it. "The metal that was used to create it is a bit of human ingenuity." The man ran his thumb over the blade to the ruby hilt. "Did you know magic has its own frequency? This material has the ability to direct and disrupt its impulses. It's the same metal we used in the geostationary satellites that we launched over every continent today."

Bren's brow furrowed in confusion, which delighted her captor. He let out a satisfied chuckle. "All we need now is a power source strong enough to broadcast our cure."

Bren's pupils dilated, and she studied Odette. "You're using sacrificial magic, warped magic. How could you?" The young witch's cheeks flushed, and her grip tightened on the book. Her eyes dropped away from Bren's.

"All Odette is guilty of is using magic for its only worthy purpose, to equalize all of us. It was her genius idea to bind these two materials and use you as the key." He tapped the ruby hilt. "This will channel your wretched energy to the satellites. From there they'll perpetually direct the magic streaming in from the universe away from our planet."

Bren's next words came out as a whisper, "This is madness. You're sentencing us all to death."

He grabbed her chin roughly. "You think us so simple, don't you? We're leaving one spot open for magic to pour in. Your precious sacred site houses the only vortex on the planet. Etabon will draw in plenty of magic to keep our core alive. We've left enough space between the satellites over Hytheis and Fortayne so neither satellite's range quite reaches there, but they'll contain magic on either side. One day, we'll find a way to convert magic into energy without it passing through a living organism. We'll channel it straight to the core so no being on the planet's surface is directly infected, but this will do for now."

This turned Bren's tears to fury. "Every magical form will suffer because of this, and that includes humans. It flows through you, too—it's your own hate that blinds you to that."

"Stop your lies, Bren. They won't save you," he gestured behind him, "but you still have the opportunity to protect your daughter."

A werewolf dragged a thrashing young woman forward and thrust her to the ground. Her tangled, flaxen hair fell in front of her bright golden eyes. Her face was streaked with tears, and she shook her head defiantly. When Bren's gaze met her daughter's, the love and grief surging between them was palpable.

"What'll it be? Your life is forfeit either way, but she doesn't have to join you."

"It's a bargain then, but know this, Leif—it can't last. Someday this darkness will come undone," Bren murmured to him.

Magic crackled around them, signifying their bargain. Leif sneered at her. "If that's what you need to tell yourself to die an honorable death, shifter."

He turned his back to raise his hands to the sky. "Let's embrace this tremendous day of reckoning. After today we'll all be of one body, one blood, and the world will have lasting peace. Human above all else!"

The bloodcurdling chant echoed through the crowd mixed with a handful of aching sobs. Everyone, besides Bren's daughter who was watching her mother carefully, was staring at Leif.

"Don't be afraid, I'll always be with you," Bren breathed. She dipped her chin to her chest and then gave her daughter a pointed look. The young woman returned a nearly imperceptible nod.

Leif returned and knelt in front of Bren and untied her bonds. "Give me your palms," he snarled.

She held them out to him, and he made a deep slice across them. Bren yelped and closed them into fists—blue light and blood leaked out.

"Now, recast through all the forms, and let your last one be human. Understood?"

Bren's breath caught. "You're using me to freeze them all in human bodies. The satellites will broadcast the curse and trap them in the final form I take."

A twisted grin split across his face. "Yes, Bren Porter, your death means rebirth for Atterah."

Bren closed her eyes, and a tear escaped and slipped down her cheek. She began to emit the soft blue light all over. Her body shimmered, as her form lengthened and sprouted fur. When the transformation was complete, her eyes flew open. In her place was a sleek red fox. She was an animal shifter. The transformation didn't stop there. Bren shifted through every single magical form, cycling through skin, scales, wings, and claws, ending in her human body.

Leif leaned toward Bren, blocking Kiera's view with his back. Kiera couldn't stay silent any longer—she felt herself trying to break free from this terrible nightmare. She screamed for him to stop, to have mercy, but none of these beings seemed to hear her. She watched as he drew his hand back sharply, and then Bren's body fell limply to the side. Above her body, a column of light shot into the sky and waves of energy rippled out across the field. Kiera watched in terror as the creatures assembled began to change as the waves crashed into them. The alarys' wings, the mermaids' scales, the werewolves' fur—it all burned away. Around the meadow, they transformed until every single one of them had become human.

When the light faded, Kiera saw Bren's daughter crawling toward her mother's lifeless body. "Let me just say goodbye," she whimpered.

Leif sniffed at her and waved her forward. "Be my guest, child. What's done can't be undone now—she's gone."

Kiera watched her drape her body over Bren's. She almost missed it but saw her slip a necklace off her mother. The way she was huddled over her concealed the action from everyone else's view. The necklace radiated a subtle blue glimmer. She caught a glimpse of it before it disappeared into her pocket—it was a gold pendant with etchings of water lilies on it, and in the center was a fox with its snout pointed to the sky. Kiera gasped, and then the meadow went black, flashing to a new scene.

This memory was lighter, not tinged with the darkness of the ones before. Kiera had been thrown further back in time. A much younger Bren, in her witch form, was sitting in a grove of trees with a box wrapped in parchment on her lap. Kiera recognized the clearing as the one that led to Etabon's vortex. A musical voice let out an exasperated laugh as they pushed their way through the willow branches.

"You better have a good reason for making me hike all the way out here, Red."

The smile that lit up Bren's face sent an ache through Kiera's heart. These memories were equally painful to watch knowing what Bren's fate would be.

"Lighten up, Lilypad! I've got a surprise for you," Bren called into the trees.

Kiera's mind startled at the girl who stepped into the clearing. Her bronze hair was unbound and fell to her shoulders. Her gray eyes glowed, identifying her as a witch. They danced with amusement when she spotted Bren leaning back against the trunk of a willow. This girl's resemblance to Rose was uncanny, but the shape of her nose and mouth were slightly off. If Kiera hadn't known these memories had taken place around the time magic was purged, over a century and a half ago, she would have thought twice.

"You tricky fox, what are you up to?" she said as she sank down beside her.

Bren handed over the parchment package. "Something for you. Well, for us really." With a jolt, Kiera saw the name elegantly scrawled on the package. *To: Lily Vandyer.*

Lily leaned her shoulder against Bren's and tore open the parchment. Inside were two shining gold pendants, both engraved with water lilies and the fox. Silver lined Lily's eyes.

"Oh Red, they're beautiful."

Bren pressed a spot on both pendants, and they popped open. She swallowed hard, looking like she was choking back tears of her own.

"You're the best friend I've ever had, Lilypad. I know it's going to be hard with us both traveling this year. Amos and I will be stationed in Renival, and you and Farren will be in Karveir, so I got us these to cheer us up. If you're up for it, I have a spell that goes with them."

Lily swiped at her eyes and grinned. "Yes, bring on the shifter magic!"

Bren held up a needle. "It's enchanted so this won't hurt." She pricked Lily's finger and then her own and let a drop of her blood and then Lily's fall into each locket. Bren shut the clasps and held them both, one in each hand. She mumbled quietly, and her fists radiated blue light.

When she was finished, she helped Lily put hers on, and her friend did the same for her. "These will let us sense each other's life forces. The magic is pure because they've been made from willingness and love," Bren said.

"This is brilliant, but I'm still going to miss you."

"Me too, but no matter what happens or how far we are from one another, we'll be connected. We can face anything because we'll remember we're not alone," Bren replied.

Lily placed one hand over her heart and the other over Bren's. "In this life and into the hereafter."

The grove flickered, then faded away.

Kiera's body hit the ground with a thud, and the impact thrust her back into the present. She rolled over, pressing her forehead into the sand and tried to suck air back into her lungs. What'd felt like an eternity to her had only been a few seconds in reality. Her body trembled as she tried to right her thoughts. She knew with a strange certainty that she'd been witness to distant memories that'd been locked within the dagger. Kiera pounded her fist into the sand. That was how magic had been ripped from all but one corner of their world. Attalin's ancestor Bren had been a shifter too, and Hallowfeld's forefather had sacrificed her to power that terrible curse. Now her essence was warning Kiera to stop Hallowfeld from committing some form of this atrocity again. Kiera held her fist to her heart, thinking of the bond between her ancestor and Attalin's. It was a love so strong it'd helped their descendants find each other. It was all so much bigger than she'd realized.

Kiera lifted her head to take in the arena. Her vision blurred and then cleared. There was a black stain against the ring wall, and ash rained down around her—all that was left of the dagger. She tried to stand and staggered, almost falling. A sharp pain spiked through her shoulder. She put her fingers to it and felt puncture wounds. When she pulled her hand away, there was a mix of blood and clear liquid. She stared down at it, and her mind scrambled to place it. Werewolf venom.

It came back to her. When she'd been destroying the dagger, Devland had leaned forward and bit her shoulder. Kiera stumbled forward, and her stomach flipped, as she scanned the pit for him. She needed to end this match and tell Attalin what she'd learned. While the blast had tossed her to the middle of the ring, it'd thrown Devland back against the far wall. He lay in a crumpled heap. Kiera limped over to him. His chest was rising and falling, but he seemed unconscious. She moved closer. Her heart ached as she scanned him—his prone form looked so much like Bren's lifeless body. She wasn't expecting it when he pounced at her.

His jaws snapped at her face, and they rolled together across the sand. Devland's claws shredded a gaping hole in her shoulder. Kiera roared, all her rage from what she'd seen coursing through her. Her eye's zeroed in on her knife buried in the sand beside them. She ripped it from the ground and rammed it into Devland's upper thigh with a snarl.

Blood gushed from his leg. The injury distracted him, and she was able to pin him down. His pupils were constricted, and he was trying to throw her off. Kiera didn't understand. He was so incensed he was inflicting more damage on himself. They were surrounded by a pool of his blood. Kiera needed to get out of the ring. She probably had less than ten minutes before it became clear his venom wasn't having the normal effect on her. She had to beat him. If she ripped the knife out of his thigh, it wouldn't take long. Kiera realized tears were trickling down her face. She didn't want to kill him. The thought extinguished the vicious fire seething within her.

Devland tried to bite at her legs, so she thrust her knee up into his chin and pulled his arms down toward her. A searing pain like the dagger had inflicted came from underneath Kiera's left palm. She loosened her grip on Devland to see what'd caused it. When she glanced down, she realized her hand had been covering the eclipse mark on his wrist. There was darkness in the mark. It was the echo of the icy hollowness she'd felt when Hallowfeld's magic had touched her. Kiera stared into Devland's eyes. She saw ire, but beneath that was fear and longing.

Her words from before echoed in her head. Have mercy. She wrapped her hand back around the mark on his wrist, letting his brand burn her. It took all her effort to focus a pinprick of her magic to it. She couldn't let her light leak out, so she gripped tight.

Kiera looked into his eyes. "I can't imagine the terrible things Hallowfeld's asked of you, but there's good in you. I can sense it."

Devland stilled beneath her. The otherworldly glow dimmed, and his pupils focused on her. The hair on the back of her neck bristled, and she could feel his buried grief surging between them.

Kiera choked, "You have to wake up and face this. It's never been the magic that creates chaos, we do. Let the light in your magic guide you back to yourself."

He let out a mournful whimper.

Her tears fell onto his fur. "I wish I could take that pain away, but I can't. I know it's easier to numb it, but you have to let it in. We're capable of terrible things when we shut out our feelings. They're what connects us all. It's what allows us to stand together, to hope for a better way." Images of Rose and Attalin rushed through Kiera's mind. "There's pain in them, but also joy—on the other side of this hate is love. I can't stop the hurting, but I can be here with you in it. That's what love is."

Kiera found herself moving off of Devland, the only point of contact was her hand on his wrist. She crouched beside him, but he didn't attack her. He just blinked up at her like a fog had cleared, and he was really seeing her for the first time. That's when Kiera realized she didn't have to beat him. Her bargain with Hallowfeld had never included her winning the match. He'd only said she needed to compete to satisfy their agreement. She reached over and gently took his other hand and placed his claws against her throat. They locked eyes in understanding, and he drew his claws a fraction closer to her neck. She'd set him up to inflict a clear death blow, but that didn't mean he truly had to deliver it.

Kiera tapped the sand lightly with her tail, but she didn't leave Devland's side. The ring's magic hissed in completion of the fight, signaling Devland as the victor. He tilted his head up at her.

Kiera gave him a soft smile. "Thank you for helping me choose a better way."

She didn't let go of him until the witches rushed over and pressed in between them to treat their wounds. When Kiera released Devland, the murkiness didn't return to his eyes and when she looked to his wrist, the mark had vanished. They exchanged one last encouraging look before multiple bodies separated them.

A moment later, Attalin was in front of her, tipping a cup of blue liquid into her mouth. "Drink this."

She did as she was told and swallowed the bitter liquid. Two witches hurried up to them, and Attalin nodded at them in recognition. One held her hands on either side of Kiera's head while the other cupped her hand over the wounds on Kiera's shoulders. The witch tending to her shoulder pulled out a syringe and injected it into the bite wound as well. She watched as another team of witches carried Devland away on a stretcher. Light poured from their hands into his leg.

"You can stand now," said the witch who'd been holding her head. "I'm not sure how it's possible, but you only sustained a minor concussion. I've taken care of it."

The skin on Kiera's shoulder had knitted itself back together, and there was only a slight tingling where the pain had been. The other witch cleared her as well, telling her the venom had been in her veins for about eleven minutes, but thankfully, she hadn't sustained any permanent damage. She thanked the witches, and Attalin ducked under Kiera's arm to steady her toward the exit. That's when she heard it. The entire stadium was chanting "mercy." Kiera gave Attalin a puzzled look.

Attalin raised her brows at the dome's measuring instrument. The needle was pressing off the scale's chart. "Well, you wanted to start a movement. They went wild when you spoke to Devland. At first, you could've heard a pin drop, but then the entire arena got to their feet to cheer you both on. I've never heard guests calling for Hallowfeld to be ousted from his position as the warden, but the entire stadium is now. People are saying that he's a swindler and chaos is a lie. He flipped over the champagne table in his suite, yelling about how you were a pathetic excuse for a shifter. When you tapped out, he stormed off, cursing about where the untapped power was and that all you were good for was using party tricks on the simpleminded. A bunch of his guards who were stationed in the suite and around the ring left with him. Apparently, something's got him extremely agitated."

She and Attalin exchanged a knowing look—their plan had been a success. He assumed she'd managed to manipulate Devland somehow, but Hallowfeld had been expecting much more power from her. Gabby met them at the gate, and she hugged Kiera softly. "Well done, Kiera. Well done." Gabby turned to Attalin, and Kiera watched as Gabby slipped the butterfly dagger into Attalin's satchel. It made sense now why Gabby went straight to Devland when the gates had opened.

She glanced over her shoulder. "I need to help the others tend to Devland. That blade hit an artery, so he'll need multiple caregivers to get him patched up, not to mention the concussion he's sure to have from the explosion as well. You girls get washed up but then go spend some time out."

Kiera dipped her chin. "So go celebrate in public, is what you're saying."

Gabby nodded in confirmation. "I'll be home late, but I'll be home tonight. Maybe after midnight. I'll see you two then."

She embraced them both, then jogged after her team. Attalin bit her lip. Kiera had to assume she was thinking the same thing. None of them could speak freely here. The fact that Gabby wanted them in a public space meant she thought it was safer for them to be among strangers than alone in the tent in case Hallowfeld decided to retaliate for the unrest that Kiera had caused. She decided to put all of it aside for a moment and turned to Attalin.

"How does it feel to know after today you're a free mermaid?"

Attalin's eyes brightened, and she linked her arm with Kiera's. "Like anything is possible."

26

UNBOUND

I took them longer than normal to make it back to the tent. Being on the lowest level of the stadium meant they bypassed a majority of the crowd letting out, but they were held up by well-wishing spectators. When the two of them finally dashed through the tent flaps, they were panting, and Attalin's cheeks were flushed. She rushed to the bookcase and grabbed the tourmaline, then whirled around hooting.

"Can you believe all of that? You could feel the thrill in the air." Attalin stuck her hands through her hair, tossing it wildly. "You should have seen Hallowfeld bolting out of there."

Kiera watched her with a sharp pang of bittersweetness. She didn't want to ruin this moment of joy for her. Attalin took her by the shoulders, her eyes brimming with tears.

"Kiera, the things you said to Devland..." Her voice tapered off as she looked at her with emotion that she couldn't quite place. Attalin angled her head to the side, noting Kiera's unease. "What aren't you telling me? What happened?" The harrowing images of Bren and the curse cascaded back into her mind.

"Let's sit down," Kiera said.

While she explained what'd happened to her when the dagger ruptured and after with Devland's mark, Attalin leaned forward in her chair, one hand covering her mouth. By the time she finished, Kiera was shivering.

"All this time, Bren has been guiding us, trying to help us understand. I think because of that curse, her essence is caught in between our world and whatever comes after. Leif Hallowfeld threatened her family; that's why she gave in, and he unleashed the curse on Atterah." Attalin let her hand drop.

She reached over and took Kiera's. "That's horrible you had to watch that." Kiera wrapped Attalin's hand with both of hers.

"What the Hallowfelds took from your family, our world, what one of them is still putting us through..." Kiera inhaled a shuddering breath. "Attalin, there are no words. It's like he's drawn to us like some warped cosmic magnet. Maybe it's the curse or the pendants."

Attalin let out a broken laugh. "I'd suffer him every time if it brought me you. He doesn't get to take that from us." She put her other hand on her chest. "I think it's beautiful that our ancestors had their connection, but I know in my heart we would've found each other even without Bren's help. Our bond is unique, it's our own. I bet they'd agree with me."

Kiera felt the hair on her neck rise, and she smiled. "I'm getting that impression too. Bren showed me the memory of the pendants for more than one reason. It was suffused with hope. It had deep meaning behind it... The necklaces could be the key to unlocking the curse on Atterah. She was wearing the pendant when it was unleashed, and when her daughter recovered it, it radiated blue light." Kiera hesitated. "What worries me is how the curse sustains itself if it inhibits magic."

Attalin shivered and touched her tiger's eye. "It must be feeding off the life force of everyone it touches. It has billions of hosts, so it only has to take trace amounts. This form of magic is sick."

Kiera's eyes narrowed on the tiger's eye. "Attalin, I want to try something, but I'm going to need you to trust me," Kiera said.

"With my life," Attalin replied.

"I believe I can destroy that stone."

Attalin swallowed hard and got up, her hands shaking. She went over to the bookcase and brought back a bag of salt and a bundle of sage. Kiera watched as she made a wide circle around their chairs with the salt and then lit the sage and set it in a bowl between them.

"This should protect you if it goes after you. If that happens..." Attalin trailed off.

"Don't think that way. I won't stop until you're safe and whatever is within is defeated."

Attalin's hands wobbled as she lifted the chain over her head and dropped it into Kiera's waiting palm. They both let out a pained scream when Kiera grasped it in her fist, but she didn't let it break her concentration. Kiera poured her magic into the stone, but something fought back aggressively. She could feel it now—this magic had been warped by hate and fear. It was feeding off Attalin's soul and didn't want to release her.

The dark magic drove back against Kiera, trying to shred through her focus. Kiera refused to give in; memories poured into her mind—ones of laughing with Jax and Wrenley, Gabby embracing her, holding Attalin's hand on the balcony, and her mother stroking her hair—she let them all in. Love and hope filled her mind until she was overflowing with it, and she pressed it out beyond herself, toward Attalin. In front of her, a black cloud emerged from Attalin's chest, slowly unknitting itself from her. The cloud drifted down into the stone, and Kiera's light sent azure cracks splintering across its surface. The darkness gave way to light, and then the tiger's eye turned to white dust in Kiera's hands.

Attalin fell forward off her chair onto her knees, gasping for air. Kiera slid off hers to join Attalin on the floor. They reached for each other and began laughing and crying at the same time.

When they'd settled, Attalin panted, "How did you know that'd work?"

"From Bren. Shifter's magic is about balance. If we can help generate curses, we can help reverse them, too," Kiera huffed out.

This sparked a thought for Kiera. "I wonder if my mom has any idea what she's wearing. From the memory, the magic in Bren's pendent appeared benevolent. She'd said it was pure because it was made from love, so it doesn't pull from a life force, it just forms a connection. But that doesn't change the fact that it's a powerful ancient relic."

"Don't you think she would've told you if she knew?"

Kiera pressed her palms to the floor. "A couple months ago, I'd have said yes," she said, her thoughts drifted to the gun, "but she's hidden things from me. It's hard to say what she'd do if she thought she was keeping me safe. Do you think your family still has their pendant?"

"I haven't seen it, but my father isn't exactly forthcoming about this kind of stuff. Next time I'm back in Tydden I can demand it from him and see how he reacts."

"The worst part is not knowing what information Hallowfeld has. I think he knew to look out for the blue light that shifters emit when they channel raw energy."

Attalin furrowed her brow. "It's a good thing you held back, because you didn't show signs of it in the arena. You said the spell book from the memories in the dagger was crimson?" Kiera nodded yes.

"I don't think it's a coincidence that when my father gave Hallowfeld a vision, he described a crimson book too. It sounds like Hallowfeld was reunited with his ancestor's creation and got exactly what he was looking for that night: knowledge about shifters."

A connection formed in Kiera's mind. She recalled Attalin saying something about a piece of fabric and inhaled sharply. "The stars and moon fabric that Bren was wearing in her hair when Leif sacrificed her, it was the same fabric you described Hallowfeld bringing to your dad when he was searching for the spell book."

Attalin paled. "All the pieces of the curse came together. Kiera, that's how my father must've been able to see where the spell book was. Bren's blood was on that cloth and he's her descendent. Hallowfeld's blood relative created that curse, and it was their physical connection that allowed my father to pierce through the curse enough to receive that vision."

Kiera shuddered. "Well, it's safe to say Hallowfeld has what he needs then to understand shifter magic."

Attalin breathed, "Your plan to conceal your power was more crucial than we realized."

Kiera swallowed the tears that burned in her throat. "I'm not sure how much time it'll buy us. If he's planning to unleash another curse of that magnitude, who knows when he'll come after me again? Right now, he may think I don't have the power he's after, but he could get desperate."

Attalin touched her forehead to Kiera's. "We'll get through tonight. We can go mingle with the crowd. Gabby's right—after that match, he won't make a move on you in public. We'll wait for her and then go from there. Maybe we can come up with a way to escape. I heard they let in some private hovercrafts from Fortayne and Renival today; it sounds like the board loosened some of the restrictions on the borders."

Kiera stared down at her hands, thinking of Bren's transformation. Before she realized what she was doing, her palms began radiating blue. "You're right," Kiera murmured, "I've seen the amount of power inside me, and I've slipped through his barrier around the site before. With Gabby's help, I bet we could do it again to get out. We'll need to wait until after sunrise, though, after you're free of your bargain and your family's safety is guaranteed."

Attalin blinked. "What about your mother?"

"She told me it'd be six weeks before she'd likely get to me. Hallowfeld doesn't know where she is either—he used the word 'resurface' when he referenced her status. The board's concealed the whereabouts of the medical team and Board Member Marcus's father even from him. For now, she's safe from Hallowfeld; but if he gets his hands on my powers, I don't think anyone will be. If we can get away, we'll have over a month to find out where she is and get to her before he does." Kiera's magic burned in recognition of her plan.

"Jade could get us a couple of motorized bikes. They won't be enchanted on the other side of the border, but they'll work like regular motorbikes, and they could get us to Tydden," Attalin said.

Kiera nodded. "I still have the bracelet. Maybe we could use it to bribe someone at one of the ports in Tydden, or if we can manage to get back near Mendinburrow, we could go to the bakery address, and they could get us to the deserts in Renival."

Attalin touched her cheek. "It'll be tough, but whatever we decide, I know Gabby will do everything she can to help us. Wherever you go, I'll go, and we'll sort it all out together."

Kiera stared at her with bright eyes. Before Attalin could say anything else, the garnet bracelet began flashing white.

"That can't be Gabby already," Kiera said.

Attalin stood to see who it was, and Kiera mumbled to the tourmaline.

When she shoved the canvas open, she found a sapphire envelope hovering outside.

Kiera flinched, and Attalin glanced back at her as she reached for it. "Don't worry, it's a letter from Jade. The garnet wouldn't have flashed white if it wasn't from a friend." Kiera sighed and Attalin brought it over so she could read it.

Hurry up and get ready! Gabby told me you two are going out to let off steam. Meet us at the Twisted Tarot. Don't waste too much time, or you'll miss Viv's opening. —J

"We've been here too long already. I don't want to push our luck. We'd better get going," Attalin said as she threw back the top on Viv's trunk and began rummaging around. She pulled out a long gold dress with a slit down the side. "Viv won't mind if you borrow this, and it'll even work for your tail," Attalin said, handing it to her.

Kiera sped to the washroom. She cleaned the ash and blood off herself, brushed out her fur, and pulled on the dress. When she came back into the room, Attalin had changed into a twinkling black dress that fell just below her knees with billowy sleeves.

"You look stunning," Kiera said.

Attalin smiled and crossed to her. She slid gold bangles onto her wrists and clipped a matching necklace on her. "Almost perfect."

She snatched up her gold eyeliner and held Kiera's chin steady to apply it. She stepped back, admiring her work. "There. Now we're ready."

Attalin snapped the top back on the eyeliner and hurried over to her satchel. She pulled the butterfly dagger out and took a clear vial of liquid off the bookshelf. She set the knife down on the ground and mouthed "sorry" to Kiera as she poured a couple drops onto the weapon. They watched as the knife turned to dust, then Attalin swept it up and poured it down the sink. Kiera wasn't upset with her—she knew they couldn't leave evidence behind.

Attalin wiped her hands off and picked up her bag. "Shall we, Whiskers?"

Kiera slipped her arm through Attalin's. "I thought you'd never ask."

The sky was bright with moonlight. The two of them stared up at it, then headed down the path. Before they turned onto the main road though, Kiera was yanked back by her tail, and then she was free-falling through space.

HAPPENSTANCE

T he moon rushed back into focus, and Kiera's knees buckled underneath her. She felt lightheaded and caught herself on a tree beside her.

A gruff voice called out, "What's this, Nash? Why'd you bring the mermaid? I said just the shifter."

Kiera tried to orient herself. She was standing in a clearing surrounded by a thick ring of evergreens.

Nash huffed, "Don't blame me that they're joined at the hip. It was the only chance I had to fade her here—the other one just hitched a ride."

Patrick had his claws to Attalin's neck. He growled, "Attalin, if you try anything, Ty will skewer your friend."

Movement caught Kiera's eye and she realized a fire faerie had a crossbow trained on her. The faerie with the bow was familiar. He was the contestant that had fought Imena in the tournament. Nash must have been tailing them and used her magic to bring them here. Attalin's arm had been linked with Kiera's, so she'd accidentally faded them both. They'd been so distracted they hadn't sensed her outside the tent. Kiera looked to the eclipse brands on their wrists. They were giving off an unsettling shadowy gleam.

Patrick stared at Kiera. "What'd you do to my cousin?"

Kiera wasn't sure how to answer. She'd seen with her own eyes that his mark had dissolved, but she wasn't going to admit that. "I don't know what you're talking about. Devland was being treated by the witches after the match ended. He's going to be fine."

He tightened his grip on Attalin. "Don't spew lies at me. You know what I mean. He was rambling nonsense about being released, and now he's gone. Hallowfeld's calling him a deserter. Where is he?"

That caught Kiera off guard. Patrick wasn't accusing her of desecrating Devland's mark, he thought she'd taken him somewhere.

Kiera held her palms up. "I went straight back to the lodging district after the match. I couldn't have taken him." Patrick's hackles rose. Kiera had to stop him before he hurt Attalin. "Does Hallowfeld know you three are doing this?"

Patrick stiffened, and he exchanged a look with Nash. "The Ascendant One is troubled. He wasn't in a state to ask us, but he'll be grateful once I prove you're not entirely worthless."

Attalin snorted. "You don't know him very well if you think he'll be happy that you made a move without his permission."

Patrick pressed down harder causing a bead of blood to pool on Attalin's neck. "Silence, nonbeliever. He'll reward us and pardon Devland if I can get this done." Patrick's eyes were blazing madly when he glared back at Kiera. "This was your second transition. Your magic should've settled by now. Why aren't you showing signs of greater power? I'll rip it out of you if I have to."

Kiera shook her head slowly and spoke evenly, "My abilities haven't changed from last visit. I don't have whatever you're after. Patrick, are you really expecting forgiveness from the same man that mutilated you with those brands?"

"This emblem was bestowed on us by the Ascendant One. Only a select few receive the honor of pledging our souls to him. The fact that you turned it down makes you less than vermin," he spat.

Nash curled her thin lips back, "Enough talk. Bite her, Patrick. We'll wait a full quarter hour this time. If she's still defective, at least we'll get the satisfaction of exterminating her for the Ascendant One."

He took a step toward her his hand still firmly around Attalin's throat. That's when Kiera saw a small cream-colored being streak from the forest's edge toward Patrick. They were all facing her, so they didn't see it coming. The tiny creature latched onto Patrick's ankle. He flung Attalin forward and doubled over in pain. Right when he started howling, a tree branch crashed down on Nash's head. Kiera heard the crossbow release and dove sideways to dodge a haphazardly launched arrow. The fire faerie had been tackled by another being and was lying motionless on the ground.

Attalin moved quickly. She gripped Patrick's skull and hissed, "Sleep until dawn."

His body hit the ground with a thump. Nash was knocked out cold, but Attalin still whispered the same order into her ear. They turned to the fire faerie, who was slumped on the ground. Attalin crossed the clearing and murmured to him, too. Their rescuers stood beside one of the trees a few feet away. Kiera's breath lodged in her throat. It was Jax.

He had his hand to the tree's trunk and was repairing the damage that his magic had caused when he brought the branch down on Nash. He turned and faced them. When Kiera and Jax made eye contact, her magic reverberated inside her. She let out a breath of surprise. Its pull was more intense than before. Kiera's intuition urged her forward. His energy felt safe and familiar.

She took a step closer, peering into his autumn eyes, and said, "Hey, Jax."

Jax's mouth gaped open. "Kie? Is that you?" he said in amazement.

"Long story, but yes. The short of it is, I'm an animal shifter, and the warden is trying to keep me trapped here," Kiera said as she scratched the back of her head.

The fox trotted up, and Kiera bent down to scratch her under the chin. "I thought that was you, Thimble."

"Thimble recognizes you, but I can't remember seeing you here. I certainly feel like I would," he said.

Kiera straightened. Attalin was beside her now, her fingers brushing Kiera's. Kiera touched her chest and spoke softly to Attalin. "It's ok, they're safe. This is the friend I was telling you about at the market. Are you hurt?" She studied the cut at the base of Attalin's throat.

"I'm alright," Attalin replied.

The tension didn't leave Attalin's shoulders though and she kept her eyes on Jax. Kiera turned back to him. "I looked more like him that day." Kiera gestured to Patrick.

Recognition glinted in Jax's eyes. "You were the werewolf with the necklace. That's right, Thimble was captivated by you." He pressed his fingers to his full lips. "That makes sense why Thimble knows you even though you were under a masking spell. She remembers your energy and smell. I thought your voice sounded funny." He stepped forward and extended his hand to Attalin. "I'm Jaxon Sage—my friends call me Jax."

She took it reluctantly and said, "I'm Attalin."

He pivoted to Kiera and reached out for a hug. When they embraced, a warm surge of energy ran up her arms. "Thank you for helping us," Kiera said.

Jax surveyed the unconscious beings around them. "You should thank Thimble. We were headed back to camp when her ears perked up. She sniffed the air and then bolted. She barely took the time to communicate that we were headed toward danger. You made quite an impression on her."

Attalin's eyes narrowed. "Seems like a roundabout way to get back to the lodging quarter."

He shrugged. "Thimble's more at ease in the woods, and if I'm being honest, so am I."

Attalin crossed her arms. "I'm grateful that you two intervened, but under the circumstances, it seems like a strange coincidence. Would you mind if I verified your intentions?"

Kiera studied the way Attalin's body was coiled with anxiety and decided it'd be best for her to trust Jax on her own terms. He gestured for her to go ahead. Attalin took his hand. "Speak the truth. Are you associated with Hallowfeld in any way? Would you harm us?"

Jax straightened. "Hallowfeld is the last person on Atterah that I'd ever align myself with. I'll never support him or his cause. I wouldn't do anything to hurt either of you. You're safe with me."

Kiera's magic flickered in her chest in agreement. Attalin looked over her shoulder at her, confirming he'd passed her test. She dropped his hand.

Kiera gestured toward the lights. "We'd better go before anyone comes looking for them."

Jax frowned down at the followers. "Can I walk you back to your tent, Kie?"

Attalin shook her head. "We can't go back yet. Our friend is a powerful witch, but until she gets back it'll be safer for us in public. Hallowfeld's followers are more likely to try something like this again if we're isolated."

Jax rubbed the back of his neck. "I think I can help with that." He closed his eyes and tipped his head back. A tawny owl swooped down and landed on Jax's shoulder, rubbing its head under his chin. He motioned for them to come closer. "This is Darrow. If you can describe your friend to him and which part of the lodging quarter your tent is in, he'll alert you when she's back and it's safe to go there."

Attalin still looked skeptical, but by the way she was studying him, Kiera could tell she didn't find him threatening anymore. Attalin hastily explained Gabby and their tent location. Darrow clicked his beak and then vaulted off Jax's shoulder back into the sky. Kiera watched him vanish into the trees.

"Will he be able to find us if we're inside a bar?"

Jax shook his head. "Don't worry, he'll make it in to wherever you go."

Kiera felt the pull of her magic twist in her stomach. "Why don't you come with us? The least we could do is get you a drink for saving us."

Attalin glanced down as Thimble leaned against her ankle. She stroked her head. "It couldn't hurt. We could use your abilities if we get into any more trouble," Attalin muttered.

Kiera smirked. It sounded like Attalin was talking to Thimble rather than Jax. He crouched down and opened the bag on his shoulder and Thimble dove in.

He smiled. "Alright, where are we going?"

Attalin was wiping away the droplets of blood from her neck with the dew off a tree branch. "The Twisted Tarot."

Jax's eyes brightened. "That's my kind of place."

Attalin's eyebrows twitched up. She was starting to thaw toward him but slowly. The three of them headed back toward the restaurant quarter.

Jax glanced at Kiera as they went. "I overheard Hallowfeld's disciples threatening you about your powers. It's really brave that you turned down his offer to join their circle."

Kiera gazed at Attalin a few steps ahead of her. "I don't think I'm brave. I would just never dedicate myself to someone who uses and hurts people the way he does, especially the people I care for."

Jax gave her a melancholy half smile. "I understand."

Kiera felt there was more to that remark, but her ears picked up the buzz of the crowds. They were getting close to the bars.

They stepped out from the forest's edge, and Kiera stopped beside Attalin. She slipped her arm into hers. "Want to try this again?"

Attalin laughed. "Always, Whiskers."

The Twisted Tarot wasn't far from where they exited the forest. They passed a couple of large tents before Kiera saw the sign for the bar. It was a giant tarot card that hung suspended above a metallic purple tent. It was enchanted to coil and uncoil in the middle. There was a long line in front of the flaps, but Attalin called to one of the beings manning the entrance.

"Raya!" Attalin waved at the water faerie.

She motioned them forward and embraced Attalin. "Jade told me to be on the lookout for you. I'll bring you to Viv's table. Welcome," she said cheerfully to Kiera and Jax.

Raya spoke briefly with the faun beside her, then the flaps peeled back, and she led them into the bar. Kiera didn't anticipate how spacious it would be inside. She stared up at the ceiling that was swathed in a multitude of sheer colorful fabrics. Suspended in between the gauzy material were tarot cards floating in and out of view. The tent was lit with softly glowing orange orbs. Kiera felt comfortable immediately. The atmosphere was shabby and welcoming, the opposite of Nautilus, which was all polished gold ornaments and spectacle. The staff here were a diverse mix of creatures in flowing garments.

Raya stopped at a table centered to the stage right off the dance floor. A sign on it read: *Reserved for Viv's guests.*

"You missed the opening acts, but Viv's on next. Jade's up at the bar—I'll let her know you're here." Raya's arm lingered on Attalin's for a moment, then she drifted away.

Kiera felt a twinge in the pit of her stomach, oddly unrelated to her magic.

Jade came over holding a tray with five honey-colored drinks spouting green sparks. "You two push fashionably late to the limit," she said.

She laid the drinks out in front of them. Jade leaned over and handed a drink directly to Jax, pausing to look him up and down. "I'm assuming it has something to do with you. I'm Jade."

He gave her an easygoing smile. "Nice to meet you, I'm Jax. Apologies for holding your friends up—we got caught up talking."

Attalin sipped her drink and watched the exchange with amusement.

Kiera flicked her tail at Jade. "Actually, it was my fault. We ended up going off the path, and Jax walked us through the woods."

Jade side-eyed her. "Why am I not surprised it was you, troublemaker? You'll have to tell me about it later. I'll be back, I'm going to bring Viv her drink."

The three of them shared a conspirator's look. This wasn't the place to admit they'd been in an altercation with Hallowfeld's inner circle. Viv and her band took the stage. Her dress was a dazzling green mirroring the sparks shooting from the drink in her hand. The bar erupted with whistles and applause. She radiated confidence, completely in her element. Kiera and Attalin waved and shouted while Jax clapped enthusiastically. Viv approached the microphone, raising her glass at them. Her wings flared out behind her.

"Thank you. This song is dedicated to two brave souls, Imena and Kiera, for challenging what it means to be a champion. We should all embrace change and show each other some love. Let's rise up!"

A jolt went through Kiera at the mention of her real name. The crowd stood all around them, cheering and stamping their feet. Viv set her drink down on the stool beside her. Her band readied their instruments, and Viv picked up her violin. Kiera's fur stood on end when she began playing. Her gift was pure magic. The crowd went wild when she started singing. At the height of her solo, green, black, and gold confetti rained down all over the bar. When she finished and bowed, the crowd thundered with approval. Jade made it back to the table completely out of breath.

"So, what'd you think?" Jade asked.

Kiera blinked away tears. "That was the most breathtaking performance. This is a real honor. I wish Imena could've seen it too." Kiera leaned her shoulder into Jade's and lowered her voice. "What if there are beings here who didn't appreciate Viv's speech or the fact that she revealed my name?"

Jade's nails curled around her drink, and her eyes sparked. She nudged Kiera with her hip. "We know the risks. They're worth it. Etabon should know you for who you truly are." She held up her drink. "To a better way." They raised their glasses, and Viv lifted hers from the stage to toast with them.

Viv's next song was cheerful and carefree. Jade threw back her drink and then ushered them onto the packed dance floor.

"Come on, we can't just stand around the table all night."

Jax set his satchel on one of the chairs. "Will you watch our drinks, Thimble?" The little fox grunted from within the bag.

The four of them moved onto the floor and twirled and swayed to the beat. Jax was a skilled dancer and took turns spinning them around. They got lost in Viv's voice. For the next hour, Kiera forgot about her powers and the curse. She was just another creature enjoying the celebration. She was winded when they stumbled back to the table. Jade waved at someone over at the bar.

She pressed her lips together, trying to hide her smile. "If you'll excuse me."

Attalin wiggled her eyebrows, and Jade pinched her arm before strolling off.

Jax leaned his muscled arms on the table. "This is probably my favorite place at Etabon."

Attalin snorted. "You've never been to Luna's, have you?"

Jax tilted his head back. "Oh, that's tough—her frothed caramels are the best."

Kiera nodded excitedly, thinking of the drinks.

A question popped into her head. "When you said you were going to do some traveling, I never thought it'd be here. Have you attended the festival before?"

He shook his head. "This is the first one I've been to. It's nice to have Thimble along, but it was still getting kind of lonely. It's much better now that you're here." Kiera returned his friendly smile.

A shadow shifted above Kiera, and she looked up. She watched as Darrow sailed between the layers of fabric above them. The clever owl landed on the table and clicked his beak at Jax.

"Your friend is back at the tent," Jax murmured.

Attalin stood. "Give me a second to tell Jade we're going." Attalin made her way across the bar to where Jade was standing with a red-winged alary.

Kiera sighed. "I had fun tonight. I wish things could always be like this. It's a crazy dream, but can you imagine what the world would be like if people like Hallowfeld or the Ruling Board didn't run it?"

Kiera's thoughts wandered to the memory of the field and what life could've been like if Leif had spared Bren, and the curse had never been unleashed. She twitched her ears and glanced around self-consciously. The atmosphere in the bar and the drinks had made it easy to forget about all the darkness that lurked around them.

Jax kept his voice low but replied warmly, "I don't think that's crazy. It sounds like a wonderful vision for the world."

Kiera shrugged a shoulder and rested her lips on her knuckles. "It's still just a fantasy. Even with everything as it is, I hate that I can't stay."

Jax studied her. "You mean because of what happened earlier tonight."

Kiera frowned. "Yes, among other things."

He hesitated but then leaned forward. "What if there was a place where you were guaranteed to be safe? Then you wouldn't have to leave."

Kiera blinked at him in surprise. The promise behind Jax's eyes reminded Kiera of a sun-soaked forest, the light in them setting the rich hues alight. Her magic flooded her veins in encouragement.

"You ready?" Attalin called from a few feet away.

Kiera wrenched her eyes from Jax's and replied, "Coming!" She stood and offered him a hand up. "Want to walk back with us?"

Jax took her hand and grinned. "Come on, Kie. Do you really have to ask?"

Kiera laughed as she turned and pressed through the crowd toward Attalin. Part of her assumed Jax was speaking in hypotheticals about staying, but her magic still sent tingles down her spine. They waved at Viv as they passed the stage, and she winked at them. When they stepped outside, the night air was cool, and the moon was directly overhead. They began walking back on the main path. It was scattered with a mix of other creatures heading to and from the restaurant district.

Jax let Thimble leap out of his bag, and she led the way twitching her ears as they went. Darrow flew overhead, letting out soft screeches. When they turned off toward the tent, they all had their guard up. Jax looked above them when they stopped at the tent and watched Darrow circle.

"Don't worry, he and Thimble would have alerted me if they detected anyone."

Attalin lifted her chin. "Thank you for your help earlier—it turns out that serendipity is real."

Jax chuckled. "Would you two want to get breakfast tomorrow?"

Kiera glanced sideways at Attalin. They didn't know yet when they'd be leaving, and they couldn't discuss it out in the open. If Gabby could get them out, they didn't know if it'd be that fast.

So, Attalin grinned and said, "Why not, Sprout? Come back early in the morning, and we'll eat here and introduce you to Gabby."

Jax turned his head to the side. Kiera swatted Attalin with her tail. "A nickname means she likes you."

He bent down and touched the ground. A flower emerged from the dirt, and he picked it and handed it to Attalin.

Her lips parted in surprise. "A dahlia. How did you know?"

Jax stuck his hands in his pockets. "Just a feeling. Plants are kind of my thing."

Attalin shook her head and nudged his arm lightly. Kiera stepped forward and embraced him. "See you tomorrow."

They turned, and Attalin pushed through the flaps.

Jax said, "Oh, Kie, wait." He pulled a leaf out of his pocket and handed it to her. "Intuition is telling me you're fond of irises, but I've been saving this."

"This is the leaf from the other day. You kept it?" Kiera laughed.

"I told you I would. Think about what I said before you make any decisions about going. We'll talk tomorrow."

Kiera's magic and maybe something else fluttered in her stomach.

2 8

UMBRA

Kiera ducked into the tent behind Attalin. Gabby's shoulders sagged with relief when they entered.

"You wouldn't believe the night we've had," Attalin said as she enfolded Gabby in a hug.

She patted Kiera's cheek, and they all dropped into chairs around the table. Gabby already had the tourmaline in her hand. She activated it and set it next to Jasper, who was dozing on the table. Nook came and pressed against Kiera's leg. Attalin and Kiera rushed through the events since Gabby had been separated from them, from the episode at the market to the serum and the memories of the curse trapped in the dagger, and the twin pendants that Kiera had seen within those memories. They explained how it was connected to their dreams and knowings. Attalin shared the news that she was unbound from the tiger's eye. When they explained the confrontation in the woods and Devland's disappearance, Gabby went pale but shook it off quickly.

"Destroying that tiger's eye was a tremendous feat, Kiera. Thank you." Gabby's voice was raspy with tears.

"I'm still getting the hang of my magic, but it's coming more naturally each time," Kiera said.

"You said you saw Bren shift into every form. Now we know what the ancient text meant by 'unsolidified vessel'. Have you tested that out?" Gabby asked.

"Honestly, with everything else going on, I hadn't tried yet, but I can give it a go."

Kiera tried to picture doing what she'd witnessed Bren do in the memories. The only forms she knew were her shifter and human body, so she focused on that. She felt her body tingle all over. When she opened her eyes, blue light enveloped her. Kiera's body readjusted, and her fur faded away. She felt her hair fall over her shoulders, and she looked down at her bare arms and legs. The golden dress hung loosely over her frame.

Attalin stared with wide eyes.

"Incredible," Gabby whispered.

Her conversation with Jax popped into her head. Kiera looked between them. "There's something else. We had so much to tell you, I just thought of it." She hesitated. "My friend Jax, he said there was a safe place I could go so I didn't have to leave. He wants to discuss it with us tomorrow morning."

Attalin's eyebrows shot up, "Do you have any idea what he could mean by that?"

Gabby pressed a hand to her face. "I think it's time you two know the whole truth. About my research with warped magic, about everything."

Before either of them could respond, the garnet bracelet on the table began flashing a deep crimson. Gabby's head jerked to the tent flaps, her eyes calculating. She raised her hand, and the black tourmaline flew up to land in Kiera's palm.

"We only have seconds. You two get in the washroom and reactivate that in there." Gabby shoved Jasper into Attalin's arms. "You need to trust me—don't come out no matter what you hear."

Gabby turned toward the entrance waving her hand behind her prompting a forceful gust to shove Kiera, Attalin, and Nook into the washroom. They quickly invoked the stone just as Hallowfeld thrust his way into the tent. He scanned the room, looking right through them, and then his seething gaze landed on Gabby. They hadn't even had time to shut the door, but the stone had adapted. The blaze had enveloped the doorway. The effect was like watching through two-way glass. They could see Hallowfeld, but they were invisible to him.

Kiera felt Attalin tense beside her. Hallowfeld's magic was in a frenzy, roiling off him in icy waves they could feel even from across the room. She shivered beside Attalin. Nook was tucked securely behind her. Kiera hadn't had a chance to shift back into her animal form. Her focus was too frayed to channel her magic properly, so, she stilled and concentrated on what was unfolding in front of her.

Gabby was the first to speak, gesturing to the kettle. "I was just about to have a cup. Would you like one?"

Kiera had never seen Hallowfeld so disheveled. He was not in his typical suit, but a rumpled dress shirt, and his hair was mussed.

His chest was heaving as he snarled, "That little beast destroyed my dagger. I need you to create a replacement weapon for me." He slammed the crimson leather spell book on the table. Kiera covered her mouth and shared a stunned look with Attalin.

Gabby raised her brows and replied coolly, "So that's a no to the tea then?"

Hallowfeld strode forward and struck her across the face. Gabby staggered a few steps back but didn't fall. Attalin jerked beside her, but Kiera held her firmly in place. If they burst out of nowhere, she knew what Hallowfeld would do to Gabby in retaliation. He didn't so much as glance their way, so the spell was working. Gabby regained her composure swiftly and faced Hallowfeld, stepping to her left so her back blocked the washroom. Her stance was defensive, but she didn't engage him.

"You're forgetting who you're dealing with, Eugene."

His fists clenched at his side. "You may be skilled, but, in the end, we know who would win out. Your power is no match for mine."

Gabby's spine straightened. "Are you sure?"

Kiera could swear there was a tiny kernel of doubt in Hallowfeld's eyes.

"I've tolerated your insubordination for too long because of your gifts, but defying my orders comes at a cost. Remember, one word, and your daughter is the one who pays the price."

Gabby's eyes narrowed.

Hallowfeld sneered at her, "Don't like that, do you? I've been too lenient with you. For your loyalty and the use of your abilities, I've allowed you not to take the mark, and I spared your daughter's life. I've ignored your transgressions for the last time. I know you didn't dispatch that sprite." Gabby didn't break eye contact.

"So, you're not even going to deny it," he hissed.

She tipped her chin up at him. "If you're in my quarters, we both know you have evidence against me."

Hallowfeld glowered at her. "Yasmeen followed the ashes you sent down the stream the other day."

Kiera and Attalin grimaced. That'd been right before they'd found out Yasmeen had returned to Etabon. She must have been going to meet with Hallowfeld when she'd seen Gabby and investigated.

"She tested some, and it came up as animal material. Explain yourself."

"Imena was no real threat to your control. She was taken care of and will never be heard from again. That's what matters," Gabby shot back.

Hallowfeld had gone very still. The temperature in the tent dropped lower, and it was like the shadows in the room were slithering toward him.

"You don't get to question my judgment. If I give you an order, you carry it out, regardless of whose throat you're slitting. Now Devland's disappeared, and you were one of the last to see him." Hallowfeld leaned forward. "You've truly forgotten who suffers when you refuse me."

Gabby squared her shoulders. "I think you're the one who's forgetting. There's no being among your followers that can connect with magic the way I can. You wouldn't have half the spells you've requested if it weren't for me."

Hallowfeld paused. "It would be a considerable loss not having access to your abilities, but if I can't control you, then you've outlived your usefulness." Hallowfeld pointed to the book, which opened itself and flipped to a page near the end. "I'm willing to give you one final chance if you perform this spell, but after that, you'll have to receive the mark."

Gabby's eyes scanned the page. "What do you need this for? Kiera doesn't appear to contain the power expected of a shifter."

Hallowfeld gave her a disgusted look. "Leave sweet Kiera to me. Her powers may not have manifested yet, but I have it on good authority she'll be the most powerful shifter to date."

Gabby furrowed her brow. "What does that mean?"

Hallowfeld was toying with her now. He drummed his fingers on his arm. "It happened when I was searching for this spell book. Caius Porter, the father of the brat you're so fond of, provided me with a vision years ago. I didn't take much notice of it at the time because I already had my shifter, but he told me I'd have need of a second. He offered his daughter up as future bait to save his own skin."

Gabby caught herself on the chair in front of her.

Hallowfeld chuckled deeply. "He said there'd be a lynx shifter coming in a few years, and she wouldn't be able to resist helping Attalin. He guaranteed an easy reaping because she's such a sentimental soul."

Kiera flicked her eyes to Attalin and felt her heart shatter as she watched the tears roll down her face.

"He must've given him that vision when I left the room that day. He saw beyond the border again and bartered with it," Attalin croaked.

Kiera wrapped her arms around her and rocked her back and forth gently.

She whispered into Attalin's ear, "It doesn't change a thing. I'd do it over again every single time."

Hallowfeld rolled his eyes. "What that vile seer didn't say is how patient I'd have to be, but I can't rush the process like last time."

Gabby had her hand to her throat. "You said you had another shifter. I assume you're referring to Nieyla."

A dark delight filled Hallowfeld's eyes. "That's right, you had a chance to meet the badger. Your pet mermaid assisted me with that one. I had her confined in the manor, and I brought Attalin in to persuade her. It didn't work—Attalin was still too weak, and the badger managed to squat in her human form and refused to transform willingly. I learned a decent amount about shifters and curses from her, though."

He waved his hand. "There were no family members to threaten her with. So, I sacrificed her in her human form. The results were suboptimal. I learned a valuable lesson that day—beings must be willing for the magic to be effective. I didn't have the right tools anyway, and it seems that shifters have to be harvested when their powers are fully manifested for the curse to work at full force."

Attalin's face drained of color as she murmured to Kiera, "I remember that day. It was only a couple of weeks after my father was thrown out. Hallowfeld made me go into a room at the manor and ordered me to use my magic on a human woman. I had to command her to release what he wanted, but her mental fortitude was too strong for my influence. That's all I was allowed to say to her, and then I had to leave. I didn't know she was a shifter; I was new to my magic and overwhelmed. I don't recall feeling her powers."

Kiera's stomach roiled, and she stroked Attalin's arm.

Hallowfeld held up a thick russet metal ring with the eclipse symbol on its raised face. It was the exact size of the brands Kiera had seen on his followers. "It wasn't all a disappointment. I did manage to forge this out of the creature's blood. It's allowed me to fuse my followers to me and heighten my powers, but the key part of the curse didn't take."

Gabby pressed her hand to her mouth.

"You're using warped magic to siphon from your follower's stores. That's how you maintain so much power." Her fist clenched at her side. "What does the board have to gain from your connection to your disciples? If I'm reading the original spell correctly, the intent was to inhibit magic."

Hallowfeld ran his hand over the open page. "You of all people know spells can be a blueprint." His eyes glittered wildly. "A framework to fit the needs of the caster. The fools on the board believe what I tell them, that I'm working on a way to convert and channel magical energy directly to Atterah's core. They owe me after my ancestors were the ones to make their world a reality, and then they cut us out of the government. They think I'm after a seat at the table." Kiera and Attalin gaped at each other.

"And you'd have me believe you wouldn't accept that seat?" Gabby said.

"Don't insult me." The entire room quivered, sending the chandelier rocking back and forth, casting shadows reeling around the tent. "I wouldn't share power with a group of sniveling humans. They can remain in their weak forms. They'll regret it soon enough. I've perpetuated their lie about chaos and magic's brutality. It's worked in my favor—the arenas allowed me to weed out the weaklings and has filled my ranks with only the strongest."

Gabby was hardly breathing, her eyes locked on the spell book. "You don't think the board will start inquiring about Kiera soon?"

Hallowfeld spoke through gritted teeth. "By all accounts, this is her first festival, and according to their system, sweet Kiera is just a werewolf. It's her classmate Cassidy they're keeping an eye on since she was documented as the shifter who trespassed. I turned her name in, along with the ticket inspector's." Hallowfeld let out a cawing laugh. "I told that foolish shifter I wouldn't divulge *her* violations—I didn't say anything about the others. I said I'd spare her classmates, and they'd have their freedom. However, the inspector was no longer one of them, so I turned him over to the board. They dealt with him as a warning to those who'd try to enter without a band. They kept Cassidy alive at my bequest for her return and the plans I have for her later this month."

Bile burned Kiera's throat, and a ringing filled her ears. Tristan had gone to school with them, but he was a year older and had graduated. How could she have missed that in her bargain? She'd been so preoccupied with protecting herself from her classmates turning her in when she'd gotten home that she'd never thought to inquire about their wellbeing. Attalin clutched her hand and whispered, "Kiera, it's not your fault."

Gabby stared at him. "What happens when the board discovers you lied to them?"

He sighed. "If they ever notice, I'll maintain it was an honest clerical error. They're all too happy to benefit from the profits of the festival. It keeps them amenable. Plus, they're so preoccupied with maintaining control on the other side of the border right now, they're not looking to what I'm doing here."

Gabby flinched. "I wasn't aware."

Hallowfeld regained his composure. "Yes, Marcus's father went and blew up one of their labs. So, they're all scrambling to see if the old man just made an error in judgment or if it was an intentional attack from another party. If you ask me, that's why you don't involve family in business. You get rid of them altogether. Such a liability."

Hallowfeld pushed the spell book closer to Gabby. "That old buffoon managed to escape the flames but wasn't out of the blast radius. They can try to piece him back together, but they gave him about a ten percent chance to recover. It's made it inconvenient where Kiera's dear mother is concerned. They refuse to tell me where they're housing them. I'll find out in six weeks if they'll be willing to hand her over." He rubbed his chin. "What I'm saying is we have time. No one's coming to fetch Kiera. I'll have acquired what I need well before then."

Hallowfeld crossed his arms. "Join me, Gabby, and I'll share my plans with you. We're going to remake this world. I'll let the choice be yours. Would you like to do the spell first or receive the mark?"

Gabby planted her feet. "Neither, you monster. I'll never use my powers to benefit you again."

Hallowfeld's icy tendrils lashed through the room. "You realize it's not just your life you're forfeiting."

When Gabby remained silent, a vein in Hallowfeld's temple bulged. "I'll give you a moment to truly consider."

Gabby's body tensed, but she didn't make a move to defend herself. Kiera realized it was because they were in the room. The only thing standing between them and Hallowfeld's magic was her. She was shielding them in case he attacked.

Attalin was shuddering in her arms. "Kiera," she breathed.

"I'm right here," Kiera murmured.

Attalin looked up at her. "I'm so sorry for everything. I want you to know there'd be no freedom without you." She leaned up and pressed her lips to Kiera's. The kiss electrified her entire body. It was as if stars were crashing down around her, burning her up and filling her with effervescent light all at once. Nothing existed outside of this moment.

Attalin drew back and whispered, "I'd go anywhere to find you, even if that's in the next life."

Before Kiera knew what was happening, Attalin had shoved her sideways farther into the washroom and burst through the shield. She thrust Gabby to the side just as Hallowfeld flung up his arm to cast a spell toward her. His eyes flared wide when he saw it was Attalin standing in front of him. He pulled his arm back, but it was too late. The curse collided with Attalin's chest, throwing her across the room into one of the bookcases. Hallowfeld was thrown back too and crashed into the bunk beds. He lay crumpled on the ground. Gabby had hit her head on the edge of the table, and a cut on her forehead trickled blood, but she was already up and moving.

Kiera raced out of the washroom toward them. Gabby skidded over to Attalin, her palm flew open, and a magnetite stone from the shelf soared to her hand. She fell to her knees and put her ear to Attalin's chest. Her eyes went wide. She pumped her hands against Attalin's chest and then breathed into her mouth.

She firmly spoke the word "restart," and the brownish-gray stone in her hand glowed bright, vibrating with electricity. Gabby held it against Attalin's chest. Kiera knelt on the ground beside them. She felt like time had stopped, and everything in the world had faded to black.

"Come on, Atti," Gabby murmured.

When the stone touched Attalin's skin, her body gave a great jolt. Nothing happened. Gabby cursed and touched the stone to her chest again. Attalin's diaphragm filled with air. That's when it hit Kiera, there had only been two hearts beating in this room before Gabby had enacted the spell in that stone. Across the room, Hallowfeld's chest began rising and falling as well. Gabby held her hands above Attalin, whispering words of stabilization and balance. Sweat trickled down her temples.

"She's alive, but the curse is surging through her now. I need to contain it."

Kiera's eyes darted between Gabby and Attalin. "What can I do?"

Gabby stared at her in desperation, and her voice cracked. "This is a coven spell. At the very least, I need another witch to save her, right now."

Adrenalin kicked in, and Kiera rested her hands on her legs, palms up, and closed her eyes. "Please hear me. Help me save her. Let your magic flow through me."

Kiera's light erupted into the room, and her body tingled. When her eyes flew open, they were glowing.

Gabby blinked. "A witch," she gaped.

"Gabby, tell me what to do," Kiera snapped.

She nodded. "Place your hands beside mine, feel your magic pulsing through your fingertips into Attalin, and repeat after me: Contain to reveal, contain to seal, contain to heal."

They repeated the phrase rapidly until a reddish-black light flared within Attalin's chest.

"We have it, keep going." They were both dripping sweat and trembling. The light turned a solid blue and faded back into Attalin. Out of the corner of her eye, she could see the same flickering happening over Hallowfeld.

Gabby panted, "She's stable."

She locked eyes with Jasper, and he dashed out of the washroom and hurried over to her. She leaned down and spoke into the charm attached to his collar. The cat fled from the tent. Gabby stood and grabbed a small clear orb from the shelf behind her and shattered it on the ground. Stones and crystals on the wall, along with other items from all around the room, began shrinking and flying into massive leather bags. The crimson book swept off the table and soared over their heads to land among the items.

Kiera couldn't move, she felt so cold. She stroked Attalin's hair. Tears blurred her vision. Her blue light flared up again, and she felt her body transform back into her lynx form, her fur returning to warm her. It was comforting. A terrible thought slithered into her mind: If they'd only made it to sunrise, maybe they could've been free. She shook it away angrily. It wouldn't help her now.

Gabby stalked over to Hallowfeld and touched her hand to his throat, and snarled, "His fate's bound to hers now. It's retribution for breaking their bargain. They're in a coma. If she dies, then he dies. I'm not sure if it's the other way around as well. This is far beyond the curse in the stone, which was an inanimate object—this is two spirits linked. If we fail to properly break the curse, she dies. We'll need experts to save her."

Kiera's bag whistled by and landed beside her. The strap placed itself over her shoulder. She looked behind her and realized the whole tent had packed itself away. A bag sat atop Jade and Viv's beds. Gabby's garnet bracelet was now a beacon of fierce red light. Her eyes flicked to it, and she said with unfathomable calm as she placed it on her wrist, "The marks have alerted his followers. His guards will be here in seconds—we have to move right now."

Gabby snatched her and Attalin's bags from the floor, throwing the straps around herself. She swiftly motioned to Attalin's limp form. Kiera leapt forward, lifting her off the ground, cradling her as gently as she could. Instead of heading out the tent flaps, Gabby's hands made an opening gesture, and the back of the tent split wide open. The sizzling of her protection spells filled the air as they dissipated. Kiera whistled to Nook, and he ran to her side.

Gabby rushed through the opening, with Kiera and Nook close behind her. Just as they rounded the tent, she heard shouting coming from inside, urgently calling for a medic. Kiera clutched Attalin closer to her chest.

Millions of thoughts raced through her head, but the one that eclipsed them all was the need to protect Attalin. She was unconscious in Kiera's arms, and sweat dotted her forehead. They kept to the shadows as they fled. Gabby had them bobbing and weaving through a maze of tents.

She was panting hard but managed to say, "We're almost there."

Kiera's night vision dialed in on Jasper's small form wavering on the forest's edge. When Gabby was close enough, the cat turned, and she followed him farther into the trees. Kiera's senses were prickled, feeling for anyone following behind them. But it was an energy further ahead that had her faltering.

"Gabby," she hissed quietly, fearing the woman hadn't noticed the presence ahead.

"It's alright. It's a friend," she rasped back.

Kiera's magic was swarming in the pit of her stomach where Attalin was curled against her. Whatever Hallowfeld had struck her with was still inside of her. They'd just trapped it for now. Kiera could feel the dark magic struggling to unleash itself.

A fog had rolled in, making their race through the forest even more treacherous. Kiera saw a figure up ahead in the middle of three larger creatures. When they got close enough, Kiera realized they were three massive elk. They snorted and pawed the ground, sending the fog swirling around their hooves. Gabby hurried around one to the being standing on the other side.

"Jasper is in my bag with Thimble. I've sent Darrow on ahead of us. They know we're coming. The way will be safe."

Recognition hit Kiera like a slap in the face.

"Jax?" She came around the elk and stared at him in shock.

He held up his hands. "I'll explain everything soon, but for now we have to go before they locate us. If they do, we'll never make it."

Jax touched each elk on its shoulder blade, and they knelt down for them to get on. He came forward to take Attalin so Kiera could climb up, but she refused to hand her over. He pulled an envelope from his shirt pocket.

"I was told to give this to you if you didn't trust me."

Kiera's eyes locked onto her name elegantly written across the front of the letter. That was her mother's handwriting. Kiera tentatively passed Attalin to him and seized the letter. She ripped it open and read,

Kiera, there's so much I should have told you. I wish there was more time. Go with my allies—they will keep you safe.

The bottom of the page had the ink imprint of the pendant. Her mother had pressed the fox and water lilies against the page as solid proof that she'd penned this message. Kiera's heart ached. Her mother had been concealing the truth from her. Rose's behavior over the last months and the secrets she'd kept had been leading to this. The ground beneath her felt shaky.

"When your mother couldn't get you safely to us outside of Etabon, her only option was for us to collect you through the festival. We had to wait for the right moment so they couldn't track you. Look, we need to go. I'll protect you both with my life," Jax said. "I'll make a bargain with you right now if that's what you need."

Kiera bared her teeth. "I'm done with bargains." She mounted the elk and then reached down and lifted Attalin into her arms. Kiera stared at Gabby.

"What about your daughter?"

Gabby looked up at her with sorrow-filled eyes. "I don't have a daughter. Attalin's the closest to it I've ever had. The night her father was banned, I made it my mission to look after her. An agent is stationed at the home in Hytheis that Hallowfeld believes to be mine. The woman he assumes to be my daughter is a plant and part of the plan to get close to him."

Kiera looked between them. "You're with the Alliance." Her magic roared through her veins. They looked lost for words. Kiera shook her head. "You don't have to say anything—I know it's the truth. Honestly, I don't care as long as they can save her. Take me to them."

Jax and Gabby mounted their elks. Gabby reached into her bag and tossed a spell into the sky to silence their journey through the woods. She led the way. Kiera kicked her elk's flanks, and they charged into the trees, Nook racing along beside her and Jax close on her heels. Moonlight flashed down through the branches turning the forest to silver. They galloped toward the Alliance. Kiera held Attalin tightly against her. She knew two things for certain: She would save Attalin even if it cost her own life. And if she survived, they were going to forge a new path for their futures, together.

ABOUT THE AUTHOR

Christina Bacilieri is the author of the young adult fantasy
The Last Refuge, the debut novel in her Stealing Sanctuary series.
She's a fan of all things magic and grew up on a steady diet of fantasy
novels and pasta supplied by her loving grandmother. Christina studied
marketing at the University of Texas at San Antonio before working
as a business relationship consultant and project manager. When she's
not reading or writing, you can find her wandering through nature or
taking in art at her favorite museums. She and her husband share their
home in Texas with two snuggly pups and an abundance of books.

You can find news and updates at **www.christinabacilieri.com**.

ACKNOWLEDGMENTS

The Last Refuge wouldn't have been possible without the support of these magical people.

Grandma, your kitchen table was the place I could always be completely myself. Thank you for seeing me and loving me just as I am. You taught me many things, but most importantly, you taught me what unconditional love is. You're forever in my heart.

Tony, thank you for filling our home with witty banter and delicious food. I couldn't have gotten through these last years without your endless humor and steadying energy. Thank you for going on this wild ride with me. You have all my love.

Mom, you were the first to read Kiera's story and believed in me from the beginning. Thank you for the early-morning coffees, late-night phone calls, and stretchy pants in Fredericksburg. Dad, thank you for all the belly laughs, especially during the times when I was close to tears with this book. To you both, it's not always easy to be a dreamer, but with parents like mine, it's not only accepted but encouraged. Thank you for teaching me to dream big.

To my oldest and best friends, Asia Richter, and Katelyn Martin: Thank you for your unwavering support and for showing me true friendship. It's the foundation on which I based many relationships in this book. Asia, throughout this journey, you not only fanned the flame of this story but protected it as your own. Katelyn, the countless hours we spent at our coffee shop sessions kept me sane. I'm eternally grateful to you both.

Thank you to my editors, Jennifer Rees, and Tenyia Lee. Jennifer, your brilliant insights and encouragement throughout the developmental and copyediting process made this story what it is today. Tenyia, thank you for expertly polishing this book so it could shine. Thank you to Kim Dingwall for this stunning cover. Your mind-blowing artwork truly brought Kiera's world to life. Thank you to Kelly Carter for designing such a beautiful interior.

Thank you to the early readers, my incredible friends, and family. Shout out to Aunt Karen and Alyssa for your encouraging feedback. A special thank you to the book community—librarians, booksellers, teachers, and bloggers for your support. And to you, dear reader, my deepest gratitude for giving this book a chance. It's an honor to share my story with you.

Printed in the USA
CPSIA information can be obtained
at www.ICGtesting.com
CBHW021013291223
2822CB00013B/8/J